For Shawna
with K
and warm
Thanks so much
for your
hospitality

LONGING TO BE FREE

Judy Austin

LONGING TO BE FREE

The Bear, The Eagle, and the Crown

JUDITH GUSKIN

Longing To Be Free: The Bear, The Eagle, and The Crown is a work of historical fiction. Apart from the well-known actual people, events, and locales that figure in the narrative, all names, characters, places, and incidents are the products of the author's imagination or are used ficticiously. Any resemblance to current events or locales, or to living persons, is entirely coincidental.

Cover and book design by Caroline Teagle Johnson

ISBN 978-0-9998967-0-3 (paperback)
ISBN 978-0-9998567-1-0 (eBook)
ISBN 978-0-99985567-2-7 (hardcover)

Library of Congress: 2018900927

Wonder Spirit Press, Florida, 2018

www.judithguskin.com
wonderspiritpress.com

Manufactured in the United States of America

For Martin Rosenthal, filmmaker, whose patience and insights were valuable, and my creative daughters Sharon and Andrea Guskin and their families for leading lives of love, compassion and commitment.

Also, in memory of Sarge Shriver who inspired so many by his work as Director of the Peace Corps, and the over two hundred thousand volunteers who opened their hearts and minds to people around the world.

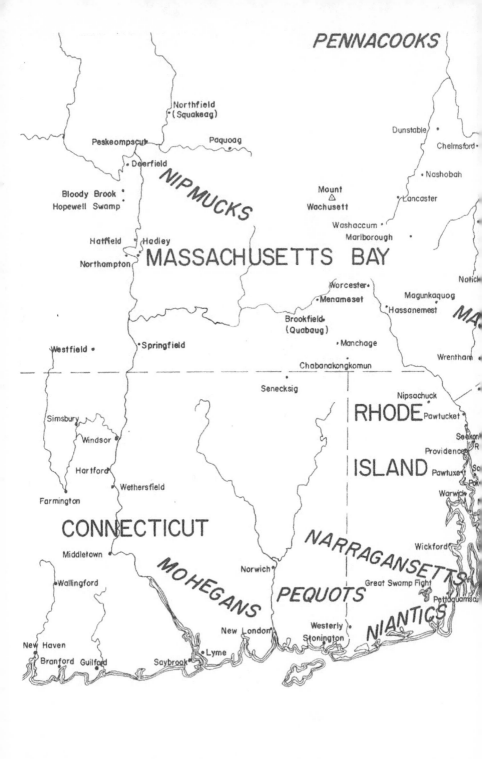

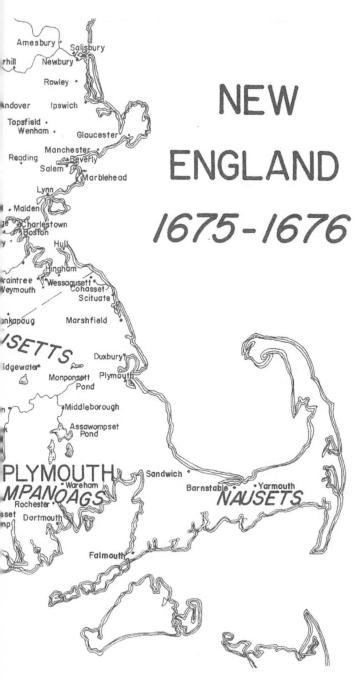

NEW

ENGLAND

1675-1676

This map is from "Diary of King Philip's War 1675-1676" by Colonel Benjamin Church" with Introduction by Alan and Mary Simpson. Chester, Conn.: The Pequot Press, 1975. Published for the Little Compton Historical Society.

"The truth is rarely pure and never simple."
—OSCAR WILDE

Preface

I started my work on this novel after I came upon a 900 year old Gothic church called Pieterskerk during a visit I made to Leiden in The Netherlands. Currently known as the church of the Pilgrim Fathers, it is also where the Reverend John Robinson, Pastor of the Pilgrims, is buried. He lived on the southside of the church. Surrounding his garden were houses for his congregants who were also refugees from religious persecution in England.

Leiden was a tolerant city and provided refuge for thousands of immigrants fleeing religious persecution in Europe. The Pilgrims were Calvinist dissenters from the state Church of England. They joined a growing population of Catholics, Jews, Moslems, Lutherans, and Huguenots during the turbulent years of the 17th century. Leiden was the second largest city in The Netherlands and its Leiden University, the oldest in the country, was attracting scholars from all over Europe. Here Cambridge educated John Robinson could converse with theologians and William Bradford took courses after finishing his work in the cloth industry.

The minister of Pieterskerk led me into the exquisite Trustee's Room. We sat at a long table in front of a huge fireplace. The walls were made of beautiful embossed leather. He told me the Pilgrims sat around this table making plans for their journey to America on the Mayflower.

I began to ask myself questions: Who were these people? How did their beliefs and actions shape our country's history and values? As Americans the Pilgrims are in our national consciousness when we celebrate Thanksgiving, but most people know little about their beliefs and actions, their continuing contacts with England during the English Civil War, or the reasons for their conflicts with Native Americans which led to one of the most destructive wars in our history, King Philip's War.

There are many threads in my past connected to this history. When I taught at Clark University in Massachusetts I supervised students working at historical sites. I visited Plymouth Plantation and the local museum to see the shoes, eyeglasses and tools brought on the Mayflower. At the Massachusetts Historical Society I examined Bradford's journal and other original documents. I studied John Milton and his times in 17th century England as well as early American writers during my Ph.D. studies at the University of Michigan.

As a fellow of the Applied Anthropology Association I spoke with friends working with Native Americans on legal issues. I worked with Native Americans improving schools and trying to preserve their native languages. One of them was Rose Shingobee Barstow of the University of Minnesota who was teaching Ojibwe. She told me of her pain when as a child she was sent to boarding school where she could not speak her native Algonquian language and knew very little English. She stayed silent and teachers thought she was ignorant. I treasure the blue beaded necklace she gave me and I'm glad native language study continues.

You can find more about me on my website judithguskin.com. I have included stories about my work in establishing the Peace Corps and AmeriCorps/VISTA as well as suggestions for further reading about issues relevant to this book and links to websites.

Judith Guskin

Major Characters

PLIMOUTH PLANTATION: Governor William Bradford, his second wife Alice, his daughter Comfort, his son Willie, Governor Josiah Winslow, Captain Ben Church

THE MASSACHUSETTS BAY COLONY: Governor John Winthrop, Deputy Governor Thomas Dudley, his daughter Anne Bradstreet, her husband Simon Bradstreet, Anne Hutchinson, her son Ned, her daughter Susanna, Reverend John Eliot, Christian Indian missionary John Sassamon

RHODE ISLAND: Governor Roger Williams, Mary Dyer, John Easton

CONNECTICUT: Governor John Winthrop, Jr., son of Governor John Winthrop

WAMPANOAG TRIBE: Chief Sachem Massasoit, his sons Wamsutta (Alexander), Metacom (Philip), Chief Advisor Hobbamock, his daughter Little Bird

NARRAGANSETT TRIBE: Chiefs Miantonomo, Cannonicus and Canonchet

MOHEGAN TRIBE: Chief Sachem Uncas

ENGLAND: Sir Henry Vane, his wife Frances, John Milton, John Lilburne

Part One

1630-1638

PLIMOUTH PLANTATION, JUNE 1630

It was so real. High orange flames leaping from house to house. Screaming children running everywhere. Whizzing arrows and thunderous guns. A woman is running, clasping an infant tightly to her chest. Her white apron and her face are spotted with blood.

He thought at first the woman was his daughter Comfort, but then recognized the sad brown eyes of his second wife Alice. Who was the enemy? Why this nightmare? He watched, helpless. He saw bloodied corpses of English and Indians scattered in a field of blackened corn husks and dead cows.

Startled by the scrapping noise of an iron spoon against the side of a kettle, Governor Will Bradford is awake. His heart is pounding and he smells smoke. He wipes sweat off his face with a corner of the damp sheet. He peers through a slit in the red bed curtain and sees a flame glowing beneath the black kettle in the hearth. He's in his bed. All is as it should be.

The horror of the nightmare fades, but its meaning confuses him. He rubs his eyes and takes a deep breath. Why this fearful dream now? Was the nightmare a warning about an Indian attack?

I'm not worried about my Indian neighbors the Wampanoags. We've had a mutually profitable relationship for over ten years. Chief Massasoit has told me about past conflicts with the

Narragansetts as well as his fear of the Pequots. He has renewed our original mutual protection treaty. As Governor I won't make decisions based on fear. My people trust me. I don't believe this nightmare is an evil omen. It's probably due to my anxiety about meeting those coming today to start the new colony.

Every morning Will starts his day praying to God that Plimouth Plantation will continue to be successful. He feels a deep sense of responsibility for this small community of farmers. They've suffered so much already for their religious freedom: leaving behind houses, family and friends in two countries, first England then The Netherlands. They've endured starvation, disease and the death of many loved ones.

He has been told the new colony, The Bay Colony, has a Royal Charter. They're better educated and will know many more wealthy investors, merchants and politicians in London than he does. His mind is a labyrinth of worries, but his faith is strong. God will decide their fate.

Once again he hears the scraping of an iron spoon against the side of a kettle. Such an ordinary sound cheers him. He pulls aside the dusty red bed curtain. Early morning light filtering through the linseed-oiled paper window provides a soft glow to this room used as kitchen, dining room, bedroom and parlor. There is a center chimney, hearth, spinning wheel, table and chairs, and this curtained bed.

Through the opening in the curtain he sees his daughter Comfort in her white sleeping gown. She's sitting on a stool, bending over the large black kettle hanging on the lug-pole over the hearth fire. She's stirring Indian porridge for breakfast. He takes a deep breath and enjoys the sweet smell of the porridge. He's feeling calmer now, knowing that his favorite child, his only daughter, is here and safe.

Her blond hair is plaited into a thick braid extending down

to her waist. She has adopted this Wampanoag custom. She has inherited blond hair and blue eyes from her birth mother Dorothy, his first wife. He wishes his second wife Alice wouldn't pull on her braid to show disapproval. Alice wants Comfort to look and behave like a modest English girl. She wants her to stay quiet and be obedient to her. She rebukes him for letting Comfort use his study to read books. He added this room to provide a quiet refuge place where he can read, write, and teach his daughter. He's so proud of her.

Dorothy would have encouraged him to teach her. Why did she die so young? Was it his fault? His chest aches; he takes a deep breath. Dorothy's hair and skin smelled from rose water. If she were alive, she would tell Comfort to use rose water now that she's thirteen, an attractive young woman, who might marry in three years.

Don't grow up too quickly, dearest girl. I don't want you to marry at sixteen. Don't deprive me of your zeal for learning. You speak their Algonquian language. The Indians love you for they know you respect their Wampanoag ways. You're helping me keep the peace.

He closes his eyes. Dorothy, sixteen, his sweet bride, is in bed. Her face is glowing in the flickering candlelight. They are in Leiden, The Netherlands, and belong to a small Protestant congregation. They left England with others who also rejected the rituals of the Anglican Church of England as being too similar to Catholicism.

How happy he was then, despite being poor. He worked long days in a cloth factory. In the evenings he taught English to Jewish refugees from Spain and Portugal who escaped the Inquisition. Everyone here was free to practice his faith. When he saved enough, he bought a small cottage on a street called stink alley. Every evening he rushed home, pulled a chair to the bedside, and watched in wonder as Comfort's so tiny fingers pressed against Dorothy's breast, nursing until both mother and child fell asleep.

The Lord blessed him with a daughter who has a thirst for learning, strong faith, respect and compassion for others, and an adventurous spirit. He's taking her with him today to meet the flotilla bringing hundreds of newcomers to this wilderness.

He hears his boys thrashing about in the sleeping loft above. The oldest, Willie, Dorothy's son, likes to hunt with Mr. Myles Standish. He's good with guns and wants to be a soldier like Myles. Alice's two boys from her first marriage enjoy fishing with him. He tries to be a worthy father, for he remembers longing for a father when he was a boy.

His father died before he was a year old, and at seven his mother also died. He was raised by two elderly uncles. At twelve he had a serious illness and stayed in bed for a year reading the Bible as well as books on history and philosophy. When he was in his teens, he joined a group of Protestants wishing to separate from the state church, and was prepared to suffer in prison because of his faith. He crossed the Atlantic in an old wine boat called the Mayflower with Dorothy, but he insisted they leave their two young children, Willie and Comfort, with Alice, a widowed neighbor. The children were too young to make the dangerous voyage. After Dorothy died, he sent for his children and asked Alice to come here and be his second wife. He adopted her two boys.

Will watches Comfort set the table in front of the hearth with a pitcher of milk, a trencher of butter, leather drinking cups, and an Indian basket full of corn cakes. Then she begins sweeping the hard dirt floor with a besom, a broom made of twigs. She's softly singing psalm one hundred fifty, her favorite, because it has verses about musical instruments she wishes she could hear. She puts aside the broom and climbs the ladder to the loft to tell her brothers to come down for porridge. When they leave, she dresses in the nook her mother sewed for her out of canvas sheets. Downstairs Will also dresses. His mended clothes are neatly folded on top of the black storage chest. He pulls on warm Irish stockings. Good. No one'll notice the stiches Comfort has sewn. He holds up and examines his scuffed shoes. Old but clean. He pulls on a dark blue shirt and over it his sleeveless russet colored jacket called a doublet. His breeches fit well, just below his knees, and they have only one small patch which is hidden by the doublet. He picks up his broad brimmed black hat and dusts it off.

In the mirror he sees a burly, broad shouldered, forty-one year old man with a ruddy complexion, dark mustache, no beard, light brown, wavy, shoulder length hair, and kind brown eyes. The hat makes him look taller and more distinguished than his usual red knitted cap. He sighs. He still looks like a farmer. Those Cambridge educated leaders and London lawyers are arriving today. Will they respect him? Do they know he could afford to study at the university in Leiden for only one year?

He hears Comfort scolding his sons about what they did in the loft. He hopes they haven't pulled down the dried herbs hanging from the beams again or overturned the barrels of corn stored there. The sons sit at the table watching Comfort spooning hot porridge into wooden bowls. She places the sugar bowl on the table. They like the same porridge the natives eat which is called "stamp", but they like it with lots of milk, butter and sprinkled all over with sugar. When she's finished serving, she turns to him. "Papa, do you want me to bring a basket of corn cakes to the meetinghouse?" she asks. She knows he usually spends early mornings praying at the meetinghouse and likes to eat his breakfast there alone.

"Yes, but first visit Hobbamock. Tell him I'd like his help adjusting the sail on the fishing boat before we take it from the brook to the harbor dock." Hobbamock, the spiritual advisor to Chief Massasoit, is coming with him, Comfort and his assistant Isaac Allerton to meet the flotilla of eleven ships arriving from England.

The main road, "the high way", leads up a hill to a square wooden building with six small cannons which is used as a church and fort. Will walks up and looks at the ocean. It's such a clear day he can see Cape Cod in the distance. Below folks are going about their daily chores: milking cows, feeding swine, goats and chickens, baking bread in the beehive shaped community ovens. Smoke rises from the chimneys. A woman bends under the weight of a wooden yoke on her shoulders which holds two pails of spring water. Women and children are in the fields picking up rocks and pulling weeds, preparing a field for spring planting. A farmer is taking tools from a small lean-to storage building behind his house. He hears the banging of the blacksmith's anvil, the grunting of hogs, the hammering of the carpenter framing a new house. He must remind the carpenter not to thatch the roof. Ever since one caught on fire, he has insisted thatch no longer be used for it burns too quickly.

He prays to God to give him the wisdom to guide this small community. He asks God to bless them with a good harvest and many beaver pelts so they can pay off a little more of the debt to their investors. He prays for the wisdom to continue to keep the peace with the Wampanoag people.

He goes behind the meetinghouse to Burial Hill to pay his respects to those who died. Half of those who came on the Mayflower died of starvation or sickness that first bitter cold winter. He'll never forget having to dole out only a quarter of a piece of bread to each person so that the meager amount left over could last a bit longer. Without the corn, geese and turkeys brought by Chief Massasoit's people they would have all died.

* * * *

Comfort has dressed in her Sabbath best: a blue blouse and skirt, a white apron and white bonnet. She's ready to visit Hobbamock's house when her step-mother Alice comes in from feeding the chickens in the backyard. What will her step-mother criticize today? She quickly tucks her braid under her bonnet to prevent Alice from pulling it.

Alice examines her and adjusts the white collar of her blouse. "Why he's insisted on taking you today, I don't understand. I said I need you to make soap."

Comfort hates making soap. What a stinking mess it is. She decides to avoid an argument. This could be the most important day of her life. She will escape quickly. "Papa asked me to bring him corn cakes at the meetinghouse after I give Hobbamock a message." She quickly puts corn cakes into an Indian basket and leaves. Alice shouts something, but she ignores her and walks towards the plantation's perimeter fence.

Hobbamock's house is only a short walk away. She crosses the common meadow where cows are grazing. There is a gate in the fence. She walks through John Howland's newly planted corn field and can already see smoke coming from Hobbamock's house. She's come this way for as long as she can remember and always feels excited about seeing her best friend.

Hobbamock's daughter Wootonekanuske, called Little Bird by the English, is exactly her age. When they were little, they cleared dirt away in front of Hobbamock's house and created an imaginary Indian village with twigs and rushes. Little Bird told her stories about the imaginary families who lived there. Over the years Little Bird has showed her how to stretch and soften deer hide, and how to identify mushrooms safe to eat. In winter Hobbamock's family moves to Pokanoket, fifteen miles away, to be closer to Chief Massasoit and his family. Called Mount Hope by the English, this is the main village of the Wampanoags and it is situated on a high promontory overlooking Narragansett Bay.

She misses her friend dreadfully in winter. If the snow isn't too deep for their horse, her father allows her to ride with him to visit Little Bird. She often helps translate for the Chief and her father in the morning, and then is free to spend the afternoon with Little Bird and Massasoit's youngest son Metacom, called Philip by the English. This boy, their age, is good at telling and acting out scary stories about bears. He says they fear bears but also honor them and see them as half-human. "They eat the same foods as we do, can stand upright, are good mothers, and were also created by the Great Spirit," Little Bird explained to her once. Philip added that he respects bears for they have great strength and courage. Now that it's spring, Philip will be coming here to visit Little Bird. Comfort intends to escape from her chores and come here to listen to his bear stories.

As she bends down on the edge of Howland's field to pick wildflowers for Little Bird's mother, she practices saying out loud words she's learned. A **wetu,** house, is made of **wuttapuissuck,** bent saplings, and is covered with mats woven of marsh plants we call cattails and the Wampanoags call a **bockquosinash.** She arrives at the house and notices that the garden has been planted with squash, corn, and beans, the three sacred crops. On a log someone has thrown the skin of a raccoon. She must ask Little Bird to teach her the Algonquian word for raccoon.

Inside the small round house she finds Little Bird sitting crossed legged on a bearskin on the raised wooden sleeping bench. She's weaving a basket. Her mother is making porridge over the fire in the center of the room. The smoke rises through the hole in the roof where mats have been removed. Comfort feels at home here.

"*Tawhitch peyauyean?* Why do you come?" Little Bird asks, putting aside the unfinished basket.

"*Unhappo kosh?* Is your father home? My father wants him to help prepare the boat and sail it from the brook to the harbor dock."

"*Anittui*, he's not here. *Cummautussakou*, you've just missed him. Mother will tell him your message." Little Bird stands and gets a wooden bowl from a corner of the room. "Here. I've picked blueberries. Your father likes them, yes?" She hands the bowl to Comfort.

"Come. I'm taking corn cakes to my father."

"*Cummattanish*, I'll come."

Her mother tells her to wear her new tunic. As her friend changes, Comfort notices Little Bird's breasts are bigger than her own. She watches her tie a wampum belt made of white and purple shell beads around her waist. She puts on doeskin leggings and moccasins. Her new tunic is decorated with flowers made from porcupine quills which have been dyed red. Comfort finds her beautiful. No wonder their friend Philip is flirting with her, she thinks, her mind full of mixed feelings of jealousy and guilt.

They walk together to the meetinghouse. Will is sitting on a bench on the men's side praying, so they sit on a bench on the women's side of the room and talk quietly.

When Will is finished, Little Bird holds out the wooden bowl. "See. Berries."

"They're sweet papa." Comfort adds. "*Weekan* is their word for sweet."

The girls talk quietly in Algonquian while he eats his corn cakes and blueberries. Later Little Bird asks about the newcomers.

"How many strangers are coming here?"

"Only three families, but seven hundred are coming to build their new village near the Massachuset people."

"Why?"

"To trade for furs and to be free to worship our Lord Jesus."

"*Sachem* Massasoit is...*wauontam.* What is the English word?" She looks at Comfort.

"A wise man."

"He says we, The People of the First Light, respect all the *manitou,* the spirits which live in everything. We must be free to keep our ways."

"I know." Will, offers her a corn cake. "Please go home and make sure your father knows he's to come to the boat." Then he asks Comfort to wait at the harbor dock. "Alice will complain, but she knows I want you come."

He smiles as he walks down the hill behind the two girls. How different they are, yet they're as close as sisters. They are talking in a mixture of English and Algonquian. They laugh, hold hands, and continue down the hill.

2

THE NEWCOMERS

The single sail of their small fishing boat is billowing in the wind. The vessel rolls and pitches in the choppy New England water. Her leaks and sail have been mended many times. Comfort holds tightly to the side trying hard to ignore the queasiness in her stomach. When they reach calmer waters, she relaxes and wipes the cold ocean spray from her face with a corner of her blue cape.

She looks at her father's anxious face. Better wait before asking questions. He takes her hand, their private signal telling her to be patient. He bends over and tucks a few golden curls under her cap.

She wants to know if these newcomers will be bringing books. If she can borrow one, she'll put it in the chest under her bed to keep it away from the dirty hands of her brothers. Her favorite book is the one with detailed drawings of the churches and bridges of London. How she longs to visit London!

"Papa, do you suppose they'll be bringing many books?"

"Hundreds. They're educated men."

"Will they build a city like London?"

William laughs. "Well, as you know my smart girl, such grand cities aren't built quickly. But, yes, someday their town, they've decided to call it "Boston", will have stone roads instead of muddy ones like ours. When you visit you won't need to wear those wooden clogs you hate so much."

She smiles, thinking of going to a new town. But who would she know there? She must make friends with a girl who lives there. "Leiden had stone roads, didn't it?"

"Yes. You'd have loved watching people walk around in colorful tunics and strange hats. People came from all over the world. I loved that about it."

"Tell me again why you left?"

"Our children were speaking Dutch and we wanted to keep our own language and culture. Besides, there were rumors about a new war with Spain. We were worried we would be forced to return to England and once again would face prison for our beliefs."

Comfort looks at the marshy banks along the shore before the boat heads out into the bay. She tries to imagine a city with stone buildings and churches. Maybe high born ladies will bring fine dresses. Would it be too impolite to ask to see inside their wooden chests? Probably so, she thinks sadly. It's windy, so she pulls her woolen cape tighter around her, and leans over the side of the boat feeling seasick.

She feels Hobbamock's hand rubbing her back gently, and she looks up at him. She loves the nest of wrinkles around his kind eyes. He wears a doeskin shirt with Little Bird's red quill work on it, and deerskin leggings. His head is shaved except for a black strip in the middle which is greased and stands up. His red headband has a single large eagle feather. He told her it makes his spirit fly high. Massasoit gave him this eagle feather after a successful hunting party.

"*Cummauchenem*? Feel bad?"

"It hurts here." She touches her stomach.

He opens the small leather pouch around his neck and takes out round pellets made of pulverized white oak bark. "Here, chew this, *wunnaks*, for stomach. Good."

"Taubotneanawyean, thank you." She doesn't like the taste, but trusts him. He knows how to make good medicine.

When she feels better, she continues to ask questions. "Will the Mayflower be among the flotilla, papa?"

"No. But there will be one that looks similar. It will also have a carved mayflower on its bow." He looks at the waves, and then wipes a tear from his eye. Yes, seeing that ship will bring back memories of that horrible sixty day voyage in the middle of winter.

"Tell me again about the crossing." There is silence. "Please, papa."

Will sighs. "A hundred of us crowded in the tween deck of the ship - one large open room smelling of sweat and urine. The weather was fair when we left Leiden on the way to Delfshaven, but after we boarded the Mayflower in Southampton the winds became violent and high waves battered the hull. It was winter, the wrong season to cross the ocean."

He shuts his eyes and sees Dorothy's pale face above a blue cape; the same one Comfort is wearing today. She stayed below, seasick, staring at black, turbulent water pounding the porthole. He'll never forgive himself for making her come, and for insisting they leave their babies, Comfort and Willie, with their widowed neighbor Alice and her two boys. Alice promised to bring his children and hers as soon as another voyage was planned. By then he hoped he'd have a proper house and farm.

Comfort touches his arm. "My mother didn't want to come. She was afraid there were lions here, wasn't she?"

He's silent, remembering the blinding snow when they finally saw land. He and a few others worked fast re-assembling this fishing boat. It had been new then, and had been stored in sections on the Mayflower. They headed towards land, hoping to find food. They found an abandoned hole in the frozen ground where Indians had buried corn. Will felt guilty taking it but the place was deserted. When they returned to the Mayflower Captain

Jones, his face solemn, asked him to come to his quarters. Why was he the only one invited?

"She's gone," he said. "Someone saw your wife Dorothy... she drowned sir, in these churning black waves. I'm so sorry, sir. A boy says she was sobbing and he thinks she may have jumped. But you know how slippery the deck is, and there was a very strong wind. We'll all pray for her soul, sir."

Comfort looks at his wet eyes and takes his hand. "She fell over, papa. It was an accident." She can't accept the fact that her mother may have killed herself. How could she have abandoned her? She's determined to be stronger than her mother no matter what happens. She'll never abandon her children.

Will pulls his hand away and searches his pocket for a handkerchief. "She lacked the courage to live in such a desolate place. I'll never forgive myself for insisting she come." He caresses the soft wool of her blue cape. "I'm glad you still wear her cape. Enough about the past. Today I must consider the future. Many things will change now."

"That's exactly what I want to talk about" Isaac Allerton says, his thin lips twisted into a scowl. Comfort doesn't like him. She was told by Alice that he had wanted to be elected Governor instead of her father and still feels resentment.

Isaac sits closer to Will, forcing Comfort to move closer to Hobbamock. "Mr. Coddington is coming on the flagship, The Arbella. He's the rich merchant I met in London who helped me acquire my new bass fishing boat."

Comfort notices her father's clenched fists and red face. "Your boat? You loaned money using Plimouth's credit to buy it. You've increased our debt when we are trying so hard to pay back our investors. It's 'our boat' and if it's lost at sea, we all lose. You knew we sent you to London to re-negotiate our debt not to buy a boat. But the boat is not the only thing I'm angry about. Too many beaver pelts have gone missing since you've been keeping the accounts at our trading post in the north. Was it just poor accounting? Did you take pelts for personal gain? All profit from pelts must go to pay our debt."

Isaac raises his voice in defiance. "It's our patriotic duty to make money from our fishing and buy English goods. Also we should be providing more timber from our forests for masts for the King Charles' warships. I'll sell fish and timber with all the nations on the other side of this vast ocean even to Catholic France and Spain."

Will ignores him and turns to Comfort. His face becomes gentler, and his voice softer. "Feeling better, my angel?" he says.

"A little." She rubs her stomach.

He nods to Hobbamock, silently thanking him for giving her medicine.

Will decides to distract her by telling her about a passenger on the flagship. "Lady Arbella, daughter of the 4th Earl of Lincoln, is coming on the ship named for her. We are going to board that ship, my sweet. This woman's mother is a patron of famous poets, so I'm sure she's brought many poetry books. You might ask her to borrow one."

Isaac refuses to be ignored. "I'm going to do business with Mr. Coddington today. I'll ask him for a new contact among the milliners who make felt hats from our beaver pelts. I'm going to supply him with timber to build his house."

Will sighs. "Isaac, why do you always say 'I' and not 'we'? We didn't come across the ocean to put money in your pocket."

Hobbamock has been staring into the churning water and sees a vision of thousands of dead herring floating in the ocean. A bad omen. He begins chanting in Algonquian.

"You be quiet," Isaac says with anger and a lack of respect.

Comfort joins Hobbamock's chanting in Algonquian.

"Speak English, girl!" Isaac barks. "You're not a savage!"

"It's a prayer," Hobbamock says in a soft, calm voice. "We're asking **Maushop**, the Giant sent by the Creator of all things, to watch over the spirits of the fish- bass, cod, sturgeon, and herring which we call **missuckeke-kequock, pauganaut, kauposh-shauog, aumsuog**. Aren't you a religious man?"

Will doesn't want Isaac to argue with Hobbamock today. "Isaac, let's thank our God for blessing us with an abundance of fish in the ocean. Lead us in prayer."

Isaac bends his head. "We give thanks unto you Our Lord. We know Thy marvelous works, and thank you for the abundance of fish in this ocean. We are humble worms and exult in Thee Our Lord. We sing praises to Thy name, O Most High. Amen."

As soon as Isaac lifts his head, he sees the anchored flotilla of sailing ships. "There they are! Look at those beauties!"

Comfort counts eleven ships. "Look at their pretty painted bows. I see red, blue, green and gold."

They use oars to go alongside the flagship which has the name "Arbella" in big red letters on its bow. When they're close enough, a rope ladder is thrown down from the ship. Comfort ties up her skirt with a piece of rope and climbs up, her father behind to help her get into the ship. On deck sailors are shouting and pulling down huge sails attached to horizontal spars and perpendicular to the keel on the square-rigger. Her father tells her this ship seems to be twice the size of the Mayflower.

Comfort has never been on the deck of such a large ship. She doesn't understand the words shouted by the sailors busy pulling on ropes: mainmast, mizzen, yardarm. She feels embarrassed when a handsome sailor throws a kiss in her direction. On her left a group of boys lean over the side of the ship watching Hobbamock climb up to the deck. They laugh, pointing to his hair. "His hair stands up like a cock's comb," one shouts. On her right a young woman walks by holding the hand of little boy who is whining for milk.

With her right hand Comfort touches the string of shells in the red knit pocket tied at her waist. It was given to her by her Wampanoag friend Philip who said it would bring luck. Perhaps she will be lucky and make a new friend.

Four men are on the deck waiting to greet them. John Winthrop, Governor of the new colony, introduces himself and then introduces the other men. Comfort stares at Reverend John Wilson. She thinks his nose is too long and is face is unsympathetic. Thomas Dudley, the Deputy Governor introduces her to his daughter Anne, a dark haired girl about eighteen years old and, standing next to her, Simon Bradstreet her young husband. Comfort likes Anne's eyes and warm smile. Mr. Coddington, the Treasurer of the new colony, remembers Isaac Allerton from his visit in London and invites him to talk in his private quarters. Winthrop invites her father to join him for refreshments in the chart room. A sailor is asked to show Hobbamock around the ship, for he has asked politely if he might see everything on what he called "this big floating island."

Anne holds out her hand. "Come. Meet my friend Arbella. I was brought up on her estate." They walk around the deck looking for Arbella. "My father was in charge of financial matters for her father, the Earl of Lincoln. Her mother was determined to educate her five daughters and hired tutors in history and literature. I was allowed to study with them. This voyage, it's been hard for her. She's had to share a crowded space with her servants. Ah, there she is, reading poetry as usual."

Comfort thinks Lady Arbella is pretty, but too thin. She admires her red dress with its trimming of white lace on the collar and sleeves, and her tiny, red leather shoes with pointed toes. Is her dress made of silk? She longs to touch it. It'll soon be spotted with mud and blackened by a smoky hearth. Those shoes are not practical. Doesn't she know she'll be living in a wigwam in a muddy meadow until her house can be built?

They chat with Arbella about the hardships of the journey and the terrible food. Arbella asks Comfort questions about food and Comfort tells her she likes to eat some of the foods that Indians eat. Her Indian friend Little Bird knows where to find wild strawberries, mashes them, adds cornmeal flour, and makes delicious strawberry bread. She offers to bring it when she visits, hoping this fine lady will invite her someday.

When Anne is ready to leave, Arbella opens a small ebony chest and takes out a blue satin ribbon. "Please take it. It's the same color as your blouse." Comfort smiles, and ties the ribbon around the end of her braid and makes a big bow. Both Arbella and Anne are charmed by how proud and happy she seems to be with this simple gift.

They leave Arbella, and walk down the ladder leading to the sleeping quarters below. "Best hold your nose," Anne says. Comfort sees a huge space filled with people and mattresses on the floor. Sections are divided by wooden boxes and canvas sheets. The only place to sit is on a damp mattress. "See how I've had to live! So what's it like living in a wilderness?"

Comfort doesn't want to scare her by telling her about the wolves and bears. "There are forests everywhere. I've learned to enjoy how the trees glisten in winter when covered with icicles and how beautiful they look in spring when the first light green buds appear on dark brown branches."

"Ah. You have a poet's eye. I wrote a poem about an Elm tree. I can let you read it. Can you read?" She sees Comfort glancing at the books piled on the mattress.

"Of course. My step-mother Alice says girls must learn to read so they can read the Bible to their children, but I love all kinds of stories. My father and I read his world history book out loud, and Mr. Standish and Mr. Brewster lend me books. Mr. Brewster has three hundred. I love Homer, a Greek poet. I read his story in the English translation, but sometimes my father and I read passages in the original Greek."

"You can read Greek?"

"Father started teaching me Greek when I was six. I'm good at languages."

"My tutors taught me Greek, Latin, French and Hebrew. I like Homer also."

"Have you read the Iliad?"

"Yes. Lady Arbella and I have read it together. Who do you like best - Helen of Troy or Andromache, Hector's wife?"

"Andromache when she speaks of her love for Hector. Don't you like the way Homer writes about Aphrodite, the goddess of love? I've not been in love yet." She looks down and takes a deep breath. "Forgive me if I'm being too bold, but I'd really like to know. Did your father choose Simon for you? I know that's how it's usually done, but I want to find my own husband."

"Well, my father hired Simon to be an assistant and he came to live with us on the Earl's estate. I was much too young to marry then, but we became good friends. We used to read my father's history books together. When I recovered from smallpox two years ago, I was sixteen, Simon asked my father if he could marry me and I agreed."

Comfort looks down. "I don't have anyone to talk to about these kinds of things. I don't like asking my stepmother Alice about anything. I wish my birth mother Dorothy was …well, she died; I don't even remember her face."

"I'm so sorry." She puts her hands over Comfort's hands. "What a strange coincidence. Dorothy is my mother's name also. Perhaps fate has brought us together. I'd like to be your friend." Anne's sincere. She never expected to find such a bright, inquisitive girl in this wilderness.

Comfort is delighted. "Yes, yes. I'd love that." She leans over and picks up a book from the pile on the mattress. "Spenser. I like his poems."

"My father bought it for me. He believes we're related to the poet Sir Philip Sidney. He encourages me to write poems. Mine are about God. Writing keeps away the darkness of my melancholy." She's quiet for several minutes, and looks away. "I didn't want to leave England." Tears fill her eyes. "Well, I'm here and truly, yes, I'd be honored to be your friend." Comfort, flattered, smiles.

Anne takes a moment to calm herself. "Now, tell me about the savages. I must confess, I was scared when I saw that strange man you've brought. Aren't they cannibals?"

"Of course not. His name is Hobbamock, and he's an advisor to the Chief of the Wampanoag tribe. His daughter, Little Bird, is my best friend. We speak Algonquian, mixed up with English of course."

"You speak their language?"

"Yes. I speak it very well. It's fun to understand their stories. My Wampanoag friends understand English, but they can't read or write it. Their own language is not even written down. Imagine that." Comfort takes the string of shell beads Philip gave her out of her pocket and gives it to Anne.

Anne examines it. "What is it?"

"Wampum. Indians make it out of quahog shells, whelk and periwinkle. It's for making promises. It's also used for money for it's a lot easier to carry than blankets and hoes when we trade for beaver pelts. Keep it. It's my way to promise to be your friend."

"How did they get these little holes in without breaking?"

"With stone tools. I broke a lot of shells trying to do it. My friend Philip lets me try only with white ones because the dark purple ones are very rare."

Anne hands her a slim leather covered book. "This is a long poem about God's creation of the world. It's by the poet Du Bartas. Keep it as a token of my friendship. I hope you'll visit as soon as my house is built."

* * * *

On the deck above, Hobbamock walks with a young sailor. Passengers stare. He touches everything - ropes, sails, the small cannons. He trades a string of wampum for a boy's grey wool cap. It's much too small and looks strange with the eagle feather sticking out from the back. The boy laughs and Hobbamock smiles.

The sailor shows him the whip staff, the large vertical arm hinged to the rudder used for steering. The twenty-eight cannons capture his interest. He has been told by Myles Standish that cannons are deadly weapons. He asks the sailor if he knows how the cannons work. "Sure. I was a powder boy in a battle against a Spanish galleon." He smiles with pride. Hobbamock is confused, but decides not to ask questions.

* * * *

In one of the few private rooms, Isaac Allerton and William Coddington are packing tobacco into their pipes. Isaac asks him for the name of a London merchant who buys pelts.

"Mr. Hughes. The price has doubled; it's a good time to sell" Coddington, says. Although he's only twenty-nine years old, he is one of the wealthiest men in the new colony. He has been appointed treasurer.

"What trade goods have you brought for the savages?" Isaac asks.

"Beads, blankets, cloth, iron pots, hoes."

"Yes. They value those things. They're asking for muskets. We don't give them any, but French and Dutch traders do. Do you know there's an endless supply of fish in these waters, sir?"

Coddington nods. "English fishing boats have been coming here for a long time."

"I've purchased that boat you suggested and can supply you with cod and bass."

Coddington thanks him. "I plan to breed cattle and horses. Unfortunately some of the best ones I've brought on the ship have died during the voyage."

* * * *

In the stern of the ship, a large table used to examine navigational charts has been covered with a green cloth and pewter mugs, beer, biscuits and salt beef are on it. Light comes in through the glass windows in this room which is in the highest part of ship.

Will removes his black hat, holds it in his lap, and begins the conversation. "I'm very grateful to you for bringing those dear souls from Leiden who will join my community. I was despondent ten years ago to have to leave so many good people behind because they had no money to pay for the journey."

"Of course, of course." says John Winthrop. "Please," he says, gesturing to the refreshments. He pours beer into a pewter mug and hands it to Will.

Winthrop has piercing steel-blue eyes, a deep, cultured voice, and a neatly trimmed black beard. Will thinks he must have been an impressive lawyer in a courtroom. His hands are those of a gentleman, not a farmer. He looks at his own rough hands, and puts them in his lap.

"We've heard good things about your small plantation," Deputy Governor Thomas Dudley says. "Although I understand you still have a great amount of debt."

Will knows Dudley has been the financial manager of the Earl of Lincoln's large landholdings. Is there condescension in his words?

Young Simon Bradstreet pushes his curly brown hair away from his wide forehead. "Yes sir. Lots of good things." He looks at his father-in-law for approval. Will thinks he is a pleasant young man. Does he have opinions of his own?

"Gentlemen, with God's blessing, we've done well," Will says. "Last winter we'd more snow than I believed possible. I feared we'd lose our entire crop. In fact, we've a surplus of corn to sell, and a few cattle to spare as well."

"Thank you. We've many mouths to feed," Winthrop says. He stares at Will with his steel- blue eyes. "Have you had any difficulty keeping order, Governor? We've brought indentured servants, poor Irish from debtors' prison, to work our fields for seven years. I expect to have the usual problems with them: drinking, lustful behavior, you know. I'll punish all who don't obey my rules. My colony will be a showcase, a beacon that shines for the whole world, a city on a hill, an example for those who come after us."

Will thinks this Governor may lack compassion. "There's much work to do in the beginning. They'll have to clear trees and plant corn. They will probably have to deal with sickness and they won't have time to engage in bad behavior."

Winthrop reaches into his pocket and takes out a small leather bound book and places it on the table. "Well, I'm prepared to keep order. I've had to deal with the worst sorts as a justice of the peace. I won't tolerate any breach of my authority. This book is my Royal Charter. I've the right to banish those who won't conform."

"Banishment, sir, is likely to divide a community; it can cause unexpected problems," Will replies. "I find that resolving conflicts fairly is the best approach."

Winthrop feels this man doesn't understand that The Bay Colony will definitely be more successful than Plimouth because they have better contacts and more money. There are likely to be thousands living in Boston before long. "Nevertheless, sir, I'll insist on conformity," Winthrop says as he puts the charter back in his pocket. "Leaders must show strength. People must fear the consequences of their actions."

Will eats a biscuit and salt beef. He brushes crumbs off the hat in his lap. He believes a leader should be flexible and listen to his people. He decides to tell Winthrop how he had to change his mind about how to divide land.

"I've had to change my ideas about land allotment. At first I insisted we hold all land in common as is the custom in many villages back home. But my men have a great yearning for their own land and desire to leave some land to their sons. Also, after experiencing oppression by our King, they had a longing for individual freedom. So, I changed my mind. Still, I insist we work for the common good and worship together, for that's what knits men's souls. It's the only way we'll survive in this harsh environment."

Reverend Wilson clears his throat and wants to speak. Will sees a man with a stern demeanor. He remembers that he's from a prominent family related to the Archbishop of Canterbury. "We've a covenant with God to establish our colony. I'll judge who's been saved by Our Lord and therefore can be counted as members of the elect, the chosen people. Only they will be members of my church. Only they will vote for our leaders. Regarding division of land, it's obvious those here should get the largest parcels. At our own expense, we've brought servants to make our land profitable."

Dudley interrupts. "As for those with different religious beliefs, we don't want them in our colony. Toleration is Satan's idea. We must protect our true church, and never let those with other ideas about God create dissent and chaos."

"Speaking of Satan," Wilson adds, "I see you've brought a heathen. How can you trust them? They're devil worshipers."

Will's anxious. He takes a moment to think, then speaks in an assertive manner. "His name's Hobbamock. He's one of the Wampanoag tribe's respected spiritual leaders. We've lived in peace with them for ten years. Gentlemen, you can, you must keep the peace with our Indian neighbors."

"Why did you choose to live so near these savages?"

"There are unexplored, dense forests everywhere along this coast. We found an abandoned Indian village already cleared near them. There were piles of bleached white human bones, and we were told those people died of some disease. The Wampanoags, during our first terrible winter, brought us food. You would be wise to show respect to the Massachuset tribe."

"But we must convert the savages," Wilson says. "It's written in our charter that we change their wicked ways. Only if they become Christians will we trust them."

"They've strong beliefs of their own. Show respect and you'll have peaceful neighbors." Will gets up and puts on his black hat, signaling a desire to leave. There'll be disagreements with these strong-willed men; today is not a time for debate. "Gentlemen, thank you for bringing our friends from Leiden. I must be off and take them to their new home."

In bed that night Will tells Alice he fears he'll have to protect Plimouth. "Many more will come. A part of our land is within their boundaries. Winthrop is a moral man, but I fear he won't listen to my opinions. These men say all natives are "devils" and can't be trusted. May God help us avoid a war." He doesn't tell Alice about his nightmare.

3

CAMBRIDGE

ANNE'S LETTER

Dear Comfort: Last winter was difficult, but this, our second winter, is even worse. I've never experienced such bitter cold. The howling wind keeps me awake all night. I can't go to church because it's on the other side of the Charles River and the raft can't go across because it has frozen. The town on our side is called Cambridge. The other side is Boston where my dear friend Lady Arbella chose to live. She died of typhus. I miss her so much.

We've built a stockade on one of the three hills in Boston, and a windmill on another hill. When I climb the hill called Beacon I can see the harbor where a wharf has been built. It's a very deep harbor and Simon says it's a blessing. We'll be able to trade with the large vessels from across the ocean. I still dream of going home, but have stopped telling Simon and my father as they get angry.

Thanks for giving Simon the poem about the passing of time when he came to Plimouth for more corn. Like the poet Sappho who wrote it, I feel melancholy most of the time. I long for spring and plan to visit you.

Your friend,
Anne Bradstreet.

She puts aside the letter, lifts Lady Arbella's red dress from the nail on the door and clasps it to her chest, using the sleeve to wipe away tears. It smells of smoke, reminding her to check the fireplace downstairs.

The wind has shifted, bringing smoke into the room. She adjusts the brown curtain that serves as a temporary damper. Coughing, she unlatches the door. A gust of cold wind brings in swirling snow.

"Close that door," her father barks, picking up several sheets of paper from the dirt floor, and putting them inside a book on his lap. He bends to pick up the blanket which was around his shoulders and has slipped to the floor.

"Look what you've done. What's wrong with you?"

"I needed air. I'm sorry."

"Now that you're out of bed, re-heat the stew."

He balances the large leather-covered book on his knees and goes back to writing. He hears Anne sobbing.

"Come, sit by me," Thomas says. He's not an affectionate man, but feels sorry for her. She's been so sad since the death of Lady Arbella.

"Remember how you would get lost on the grounds of Tatters Hall Castle? Look in the rose garden, your mother would tell me. Sure enough, you'd be with Lady Arbella, sitting on that stone bench, reading poetry. Which poet did you love best?"

"Sylvester's translation of du Bartas. I lent the book to Comfort."

"Why don't you send her your poems? Written any new ones?"

"I don't feel like writing." She wipes tears away. "Look at you, trying to write on a book balanced on your knees instead of on the beautiful mahogany desk you once had."

"That life is over. Be grateful you've shelter and food. Our servants are starving and freezing in tents. Bridget is living like a savage in a wigwam, and her infant son has just died."

"I pray I don't bring a child into this world."

"Don't say that. A child is a gift from the Lord."

Simon enters, stamping snow off his boots and brushing it off his coat. Anne takes his wet coat and drapes it over a chair near the fire.

"We're running out of food again. Winthrop wants me to return to Plimouth as soon as possible, but there's going to be another blinding blizzard." He stands before the fire rubbing his hands together.

"Anne, go upstairs and give your mother her cough medicine" her father says.

Thomas waits until Anne is gone and confronts Simon.

"Why didn't you greet your wife, Simon?"

"I had Winthrop's message on my mind."

"Don't you see how she is?"

"Of course. Her hair is always tangled, she cries herself to sleep holding that red dress." He pulls off his boots and wet socks and places them near the fire.

"We've plenty to endure without the Devil sealing Anne's soul. She's too melancholy. Women like Anne can drown in sadness."

"She must bear loss like the rest of us" Simon says, continuing to spread his wet sock out on a chair, then standing, his back to Thomas, looking into the fire.

"Be kind to her, young man. Hold her close. Look at me. Do I have to spell it out?"

"She'll only push me away." Thomas sees tears and embarrassment.

"Keep trying, son. She needs you."

Later that night, they're startled by explosions created by a small sack of gunpowder which was placed too near the hearth. Anne wraps her mother in a blanket and helps her go into the cold darkness. Simon and Thomas throw snow on the fire and put it out.

Exhausted and shivering, Anne slides under the quilt next to

Simon. He whispers "Never doubt my love." He kisses her neck several times, and she feels her body relax and respond. It's been a long time since she has slept entangled in his loving arms.

In the morning, she adds a poem to her letter to Comfort. It's about spring.

Under the cooling shadow of a stately Elm
Close sat I by a goodly River's side,
Where gliding streams the Rocks did overwhelm.
A lovely place, with pleasures dignifi'd.
I once that lov'd the shady woods so well,
Now thought the rivers did the trees excel,
There would I dwell.

4

PLIMOUTH

Three years have passed since the Bay Colony fleet arrived in New England. Comfort is sixteen. She sits near a window and watches the morning fog disappear. Next to her are two books, John Speed's "History of England", and Sir Hugh Plat's "The Jewel House of Art and Nature". On her lap is a large map of London.

"So there you are," Alice says, putting down an earthenware pot she had just washed. "Hiding in books again, and I've so much to do before our Bay Colony guests arrive." She picks up a book. "Well, at least this Plat book is practical. You can learn how to keep moths from wool cloth, and how to preserve food. You don't need to read the history book; girls don't go to school." Alice takes up the map. "Why are you studying a map of London? Planning on stowing away on the next ship?"

I'd like to, Comforts thinks. "Please let me show you something." She takes the map back from her mother. "See, this is Whitehall Palace. My friend Anne wrote that she went there when the new Banqueting House was being built. I wish I could see it."

"Oh, stop dreaming young lady. Your destiny is here; make the most of it. I had to accept the death of my first husband. I thank our Lord every day for inspiring your father to marry me. John Alden Jr. has a mind to marry you. Accept him. It's time you had a household of your own."

"John always smells from pigs. I told you, I don't want to

marry him."

"It's your father's fault, filling your head with things women don't need to know. Now put those books back in his study and come help me make a beef stew for our guests."

Why does her step-mother still treat her as if she's a child? She goes into the garden and pulls up carrots, gathers Good King Henry, a kind of spinach, and picks some Costmary which her father uses for making beer, and marjoram and hyssop to sprinkle into the stew for flavor. She helps prepare the stew.

At last their guests from Boston arrive. She watches her older brother Willie organize the procession up the hill to the meetinghouse. He looks so handsome with a long sword at his side and a wooden powder bandoleer slung across his blue coat.

The ministers, Reverend Roger Williams and John Wilson, wearing black coats and black hats, are in front. Following them, are the Governors, Deputy Governors and the Assistants. Winthrop, Dudley and Simon walk first, and her father follows with Elder Brewster. Behind them walk the rest of the men, then the women. Last of all come the children, boys first, then girls. Anne helps Comfort keep the youngest children quiet. Finally everyone is in line. Comfort's younger brothers beat their small drums providing a solemn rhythm for the procession.

When they reach the meetinghouse, the men sit on the benches on one side, the women on the other. The children stay in back. Comfort and Anne keep all the children quiet.

"I'm pregnant," Anne whispers. "You must come to Boston to help with the baby. My father and Mr. Winthrop have approved already."

"I'd love to," Comfort replies, glancing at her mother. Alice is putting a finger to her lips, shaking her head, warning her not to talk. Can she get Alice's permission? She asks many times already, but now perhaps Alice will agree. Comfort feels Alice is tired of arguing with her.

Reverend Roger Williams, a young man of thirty-three, is the new preacher at Plimouth. Governor Bradford was happy to have a Cambridge University educated clergyman living here. Today is the first time Roger is preaching to guests from the Bay Colony. He clears his throat, then nervously pushes strands of long black hair away from face. What he's about to say today will not please everyone, but he feels he must follow his conscience.

"His Hand has made and formed the whole fabric of Heaven and Earth. He hath hung out the Globe of His world, hung the Earth upon nothing, drawn over the canopy of the starry Heavens... Seas he hath made, and the vast mountains, these trees, and soft breezes around us. They are all His work."

He lifts palms up to the heavens as if to embrace the world. "He's a poet like you" Comfort whispers to Anne. She knows this will not be controversial.

"Indians have souls just like us. Of one blood...God made all mankind."

Now she watches as Wilson, Dudley and Winthrop shake their heads in disapproval. She notices that Roger is aware of their disapproval.

"I do strongly believe that one cannot impose their sense of truth on others. For he who imposes truth is no longer concerned with truth but only with imposition. Each must find truth within his own soul, in his own way. Those who mistake their own assurances for divinely appointed missions, and so forget the sanctity of others' persuasions, as to try reducing them to conformity, commit in the face of the Divine a sin more outrageous than other crimes. We've had enough of such conformity in old England. Let us keep ourselves from it in New England."

Why are they upset? Didn't they hate being forced by the King and Bishops to conform to rituals they didn't like? Comfort sees that Winthrop is particularly upset.

Roger's concludes his sermon, and Comfort is delighted with his words.

"Faith is an inward power; it causes the Divine Father to shine in our hearts. We are resurrected by God's grace, and we are given a new heart. We must have an open mind, and an open heart. A blind mind can no more grasp heavenly things than a blind eye judge colors. This world is the reflected Light of God's son, and we must seek His wisdom to prepare ourselves by His Grace for Heaven. We bless you Lord for giving this world to us and pray that we will be worthy of your Grace. Amen."

"Did you like the sermon?" Comfort asks Anne.

"My father didn't," she replies.

Can't you think for yourself? Comfort thinks. But she doesn't say anything.

After the sermon, everyone walks down the hill to the harbor for the Sabbath meal. Long boards have been set on trestles to make tables. Comfort brings out wooden trenchers with round loaves of warm bread, earthenware bowls of beef stew, spoons, and pewter tankards for her father's homemade beer.

Suddenly it's quiet as guests see Hobbamock and his wife who've walked through the gate in the fence and are carrying a roasted turkey on a wooden tray. Captain Miles Standish invites them to sit at his table. He and Hobbamock are friends.

A few minutes later Little Bird and Philip ride up on a black horse. They speak briefly to Hobbamock, greet her father politely, and stare at the guests, then leave again. Comfort envies their freedom to come and go as they please. Little Bird is holding tightly to Philip's bare back as they ride off. Comfort admits to herself she's jealous of Little Bird. Philip is a handsome, muscular young man. Little Bird has confessed to her that she wants to marry him.

After the meal, Roger wants to visit Hobbamock's compound.

Comfort asks Hobbamock in Algonquian if it would be alright.

"Of course, *cowammaunish*".

"What did he say?" Roger asks. He's been learning a few words since living here, but doesn't understand this one. He's good at learning languages and wants to be fluent in Algonquian.

"He calls me 'daughter'. Don't tell my mother, for she doesn't approve."

* * * *

After the meal, Comfort and Roger walk to Hobbamock's house. They sit on a bearskin covered sleeping bench. Roger offers Hobbamock some Virginia tobacco. "It's not as harsh as the Indian kind," he informs Comfort.

"I like it, *netop*," Hobbamock says. "Thank you for sharing it with me."

Roger is happy. Hobbamock has called him *netop*, a friend.

Hobbamock, his dark eyes shining with pleasure, fills his long stemmed stone pipe again. Comfort thinks he's a handsome man. She likes his bronze colored skin and his long, shiny black braid. He's wise, kind and respected by his people and her father.

He and Roger take turns, passing the pipe to each other, smoking in silence. Comfort watches them. Little Bird hasn't returned home and she's bored. Soon she asks Roger if they can return.

"Why does Hobbamock live so close to us?" Roger asks, as he passes through the gate in the fence.

"He helps my father understand what Chief *sachem* Massasoit is thinking and also reports to Massasoit. He's a *powwaw*, a spiritual man and sometimes he goes into a trance and sees what will happen in the future."

Roger shakes his head. "We can't know the future. I believe strongly if we follow our own conscience, we'll do what's right."

When they arrive back at the Governor's house, they see the Bay Colony guests getting ready to return to Boston. Anne hugs Comfort. "Please try to come to Boston to help me when my baby is born."

That night, Comfort pleads with her step-mother to allow her to go to Boston. Alice, as usual, refuses. Angry, she walks up the hill to the meetinghouse, looks up at the star filled sky, and asks God to help her find a way to live a more exciting life.

5

PLIMOUTH

"There's going to be a wedding tomorrow!" Comfort says, catching her breath after running up the hill to the meetinghouse to talk to Roger Williams who is practicing his sermon.

"Here?"

"No. Mount Hope. You must come. The village is at the end of a rocky peninsula, on a high hill that overlooks Narragansett Bay. It's often very windy, but I love it there. My father often takes me with him when he needs to see Chief Massaasoit. Philip and I sit overlooking the bay and he tells me stories about bears."

"Who's getting married?"

"Wamsutta. We call him Alexander. He's Philip's older brother. He's marrying Little Bird's half-sister Weetamoo."

He writes Wetamoo and Wamsutta in the little book he always carries in his pocket which is filled with Algonquian words. "Tell me the word for 'husband' as well as the one for 'wife'. I want to write these in my book."

"*Wasick* is husband and the word for wife is *weewo.*"

Roger tries pronouncing them, and she corrects him.

"The word for brother is *weemat.*" He writes this down as well, then he asks her to explain the succession of leadership of the tribe.

"The oldest, that's Alexander, will be chosen *sachem* when Chief Massasoit dies. Then, when he dies, Philip will be *sachem*. If a *sachem* only has a daughter, no sons, she can be a squaw Queen. Several of the Wampanoag bands have *squaw sachems.*"

"I would like to meet a *squaw-sachem,*" Roger says.

"Oh you will. I'll introduce you to Awashonks. She's a cousin of Philips, and *squaw sachem* of the Sakonnet band. I visited her with my father. Our canoe stopped at a place they call Toothos. It is very beautiful. In winter she lives in Tompe Swamp. She's very friendly to me and my father."

* * * *

Hobbamock and his family are packing all their things, and Roger and Comfort are helping them. After the wedding the family will be staying in Mount Hope for the winter. Roger helps them remove the woven mats that form the walls and roof of their *wetu,* and Comfort puts these in a pile. Only the bare bent poles of the structure are going to be left here to be used next summer. Comfort visits this empty place during the snowy winter days when she misses her friend. She tells the bare trees and frozen grass all the secrets her heart longs to share with her absent best friend.

Little Bird takes out a deer's shoulder blade wrapped with sinew around a stick. Then she takes a piece of soft deerskin to protect this sharp tool used to drill holes into shells to make wampum. She tells Roger this tool is also used to sew shell beads on moccasins to make them pretty. Comfort smiles, proud of her friend's artistic abilities.

"I'm sharing a *wetu* with Philip this winter," she tells Comfort. "I'm so happy." She laughs aloud, then covers her mouth with her hands, realizing her friend will be surprised about this practice of trial marriage. "Surely you've noticed he loves me. We'll live together for a year to make sure we want to marry."

Comfort remembers when Little Bird called Philip *wagwise,* mischievous fox, then took his hand and followed him into the woods. She was jealous when she realized they weren't going to return and guessed what was happening in the shadows.

Roger asks Comfort questions as they work bringing out from the *wetu* pottery and baskets. "When's a boy considered a man and allowed to marry?"

"After he completes his vision quest. He must fast in the woods and live alone for two months. Philip told me during his vision quest he saw a blue light and was visited by his spirit helper, a huge brown bear. I'd be scared to death if I saw a bear, but he wasn't."

"Did he kill it?"

"Yes. Its hide is on his sleeping bench. That wooden bench wouldn't be comfortable without it. Surely you've seen the bear's claws on the leather band he wears around his neck? It's proof of his courage. He says the bear's strong spirit is now living in him."

"Is having a bear as his spirit helper considered special by his people?"

"Yes. Wampanoags call bears 'brothers'. I heard a story about a girl who married a bear. Bears can stand on two legs like us, and reach up with their paws for berries. Little Bird says bears are wonderful mothers to their cubs. She's told me many bear stories."

"What does it mean if someone has a bear as his spirit guide?"

"Hobbamock says Philip will be a great leader. Bears are honored by the Great Spirit, *Maushop,* and Philip will be honored by their most powerful God."

"We Christians think bears remind us about the renewal of life after death," Roger says. "The bear hibernates in winter and is alive again in spring. In England a man wearing a bear costume made of straw dances with young girls in the spring. He's called the Shrovetide Bear. Many villagers give him money and food to insure a good harvest. I once saw a girl take straws from his costume and put them in her chicken coop to ensure that her chickens lay more eggs. Of course that's just superstition."

"Why are there so many stories about bears?"

"We humans are dependent on the cycle of nature. We wonder about death and hope for rebirth."

"Philip believes there are gods—*manitou*—in animals, plants, and even in rocks. He believes *Maushop*, a benevolent Giant, was sent to watch over Mankind."

"Do you know any stories about *Maushop*?" Roger asks.

"Well I was told *Maushop* once split open an ash tree and the First Man stepped out."

"And Eve? What do they think about the creation of the first woman?"

"Philip says that *Maushop* created Woman because First Man needed someone to carry his water, plant his corn, cook his food and nurse his babies. I told him a wife has wisdom to offer, if he cares to listen to her. He teased me about that, but I know he respects Little Bird's ideas. She told me so."

"Tell me about *Maushop*,"

"He freed streams from the swollen belly of a giant frog. He captured the Wind Eagle, but the world fell into a stifling calm, so he loosened the eagle's wings again and cool breezes wafted once more. He made all the animals and taught men how to track and snare them. He taught us about the stars. And when the world was created and fit for humans, *Maushop* went to live in the forest with Grandmother."

"Do you know what Philip believes about our people?"

"He says my father promised to protect the Wampanoags from their enemy, the Narragansetts, and someday it will be my turn to keep the peace between us and his people. But how can I? No woman can be chosen to be Governor. He made me promise to try."

6

Mount Hope

Comfort holds on tightly to Little Bird's waist as they ride a golden mare with a white mane to Mount Hope. She smells bear grease which has been mixed with soot to enhance the blackness and shine of her friend's hair. The smell reminds her of the time Philip asked her to spread it on his back to keep away mosquitoes. Now Little Bird will be doing that for him.

"Tell me again the story about Ahsoo and her beautiful voice."

"Once there was a woman called Ahsoo. She had a pointed chin, sharp as the beak of a loon, and a crooked nose, and eyes like a frightened doe. She wasn't pretty, but she had a pleasing voice."

"Did she sing?"

"When she sang, birds paused to listen to her. One of those lured by her singing was Trout Chief, a big fish. He followed her voice inland from the sea, swimming so fast that he died."

"What does this story mean?"

"It reminds us of the spawning season when older fish die. We call that month 'Spearfish Moon Days'. You call it 'April'. Why?"

"I've no idea." Comfort thinks English stories are about the dangers of the wilderness, like the story of Red Riding Hood and the bad wolf. Do we fear nature? Her mother feared this wilderness was full of lions. She'd rather believe like the Wampanoags do that animals have spirits and are our cousins and everything alive must be in harmony.

They cross a stream, then climb a hill to Mount Hope. Comfort sees fields of corn entwined with beans. Squash has been planted between the rows. There is a field of bright orange pumpkins. Women, cradleboards strapped on their backs, bend down to harvest the multicolored corn.

As they enter the village a domesticated wolf-dog chases their horse. Two old women who are sewing deerskin tunics under the shade of a birch tree shout a greeting to Little Bird. She gives her horse to a boy, and they walk among *wetus* which are built in a circular pattern around a large field, the sacred ground. Mats from the top have been removed to let autumn breezes into the *wetus*.

Several gray-haired men sit in front of the council lodge throwing sacred tobacco into the fire. Chief Massasoit and her father are talking. Roger and her older brother Willie are sharing a pipe of tobacco with Hobbamock. Philip and Alexander are talking quietly and she can't hear them. She remembers that Little Bird has asked her to call them Metacom and Wamsutta today.

"Metacom, Metacom, Metacom" Little Bird says in a soft, coy voice to him. He gives her braid a little tug. "Wootonekanuske, why are you late? Didn't you miss me?" He is wearing two flaps of deerskin tied at the waist called a breechcloth, and his muscular chest shines with sweat.

"Ah, Sky Eyes, welcome," Metacom says. "Wamsutta and I've been racing all morning. I, of course, won every race as usual. We're going to cool off in the river. Little Bird and you must join us for a swim."

Comfort looks at her father. "Only watch if you want to go," he says. He's preoccupied with how to tell Massasoit that many more ships are arriving this fall with thousands of new English settlers. Small villages are being set up around Plimouth and Boston.

At the riverbank, she sits on a log watching her friends

splashing in the water, their strong bodies glistening in the sun. How she longs to join them! She is hot in her long-sleeved shirt and long skirt. She walks to the edge of the river and splashes cold water on her face then decides to return to her father. Perhaps he'll need her to translate.

Will is tossing a handful of ceremonial tobacco into the fire. Massasoit passes him the long stemmed ceremonial pipe and he puffs it and passes it back.

"I'm happy your son is marrying the daughter of our good friend Hobbamock," Will says. The gifts he has brought are on the ground nearby. He has brought Massasoit an iron kettle for his wife, a large green cushion for himself, and a trumpet to announce visitors as the English do. He also gives him a copper bowl and copper bracelets as wedding gifts for Wamsutta and Weetamoo.

Massasoit smiles but doesn't speak. Will is used to his long silences. The Chief signals to a boy who takes the gifts into the longhouse. Finally he speaks.

"My friend, speak the truth. How long will these strangers stay in my country?"

"They'll raise children, and grandchildren. Know in your heart, our King across the great water wishes your people friendship. Haven't we been good neighbors?"

Massasoit fills his pipe again with a mixture of tobacco and a powdered red bark. Finally he speaks again. Comfort helps translate a few words her father doesn't know.

"You're strangers in our land. Your cut down too many trees and the deer flee. You allow men to own more land than they need, and to give it to their sons forever. That's not our way. The land must belong to all the people. Only I decide how much each family needs to use."

Will takes the pipe when Massasoit passes it to him. He's not sure what to say and feels sad. He had wanted to have Plimouth's people share all the land, but each man coming here wanted his own property.

After another long silence, Massasoit continues. "I hope these new strangers have as much peace in their hearts as you have in yours, my friend." Then he gets up and they follow him into the longhouse. The wedding is about to begin. Comfort sits with the women on one side of the large room and her father sits with the men and next to Chief Massasoit as an honored guest.

Hobbamock starts the ceremony. He tells Wamsutta, now dressed in doeskin pants and a shirt painted with pictures of horses, to wrap his bride and himself in a large deerskin. Now they're bound together as husband and wife. Hobbamock then takes out of the pouch around his neck a special tobacco. He chews it then dances in a trance. He sings to them and tells them he has had a vision of them and they will always love each other.

After the ceremony, the young and old people dance to the beating drums. Comfort watches Metacom and Little Bird dance, sees their legs move to the rhythm of the drumming, their joy. She longs to join them, but knows her father wouldn't like it. She wonders if someday when she marries she'll be allowed to invite her Indian friends to the wedding.

7

PLIMOUTH

Alice is awake. It's still dark. She takes a coat and goes outside.
She sees a yellow crocus in a patch of melting snow. At last spring
will come. It's been a difficult winter. Twenty of our people have
died of smallpox. Many more Indians have died. Roger and Mary
want to leave after their baby is born. There were fewer cases of
smallpox in Salem where he's going to be a preacher. She won't
be sorry to see him leave. His opinions about God and his relationships with the Indians have not pleased her. Because of his
desire to learn the Algonquian language, Comfort has spent too
much time taking him to visit the Wampanoags.

She is cold, so goes inside. She decides to look at Comfort.
Her step-daughter is at a critical age. Soon she must arrange a
marriage for her. Alice sees she's sleeping peacefully, the new
diary by her side. Simon Bradstreet brought it as a present from
Anne for Comfort's seventeenth birthday. This girl wastes her
time writing in the book rather than helping me weed the garden.
What on earth does a young girl write about? Curious, she picks
up the diary and opens it at random. She reads about a visit to
Mount Hope last August.

COMFORT'S DIARY

*Roger and I watched them make a large canoe. A large tree was cut
down and burned out in the center before we arrived. Roger drew*

sketches of the men working, but I was bored so I decided to find Philip and Little Bird. Little Bird wasn't home, but Philip seemed delighted to see me. I rested on the sleeping bench watching him make arrows, then I fell asleep. When I woke up, he was lying next to me. I was startled but he smiled, and touched my cheek gently.

*"I'll never hurt you Sky Eyes. You were created by **Maushop** to teach me that English people can be kind. You are a beautiful woman." He touched my hair gently. "Ah **netop**, we wish you could marry our friend and come live here in Mount Hope."*

We both got up and went to find Roger. He was drawing the finished canoe. I don't know how many men can fit into it, but Roger thinks twenty men. He wrote that in his book.

Riding back home with Roger, I longed to tell him what Philip said, but feared he would tell my mother. I wish I was marrying Philip. I mustn't be jealous of my best friend. I should go to Boston and live with Anne, for my feelings are not proper. If only Alice would let me go.

Alice doesn't want to read any more of the diary and places it back on Comfort's mattress. She returns to her bed and gently touches Will's arm.

"Are you awake?"

"I am now. What's wrong?"

"I'm afraid our daughter will get herself in trouble."

"Why?"

Alice told him what she read in the diary. "He could have…"

"Nothing happened. Calm down."

"We need to choose a husband for her," Alice says. "John Alden Jr. is interested and suitable, but she doesn't like him."

"I won't force her to marry someone she doesn't love."

"Do you want her to marry one of the devil's children?"

"Please don't call them that. Anyway, Little Bird and Philip are going to marry."

"I don't want Indian grandchildren. Even if the Indians convert, I don't want those people as my kin. I won't have it."

"What do you want me to do?"

"Let's send her to live with Anne Bradstreet. Mr. Dudley's a strict father. Maybe he'll find a rich merchant who'll agree to marry her."

"She's wanted to go for a long time. She can keep me informed about affairs in Boston. I've an uneasy feeling now that they've set up a trading post in the north in competition with ours. Tell her she has our permission to go."

"I hope she doesn't break your heart, Will. She's a stubborn, willful girl. I'll be glad when she has a husband who'll insist she behave as a proper wife."

* * * *

Roger and Mary come to visit the next morning. Mary is going to give birth to their first child soon. Alice will be midwife and Comfort will assist.

"Did you know about Indians when you were growing up?" Comfort asks Roger.

"When I was a young man I saw an Indian princess named Pocahontas. Captain Smith wrote a book about how she saved his life. He's known to exaggerate, but I believed him about this and was excited to see her."

"What did she look like? Did she speak English? Did others come with her?"

"Not so many questions all at once, dear" Alice says. She frowns, but Roger says he doesn't mind her questions.

"Where was she when you saw her?"

"I went with my father to La Belle Savage Tavern and Inn near

St. Paul's Church. It was Christmas, and I remember the room was filled with the smell of pine. There were candles in the windows. I loved the red holly which was hanging from the beams."

"Was she in the tavern? I thought women were not allowed."

"She was upstairs getting ready for a procession to the palace. Queen Anne invited her to tea. I wanted to catch a glimpse of her carriage, so father told me to go outside and wait until she came out and watch it leave. He didn't like all this fuss about her. He said she was only invited in order to help the stock company raise money for Virginia and find investors interested in tobacco farms. Her husband was an English tobacco farmer."

"I don't approve of marrying with savages" Alice says. "Don't you agree? We must marry our own kind." Alice can't resist looking at Comfort.

"Indians find us too ugly; we are far too hairy and pale to be attractive to them," Roger says laughing.

"What did she look like, this princess? Did Queen Anne send a golden carriage for her?"

"I'll tell you what I remember of that wonderful day. I never forgot it. There were boys dressed in gold coats, marching four across, banging on small drums in front of the open golden carriage. Hitched to it were four white horses wearing large white feathers on their heads. She came out of the Inn and sat in the carriage."

"Who sat in the carriage with her?"

"Her uncle, a *sachem*, and his wife. He wore a brown bearskin around his shoulders and his wife wore a white fox cape. She held Pocahontas' small son on her lap. He looked just like an English boy. Did you know she was converted to Christianity?"

"No. What was she wearing?"

"She wore a cape with a lace collar, and a tall black hat and she carried a scepter with feathers on the top of it. Her husband wasn't invited to the palace because he was a commoner, not royalty."

"Did she stay in London a long time?"

"No. She died there. Her son remained with her husband's brother. He is still there, and is being raised a Christian. He may come here someday to get his inheritance."

"I hope she didn't have smallpox. It's so painful a death," Comfort says. "Little Bird's brother has it now. It's so sad."

"Don't talk about it," Alice says. "We're all scared enough as it is."

Roger puts his coat around Mary's shoulders. "I pray this horrible sickness will end quickly."

"We must pray for the Indians too" Will adds. "I've seen pox all over their bodies. Many are too weak to eat. Half of those who get it die."

"I've heard many here say it's God's will. They feel the Wampanoags are dying so we can have their land and properly improve it. They feel God wants us to prosper" Roger says. He's angry. "We must be more compassionate. I'll write a sermon about this tonight."

8

Hobbamock's Compound

Hobbamock's son has died. Roger's head is bowed in silent prayer. Comfort leans against her father's shoulder. In front of them is a freshly dug hole. Behind them, in a pile, the poles and mats of Hobbamock's *wetu* are on the ground, discarded. The family is leaving and their house can no longer exist in this spot. This is the Wampanoag custom when someone in a family dies.

Little Bird has come to the funeral. She has loosened her long, black hair. She has slashed the front of her doeskin tunic with a knife as a sign of mourning. She has rubbed her face, arms, and legs with ashes. She stands, looking into the hole. It will be a long time before she can decorate her body with jewelry or put red paint on her face, or use bear grease to make her hair shine. Her wedding to Metacom has been postponed.

Little Bird's mother is kneeling on the ground. Her naked upper torso is blackened with ashes. She is sobbing and watches two old women wrap her son's pock-marked body in large woven mats.

Metacom and his friends lift the bundled body and place it in the hole. They sit in silence. He glances at Comfort and her father. His angry face chills her soul. Surely he doesn't blame them? He asked her once why fewer of her people get sick with smallpox, but she doesn't know. Her father puts his arm around her shoulders, and tries to calm her, but her tears keep falling. Roger hands her his handkerchief.

A gray-haired *pawwaw,* wearing a cape covered with eagle feathers, begins chanting, and dancing. His feet create dust clouds as he stamps the dry earth round the gravesite in a trance.

When she first heard his chanting early this morning, she thought it was a howling wolf. Then she realized Beaver, the brother of Little Bird, must have died.

Hobbamock moves around his son's grave sprinkling sacred tobacco into it from each of its four sides. Metacom places Beaver's things into the grave: a bow, a sheaf of arrows, a clay tobacco pipe, and a wampum belt with alternating lines of dark purple and white shell beads. All these belongings will go with Beaver to the place they call the Southwest.

"Do you know what they believe about Heaven?" she whispers to Roger. He has been asking questions about their religion.

"*Keihtan*, the Great Spirit, lives where all dead people go, not only good people. Life is just as it is here, even better, with all pleasures of the flesh. They don't believe in a Judgement Day. They may think differently, but feel the pain of loss just as deeply as we do."

After the funeral, women serve fish stew to the men. The women will eat what is leftover. Little Bird pushes away a plate that Metacom offers her.

Comfort wants to hug her, to tell her how sorry she is, but doesn't dare. She has never felt so strongly that she is an outsider.

She, her father and Roger decide to leave. As they walk through the palisade gate, she hopes Little Bird will still be her friend. She's leaving for Boston soon and won't be able to write since Algonquian doesn't have a written language. Little Bird speaks English well, but can't read it. Comfort will never forget how she looks, bent over, frail, and weighed down by deep sorrow.

9

PLIMOUTH

"Dress quickly. Mary's baby is coming," Alice shouts, waking Comfort from a dream about being on a ship going to London.

When she comes downstairs, she sees Alice sitting on the floor in front of the oak chest, carefully preparing burnet to staunch excessive bleeding, and making a plaster of tansy, mugwort, chamomile and hyssop. Comfort helps her wrap everything in clean clothes which have been boiled and dried in the sun. They hurry to Roger's house to help Mary deliver her child.

Roger has reason to be anxious. It's his first child. He is sitting in front of the hearth praying silently while in the other room Mary is moaning in pain. "Please God let her and the child live.

"Push again," he hears Alice say. "I can see the baby's head."

Roger hears a baby crying. He thanks God that his child is alive.

"Hold your healthy daughter." Alice says, bringing him the infant wrapped in a clean white cloth."

He looks into the sweet sleeping face of the baby in his arms. "How's Mary?"

"She didn't lose too much blood, so she'll be fine. Comfort will come tomorrow and bring her some chicken broth."

The next month Roger is preparing to take his family to their new home in Salem. Comfort will go with them to

Cambridge, to live with Anne and Simon Bradstreet.

One day Alice gives her a gift of paper, ink, and a quill pen.

"Be obedient, do what they ask you to do, and don't ask too many questions," she says. "Simon will bring me your letters when he comes here."

"I'll tell you everything. I promise." She hugs Alice.

That night Alice tells Will that she's anxious Comfort might do something in Cambridge to bring shame to his reputation.

"I trust her." He can't sleep wondering if she'll ever return to live here again. He will miss her.

10

CAMBRIDGE

COMFORT'S LETTER

Dear Mother: I'm so sorry I haven't written sooner. I'm happy and very busy taking care of Anne's baby Sammy. He knows words, but can't always say what he wants. He makes fists and screams "no" if I don't do what he wants. I'm getting good at caring for this demanding boy.

Anne is grateful for my help. From time to time she gets melancholy, so I take Sammy to the Common, a meadow where cows graze. I'm sad Anne suffers from this affliction. Some believe the Devil sends it, but I believe these dark times come because Simon is gone away on business so often.

There are many villages being established near Boston. Simon told me over four thousand people live here now and hundreds more arrive from London every few months. Newcomers build their own meetinghouses. Mr. Dudley doesn't like that because he wants Reverend Wilson to judge if those newcomers are godly enough to live here. Dan says they turned away a ship bringing over a hundred people last month because they were not thought to be morally fit to stay.

You should see the frightened faces when Massachusets Indians come to trade with pelts slung over their naked shoulders. Mothers grab their children's hands and pull them away even though the Massachusetts tribe is friendly. My friends Little Bird and Philip would be uncomfortable here. Do you know if they've decided to marry? I must go to their wedding.

Last month Anne asked her Irish servant Dan to show me around

Boston. *He took me across the river on a Thursday, Lecture Day. On this day folks from all the small villages come to First Church to hear Mr. Wilson's sermon. There's a market near the harbor where they shop and sell animals and food. Many large ships are always in the harbor. Dan says Boston will be a center of commerce for all the colonies.*

Dan took me up the Muddy River by canoe. Such large farms! Mr. Winthrop, Mr. Dudley, and Mr. Coddington have the biggest ones. They've brought several indentured Irish servants to work on their land. They justify allotting the best land to themselves because they have more servants. Governor Winthrop has six hundred acres in one area and fertile land along the north shore of the harbor. Irish servants can't own land. Some of the artisans, carpenters, tailors, and sailmakers have been allotted small gardens.

You'd love Town Cove! There are many shops all along the harbor. There's a dressmaker who has drawings of the latest fashions in London. I saw rolls and rolls of colorful silk and linsey-woolsey. Can I have money to make a new dress? I can't wear my old Sabbath dress. It's way too tight across the bodice. Please...

I saw a bookseller with books recently published in London. Imagine that! I'm thinking of buying Mr. John Smith's new book for father for his birthday as I know he has his other book.

I'm invited to a dinner party at Mr. Coddington's house tonight. I'm so excited to see inside it. It's the only brick house in town, and Anne says they have lots of pretty things.

Anne will lend me one of her dresses for tonight. She wants me to find a young man to marry so I'll be able to stay here. I'll learn so much from the educated people here if I could stay. Please don't worry. I'm not in any hurry to marry!

Love,
Comfort

* * * *

So this is how a rich merchant lives, Comfort thinks as she sees the Coddington house. Two large silver candelabra, each holding six candles, light the long oak table on which have been placed delicate porcelain dishes with pink flowers. There are tapestry cushions on the high backed chairs. Fragile wine glasses sparkle in the flickering candlelight. A large gold framed mirror hangs over a handsome chest with gold inlaid flowers. Armchairs and small tables covered with Turkish rugs flank each side of the large stone hearth. In one corner of the room there is a spinning wheel and beside it a basket overflowing with blue and purple wool. It's the most exquisite room she's ever seen.

"Tell me about Mr. Coddington," she whispers in Anne's ear.

"Well, he's a successful wool merchant and his wife Mary plays the violin. Come, I'll introduce you." She takes Comfort's hand.

"Mary, meet my friend Comfort Bradford, the Plimouth Governor's daughter. She's staying with me. She has a special talent for languages, reads Latin and Greek, and has inspired me to write poetry again. Best of all, she calms my baby's wild nature."

"Welcome. I'm glad you read literature. You must get to know John Winthrop Jr. for he has brought over a thousand books, including many in Latin and Greek. We've many graduates of Cambridge University here."

Mary points to a young man. "That fellow will provide musical entertainment for us after dinner. He plays the viola da gama beautifully. You play an instrument also, don't you Anne?"

"I played the harpsicord when we lived in Lincolnshire, but father says it isn't modest for a woman to perform in public so I only play for family."

"The music tonight was written for a masque I attended in a nobleman's house. But now please excuse me, for I must ask the servants to serve dinner."

What is a viola da gama? Comfort wonders. What's a masque? How confident Anne is. She wishes she'd grown up in London. Reverend John Cotton walks over to Anne. "This spring a family is coming who attended my church in London. The mother, Anne Hutchinson, is an extremely pious woman. Her father, a preacher, went to jail for the right to preach our Calvinist doctrine. I'd be grateful Anne if you'd make her feel welcome here."

"Of course."

He recognizes Comfort. "I understand your father taught you to read scripture in the ancient languages."

"Yes." She's pleased he knows she's able to read Greek and Latin.

"Anne Hutchinson knows both languages also. She organized meetings for the women in my London parish and I hope she'll do the same here. Perhaps you will attend."

Mary Coddington announces dinner is served. As they walk to the table, Anne points out John Winthrop Jr. "His wife and young daughter died last winter so he's looking for a new wife. You must borrow books, everyone does."

Are those small plates for bread or dessert? Comfort, confused, decides to copy everything Anne does.

Reverend Cotton says the prayer: "Let us lift up our eyes and hearts to God in Heaven to bless us poor worms under His feet. Thou, who feed every living creature, make our food to be a staff to sustain our faint and weary bodies and feed our souls, and help us rejoice in the Lord, Amen."

Throughout the meal, Comfort remains quiet, too nervous to talk. She listens as John Cotton talks to John Harvard. "When can we establish a university?" Mr. Harvard asks.

"Soon. We'll need more educated clergy."

"In my view, a university shouldn't only teach religion but also languages, philosophy, and the new sciences like astronomy. If that's the kind of institution you're planning, I'll donate money to get it started."

What does "the new sciences" mean Comfort wonders?

After dinner a young man appears with a viola da gama. He says his friend John Milton, a poet, wrote the lyrics for this song which is part of a masque. Mary Coddington tells them she saw it at Ludlow Castle the home of Lord Bridgewater. It was performed to celebrate his appointment by King Charles as the administrator of Wales. "The Lord and his children sang parts in it," she says.

"What's a masque?" Comfort whispers to Anne.

"It's a story told with music, poetry, and dancing. They're only performed for the King's pleasure or in houses of rich nobles. I saw them when I lived with Lady Arbella."

"It's called Comus," the young man says. "That was the name of the ancient Greek god of revelry, son of Bacchus, the god of wine and the witch Circe. In this masque an ugly man tries to get a beautiful lady drunk in order to get her into his bed."

"Circe's gave herbs to Odysseus so he would stay with her and not return to his wife Penelope," Anne says. Comfort says she knows the story.

"Does the beautiful woman remain chaste?" Reverend Cotton asks. He doesn't think this is a proper story for a dinner party.

"Of course she does. These lyrics aren't bawdy, sir. Mr. Milton is a pious man. His lyrics indirectly criticize the King's court for indulging in carnal pleasures. Temptations are a theme of his poetry."

At the end of the evening, Comfort is relieved she didn't make any inappropriate comments. If she can't go to London, at least she can learn from educated people here. But will she be accepted? The only way is to marry the right husband.

Beacon Hill

Comfort and Anne have taken Sammy on the ferry across the Charles River. It was difficult, but they climbed up Beacon Hill to pick wild blueberries. There are three hills in the center of town. The middle one called Beacon Hill is the highest at one hundred and fifty feet. From here they will be able to see tall ships arriving from London in the harbor. This hill will be used to build a warning fire to be seen by many should enemy ships invade. There aren't many trees, for Indians cleared this area long ago, but it's a good place to find wild blueberries.

They stand at the top and marvel at the beauty of the shimmering harbor below. Sammy loves to see men unloading barrels of imported goods, fisherman mending their nets, and passengers disembarking from large sailing ships. Sammy loves to find the blueberries and mushrooms.

An hour latter he's tired, so Comfort spreads a quilt on the ground. He puts his head in her lap, sucks his thumb, twirls a curl with a finger, and quickly falls asleep. "I'd love to hear the love poem you've dedicated to Simon." Anne recites it.

If ever two were one, then surely we,
If ever man were loved by wife, then thee;
If ever wife was happy in a man,
Compare with me, ye women, if you can.

I prize thy love more than whole Mines of gold,
Or all the riches that the East doth hold,
My love is such that Rivers cannot quench.
Nor aught but love from thee, give recompense.

"I hope I'll be blessed with a husband I love as much as you love Simon."

"What kind of a man do you hope to marry?"

"Well, one thing, I don't want one who raises smelly pigs! He must be educated and take me to London. Of course, he will be affectionate. I don't want a man who's afraid of my Indian friends."

"Hasn't your mother someone in mind?"

"I'd rather be a thornback and remain single forever than marry that boy."

Suddenly they hear six blasts of a trumpet followed by musket shots announcing the arrival of a large ship. The commotion wakes Sammy. Comfort takes his chubby hand and they look down at the harbor.

"It's The Griffin. See the three masts, Sammy?" Anne tells him. "My father said 200 are coming on it. Let's fold the blanket and go down to watch the ship unload."

"Perhaps your true love will be on it," Anne teases, as she puts Sammy's shoes on. "Let me fix your hair." She takes out a wooden comb. "Such beautiful hair should be free to catch the sun's light."

Sammy reaches with his sticky hands and grabs Comfort's hair. "Ouch! You'd better carry him."

Anne puts Sammy on her hip and they start down the hill. Then Sammy wants to walk, so their pace is leisurely as he stops often to study flowers or point to butterflies.

"Look," Anne says, "Keayne's warehouse taking in lots of barrels. I wonder what is in them. Simon says he's going to get wealthy from provisioning ships. I hope he's brought quality linsey-woolsey. I'll have to find out if the dressmaker's shop on Town Cove gets some."

"See Thomas Fowle's shop, Sammy, where sails are mended." Comfort says. Sammy's busy gathering pebbles and putting them in his pocket.

"Fourteen investors have helped us build this wharf" Anne says. "Simon told me they plan to have many more as commerce will be expanded because our harbor is perfect for the largest ships."

A tall, young man climbs out of a one of the small boats. He is carrying a red haired baby. He walks up to them. "Hello. I'm Ned Hutchinson. Would you ladies please be kind enough to hold my sister Susanna for a few minutes? I must get my brother to help me with the chests. I'll be right back."

Comfort takes the child. Susanna immediately grabs her nose. Comfort laughs. The child laughs, and Sammy laughs. "How pretty you are, Susanna." Sammy grabs her hand too hard and she cries. "She's too little to play, Sammy." Anne takes Sammy for a walk to watch barrels going into the warehouse.

Ned talks to a tall woman about forty-five surrounded by many children. Anne Hutchinson is introducing her children to Reverend Cotton. He greets each child. The youngest girl hides behind her mother's skirt.

"My, what a large family you have Susanna!" Comfort says after she counts thirteen of various ages.

"So nice to see you again, Mistress Hutchinson," John Cotton says. "I'm looking forward to having you and your husband in my church once again."

Ned returns to Comfort to collect Susanna. "Thanks for minding Susanna. Land at last. I'll never be a sailor." He has curly brown hair, blue-grey eyes and a warm smile. She finds him attractive and thinks he's close to her age, but certainly can't ask him.

He takes Susanna. "Forgive me for being bold, but you've beautiful eyes. I've neglected to ask your name." Will she think he's flirting? Well, so what if he is.

"Comfort Bradford. I live with my friend Anne Bradstreet." She blushes, and touches her hair.

"My father's a wool merchant. My mother's over there. I see your friend is getting introduced, so why don't you also come to meet my mother."

Mistress Hutchinson pushes stray gray hairs under her white cap. Her blue-grey eyes are the same as Ned's, and her gaze reveals self-confidence. She greets them politely, but says she must supervise the unloading and takes her younger children with her to where sailors are stacking large wooden trunks. Ned and his older brother are busy arranging for transportation with the driver of a large wagon.

"I'm hungry mommy," Sammy says. Anne gives him a biscuit kept in her pocket for such times, and they walk towards the landing to get the ferry back across the river. As they wait, Comfort thinks about Ned. When will I see him again? I think he's about eighteen.

"You're dreaming," Anne says. "Are you thinking about that handsome young man?"

"His sister Susanna's pretty. I loved her red hair, didn't you? I'd like to see her again."

Anne laughs. "Let's give him a little time to settle in, then we'll arrange to see him again."

12

BOSTON

Comfort sees Ned at church and town meetings. He smiles but doesn't speak to her. She nervously checks the announcements to see if he has informed the community he has plans to marry. A man must tell people his intention at three different meetings before the magistrate will marry the couple. A civil ceremony not a religious one is performed. His name is not listed, but that doesn't mean he isn't courting someone. He could have met a girl on the ship coming across the ocean. She knows a couple who married soon after they arrived.

She searches the crowd for him at the Thursday market held after the Bible lecture. There he is, at a stall buying meat and putting the package into the basket held by a pretty girl with long black hair. She finds out that evening from Anne Bradstreet's servant Meg that the girl was Ned's older sister Faith.

Months pass. He doesn't contact her. She decides he's just not interested. Perhaps she's not pretty enough or her father's not rich enough or…well something. He would have contacted her already if he were interested in her. Ned knows where to find her, doesn't he? She tries unsuccessfully to forget his intense blue-grey eyes.

She's become obsessed. She takes Sammy to the meadow called 'the common' one evening just before sunset. It's a time when courting couples walk around holding hands in public.

Perhaps he's there with a girl. He isn't. She's upset with herself. She tells herself to stop thinking about him. Maybe it's her desire to be in love that she's longing for, not a boy she doesn't really know.

"I will not marry someone I do not love" she tells Anne. "My step-mother continues to write praising John Alden Jr.'s fine qualities, but I can never love him."

"Seventeen isn't too young to marry," Alice writes. "Your friend Miss Bradstreet was sixteen when she married Simon. Did you know Simon worked for her father and he arranged the marriage? My sister Mary is a thornback. Don't be like her and remain single." Comfort wonders if Aunt Mary was ever in love. She isn't an attractive woman, but she is kind.

She wants to write to her father and ask him to stop her mother from writing to her about marriage, but she doesn't do so because she knows he's very busy these days with important problems. He's bought a small parcel of fertile land from one of the Connecticut River tribes. Now he fears there may be a conflict with the Dutch fur traders in that area. Also the squatters from Boston are settling there. They've found the land in the Bay Colony too rocky for farming. Wealthy London investors are sending people to claim land in the Connecticut valley.

Her friend Anne Bradstreet wants to stop her obsession with Ned. "Affection can follow marriage," she says. "You can't remain here as a single woman for very long before the gossip starts about whether or not you're still a virgin, and my father wouldn't like that at all. Why not consider John Winthrop Jr.? He's a widower, quite intelligent, and shares your love of books. I hear he's leaving for London soon to try to find a suitable wife. Visit him before he goes."

Comfort agrees to pay a visit to John Winthrop, Jr., the Governor's oldest son. She's been interested in seeing his vast book collection for a long time.

* * * *

She finds his house easily and sees it has a lovely rose garden just as Anne has described it to her.

"Welcome Mistress Bradford. You've finally decided to visit. Anne has told me you read Latin and Greek. I've many books in those ancient tongues and you may borrow as many as you wish. Not many girls here have been educated well by their fathers. I see you're not only pretty but have a good intellect as well." His smile is warm. She's flattered.

They sit in uncomfortable silence for several minutes, looking at each other, not sure how to begin to get to know each other. Both are aware that Anne is hoping they will like each other. He needs a wife; she needs a husband.

"I love books. My father started to teach me Greek when I was only five. I like stories and history. My favorite book is about London and it has wonderful drawings and maps. I hope to travel there someday. I'd love to hear about your travels sir"

John looks at her breasts. Perhaps a button has come undone. No. She blushes.

"Well, I studied at Trinity College in Ireland when I was sixteen," he says. "Afterwards I toured the Mediterranean on a merchant ship. I've seen Turkey and Holland. I love Italy. Perhaps we can go there together someday."

She smiles. Pleased, he gets up and places a log on the fire, then returns and moves his chair closer to hers. "Don't call me 'sir.' I'm only a little older than you. Call me John." He moves his chair even closer and takes her hand. "How old are you?"

"Seventeen." She pushes her chair away from his.

"Ah. Old enough." He touches her cheek gently.

Why does Anne think she would want him for a husband? True, he's educated and might take her to see the world, but he's not so handsome and he smells from tobacco. She must be polite. How can she let him know she is not attracted to him?

"I read about scientific experiments in chemistry, astronomy and especially practical new technologies. I've always been curious about how things are made – medicines, telescopes, those silver buttons on your dress." He dares to touch one of her buttons. She blushes and bites her lip, thinking that if he does this again she'll slap his face and then she won't be able to use his library.

"I'm twenty-seven. Does that seem old to you, my dear?"

"No sir, I mean, John." She decides to focus on his interests so he won't get personal. "I heard you want to make iron goods in Boston so we won't have to import them from London."

"Yes. We can make nails, guns, farming tools here, but we will need to make iron first. I plan to start an ironworks. Do you know what that is?"

"Well, I suppose it's where you make iron." She yawns, then she feels embarrassed. This doesn't interest her at all. She'll force herself to be polite.

"It's a factory with extremely hot furnaces that work all day melting iron ore. I've found an iron bog. We've plenty of timber for heating the furnaces and water for processing. You must dredge; get water out of the mud before putting it in the furnace." He notices she's looking about the room.

"I see I'm boring you, my dear."

"Not at all. But, I was wondering where your books are. I'd like to see your library. Anne says it's enormous. "

He sighs, realizing she's bored talking to him about practical science even though he's passionate about it and wants to spend his life studying science and manufacturing things. He'd hoped to have wife who shares his interests. They walk through the house to the library. "As you can see, I've over a thousand books." She can't believe her eyes. There are wooden crates filled with books stacked up one on another reaching to the high ceiling. There are chests filled with unpacked books along one wall.

"The ones in Greek and Latin are on the top, so use the stool and be careful. Borrow whatever you want, my dear. But first, let me show you my telescope. I bought it in Italy when I went to see Galileo."

Now he has a chance to get physically close to her. He gently touches her back, then guides her to the small telescope near the window. "It's an amazing instrument. Someday I hope to be the first to discover a new planet." He touches her hair. "You're a beautiful woman, Comfort." He puts his arm around her, and tells her to look through the telescope.

She smells tobacco on his breath and pushes his arm away, then looks into the telescope. She doesn't understand what it is used for or what a planet is and she is reluctant to ask him questions that would show her ignorance. She remains quiet and walks away from him and sits in a chair nearby. He sits down, keeping his distance.

John realizes she's not attracted to him. She thinks he's too old. "I'll be leaving for London to raise money for the ironworks. I hope to bring back a new wife. You may borrow my books, young lady. Please feel free to come here while I'm gone; my servants will let you in." He sighs. She is a pretty young girl, but he must find a more suitable, more mature woman who shares his interests.

"I hope you have success finding a new wife, sir."

John says goodbye and leaves her to browse among his books. She pulls over the three legged stool and climbs up to read the titles of the Greek and Latin books in the top crates.

The door to the library opens quickly, startling her. She tumbles off the stool, scattering books on the floor around her. She sits on the floor, stunned and confused, her skirt high on her thighs. Another book falls on her head.

"Oh no! Are you alright?" Ned Hutchinson bends down and looks at her.

Confused, blushing, she looks into Ned's blue-grey eyes. She recognizes him and is delighted that he's here. She pulls down her skirt.

"I'm so sorry. I didn't mean to startle you. You're not hurt, are you? Here, let me at least help you up. "

He's gentle, yet strong and smells of cinnamon, not tobacco. "I was trying to get the books from the top." They both pick up the books and put them on the table.

She takes off the blue satin ribbon which has fallen off her hair and ties it around her head again. "I must look a mess."

He has been watching her carefully. "You've beautiful hair." He sits next to her at the table. "Have you come to borrow a poetry book for Mistress Bradstreet? You do still live with her, don't you? I've seen you on the commons walking with her and her baby."

"Yes, I live with her, though I'm here to get a book for myself." Does he think she's Anne's baby's nursemaid? She picks up one of the books on the table. "Actually, it's this one I was hoping to find" she says, holding it out for him to see.

"It's Homer's 'Iliad' and it's in Greek. You can really read this?"

"Yes." She wonders if he likes smart women. Her step-mother has told her men aren't interested in women who are smart; they want a wife who will obey them. Then she remembers that Reverend Cotton told her that Anne Hutchinson is an intelligent woman who was educated by her father, a well-known minister. He said that if Mistress Hutchinson had been born a son, she would have been a minister.

"I'm impressed. I wanted to see you, but mother has kept me very busy overseeing the carpenter's work. We're a very large family, and many beds and chests had to be made. We're settled in now, so mother's about to start holding Bible classes in our house again just as she did in London. I'm sure she'd be happy if you'd attend. Let me put the books you don't want to borrow back in the crate." He picks up a few books from the floor and puts them away.

Comfort hands him books as he stands on the stool and puts them back. All this time she thought Ned was avoiding her, but now she knows he was just too busy.

When they finish the task, they sit at the table. He opens the book written in Greek and reads the first words of Homer's long poem: "RAGE: SING, GODDESS, ACHILLES' RAGE, BLACK AND MURDEROUS. See I can read Greek. But why do you want to read about war?"

"I want to understand why men fight."

"I believe greed causes war, whether it's for gold, land or furs. Homer says they fought the Trojan War to win back Helen of Troy, the most beautiful of all women, who was seduced by the handsome Paris. While I'm not sure that was the reason, Eros, Love, it's powerful. Have you ever been in love?"

She blushes, shakes her head. "No."

He looks into her eyes. "Well, I haven't either. I'm eighteen now so it's time Cupid's arrows find my heart." He touches his breast. "Ah, yes, my heart is beating faster right now. Something is happening." He smiles. "How old are you?"

"Seventeen."

"When I was thirteen I studied Greek and Latin to prepare for Cambridge University. My heart was set on studying science and mathematics. Mother insisted I follow her here, so I had to give up my dreams. I come here frequently to read science books. John and I like to discuss the new discoveries. It's amazing what people like Galileo are discovering about the stars."

"So now that you've come here, what'll you do? Will you be a farmer?"

"No. I'll be a merchant like my father and grandfather. William Coddington has already asked me to work with him in his shipping business. I'm learning navigation and accounting. When I'm rich I plan to buy my own ship to use for trade."

"My father wants me to continue my studies even though I'm a woman. He says I have a special talent for languages."

"I believe women should be taught to read many things. You remember the baby Susanna? You held her when we just arrived. Well, she's too young, but I'll teach her. She's our youngest, and we all adore her."

"My step-mother says the Bible is the only book a woman needs to read. She says no one'll marry me because I prefer reading books to making soap."

"Well, you don't want a husband who's not clean, do you? He'd smell awful in bed" Ned says with a twinkle in his eye. "I'd hate making soap. What awful smells! When I marry, I'll have servants to make soap. I want my wife to help me with my shipping business."

Ned searches for a book and finds it. "This was written by Galileo, the scientist who invented that amazing instrument" he says, pointing to the telescope. "It's called "The Starry Messenger". Galileo arranged glass lenses so that objects far away are magnified. He says there are so many stars we can't ever see them all. Stars are important for navigation, especially the constellation called Ursula Major which never sinks below the horizon. Ursula means bear and some say it looks like one. I'll be an expert navigator someday."

Ned motions with his hand for her to come closer to him and she does. "It's not dark now, but one evening, I'd love to show you how the stars look through this telescope"

He holds it steady while Comfort puts her eye to the telescope. She's embarrassed by the flush of desire she feels when she senses his breath on her neck. Oh how shameless she is, longing for him to kiss her neck. This is quite a different feeling than when John stood close to her. He takes her hand and they sit again at the table.

"My Wampanoag friend Philip told me about stars called the *mosk* which means bear. It might the same stars you call Ursula, but I know very little about stars. I do know a lot about plants from my Indian friend Little Bird. I help my mother make poultices when she's helping women with childbirth."

"My mother is also a midwife. I want to learn more about plants. Do you think we could meet here in the evenings? I'd love to show you the stars and you could teach me about plants."

They decide to meet one evening a week. They look through the telescope and also discuss botany. He brings a book into which she draws pictures of red lilies that flower in June, and something called alder tongue from which an ointment is made, and another plant called water-suck-leaves which can be used for burns and to draw water from swollen legs.

After a month of these evening study sessions in the library, Ned kisses her. She lets herself melt into the warm, sweet pleasure of her first kiss. He says this kiss is meant to show her how much he appreciates her help learning botany, but she's sure botany is not what's on his mind, for he continues kissing her with greater passion at the end of each meeting. Cupid's arrow has indeed found its way into their hearts.

* * * *

Comfort attends Anne Hutchinson's Bible meetings. She's inspired to see a woman who expresses her views with strong

conviction. She likes the fact that so many folks are coming to
hear her talk about God's spirit within everyone, men and women,
rich and poor people. After her sermon, they ask her advice about
their problems and, with kindness and attention, she listens and
they leave calmer and more hopeful about the future.

One evening Anne Hutchinson learns Comfort has assisted
Alice as a midwife and she wants to learn about the medicines
Alice uses for pain and to stop bleeding. She also likes the way
Comfort quiets red-haired Susanna.

Comfort doesn't tell her parents she's in love with Ned. What
if they disapprove?

13

CAMBRIDGE

"Most girls in Boston wait until they're twenty," Anne Bradstreet tells Comfort. "Don't be in a hurry to marry Ned even though you feel you love him. Have you heard the gossip about his mother? What she says is heresy."

"She's a very pious woman. More people come to hear her speak every week."

"You don't understand, Comfort. She isn't an ordained preacher. The words in the Bible are God's words and our ministers are the ones to interpret those words. People shouldn't listen to a woman's claims of visions and prophesies."

"Reverend Wilson is spreading this gossip. They don't like each other."

"She's even been criticizing how Winthrop's governing our colony. My father says women shouldn't meddle in colony affairs. She says our minister is going to send everyone to Hell because he is preaching that salvation is based on good works rather than God's grace. She's making the magistrates very angry."

"The men and women who come to her meetings love her." Comfort feels angry. Why does Anne always agree with her father's intolerant opinions? Why doesn't she think for herself?

"Men shouldn't even come to her meetings. You're naïve to think women can have influence here. Women should only share their opinions privately among the women in their quilting and childbirth meetings.

"Oh Anne, it is just malicious gossip. Governor Winthrop lives across the lane from her. I've seen his scowling face in his window many times as he watches people flock to the Hutchinson house. He's jealous that she's so popular."

"Don't be silly. This is an important problem. My father tells me she's spreading the heretical beliefs of a group called The Family of Love in Germany. They believe that revelations are more important than the Bible. Lustful things happen during their meetings. My father thinks Mistress Hutchinson has been infected by their heresies and lustful things happen during her meetings also." She knows her friend is distressed, but isn't it her duty to protect her friend from this? Her father has threatened to banish Comfort from her house because she's attending those meetings.

"It's all lies, all of it." Comfort can't hold back tears.

Anne hands her a handkerchief. "I'm sorry I've made you cry. Maybe nothing bad will happen, but you have to consider what people are saying."

"I don't care what they think."

"Well you must care. Be careful that your passion for her son doesn't get out of control, and that it doesn't blind you to what's happening. Keep your behavior at all times appropriate. Desires must be fenced in and controlled like flowers in a proper English garden."

"I'm a virgin and will be one when I marry, if that's what's on your mind. Oh Anne, trust me, and please don't write to my parents about any of this."

Anne walks to the stairs. "We need to put Sammy in bed for his nap." She goes up, and Comfort follows her.

As they lie in bed with the sleeping boy between them, Anne confides that she's pregnant again. "I fear dying in childbirth. Mistress Hutchinson and her assistant Mary Dyer are respected midwives. My father doesn't want me to ask their help with the birth."

"I'll help whoever you choose to be midwife. Please promise not to write to my parents about Ned or his mother."

"I won't. If my father or yours insists you go home now, I'd miss you terribly."

Ned and Comfort take care not to show their affection in public. They take Susanna and Sammy with them to Beacon Hill to search for plants for Ned's botany collection. When the children sleep, they kiss in the shadows of the trees. They read Shakespeare's love sonnets. When Ned says: "Shall I compare thee to a summer's day?" she feels he wants to kiss her. No one is looking. He holds her face gently and kisses her.

Alice has written that Little Bird and Philip are getting married next week. Comfort decides to accompany her father to Mount Hope. The night before she leaves, she dreams of Little Bird asking her: "Have you enjoyed love's pleasures yet? Philip and I have lived together this year and know how to give each other pleasure." When she wakes, she is excited about seeing her Wampanoag friends.

14

PLIMOUTH

COMFORT'S DIARY

I guess once you leave home nothing seems the same when you return. I hate the smell of pigs and cows, and hate swatting flies. My parents are getting old. Alice is having difficulty walking, and her hair is turning gray. She still orders me about as if I'm a child.

Father is angry Winthrop has not agreed to his idea of a joint trading post in the Connecticut River valley. They are competing with each other for the loyalty of the local river tribes as well as competing with the Dutch and the French traders for beaver pelts, the commodity that provides the most wealth.

I miss the closeness I once had with father. I feel guilty about not telling him about Ned.

*Yesterday I saw smoke curling skyward outside the palisade so I went to visit Little Bird's mother. She was happy to see me. She gave me powdered bark for Mistress Hutchinson saying it would heal muscle pain. I gave her a copper bracelet and red glass beads. She loves anything red. I learned how to say ire **peeyaush netop, mattapsh yoteg,** come, friend, and sit by the fire.*

Willie, father and I leave tomorrow for Mount Hope. I can't wait to see Little Bird and Philip.

15

MOUNT HOPE

Little Bird invites her into her *wetu*. Comfort admires the hangings painted with blue birds, the finely woven baskets with abstract designs, and the large clay pots filled with corn. The space is small, but her friend's talents have made it a comfortable home.

"During the many days of snow last winter I painted these birds. Chief *sachem* Massasoit gave us these baskets, and my mother made the pots. Feel how soft this is," she says, taking Comfort's hand and putting it on the brown bearskin covering the sleeping bench. "Good for making love."

Metacom arrives wearing only a breechcloth and his bear claw necklace. He looks strong and handsome. "Welcome Sky-Eyes" he says. When she calls him Philip, he asks her not to use his English name anymore and call him Metacom.

"Little Bird and I must now welcome all the *sachems* of the bands. They've brought us wedding gifts."

Comfort looks around the *wetu*. There are arrows tied together with a snake skin lying on the floor next to his bow. Metacom once told her the best arrows are made of elder, the best bows of hickory, and the bow string should be made of strips of deer hide. Melted horn is used as glue.

Little Bird's wedding clothes are set out: doeskin leggings, a long doeskin cloak painted with blue birds, and a pair of moccasins decorated with porcupine quills sewn into little red flowers.

Little Bird returns with her mother who will help her dress. Comfort's surprised when Little Bird doesn't braid her hair, but leaves it cascading down her back.

"It's time," her mother says, and leads the way through the village passing children and barking wolf-dogs. Where are all the women? Comfort usually sees women sitting together sewing, gossiping, or nursing babies.

They arrive at the special longhouse used only by women during their monthly "moon time." As soon as a young girl bleeds, she's invited to join other menstruating women and spend several days separate from men. It's seen as a spiritual time, as well as a time for sharing wisdom. Today it's crowded. Comfort is given a place of honor next to her friend's grandmother. Little Bird and her mother stand in the center of the room.

Chief Massasoit's wife walks into the center of the room carrying a knife. Little Bird's mother holds out her daughter's long black hair and she cuts it short. It now just touches Little Bird's shoulders. Comfort watches the shiny black hair fall to the dirt floor. Then she places a leather necklace with a small carved turtle around Little Bird's neck.

"You'll give me many grandchildren, daughter of the turtle clan; some will be excellent hunters, and some will plant the sacred crops of corn, beans, and squash."

Little Bird explains to Comfort later that her hair was cut to show other men in the village that she's married. "If another man tries to take me to his bed, he'll be sent away. When Metacom is Chief **sachem,** he's allowed to take more wives, but he has promised he won't."

The drums call everyone to the sacred ground in front of the Council Lodge. Comfort sits next to her father, Roger Williams, and her oldest brother Willie. They sit to the left of Chief Massasoit, a place of honor. Metacom is sitting on the Chief's right, and Little Bird and her mother sit behind the men.

More than sixty guests and their families sit in a large circle. The Chief's advisor Hobbamock and the *sachems* from the bands sit directly across from Massasoit.

A gray-haired elder enters the circle. He wears a long cloak covered with eagle feathers and holds up the sacred medicine bundle attached to the top of a pole. He walks to the center of the circle and stands in silence before Massasoit. He speaks to him then moves into a circle dancing and chanting.

"I don't understand his chanting," Comfort whispers to Roger.

"He's speaking the language of the spirits" Roger replies.

"Do you understand it?"

"No. It might be the names of various *manitoo,* spirit gods," Roger whispers. "I've counted thirty two of these *manitoo.* They even believe rocks have a spirit. This is their way of giving dignity to all things in nature."

Suddenly the men strike the ground with their hands or sticks.

One of the honored guests, a gray-haired *sachem*, sits in front of Massasoit and says a few words, then gives him a wampum belt made out of *suckkauhock,* rare and valuable dark purple shells. People show their approval by hitting the ground. Then the old man gently touches both sides of the shoulders of his Chief *sachem* to show great respect.

"He said *sontimooonk, ninnimissinouk, cowaunchamish,*" Comfort tells Roger, "which means great leader, of all our people, I pray for your favor."

One by one other *sachems* from all the small bands present Massasoit with gifts in honor of his son's wedding, and repeat the gestures that old man made.

One man brings a painted clay pot filled with corn, another man a bundle of arrows, then one holds out a headband with five large eagle feathers, and his son brings a doeskin cape. Massasoit gives the cape to Metacom who puts it on one shoulder. When all the important guests have presented gifts, Hobbamock nods to Governor Bradford. He tells Massasoit the **wautaconuaog** brings gifts for Metacom."

"They call us coat men," Comfort whispers to Roger.

"I know. They admire our warm coats."

Will sits on the ground before Chief Massasoit and speaks to him in English.

"Chief Massasoit, I'm honored to be invited to your son's wedding. I'm giving him this gun to help him provide deer for his family. It shows my trust and respect. May our people continue to live in peace." He places the gun on the ground. Massasoit picks it up and gives it to Metacom who gives it to his brother Wamsutta to hold.

Massasoit stands and motions to Metacom to stand next to him. Massasoit is wearing a long cloak of moose hide embroidered with shells. Around his waist is the wide wampum belt decorated with dark purple and white diamond shapes, the symbol of his status as Chief **sachem**. Metacom is wearing the deerskin cloak over one shoulder, a breechcloth, and a headband with three eagle feathers.

Massasoit speaks in Algonquian. Comfort translates for her father, her brother Willie and Roger. "We are pleased our son has chosen to tie our family to the family of our great **piensok** Hobbamock. We welcome Little Bird as our kin. She has lived in our hearts for many seasons. I will not make a long speech, for who can listen if they smell venison roasting?" He smiles.

The gray-haired **pawwaw** now asks Little Bird to stand next to Metacom. He circles the young couple, singing and dancing, his long gray hair flying, as he moves quickly. Then he takes the deerskin cape from Metacom's shoulder and wraps it around them both, uniting them in marriage.

Women bring food and wooden bowls. There are the sacred three foods - corn, beans, and squash - as well as roasted venison, multicolored corn, berries and nuts.

Afterward, the games begin. Young boys play a dice game using stones painted white on one side. Comfort notices her father scowling. He doesn't approve of gambling, only games of skill. He smiles when he sees boys playing with a hoop.

One of the boys rolls a hoop made of green hickory with a mesh of willow strips inside it. He rolls the hoop fast along a path made in the dirt. There are many boys alongside the path who try to shoot arrows through the hoop as it passes. The boy who can put his arrow through the hoop then gets a turn to lift the hoop and throw it over arrows sticking in the ground. He can keep those arrows he has encircled with his throw. Boys cheer when a boy wins many arrows.

Later there is a wrestling match between her brother Willie and Metacom. Everyone shouts as they watch the young men show their strength. Willie is the same age as Metacom and just as muscular, but not as tall. Wrestling is considered a good way to promote strength and skill.

Willie takes off his coat and shirt, and gives them to Comfort. His white skin looks strange to the Wampanoag young girls who point at him and laugh.

Metacom takes off his doeskin cape and gives it to Little Bird. He crouches and circles Willie. His sinewy arms grab Willie's arms and hold them behind his back in a powerful lock. Willie breaks the arm lock with a single motion that flings Metacom to the ground.

Metacom and Willie circle each other again. They're straining and sweating, holding each other, then breaking away. Finally Metacom throws Willie to the ground and bends both his arms behind him and locks them there.

After Metacom wins the wrestling match he walks around in a circle smiling in triumph. Willie, his body covered with dirt, bows to him.

When it's time for their English guests to leave Mount Hope, Little Bird gives Comfort a pair of moccasins with red flowers made from porcupine quills.

"For you, Sky-Eyes, *weticks*, sister."

"*Taubotneanawayean*, thank you." She clasps them to her chest.

16

CAMBRIDGE

After Metacom's wedding, Roger brings Comfort back to Anne's home. He's surprised to see John Winthrop sitting with Simon Bradstreet. On the table is a pamphlet Roger has written about the legality of Indian ownership of land and the necessity of buying their land.

"Please help Anne get refreshments," Simon says to Comfort. "We've important business with Roger."

Anne gets up and puts Sammy into the bed next to her. She and Comfort take down pewter tankards, fill a copper pitcher with homemade beer, and put salt beef and bread on a wooden trencher. They serve the food then sit in corner of the room where Sammy is sleeping soundly. Anne whispers "Later I want to hear about the wedding."

"So, Reverend, you're back from the savages. Did you learn holy things?"

Winthrop's fists are clenched.

"I'm learning their language and beliefs," Roger says, taking out of his pocket his notebook. "I've collected words that'll help us trade with them and perhaps convert them. We need to know and respect their beliefs if we're to bring them to our Lord. Forced worship stinks in God's nostrils."

Winthrop is irate. "That's not what I want to talk about. I want to discuss this," he says, picking up the pamphlet. He reads aloud from it: "Boast not proud English of thy birth and blood, thy brother Indian is by birth as good. Of one blood God made him and thee and all."

Roger puts his notebook in his pocket. He knows this flowing anger will grow stronger as Winthrop discusses his views on Indian land ownership. He's ready for this, expected this outrage, but had to follow his own conscience. "Just because the King gives us land it doesn't mean we own it. The King can't give us what he doesn't own. We must buy land from the Indians who are the rightful owners of it."

"What rubbish! Why do you want to cause chaos and dissension amongst us? Tell me young man why you wrote it. It's my duty to keep order. It's clear you've no interest in respecting my authority. Perhaps you don't belong here."

Roger takes a deep breath. "I must follow my conscience, be free to speak and write what I believe. You knew my mentor Chief Justice Coke, so it shouldn't surprise you he taught me that neither civil nor church government should come between a man and his conscience. We both know many in London who were jailed for their beliefs. This must not happen here."

"How dare you lecture me, young man. I'll not abide such arrogance. You're challenging the legitimacy of my charter which says this land is ours to settle in His Majesty's name. I insist you destroy this pamphlet. Don't forget you need my permission to stay here."

Their loud voices wake Sammy who stretches his arms to Comfort to pick him up and hold him. Anne hates conflict, so she doesn't want to stay and hear this argument. She goes upstairs. Comfort makes the boy comfortable on her lap and he falls asleep.

Winthrop tries a different approach. "Roger, I've difficulties enough with angry newcomers demanding more land. We improve the land, make this land profitable, the savages don't do so. It is vacant land, and God sent us here to make it an Eden. Have these savages convinced you to follow their wild ways? They're agents of the devil."

"John, please be calm," Simon says, handing him a tankard of beer. "You've been ill. Only a few men have seen Roger's pamphlet."

Roger won't be silent. "They're good people. Like you, John, they care about the poor. There are no beggars among them, no fatherless children who are not provided for. They share what meager food they have with everyone and are not greedy."

Winthrop argues with him. "What've they done to improve this land? Haven't you noticed how idle they are? The men sit around, while their women work in the fields. They've no sense of moderation. They're Satan's tools. They'll cut off your scalp in a minute if they believe they can get away with it. We must never let them think they can."

"Just because they're heathens, doesn't give us the right to steal their land. Their Chief *sachems* know the boundaries of their land and only they can sell it. Are we to behave like the papist Spaniards who take what they want and enslave or kill the natives? I heard your brother-in-law say he want to make slaves of them. No, John, we must be more compassionate."

Winthrop can't control his anger. "Don't be naïve. These are dangerous times. If we challenge England's right to colonize this place, he'll take away our charter, independence and religious freedom."

"I came here to seek freedom of conscience and freedom of speech," Roger says.

Winthrop bangs his fist on the table. "I won't allow you to share this pamphlet with others. I absolutely won't permit it!"

Comfort watches Roger wipe the sweat off his face with a handkerchief. Would she be able to defend her beliefs so strongly?

Roger continues. "Why can't you negotiate a proper land deed with the tribal chiefs? They accept little enough for it... coats, iron hoes, woolen blankets. They want to trade for these things. If we treat them with respect, we can get what we want."

Simon, as usual, tries to use reason to get agreement. "Roger we need to maintain unity. Hundreds of newcomers come here every few months and demand land. John's our Governor. Respect him."

Winthrop stares at Roger. "You don't respect me do you?"

"I care about you John and your oldest son is my friend. This isn't personal."

"Then destroy all copies of this treatise. Take an oath that you'll stop writing about Indian rights."

"The only oaths I swear are to my God. Are you going to banish me?"

"I can't have chaos!"

Thomas Dudley comes in. "Savages have killed Captain John Stone and eight of his men. We must discuss our response. We can't let the murderers get away with this."

John looks at Roger. "Tell the bloody details to Roger. Write this in your notebook."

Roger's worried. "Which tribe was responsible? Do we know why they attacked?"

"Pequots. Who can know the motives of these barbarians? What do you know about the Pequots?"

Roger sighs. "The Wampanoags call them "killers of men" and the Narragansetts "destroyers". Both those tribes have fought with the Pequots over territory. The Pequots dominate the fur trade with the Dutch. I've heard that the Pequot have disputes among themselves about leadership." Winthrop needs him now, so perhaps he won't be banished.

"I've never liked Stone" Winthrop says. "He was a privateer in the Caribbean and is a drunkard and adulterer. Because his family in London is influential, he felt he could do what he wanted here."

"We can't let the savages think they can murder our traders without consequences" Dudley says. "They must turn over the killers, surrender them to English justice. We must show strength."

Roger is alarmed. "We don't know yet who killed these men or why. Were the Dutch involved? How can we act before we find out why this happened?"

Dudley has already acted. "I've told Captain Underhill to mobilize men sixteen and older and increase their training." He turns to his son-in-law. "Simon, you must find out how much gun power we have and if we must make more."

"I'm worried about defending so many scattered villages. People will be afraid," Simon says.

"Tell them to pick a house in each village to use as a garrison house" Dudley replies.

"What if Stone kidnapped a squaw? Give me time to try to find out what may have caused the violence." Roger says.

"You're not in charge," Winthrop shouts at him. "People should be frightened of these barbarians. We can't trust them." Then he picks up Roger's treatise from the table and, with deliberate formality, throws it slowly, page by page, into the fire. Small burned pieces fly into the air. "You create dissention when what I need is unity."

Roger gets up to leave. "I'm going to find out what the Narragansetts think," he says. "We don't know what past conflicts or alliances will determine their actions. Before we start a war that could involve several tribes, we must know who might be on our side."

After all the men leave, Comfort remains downstairs holding the sleeping boy. The room is dark and cold. Will the Wampanoags join this conflict? Ned is in the militia under Captain Underhill's command, so he will fight. And her brother Willie is a soldier under Captain Standish. Is her father too old? They could all die.

She is remembering reading Homer's poem "The Iliad" with her father. "One war creates conditions for another" he said. Eventually Troy was completely destroyed. Could that happen to Boston?

She cried when they read about Andromache. Her husband Hector was dead, and was holding her boy and thinking about his future. She said that before the Trojan War her boy had food, a soft bed, and a safe place to play. All is lost because he no longer has a father to protect him.

Comfort picks up Sammy and carries him into her bed upstairs. She's thankful to have him sleep near her. Listening to his calm breathing, she falls asleep.

17

BOSTON

Comfort walks along the narrow streets on her way to what people call "the common", a meadow used by those who don't have their own grazing land for cattle. It's almost sundown and the evening breeze cools the humid summer air. Ned is training the youngest boys in the militia in this meadow and she's going to meet him. She's anxious to ask him about Anne Bradstreet's warning about his mother. Why did this attack on Mistress Hutchinson have to happen now, just when everyone is worried about a possible war with the Pequots?

It's all so complicated. The Pequot *sachem* isn't willing to hand over the murderers. John Winthrop Jr. has just returned from London with a contract from Lord Say and Lord Brook, two wealthy investors, to establish a new colony in that area controlled by the Pequots. He'll be its governor. His father bought land from tribes along the Connecticut River and said beavers are plentiful. People from The Bay Colony are squatting on fertile land near the river because they're dissatisfied with the land allotted to them.

Now, on top of everything else, Anne Hutchinson is being attacked. Will she be sent home? It doesn't seem fair that this is happening to her now!

All boys sixteen and older have to join the militia and its Ned's duty to be in charge of those sixteen or seventeen. He has told her he thinks some are only thirteen. He doesn't think they'll be disciplined enough to be good soldiers. Captain Underhill has said he wants to combine the Boston youth with those from the new villages of Roxbury, Dorchester, Weymouth and Hingham to form a South Regiment. Ned worries that his boys will not be as well trained as those from those other villages.

Comfort hears gunshots and walks faster. "Better move to the side, my dear," says a tall woman with a babe in her arms. "Fairbanks is coming."

Comfort knows Richard Fairbanks who is the herder of cows. He must drive them in the mornings, after the milking, to the meadow in the center of town to graze on the grass and bring them back to their barns before evening. Each family is allowed only two milk cows because there is limited pasture land available for grazing. She sees him and the cows coming around the corner. The common has been cleared of cows, so militia has use of the meadow.

Ned is supervising the boys as they practice shooting. She hurries to stand where fathers and little brothers watch the activities.

A boy is trying to balance his heavy gun on the sticks needed to support it. The gun falls. Ned tells the boy that if that gun had powder in it, he might have shot himself.

Other boys have taken apart their matchlocks and are cleaning them. Ned goes over to them and asks them to do a better job. "They'll misfire if they're not cleaned well," she hears him say.

Further away, two boys are playing with pikes, knocking these sharp pointed sticks together. A pike has scratched a boy's leg and it's bleeding. Ned ties his handkerchief around the wound. It's not serious, but he chides them for playing with them.

"They're weapons, boys. They're to be used if your guns get wet. Guns are no good in the rain or if you drop them in a swamp."

The fathers, standing next to Comfort, ask questions. How will the Indians fight? How many warriors do the Pequots have? Have the Dutch given them guns? Can they make gunpowder? Are the tribes who live along the river going to join the Pequots? Good questions, she thinks, but wonders if anyone knows the answers.

"Indians won't fight in a line. They'll ambush our sons," an older man says. "Our sons will get bitten by insects and snakes and have to creep through muddy, tangled roots," says a younger man. Suddenly there is silence, as each father considers the dangers their boys will face.

Now that its twilight, Ned sends the boys home and walks with Comfort along the shoreline to Town Cove, the place at the harbor where the city is divided into the North End and the South End. The shops along the shore are closed for the night. They sit on a bench in front of the sailmaker's store. Sails which need mending have been rolled up and are piled against a wall. It's cool near the water.

"Anne Bradstreet says there's nasty gossip about your mother's meetings," Comfort says. "She's warned me to stay away. Mr. Dudley thinks she's preaching heresy. He may ask me to leave Anne's house if I keep going to hear your mother. Are you worried about this gossip?"

"Not at all. Pastor Cotton has known her for years; we belonged to his parish in London. His beliefs are the same as hers. Besides, my father is a Deacon of the church. Why not stay with us? You could take care of Susanna."

"I'd love that. We'd see each other every day."

He kisses her passionately. They hold hands and walk back to the Bradstreet home, slowly, so grateful for these sweet moments alone.

18

Boston

Anne Hutchinson's house is just across the lane from Governor
Winthrop's house. Like the others, it has been framed in wood
and covered with unpainted gray clapboard. It has a steep roof,
and several small windows. There is a large chimney and a huge
fireplace on the first floor where Anne's meetings are held. The
bedrooms are on the second story. In the addition in back, are
bedrooms for the servants. Comfort is now living in one of
these rooms. She's glad it's near the kitchen so she can enjoy the
warmth of the hearth on cold mornings.

The Bible meeting is the highlight of the week for the household. More than eighty people attend, men as well as women,
though such meetings are supposed to only help women understand Reverend Wilson's sermons. Rich merchants like William
Coddington attend as well as a shoemaker, dressmaker, carpenter,
and blacksmith. Everyone's glad to discuss the Bible readings
Anne Hutchinson selects.

Comfort and Ned help the servants set out benches. Ned lights
the fish-oil sconces creating a soft yellow glow to the walls. A
servant wipes the large mirror clean. Comfort takes pleasure in
putting flowers on the table. Today she has picked orange lilies
from the garden and placed them in a blue pottery pitcher. She
makes sure the Bible is opened to the selected passage.

When Anne Hutchinson goes to the door to welcome her

guests, she sees Mr. Winthrop's scowling face in the window of his house across the lane. He's watching Henry Vane arrive. Despite his youth, Henry has recently been elected Governor because of his connections to the court. Winthrop thinks Henry can influence the King not to interfere in the colony's affairs. He fears the King will appoint someone to control his colonies as he did in the Caribbean. Anne hugs Henry hoping Winthrop is watching.

Henry's twenty-five and has long blond curly hair which he's always pushing behind one ear to keep it out of his intense green eyes. He had a conversion experience when he was in his teens. His father is finance administrator on the King's Privy Council, advisors the King uses in order to bypass Parliament and the courts. Henry is a "Seeker", doesn't belong to any sect, and has opposed the rituals of the state Anglican Church. His father urged him to leave England because King Charles I arrests men who reject the Anglican Church.

Comfort likes Henry. He's self-confident and friendly to everyone regardless of their social status even though she knows he comes from a high born family. Comfort thinks he's handsome. She can see that Ned's jealous when she talks with Henry after the meeting is over and Henry is clearly reluctant to say goodnight to her.

Anne Hutchinson greets her followers by name, asks a farmer about his children's health, hugs a woman recently widowed, greets a woman whose child she helped bring into the world as a midwife. So many women have been grateful for Anne's help during childbirth.

Anne reads from the Bible, and then she answers questions. She talks about God's spirit and says it is within her and can be in everyone. "You too can feel God's grace. Have faith and you will feel His spirit as strongly as I do."

At the end of the meeting there is a discussion about a war with the Pequots.

"I won't let my sons join the militia" a woman says. "I don't want war."

"I'm afraid of savages. We should destroy all of them before they burn down our towns," says another. "They're the Devil's children."

"Why do they want war?" asks a man. "They benefit from trade with us."

"I agree with Mistress Hutchinson about her opposition to the appointment of Reverend Wilson as chaplain to the soldiers. He preaches about good works, not God's grace."

After everyone has gone home, Ned and Comfort sit near the dying fire and eat apple cinnamon cake and drink tea.

He takes a book of poetry from his pocket and reads a poem aloud.

"To the Virgins to Make Much of Time" by Robert Herrick.

Gather ye rosebuds while ye may,
Old Time is still a-flying;
And this same flower that smiles to-day'
To-morrow will be dying.

He puts the book down, and tilts her face up with his hand and kisses her. "You're my beautiful flower." He hugs her so tightly she can't breathe. "Now let's enjoy our youth," he whispers in her ear. They kiss again. She wants to let herself melt into his embrace but can't help worrying that someone will come down the stairs and see them.

19

Salem

Roger lives in a village called Salem just north of Boston on the coast. The village's name is based on the Hebrew word "shalom" meaning peace, but Roger house is far from peaceful today. Mary is giving birth to their second child. Midwives Anne Hutchinson and Mary Dyer have come to assist the birth and Comfort is also here to help.

Ned brought the women here in a wagon and wants to use this opportunity to ask Roger questions about the impending war with the Pequots. He and Roger are drinking beer at a table in front of the hearth. The red curtain on the window is closed, so the room is dark. Two out of ten women die in childbirth and Mary was bleeding earlier this month, so Roger is anxious. He cannot imagine life without her. If he is banished, he'll be forced to move in winter with two small children. Where will they go?

Ned is asking important questions. "If there is a war with the Pequots, will it be a just war?"

Roger hears Mary crying out in the next room and can't concentrate.

"Why must I lead young boys into the damp confusion of a muddy swamp where Indians wait to kill them if the cause isn't just?"

"A soldier obeys orders. But you should consider morality before the war begins and here's no shame in confessing your doubts."

"Will the Narragansetts fight against us also?"

"We'll be vastly outnumbered if they do."

"Dutch traders give the Pequots guns, but do they know how to make gunpowder?"

"I'm sure they'll try to make it. I still hope we'll try to negotiate. If Winthrop thinks attacking the Pequots won't have consequences for our relationships with all the other tribes, he's wrong. We may not experience them for many years, but all wars have consequences."

Suddenly Roger's daughter called Little Mary comes in and climbs on his lap. She's frightened by her mother's cries. Roger kisses her forehead and gently carries her over to the quilt on the floor. She hugs a doll made of cloth and falls asleep.

"Why haven't the Pequots turned over the murderers of Stone?" Ned asks.

"Because they don't know who murdered Stone. They're probably lying. The killer may be someone important, perhaps a *sachem* of a river band that pays tribute to them. Maybe they don't want to submit to our rules of justice. They have their own."

"Captain Underhill feels we must show strength now."

Comfort comes in holding bloody cloths. "Where are the boiled cloths?"

Roger points to a basket of cloths boiled and dried in the sun in preparation for this day. "I'm so grateful you're here," he says. Comfort takes the cloths into the bedroom. "It's going be a little longer. The baby has not turned around yet."

Roger gets up and paces the small room. He sighs, and then continues talking to Ned. "I think the Wampanoags will stay neutral. They've had a good relationship with Governor Bradford for over fifteen years." He fills his pipe with tobacco.

"We must secure the safety of our families, but I don't believe we should think God is on our side."

Ned nods. Then he sees his mother. "May I help?" he asks.

"No. She needs you Roger. She must have strength to push hard now. I see the baby's head."

Roger sits by Mary and sees how scared she is. "I'm here, darling. It's almost over." He holds her hand.

Comfort mixes a plaster of tansy, mugwort, chamomile and hyssop. Mary Dyer tells her to mix in some sanicle, burnet roots, and parsley.

"The pains cut like knives. Pray for me, Roger" Mary pleads. Roger prays. Then Anne tells him to leave.

"You've asked me how to judge if a war is just" Roger says, puffing on his pipe. "Well, I think it matters who started the violence first. If it's a war against a tyrant, and his people want to be free, then it may be considered a just war. War shouldn't be started to take gold or land from the rightful owners. If authorities send boys to fight in a war that they know beforehand isn't just, the death of those boys will weigh heavily on their consciences for the rest of their lives."

"Can't you negotiate with the Pequots?"

"It's hard to negotiate if there's no trust on either side. Winthrop and Dudley hope strong action now will prevent another war, but I don't know. It might cause one."

"I recently read a book by a man named Descartes, a philosopher and a mathematician. He has developed new ways of applying reason to problems. Can we apply reasoning to the problem of war?" Ned asks.

They hear a baby crying. "You've another beautiful daughter Roger" Anne calls out. "Come in and hold her."

Roger holds the tiny infant swathed in a white cloth. "I'll name you Freeborn for you've been born free from a King's tyranny." The child stops crying and opens her eyes.

The women clean the bedroom, pack up their things, and

then leave.

The house is quiet. Roger is the only one awake. He prays.

"Lord, you have sent me to a better place than corrupt England but there are problems here in New England also. There was no separation between church and state in England and there is none here. Our leaders don't like me because I have a different view of the natives. I believe they're not devils and deserve our respect as human beings. Lord, give me strength to follow my conscience. Give my new daughter Freeborn the heart of a lion and the sweetness of a lamb. She'll need both qualities to survive in this new land."

20

BOSTON

The Pequot *sachem* has come to Boston to negotiate. Roger and Henry Vane wait for him with John Winthrop. Roger is asked to translate. Twenty men from the Southern Regiment, including Ned, stand guard, inside and outside, commanded by Captain John Underhill. They carry guns and swords.

Chief *sachem* Sassacus is short, but has muscular arms and legs. He wears a bear skin over one shoulder of his deerskin shirt. A fox tail is attached to his long hair. His breech-clout is tied around his waist with the skin of a snake. His face is painted with black dots on his cheeks and black lines on his chin. He has many tattoos on his legs and upper arms. Ten warriors in black paint have come with him.

Ned is frightened. Black is the color of war. Are they just pretending to want peace? Will they attack now?

Everyone waits until Chief *sachem* Sassacus is ready to talk. He lights his long pipe and stares at the guns and swords carried by the militia. He stares into the eyes of the men sitting at the table.

The Chief *sachem* finally speaks. "*Manowesass*" he says. Roger, translating, says "I fear no one." Sassacus points to the English soldiers. " *Nnickummaunamauog*, I shall easily vanquish them. *Kekuttokaunta*, Let's talk." He turns and says something Roger doesn't understand to his warriors, and then remains silent.

Finally he continues. "I would turn over the murderers of

Stone," he says, "but I don't know who they are."

John Winthrop frowns. "Once again you lie." He tells Roger to translate.

Roger is afraid to call the Chief sachem a liar, so he says *nonantowash*, you speak plain, instead of *cuttiantacompawwem*, you're a lying person.

"Give us 100 fathoms of wampum as a penalty because you haven't brought us the guilty ones," Winthrop demands.

It's a huge penalty. A fathom of wampum is six feet of shell beads. It's worth more than ten shillings, twenty if the dark purple shells are included. This is an unreasonable request. Roger translates Sassacus' reply.

"*Nquit pawsuck*? 100 fathoms? *Cosatumawem*, Too much. *Nonanum*: I can't pay. *Noonat. Noonamautuckquawhe* , I don't have enough. You're a greedy nation."

Sassacus pulls some wampum strings with white and cockleshell beads from a pouch around his neck and throws them on the floor in front of Winthrop. "*Tauguock cummeinsh*, I will give you money." Sassacus stares at Winthrop. He's very angry.

"*Kemineiachick*, Murderers! *Wepe kunnishaumis*, You killed my father, Chief *sachem* Tatobem. Stone was killed in revenge for his death," he says. "*Achienonaumwem*, We must revenge my father's murder. I speak truth."

"Do you have proof?" Winthrop asks.

"*Wompesu*, a white man. *Wautaconquog*, a coatman. Then he looks at each of them, Winthrop, Underhill and the soldiers. "You all look alike, " he says in English and laughs. The other Indians also laugh.

"*Nummusquantum*, I'm angry" he says to Winthrop. Then he says something to his warriors that Roger doesn't understand. Then the Pequot warriors turn and leave.

"Captain Underhill, escort these savages out of my colony,"

Winthrop shouts. "I don't trust any of these devils."

"I've heard that a Dutchman killed Tatobem" Roger says, "but perhaps it was Stone. We'll never know. There's been conflict among the leaders of this tribe. Some Pequots have joined the Narragansett tribe because of disagreements with Tatobem. Now they might convince the Narragansetts to join with the Pequots against us. We must move quickly and convince the Narragansetts to be on our side."

"Are you making these decisions?" Winthrop shouts, his face red.

"You don't want my help?" Roger asks and when there is no answer he starts to leave.

Henry grabs his arm. "Please don't go. You know these Indians better than anyone in this room," Henry says. "I'm still Governor and I want your help. Please share what you know."

Roger sits down. "There's another tribe into which Pequot leaders have intermarried. They're called Mohegans. Their Chief *sachem* is called Uncas. He wanted to be Chief *sachem* of the Pequot tribe due to his marriage to Tatobem's daughter, but he was rejected so he is Sassacus's enemy. Perhaps he will be on our side. So you see, Henry, its complicated and unpredictable. War usually is. Please, let's take time to understand this situation and see if we can have the Mohegans and the Narragansetts on our side."

"John, let's delay," Henry implores. "We must try to get the other tribes on our side."

"Don't tell me what to do Henry. Both of you should go back to England. I'll ask Comfort Bradstreet to translate from now on. She won't tell me what to do."

"I'll leave in spring," Roger tells him. "I've two young children and it's too dangerous to leave just as winter is beginning." He gets his coat and leaves. Henry follows him out.

When Roger arrives home, everyone is asleep. The Narragan-setts have indicated they're willing to sell land to me. It's going to be a hardship for Mary and the children. First, I must first find out if the Narragansetts will support us.

He sits by the fire and rubs his aching leg. It's never healed and is a constant reminder of his time he spent in a London prison for his religious views. A soldier hit his leg repeatedly with a stick. No, he won't go back to corrupt England. He takes out his pipe and a small pouch of Virginia tobacco and fills the bowl. His hands are shaking.

Roger is sad and thinks that if he should perish because of what he believes, it's but a shadow vanished, a bubble broke, a dream finished. But his children mustn't die. They're the hope of this great experiment in freedom.

21

BOSTON

Mistress Hutchinson's house is so crowded people are standing in back and on the sides of the room holding their wet coats. Ned welcomes them, collects their coats and takes them upstairs. He's tempted to lie down on his bed and skip his mother's talk this evening. Militia training has stopped for a while due to rainy weather, for the guns mustn't get wet. Ned struggles with his fears about the impending war. He can hear his mother downstairs talking about her revelations again. He wishes she wouldn't; it's sure to get her in more trouble. He listens to her, biting his nails, a new habit Comfort hates, but he can't seem to stop. He sighs and returns downstairs and stands by the wall next to Comfort.

"I've had a revelation," Anne is saying. "A time of darkness is upon us, but there'll be joy born out of great pain. Just as a newborn babe brings its mother joy after a hard labor, so will Our Lord help us through these coming travails and show us a way to peace. You must have strong faith. If you do, the Lord Jesus will reward you with His Grace."

Ned looks at his mother. Why is she putting all of us in danger by being so outspoken against Pastor Wilson's appointment as chaplain? Why can't she be silent like most women? She dresses appropriately - white collar on a grey dress, just a touch of lace, an appropriate bonnet. But she speaks too strongly about having direct communication with the Lord. He doesn't believe in these revelations. He sees her face is flushed. He wonders if it's because the room is too hot or, as her followers strongly believe, she has spoken directly with Christ.

"The Holy Ghost dwells within each and every one of you. Have faith and you'll experience Him in your own heart. You don't need Reverend Wilson to tell you whether you'll go to Heaven or Hell. Our Lord is listening to each and every one of you. Close your eyes for a few minutes and feel His Spirit inside yourself."

Ned sees bliss on the faces of everyone. Henry Vane looks ecstatic, as does William Coddington. They're moving their lips in prayer, believing the Lord is listening to them.

"I admire your mother so much," Comfort says. She realizes then that Ned fears his mother's behavior will lead to exile for his family. He doesn't believe prayer will prevent his death in a muddy swamp. She sees confusion and fear in his face.

Anne Hutchinson closes her Bible. "Remember Reverend Wilson shouldn't be chaplain. Tell your friends to protest, to prevent their sons from joining Underhill. It has been revealed to me that this war will lead to an even bigger war."

The meeting ends. Ned brings down their damp coats. Men pull on woolen caps, and women wrap wool shawls around their heads and necks. The rain has now changed to snow. Cold blasts of wind and snow enter the room through the open door as people leave. His mother goes upstairs to bed.

Ned and Comfort put away the benches. They sit before the dying fire.

"I visited Anne Bradstreet yesterday. I want to remain friends with her despite this difficult time. She's warning me the magistrates will punish your mother for talking against Wilson, for dividing our community. She said that in England women like your mother are burned alive as witches. That could never happen here, could it?"

He takes her into his arms. "Shush, my darling. Don't be afraid. Reverend Cotton will defend her. He has known her for years. He won't let harm come to her. And if we're separated, I'll still love you, and come back for you."

"Can't Henry help? He's still Governor."

"In name only, I'm afraid. He says he's leaving Boston in the spring. His father has asked him to return to the court. Go, get some sleep, dearest. I'll sit here a bit longer."

Ned thinks about Galileo who was put under house arrest in Padua, Italy until his trial for heresy by the Inquisition. They forbid him to write that the sun, not the earth, is the center our universe. They said what he wrote went against the Bible's truth. But Galileo recanted and was allowed to continue his work. Will his mother recant? Stop speaking of her revelations? Stop criticizing Wilson and this war?

22

BOSTON

COMFORT'S DIARY

Winthrop will put Mistress Hutchinson on trial for heresy, we don't know when. If I dare to defend her, I think I'll be banished too, as I'm considered a "sojourner" and need permission to stay.

Thomas Dudley believes tolerance will destroy this colony. He hates democracy and freedom of religion. Everyone must believe and practice their faith only as he, the other magistrates, and Reverend Wilson say they should. He carries a slip of paper in his pocket which says tolerance and democracy are "poisons." Mistress Hutchinson will not get a fair trial.

Susanna cries a lot these days. She knows something is happening. She is only able to sleep if she sleeps next to me. We have a strong bond.

If this family is banished, many others will decide to leave and begin a new settlement elsewhere. Mr. Coddington has promised he'll lend people money to build new homes. More than eighty families have said they'll leave. They don't know where they will go, but have been thinking about moving into Narragansett territory.

Will I be brave enough to support her? I will have to return to Plimouth if I do. Ned and I feel we're too young to marry. Will our love survive a long separation?

She closes her diary. She looks out the window and sees a man coming up to the house on his horse. She hears Ned let him in, and goes to see who it is that has come even though it's snowing hard.

It's John Sassamon, the Christian Indian who assists Reverend John Eliot in Roxbury. He's a friend of Roger Williams.

"Captain Underhill will arrest Roger tonight. Winthrop wants to force Roger and his family to leave the colony tomorrow on a ship headed for Barbados."

"What will he do?" Comfort asks. She doesn't want him to leave.

"He won't go. Chief *sachem* Massasoit has invited him and his family to spend the winter at Mount Hope. They must leave immediately. He wants you to come with them, Comfort, for you know the Wampanoags and will help Mary and the children stay calm. Will you come?"

"Yes. Ned, can you take your father's wagon? It's bigger than Roger's and they'll need to take belongings with them: their bed, a cradle, kettles, and clothing. How scared Mary will be."

"Sure. I'll hitch the horses." He grabs on his coat from the hook and pulls on a black wool cap. "Bring blankets. Leave a note for my mother explaining why we've gone, and say we don't know how long we'll need to stay."

Comfort collects blankets and writes the note. Susanna's asleep. She kisses her forehead and thinks about Roger's children and wife. They'll be frightened. Well, they'll learn Wampanoags are kind and hospitable people. She'll ask Little Bird to help Mary and the children adjust.

23

MOUNT HOPE

"Don't get so close to the river," John Sassamon shouts over the whistling wind. Ned is encouraging the horses to go faster along an icy river road along the Taunton River. John is sitting beside Ned in the front of the wagon. "The horses will slip into the icy bay. It happened last week. A family drowned. I was the one who found them."

Roger and Mary huddle under a blanket in the back of the wagon. They're wearing several layers of clothing and they feel the biting cold wind on their faces. Bundled in a sheep skin, the baby Freeborn sleeps in Mary's arms. Comfort sings softly to the whimpering toddler cuddled against her.

"I'm hungry. Are we there yet?" Little Mary asks.

Roger knows they haven't yet reached the Quequechan River where there are waterfalls. That river ends at the mouth of the Taunton River which then flows into Mount Hope Bay.

"The Indians will give us food. They don't let anyone go hungry or unsheltered. Be patient, dear girl."

Finally they see the snow covered palisade fence of Mount Hope. Smoke is rising in the air above the *wetus*. There is no one outside except for three Wampanoag men on horseback riding out to see who has come. Metacom is one of them.

"Sky-eyes! Welcome. Little Bird will be happy to see you." He smiles and leads them to Chief *sachem* Massasoit's longhouse.

As soon as they enter, they smell venison stew. Comfort tells little Mary to watch Little Bird braiding her mother-in-law's long grey hair. Little Bird smiles and invites the girl to come closer, but little Mary moves away and grabs her mother's hand.

Metacom signals to Mary who is holding the crying infant to go to sit on the sleeping bench. Little Mary follows and caresses the soft brown bearskin. She's still frightened but sees people are friendly. The infant stops crying.

"Welcome. Eat, Roger. We have plenty of venison stew," Massasoit says in English.

"*Taubotneanawayean*, thank you," Roger replies.

They are all given a wooden bowl of stew and wooden spoon. After everyone has eaten, Massasoit's wife wants to examine the baby. She touches the baby's fingers gently, and speaks to it softly. "*Tahossowetam*, what is its name?"

"Freeborn" Roger says. The infant stops crying and smiles.

"His skin is so pale," Metacom says. "I'll call him Snow Owl."

"It's a girl," Comfort says.

"She is Snow Owl," Metacom laughs. "I like girls named after birds," he says pointing to his wife.

Little Bird gives Little Mary a doll made of woven grasses. Then she whispers in Comfort's ear. "Is the one called Ned your lover? He's handsome, well, for a coatman. Is his chest hairy? Do you live together?" Little Bird asks in Algonquian.

Comfort nods yes. She's glad Ned can't understand what her friend said.

Roger has brought Chief Massasoit a gift, a red wool coat with silver buttons. The Chief *sachem* tries it on. It fits. He touches the silver buttons and smiles.

Metacom brings a trumpet, a gift from Comfort's father years ago. He blows it startling the baby who howls.

"You blow this when guests come, don't you?" He's proud to

be honoring their custom.

"Your **wetu** is ready" Little Bird says. They put on their coats and follow Metacom through the quiet village to a place that has been prepared for them.

Metacom lights a fire. "You'll be warm here," he says and leaves.

Mary looks around the room: a dirt floor, a sleeping bench with a bearskin, a clay pot filled with maize, and bark boxes for storage. There is a small wooden table, two wooden stools, three clay bowls, and an iron kettle. Her eyes fill with tears.

"We're safe here, my love. We're not being tossed around in rough seas and sent to an island far from here. These Indians are rightly proud of their kind hospitality. We must thank our Lord for their help and protection." They pray.

Roger takes the sleeping baby from her arms and puts her in the cradle they brought with them. Their older daughter has already climbed up on the sleeping bench and fallen asleep.

"In the spring we'll build a new home among the friendly Narragansetts. Remember, I showed you the deed? We'll have fertile land and I promise you I'll start that apple orchard you've wanted. Our land has a fresh spring, and I'll dig a pond. I'll teach our girls to swim. There's a river called Mashassuck nearby. I'll build a canoe, and teach you how to paddle. I intend to call our new home Providence."

He tells Mary to lie down next to their daughter. He takes off her shoes and wet stockings and massages her cold feet. He continues to talk calmly about their future.

"We won't be alone. Our friends are coming: the Harris family, William Arnold's family, Robert Cole, the Throckmortons." He tucks a blanket around her. "Dream of the Eden we'll be living in when flowers bloom again." He kisses her. She smiles and turns toward their daughter and goes to sleep.

They've brought a chest for their clothing, his Bible, a Latin dictionary, a couple of quill pens, some ink and writing paper. Roger unpacks the fish oil lantern, puts it on the table, but doesn't light it. He takes out a pouch of Virginia tobacco, fills his pipe, and smokes. Now it smells like home.

* * * *

Little Bird invites Comfort and Ned to sleep in her *wetu*. "*Cow-wetuck, takitippocat, wasick, netop,* let's sleep, too cold to talk, you've a lover, my friend." There are two sleeping benches in her house. Little Bird and Metacom will sleep on one and Ned and Comfort on the other. Metacom has not yet come inside to sleep.

Comfort and Ned remove their wet coats, shoes, and stockings, but leave their clothes on. They snuggle together under their blanket and listen to Little Bird singing softly.

"This singing will go on for quite some time," Comfort whispers. "It's their custom." Cuddling together with our clothes on is not immoral. I don't need to feel guilty. She is exhausted and is quickly asleep.

* * * *

In the dark outside the *wetu,* the snow has finally stopped but the wind blows snow around. Sassamon and Metacom sit around a fire sharing a long stemmed pipe of Indian tobacco. Metacom is upset with him but he isn't sure why.

"So, you believe in Jesus?" Metacom asks.

"Yes. I pray to Lord Jesus. I'm an orphan and was raised by kind Christians. I've adopted their religion."

"And all the *Manitou*? Do you still believe there are spirits in all things? That we must be in harmony with nature?"

"Yes. But Lord Jesus is a powerful God."

"These coat men, are they more powerful than our people?"

"Yes. If there is war, will you join the Pequots? Will you fight against the coat men?"

"The Pequots are our enemy, but I don't want to fight them. Someday, when I'm Chief *sachem*, I will tell my people not to be Christians. I want them to respect me, their *sachem*, and follow our ancient ways, the customs of the Dawn People."

Metacom stands up and throws handfuls of snow on the fire. He points to a *wetu* nearby. "That family is visiting kin. You can sleep there, Praying Indian."

24

THE SAYBROOK FORT

Ned is on a sloop on the Connecticut River heading toward a small English settlement at the mouth of this river. He has been ordered by Captain Underhill to meet with Lieutenant Lion Gardiner who's in charge of protecting a fortified settlement. Because it is Pequot territory, Ned was ordered to find out what reinforcements are needed. Now that winter is over, preparations for war have been resumed.

John Winthrop Jr. told him a group of men who are members of the House of Lords and their rich merchant friends have financed this new settlement. They're friends of the Earl of Warwick, President of the Council for New England, a committee of the House of Lords. They meet in Broughton Castle, owned by the Earl, to support Puritans opposed to the oppressive religious policies of Archbishop Laud and King Charles I. They have hired John Winthrop Jr. as Governor of this new enterprise.

Lord Saye and Sele, (William Fiennes) and Lord Brook, (Robert Greville) are investors so this small settlement is named Saybrook after them. They've hired Lion Gardiner to oversee the building of houses and fortifications. Eventually they hope to have a town here populated by "men of quality" like themselves. At this point only twenty-four men and their families live here. There is land outside the fort set aside for planting crops, and a good harbor. The sloop Ned Hutchinson is arriving on has no problem navigating into the harbor.

Ned wishes he could share in profits such men make here and in the Caribbean. These Lords have planted tobacco and cotton on two islands, one called "Providence Island", off the Spanish Mosquito Coast, and another called "Somers Isles." John Winthrop Jr. told him that the tobacco is of poor quality so they are planting sugar cane. Since the indentured laborers return to England, they've begun bringing African slaves.

Lieutenant Gardiner greets the sloop. He's an engineer and master of works of fortification who lived in Rotterdam in The Netherlands and worked for the Prince of Orange. He's brought his Dutch wife Mary and his master worker with him. The fact that he speaks Dutch is helpful since Dutch traders have a post in this area.

Gardiner is disappointed to see that Ned hasn't brought other soldiers. When the gate in the wooden palisade is opened, Ned sees barracks and a building with quarters for the twenty-four men and their families stationed here. There's a pond, a vegetable garden and a storehouse. Two small cannons are placed on a ten-foot-high mound in the middle of the compound. They're pointed at the mouth of the river.

Gardiner introduces Ned to his wife, a cheerful young woman who cooks porridge for their supper. "We don't have beer or bread, or enough warm clothing. War is like a three-footed stool: you need men, food, and guns, or the whole stool collapses. I need more of all three."

"I'll tell Captain Underhill to send supplies, sir."

"They want me to protect the widely scattered squatters from The Bay Colony from the Pequots, so they need to give me what I'm asking for before the fighting starts."

Gardiner thinks the leaders in Boston want to claim the whole Connecticut valley. Maybe that's why they supported the squatters. He must inform those Lords in London.

That evening a man named Gallop, one of the squatters, arrives with his two young sons and two Indian captives. He pushes the two Indian boys forward towards Gardiner. They stumble and fall. He pulls them up roughly and they curse him in their tongue.

"Pequot savages, sir. They've murdered another trader. We must teach these savages a lesson. They can't get away with killing Englishmen."

"Tell us your story. I'll decide what action to take," Gardiner says.

"My small boat was bobbin' in rough waters near Block Island. There wasn't much wind, and with torn sails, well sir, I wasn't moving fast. We slept poorly. Edward, my youngest, is ten, and John here, he's just turned thirteen." He puts his hand on the younger boy's head. "They're brave lads, sir."

"I'm sure they are," Ned says.

"John saw it first...an English boat crawling with savages. They were on the deck. One was climbing up the mast. I tried to get closer."

"Did you recognize the boat?"

"Not at first. Knew it was a trader's, for there was a mess of goods on her – beaver pelts, tools, blankets, and such. Later I recognized it as Oldham's."

"I've met Oldham. He trades with the Narragansetts. Did you see him?" Ned asks.

"Before I could climb up and have a look, a drunken savage spotted us, and points a musket at my boy Edward here. Thank God it misfired. I pushed my boys down into my boat. Then a gust of wind pushes us closer and this savage here, the tall one, starts waving an English sword above his head." He waves his hand as if it's a sword, and the Indian boy spits at him.

"When my boat drifts and bangs the side of that boat, and several devils jump overboard, splashing about frantically, and go under for good."

"It was awful, sir," says Edward. "I ain't never seen men drown before."

"Go on Mr. Gallop," Gardiner says.

"Then I and my boys jump on. John junior here pushes one overboard while I grab these two, throw a blanket over their heads, and tie the bottom of the blanket with rope. They're slippery, they are, these savages, and clever at getting loose."

"Did you find Oldham?"

"Yup. His naked, cut up body was under a sail, and his severed head left on top of it. I tossed what was left of him overboard and said a prayer. We mustn't let them devils get away with this."

"Go home. Leave these Indian boys. We'll see they're punished," Gardiner says.

The next morning he tells Ned to take these Indian boys back to Boston. "Find out if they really are Pequots. And tell Underhill I was promised two hundred soldiers for this fort. Tell him to come here with reinforcements."

On the voyage back to Boston, Ned is anxious. Will the murder of a second trader mean war with the Pequots will begin soon? Maybe there can be one last attempt to negotiate.

25

BOSTON

The interrogation of the two Indian boys takes place in John Winthrop's house. Will Bradford comes from Plimouth, and Ned and Henry Vane are present. Henry has a letter from Roger Williams about the Narragansetts. He knows the leaders and lives in their territory. He suggests Comfort translate.

The Indians insist they're not Pequots. They say their tribe, the Niantics, has split into two groups. The Eastern Niantics live on Block Island and pay tribute to the Narragansetts, and the Western Niantics pay tribute to the Pequots and live near them.

Roger Williams's message confirms their claim. He writes that the two Chief *sachems* of the Narragansetts who share power, an uncle and his nephew, want to be the ones to punish these Eastern Niantic boys. Oldham was killed because of competition between Niantics and Pequots over trade with the English and Dutch. This is a matter to be resolved by the Indians and the English should not interfere.

"This Oldham fellow was a drunk," Will tells Winthrop. "He used to live among us, but when he kidnapped a squaw we refused to let him stay. Let's not go to war over such a scoundrel."

Henry Vane agrees and asks for one more try at negotiation with the Pequots. "Chief Sassacus has paid more of his indemnity, but says he can't pay the rest. We should try to meet with him again." He sees Winthrop's grimacing face.

"We must know what actions the Narragansetts will take," Ned says.

"My Wampanaog friend Metacom says the Narragansetts have fought with the Pequots for years over tribal boundaries," Comfort adds.

"How many Narragansetts are there?" Henry asks.

"Metacom says they've thousands."

"Gardiner believes the Pequots have at least five thousand," Ned says. "Do the Narragansetts have more than that?"

"Twice as many." She blushes when Ned looks at her and smiles.

"If they join forces, it'll be a disaster," Will says.

"Perhaps we should let Chief *sachem* Canonicus of the Narragansetts negotiate with the Pequots. He told Roger he'll give us a hundred fathoms of wampum if we let him do so." Henry says.

"We must show strength." Winthrop replies. "We must be in charge."

Because Will is adamant that they must gather as much information as possible before starting a war, Winthrop reluctantly agrees to let Roger to set up a meeting with the Narragansetts. Ned and Henry will attend that meeting.

* * * *

Before going back to Plimouth, Will insists Comfort talk privately with him. They walk along the harbor. He tells her that Mr. Dudley has written to him to inform him that Anne Hutchinson will be put on trial for heresy.

"You must come home now, before her trial. I don't want you involved."

"But what if the Pequots want to negotiate? I must help translate."

"No." He sits on a bench and she sits beside him.

"There's another reason I want you leave. I saw you blush when Ned looked at you. You're in love with him, aren't you?"

"Yes, papa. He loves me also."

"It's my fault. I never should've let you move into his house. You must leave as soon as possible."

Comfort feels guilty and looks down, watching two gulls fight.

"Look at me. Have you ruined your chances of a good marriage?"

She blushes and stays quiet.

"You know what I'm asking. Has he taken advantage of you? I want the truth."

"I'm a virgin and will be one when I marry. Ned would never hurt me. You should see how good he is with his baby sister. Oh, do come meet Susanna, papa. They say redheads often have a temper, but she doesn't. She's so sweet. Do come. I'm sure you'll fall in love with her in an instant!"

"Stop trying to distract me. Listen, his mother's not only preaching heresy, but she's also telling boys not to join the militia."

"But I know you don't want this war either, isn't that so, papa?"

"The decision to go to war isn't a woman's business. What she's doing is dividing a community that must be united at a time of possible conflict."

Comfort can't think of a way to convince him to let her stay.

"Did you walk out with her during Wilson's sermon when he refused to answer her questions? You know women aren't allowed to ask questions in church."

"I didn't." She doesn't tell him she got up to leave, but Anne Bradstreet pulled her back down. She called her friend a coward for being afraid of her father's anger. Tears are now flowing down her cheeks.

"You're not yet even eighteen years old and don't understand. You're not going to change my mind, young lady, with words or tears." He hands her a handkerchief.

"Can't I stay here if I move back into Anne Bradstreet's house?"

Will is silent for a long time. Finally, he sighs and takes her hand. "Will you promise to stay away from Ned and not speak publically about supporting his mother?"

"I promise."

"I love you. Please obey me."

"I will, papa."

26

BLOCK ISLAND

"It's time to show strength," General Endecott says to Winthrop. "We shouldn't wait to learn what the Narragansetts might do. I'll take ninety men and destroy the village on Block Island where the killers of our traders live."

This island, less than ten square miles, south of Narragansett territory, is home to the Eastern Niantics. Ned and the other soldiers under Captain Underhill are part of the attack force.

It's a gray dawn when Ned leaves for Block Island. The sea throws him and the other soldiers about as if they're a small piece of flotsam. Many in the crowded pinnace are seasick and hold their caps over their noses. Ned chokes from the smell. Ned sits across from John Sassamon. I'll stay near him, he thinks, for he knows better than I how to survive in the dense tangled growth on this island.

The sun is just breaking through the morning fog when they pull their boats onto sandy shore. They find the village, but it's been recently abandoned; fires are still smoking. Ned, following behind Sassamon, crouches, runs, and trudges through dense bushes surrounding a small pond.

Suddenly arrows are flying towards them from all directions. He's scared and shoots his gun into the bushes wildly, without seeing who is attacking him. The smoke from muskets makes it hard to see. When it clears, the Indians have disappeared into the woods. Fourteen Indians have been killed, but the rest are gone.

General Endecott orders them to return to the empty village. "How can I fight an enemy I can't find?" he yells. "Burn it all. Destroy their cornfields. Let them starve."

Ned sees Captain Underhill running after wolf-dogs, cursing them. The pitiful creatures are howling. He catches one and cuts its stomach open, then chases the remaining dogs around the burning wigwams. One dog, whimpering, tries to run on three legs.

Underhill screams at Ned: "Do it, you idiot. Kill it. They'll not have their dogs, their houses, or their corn."

Ned hesitates, so Underhill finishes it off himself with his sword, splashing Ned's face with its blood.

"There is no more to be done here. Return to the boats" Endecott says. But he's too angry to head for home and wants to find a Pequot village to destroy. He orders the soldiers to head towards Fort Saybrook.

When they arrive Endecott leaves the soldiers in a meadow in front of the Fort while he goes in to consult Lieutenant Gardiner. The soldiers are exposed should there be an Indian attack. Gardiner says he'll cooperate.

Endecott intends to lure *sachem* Sassacus from his safe haven by sending John Sassamon to tell him to come to the fort to negotiate a new peace treaty. They expect him to bring his sons with him, as he did in Boston. Endecott will take his two sons hostage and insist Sassacus turn over Stone's murderer if he wants to free his sons.

Two hours later Sassacus and three hundred Pequot warriors armed with guns and bows and arrows surround the meadow where Ned and the other boys are resting.

Sassacus is screaming something they can't understand. His head is shaved except for the middle where hair is straight up and painted red. Sassamon tells Ned that he's demanding they all disarm before he'll speak with Endecott.

"No harm will come to you or your warriors if you will negotiate," Endecott says. "We will not shoot, but we will not disarm."

"Why are you again threatening to attack us?" Sassacus asks. "We signed a treaty in Boston."

"You didn't give us the killers of Stone and you didn't pay all the tribute you owe."

"Why should I pay? We're not inferior to you. Only less powerful tribes pay tribute. Answer me coat man. Do you kill women and children in war?"

"Yes!" Endecott hopes this answer will scare him.

"So we'll kill all English like we kill mosquitoes." He slaps his arm. "Then we'll take away all your wives, children, horses, cows and hogs."

"That won't be lucky for you," Endecott replies. "Our women don't work as hard as yours, our cows will spoil your cornfields and our hogs will destroy your clam banks."

Sassacus spits on the ground and says something to his men. They all quickly turn and go into the woods. As soon as they reach the cover of the thickets, they fire hundreds of arrows and disappear. Endecott searches, but only finds another abandoned village to reduce to ashes.

27

NARRAGANSETT VILLAGE

After the events in Pequot territory it is important to find out whose side the Narragansetts will be on. Ned and Henry consult with Roger who sets up a meeting with the two *sachems* Miantonimo and Canonicus. They share the leadership of the tribe.

They stay overnight in a longhouse waiting for an answer. Unfortunately, four Pequot warriors are there to try to get Narragansett support. They must all sleep there for the night. An answer will be given the next morning.

Ned is much too frightened to sleep. He looks up at the stars through the opening at the top of the longhouse. In the moonlight, he can just make out those four Pequot warriors. Two are asleep on the floor, but the others are sharing a pipe of tobacco. All night Ned's been worried that they'll slit his throat with their sharp knives or bash his skull in with their clubs. How can Comfort be friends with these dangerous savages?

He's jealous of Henry Vane who told him yesterday that he has made plans to return to the court in London. How lucky Henry is to have been born into an aristocratic family. Soon he'll be walking in the exquisite gardens of King Charles, enjoying the company of beautiful women, sipping Madeira wine and eating pheasant at the King's banquet table. Meanwhile he'll be still here fighting savages. That is, if he lives through this night.

Ned hears Roger next to him praying. Does he think the

Narragansetts will decide against us? He closes his eyes and tries to pray, but he doesn't have faith that God will intervene to save his life.

Ned opens his eyes. Dawn at last. He sees two Narragansett girls cooking stamp. They wouldn't feed us porridge if they were going to kill us, would they? he thinks. But what if the food is being poisoned? Ned is surprised he feels hungry despite his suspicions.

Stamp is served to everyone. Then Chief Canonicus and his nephew Miantonimo signal the four Pequot men to follow them outside.

"Should we run now?" Ned asks Roger.

"Be patient. We'll know soon."

Chief *sachems* Canonicus and Miantonimo return without the Pequots. They say something to Roger.

"They will join us," Roger says, smiling. "There are conditions."

"What conditions?" Henry asks.

"They want captured Pequot women and children be given to them. They want to protect them from being sold as slaves and want to adopt them into their tribe. They say it's their custom."

"I believe we can agree to this. Anything else?" Henry wants this treaty to be signed before he leaves for London.

"They want to be free to hunt in conquered Pequot forests. They've fought over hunting rights in this area for years. If we accept these conditions, I believe they'll be brave, trustworthy allies," Roger says.

"I'll urge Winthrop and Dudley to accept these demands," Henry says.

Miantonimo says he'll come to Boston to sign a treaty if these conditions are met.

"*Cowauontam*, you're a wise man," Miantonimo tells Henry.

Before Ned and Henry leave for Boston, Roger tells them

that the Narragansetts are willing to sell land on the north part of Aquidneck Island to English settlers who want to be good neighbors and traders.

"How much wampum will he want?" Ned asks. He knows his father wants to buy land somewhere in case they're banished from the Bay Colony after his mother's trial.

"Only a few fathoms of white beads worth about two hundred forty shillings. *Sachem* Canonicus also wants two red woolen coats with silver buttons for his sons and three sharp hunting knives. Oh yes, I almost forgot, he wants a large bag of sugar. He loves sugar."

Soon after this meeting, Miantonimo signs a peace treaty in Boston. The Narragansetts have agreed to deny safe haven to Pequot warriors. They will be given captured Pequot women and children, and have guaranteed rights to hunt in Pequot forests.

28

FORT SAYBROOK

The Pequots have attacked Wethersfield, a village of squatters close to Fort Saybrook. Lieutenant Gardiner reports they've slaughtered nine, including women and children, and kidnapped two young girls. He thinks the girls were taken to a Pequot fortified village somewhere on the Mystic River. He's willing to try to rescue the girls, but only if he is given reinforcements.

"I was down by the river when a small boat sailed by with the two girls. The savages mocked us by using a sail made of a bloodied English dress and screaming loudly as they passed."

"Reinforcements for the fort are coming," Captain Mason tells him. "Captain Underhill is bringing twenty, and I'll come with eighty."

"The Mohegans have offered to be our guides," Gardiner says.

"Can they be trusted?"

"Yes. Chief *sachem* Uncas hates Sassacus. Uncas is married to his sister. When the father was murdered, he thought he'd be chosen Chief *sachem* based on his wife's lineage and wants revenge against Sassacus who usurped his power. He leads the Mohegans and knows the swamps where the Pequots build fortified villages."

29

Plimouth

Its early evening and smoke from cooking fires rises into the cool evening breezes coming from the harbor. Fish oil lanterns have been lit in the houses below. The blacksmith's shop is quiet.

Will Bradford and Miles Standish sit in silence in the meeting-house above the town. Will is thinking about the boys who'll soon leave to fight the Pequots. His son Willie will be among them.

"Miles, I'm reluctant to send you and our boys to fight these Pequots or pay the tax Winthrop demands from us for this war The Bay Colony started."

"I'm glad our friend Hobbamock says the Wampanoags won't be involved" Miles says.

"One war often leads to another. Those with revenge in their hearts won't live in peace. We who know history understand there will be consequences in the future."

"Winthrop wants fifty of our boys."

"He refused to provide protection for our trading post in the north. Instead of helping us scare those Indians armed by the French, he established his own trading post and is competing with ours for furs."

"I'll hold off sending our boys for as long as possible," Miles says. "Let's see how things develop. I fear the Indian tribes along the Connecticut River will support the Pequots."

30

Boston

Winthrop orders Captain Underhill to arrest Mistress Hutchinson. "I saw all those people going to her house last night and I won't tolerate it. She's an unruly, arrogant woman who's usurped Reverend Wilson's role as preacher and mine as the one who determines policy here. Arrest her tonight. I'd like to rid the colony of all her followers."

Over eighty people are discussing the war with the Pequots with Anne Hutchinson when Captain Underhill arrives to arrest her.

"You are under arrest for disturbing the peace of this colony. Tell all these people to leave. I've been ordered to take you to Reverend Welde's house. You're to remain there under arrest until your trial for heresy is concluded."

"You're a traitor," one woman shouts. "You've attended these meetings pretending to be pious. Shame on you."

"We'll support you. If you are banished, we will leave and follow you to Aquidneck Island where we can worship as we wish" says a man. "Your husband came with a small group of us and we have found suitable land."

"God has told me this would happen. He has a purpose even if we don't yet know what it is," Anne tells them.

"You'll go to Hell for this, John Underhill," a man says. "She's a saint."

Henry Vane wishes he could stop this trial, but knows he no longer has influence.

* * * *

When Comfort learns of the arrest she tells Anne Bradstreet she wants to speak out against this injustice. "If I were a man, I'd organize a protest meeting against Winthrop and your father."

"Don't you dare. You mustn't interfere. You promised your father. My father will send you home immediately. We women only have power in the private sphere. Corinthians says the man is head of the household. Eve's pride caused Adam and Eve to be exiled from Eden. Mistress Hutchinson's pride has caused her downfall."

"Eve didn't force that apple down Adam's throat. Mistress Hutchinson is brave and I admire her. It takes courage to follow your conscience when you know others have all the power to decide your fate."

"You've no influence Comfort, so there's no sense in trying to change things."

"I'll lose Ned." She starts sobbing.

"Don't cry. I'll help you find someone else. You're only seventeen."

Comfort decides that night to disobey her father. She'll visit Ned and his mother, show them she loves them, but won't do anything publically that will get her sent home.

Anne's right. She can't stop this trial. Mistress Hutchinson will defend herself very well. She's very intelligent and knows the Bible as well as any man. Maybe Reverend Cotton will continue to support her. He knows she followed him here because of his beliefs and was a member of his parish in London. Her beliefs are the same as his, aren't they? He will help her.

31

ROXBURY

Anne Hutchinson has been under house arrest for four long months. Her trial starts tomorrow. It's been hard for her family to walk to Roxbury, a neighborhood two miles from Boston, situated on a narrow strip of land called The Neck. She misses the familiar chaos of her busy household. She spends her lonely hours in this small, all too quiet, room reading the Bible.

The local ministers, Thomas Welde and his assistant John Eliot, come often to interrogate her about her faith. They're not sympathetic and she fears they'll use what she has told them against her during her trial. She doesn't have a lawyer, but is confident she'll be able to defend herself.

Will Winthrop dare accuse her of having sexual orgies as that group The Family of Love is rumored to engage in? No one could think she'd engage in such debauchery. Her husband may hear this filthy gossip during the trial. At least they haven't said she's a witch. An older woman was accused of witchcraft in this colony last year.

She looks out the window. It's raining hard. She's startled by the flashes of lightning and loud thunder. She lights a candle on the small table near her bed. She remembers Susanna is afraid of thunder.

She prays: You've chosen me Lord to spread your truth. Your Spirit guides me. Whether rich or poor, sinner or saint, all must have faith in your Grace. My father preached the truth and was jailed in London for it; it's now my turn to suffer for my faith. I'll be strong because your Holy Spirit is within my heart.

* * * *

Anne is resting when Comfort and Mary Dyer arrive with Susanna. They take off wet coats and shoes. Susanna climbs on the bed and cuddles against her mother's side. "I miss you mama."

Anne rubs her back. "I know sweetheart."

"Do you have a proper dress for tomorrow?" Mary Dyer asks.

"Ned's bringing one. Don't worry, I won't look like the Jezebel they accuse me of being."

"How ridiculous!" Comfort is furious.

"This is the thanks I get for bringing fifty of their babies into this world."

"I admire your courage" Comfort says.

"I must be true to what has been revealed to me."

"Reverend Wilson says we are Satan's puppets because we've helped deliver a few deformed ones," Mary says. "I was told to bury my deformed fetus and not to tell anyone. Reverend Cotton said some will see it as a sign that I'm a witch."

Comfort looks out the window. "Look, the sun is shining. A good sign. Now your followers will find it easier to attend the trial."

Ned comes in, opens his knapsack, and shakes out a simple, dark blue dress with a white collar and a white bonnet. He lays them carefully on a chair. He hugs his mother.

Henry Vane and Anne's husband William arrive together. Henry's hair is unkempt, and William's eyes show a lack of sleep. "I'm so sorry I can't protect you," Henry tells her.

Anne tells Henry and William to organize a meeting. "Winthrop's brother-in-law wants to sell captured Pequot children into slavery and send them to plantations in the Caribbean. People should protest this immoral action."

"Now dearest," her husband says, "save your strength."

She rubs her stomach. "I suppose they'll be shocked to see I'm with child again at my age." They chat about family matters and the war, but don't stay long.

Ned asks Comfort to go for a short walk. He kisses her in the apple orchard behind this house. "Whatever happens tomorrow, I'll never stop loving you."

32

BOSTON

Anne Hutchinson stands below the wooden platform in the meetinghouse. She looks at the faces of the ministers and magistrates seated above. Dudley, Simon Bradstreet, Winthrop and Reverends Wilson and Cotton wear long black robes. Their faces are somber. They will challenge her and she's ready to defend herself.

Ned is sitting in front next to his father. "She looks radiant and strong" he says.

"Her face glows when she's with child," William replies.

Comfort, sitting two rows in back of them with Anne Bradstreet, notices the gray in her hair and turns and sees the shocked faces of women realizing Mistress Hutchinson is pregnant. She's worried the stress of this trial may cause a miscarriage. She turns and looks at Mary Dyer in the back of the room. Mary will help her.

"Remember, you've promised you won't talk" Anne warns. Comfort wishes she could sit with Ned and hold his hand.

"Don't even think of speaking to Ned."

"I'll look at him as often as I want to, but I'll stay silent."

"She's brought these troubles upon herself."

"Her meetings were in her own home. She interpreted Bible passages."

"Hush. Let the judges investigate."

"Why are they prosecutors, judges and jury? Do you think it's a fair trial?" She's angry. Anne sighs, and then takes her hand. "We have no power to change things, dear friend."

Winthrop clears his throat and asks Reverend Cotton to begin the trial by reading a selection from the Bible. Cotton reads from Proverbs 31:10-29.

Who can find a virtuous woman? The heart of her husband
Does safely trust in her, so he shall have no need of spoil.
She will do him good and not evil all the days of her life.
She stretches out her hand to the poor; yea, she reaches
Out her hands to the needy. Strength and honor are her
Clothing; and she shall rejoice in time to come. Her children
Arise up, and call her blessed; her husband also, and he praises her.

Did he choose this passage to shame her? Comfort thinks he will betray her.

He continues. "I will now read from Paul's first letter to the Corinthians, verses 34 and 35." He reads, looking at straight at Anne Hutchinson.

"Let your women keep silence in the churches...and if they will learn anything, let them ask their husbands at home, for it is a shame for women to speak in church."

"And now, this is a passage from 1 Timothy 2, verses 11 and 12."

"I suffer not a woman to teach nor to usurp authority over the man, but to be in silence."

Winthrop is sitting in the largest chair on the platform, the only one with cushions. As the Governor, he must present the charges.

"Mistress Anne Hutchinson, you have not been silent in the church, but that is only one of many charges against you. You will now hear all the charges against you."

Winthrop says there are twenty-nine issues of heresy. The most important accusation is that she claims she has direct revelations from the Lord, revelations which tell her about future events, and which she says are as infallible as the Bible itself.

"Do you deny this?"

Anne doesn't deny these accusations but challenges the legitimacy of the trial. "Your institutions and your actions hide hypocrisy. I contest this trial and challenge this court. You do not try me fairly, but wish to entrap me."

"We only wish to help you out of Satan's snares," Dudley says.

Mary Dyer, sitting in the back, stands up and shouts: "Give this woman a fair trial! We demand it as English citizens. She should have a lawyer and there must be two witnesses for every charge."

Another woman stands up: "She's delivered our babies, and prayed with us when we lost our sons and daughters to smallpox. She's a good, pious woman. Why are you punishing her?"

"Quiet or you'll be thrown out of this room!" Dudley says. "I won't allow anyone to disrupt these proceedings!"

Ned has turned around to look at Comfort. She sees he's scared.

Cotton addresses his old parishioner more gently now. "You're right to say that only with strong faith in Christ is there a foundation for good works for the two must go hand in hand or there's hypocrisy," he says. But then he pauses and wipes the sweat off his forehead. "But you've usurped the authority that rightly belongs to an ordained minister. We cannot have a moral community without respect for our ordained preachers."

He pauses, looks at Winthrop, and continues in a louder, angrier tone of voice. "You are puffed up with Eve's pride and have forgotten your place. I've known you a long time, and it makes me sad that you've ignored warnings to stop your disruptive behavior."

"To be betrayed by you is the worst betrayal of all," Anne replies.

"You taught me that only when we have strong faith in His Grace can we can love others and be good Christians. It is not you, but Reverend Wilson who's preaching falsely, leading people towards hypocrisy. You inspired me to come here. I share your strong belief in God's Grace and His Spirit within all people." Her heart was breaking as she knew now that the magistrates had convinced him to condemn her. Many of her followers may doubt her. She can't abandon her faith, be a hypocrite. The Holy Spirit is testing me to strengthen my faith. Whatever happens now, my life is not my own. God has a plan even if I don't understand it.

"She's trying to divide the ministers," Anne Bradstreet whispers to Comfort. "It won't work. They've been meeting in my house and are united against her."

"I knew they'd pressure Reverend Cotton before the trial to find her guilty."

Reverend Wilson stands up. He points a bony finger at Hutchinson. "You mislead people and cause them to drown into a sea of licentiousness and sin by your false words. People must look to their own salvation now. They must denounce you or Satan will tear their very bowels out. You'll not usurp my authority, you wanton woman, for you are possessed by the Devil!"

There is murmuring throughout the room. Some are saying she's a witch, while others are saying she's a saint and not a devil.

Ned looks at his father's sad face. "Don't worry, my son," William whispers. "She's not on trial for witchcraft, but only for heresy. They won't burn her. They'll likely banish and excommunicate her. She expects it and I know she'll be strong."

Mary Dyer's voice rings loud and clear once again from the back of the room. She is standing up. All eyes are on her. "She speaks from the heart of God's Love and His Grace. It's you who speak falsely."

"If she were a man, you would never accuse her this way," shouts a woman.

"We love you Anne Hutchinson" shouts an old man. "Those who judge you today will burn in Hell for these false charges!"

Winthrop bangs repeatedly on the table to restore order. He demands no one else stand or shout. He orders Captain Underhill to remove anyone who does so from this room. He tells Anne to be quiet and reads the verdict.

"Mistress Hutchinson, you've spread the venom of your opinions into the vital organs of the people, spreading pride, insolence, contempt of authority, and sedition. We're at war with fierce barbarians, yet you dare challenge our authority. There is no place in this community for you or others like you. You are banished."

Anne remands strong. "It's not God's will to fight this war against the Indians. It is not God's will to appoint Reverend Wilson as chaplain."

"And how do you know God's will?" Dudley demands.

"He has spoken to me."

There is shocked silence.

"They'll surely excommunicate her now" Ned whispers to his father.

"She must follow her conscience, speak the truth as she knows it," he replies.

Anne Bradstreet whispers to Comfort. "Stay quiet. You've promised." She reaches for her hand and squeezes it. "I feel your pain; I really do. It's sad that it's come to this."

Winthrop continues with the verdict. "Mistress Hutchinson what you have spoken is heresy. It would be a dark stain on our conscience if we persist in letting such a misguided woman as yourself to scatter the poison of your errors, to broadcast these errors to others, and to send them to eternal damnation."

"This trial's a mockery!" Mary Dyer shouts. "You decided the verdict months ago. Many people will follow her wherever she goes. Your church will lose many members for your actions on this day. You'll be sorry you did this."

Winthrop nods to Captain Underhill and he goes to Mary, takes her arm and escorts her outside.

Winthrop continues. "For your hardness of heart, your lack of remorse, your foul and filthy opinions, and your disturbance of the public peace - for all these reasons - I hereby excommunicate you and banish you and your family for the common good. Those who object must leave our colony as well. Everyone must follow an orderly procedure in doing so. I demand you hand in all guns and sell your property as quickly as you can. Those who don't obey will be arrested."

A woman gets up. "It's you who are splitting this community, John Winthrop. The Lord will punish you. Mistress Hutchinson is defending our freedom to follow our conscience. We don't want to stay here." She walks out and many follow her.

"Order! Order!" Winthrop shouts. "I want all unruly people out of my colony."

Captain Underhill takes Mistress Hutchinson's arm gently and leads her to the door. He'll take her back to Reverend Weld's house where she'll have to remain until her family is ready to leave. He whispers: "you're a brave woman."

She stops at the door, turns and looks at Winthrop. The room becomes quiet as people wait for her to speak. "You'll find out, John Winthrop, that I speak the truth. It was revealed to me long ago that you would plot against me. The Lord bade me not to fear."

Then she addresses all those who judged her in a confident, loud voice. "All of you who have condemned me have power over my body, but only Our Lord Jesus has power over my soul. God will punish you and your children, and their children for this hypocrisy. It's better to be cast out of this church than to deny Christ. God will ruin you and your descendants, and this whole colony!"

Someone shouts "a prophecy, a terrible prophecy."

Reverend Wilson says: "I deliver you to Satan!"

Dudley shouts to Underhill: "Remove this woman now!"

Outside her followers discuss selling their homes, cattle, and farms and moving to Aquidneck Island. They will help each other. Sufficient land has already been purchased on that island. They paid forty fathoms of wampum beads, ten coats, and twenty hoes to the Narragansetts for fertile land. Others aren't sure when they can leave for their sons are at Fort Saybrook training with the militia which is preparing additional attacks on the Pequots. Still others feel that if Reverend Cotton has condemned her, he might be right. They are unsure what they'll do. They feel for Anne. They saw her pain when he deserted her.

Ned is also unsure what to do. Isn't it his duty to continue to lead the boys he has trained in the militia? Isn't he obligated to protect the people in Boston and those living in the villages in the surrounding area frightened they'll be attacked any day now? It will take time to sell their house and farm. His father urges Ned to continue to do his duty to his boys until the arrangements for the sale of their property is completed.

"This trial wasn't fair," Coddington tells Nicholas Easton and his son John as they leave for home. They all intend to follow her to Aquidneck. "Please come with me to settle the southern part of the island where there is a possibility for a fine harbor that can be used for commerce." John and Nicholas agree to go with him.

John Easton stops when he sees Comfort dabbing at her eyes with the end of her sleeve. He takes out his handkerchief and tells her to keep it. "They're wrong about Anne Hutchinson. My father and I intend to follow her and make a new life with her and Roger Williams. Please remember, young lady, you're welcome to join us now or in the future. We intend to settle in the south of the new colony where there is a good harbor. I will personally see to it that you'll be comfortable there." She looks into his sympathetic handsome face and sobs. He opens his arms and she lets him hold her until she can control herself. Then, embarrassed, thanks him for his kindness, hands him back his crumpled, wet handkerchief, and rushes away.

As she walks back to the Bradstreet house slowly, she is furious with herself. Why didn't I dare speak out against the magistrates? Why did those who fought for their own freedom to worship need to banish her? Is it to keep their power? And will she always be a coward? She feels empty, abandoned. She will lose Ned.

33

A Pequot Fort Near The Mystic River

Rivers are essential for all commerce in New England. The Dutch and English build trading posts near rivers. Indians paddle these waters in their huge canoes bringing bundles of pelts. The Dutch have a fortified trading post near the Mystic River called The House of Good Hope. Indians trade a great amount of beaver for guns. It is in Pequot territory. The Narragansetts claim this land once belonged to them.

English farmers have established the towns of Windsor, Hartford and Wetherford just a few miles north and south of the Dutch trading post. Winthrop's summer home, Ten Hill Farm, consists of 600 acres on the southern bank of the Mystic River. Winthrop has chosen this area for shipbuilding. Three ships have been built. The most recently built is named Desire and was used for fishing, but is now going to the West Indies to bring back salt, cotton, tobacco, and a small number of African slaves.

North of the estuary where tides bring in salt water, the water is fresh. Fish are plentiful: cod, haddock, mackerel, bass, and alewives. The Mystic River is named after "Muhs-uhtug" in Algonquian meaning "great tidal waters". Twice daily tides make it an appropriate place to build mills powered by water to grind grain and saw wood.

The fighting against the Pequots has remained limited. Too much is still unknown : the number of warriors and guns, whether or not the Indians know how to make gunpowder, how much the colonists can trust their Indian allies.

William Bradford fears the war will spread to Plimouth. "Will it spread to my colony?" He asks Captain John Mason for his opinion.

Captain Mason answers: "I don't know."

The two young girls who were captured by the Pequots have been exchanged for Pequot prisoners thanks to Dutch help. While captive, they claim they were ordered by Pequots to make gun powder, but they didn't know how.

So much is at stake: the use of fertile land and water resources, the profitable trade in furs, especially beaver pelts, and a show of strength that will hopefully lead to control of this area. To some English, this is a holy war, good against evil, God's elect against the Devil's puppets. They feel war against these barbarians is inevitable.

The Pequots must prove they won't be forced to obey these strangers who don't understand or respect who they are, what they believe or their tributary relationships.

Captain John Mason wants to escalate this war now. "I'll organize a surprise attack on the large Pequot fortified village called "Siccanemos".

Will Bradford is delaying sending his boys. He wants to see for himself how large a force has been assembled on the western side of the Mystic River before telling Standish to bring the Plimouth militia there.

When he arrives Captain Mason tells him he has ninety men, seventy Mohegan allies, and four hundred Narragansetts. The Mohegan allies say they know the way into the fortified village. The surprise attack will begin at dawn.

It's a hot, dark night, and there is only a sliver of a moon. Will sees boys lying here and there on the grass, cleaning their guns.

He leans against a tree. The bark of the tree feels rough against his aching back. What is he doing sitting on this cold, damp ground? Will this violence tomorrow lead to more violence?

He remembers what he saw yesterday. He came to a small village after Indians had attacked. He saw slaughtered cows, slashed open and covered with flies, women, children and men hastily buried in freshly dug graves. He saw survivors walking slowly away, clothing tied in rolled up blankets on their bent backs, trudging towards the few garrison houses in a nearby village. He can't forget their desperate faces.

The Narragansett Indians have come here with *sachem* Miantonomo and the Mohegans are led by *sachem* Uncas. These men hate each other so he's been told, but he doesn't know why. Will their enmity prove dangerous for us?

He's surprised to see Ned Hutchinson. Ned's family must still be in Boston. Perhaps they can't get a good price for their large farm. Perhaps their new home on Aquidneck Island isn't finished. Will hopes Ned won't die today. That would break his daughter's heart.

At daybreak, the Mohegans lead them to an Indian path and they walk for two miles towards the Pequot fortified village. Most of the Narragansett and Mohegan allies stay in the rear. The strategy is to make two circles around the village: an inner one close to the tall interlaced poles of the palisade which will be composed of English boys, and an outer one which will be composed of Narragansett and Mohegan warriors. This way the English boys won't confuse the Pequot enemy with their own Indian allies.

They arrive at a cornfield at the foot of a high hill. **Sachem** Uncas, the Mohegan, tells Captains Mason that the fortified village is at the top of this hill. It's large and hundreds of people are living there. It's fortified with a long fence twelve feet high made of thick young trees. Between those are holes through which the Pequots will be shooting arrows at them. Uncas points out two entry points, both of which are piled with thick bushes.

Uncas tells Underhill to order his men to clear the bushes away from one entrance so they can get in quickly and attack while people are still asleep. Captain Mason's men will climb over the bushes at a second entrance and set the wigwams on fire. This will create terror and confusion.

From the moment it begins, the Pequots warriors respond by shooting guns and sending hundreds of arrows towards the invading men. Some manage to fight their way out of the village, leaving their wives and children behind. They believe that the women and children will be captured and enslaved, but not killed. This has been the case in wars between the tribes.

Wigwams burst into flames. Women and children flee burning homes. There's no place to hide as a strong wind spreads the flames. Elderly men and women roll on the ground in pain. Within a half an hour the entire village is in flames.

Will watches as Ned encounters a young girl whose hair is on fire. Captain Underhill shouts to him: "Shoot her Ned. Don't let anyone get away." Ned can't do it. Others near him are shooting women, old men, and children.

Some of the wives and children try to follow their husbands who are squeezing through the tall poles of the fence. The English soldiers on the other side of the fence are slashing them with swords dripping with blood. The Narragansetts are refusing to participate in this slaughter of innocents. **Sachem** Miantonimo is horrified.

At last it's over. The English soldiers and their Indian allies return to the meadow below the hill to care for their wounded. Will helps bandage a boy's leg. He looks up and notices Ned leaning against a nearby tree, his shirt splashed with blood, sobbing.

He gets up and puts his arms around him. Ned wipes his eyes with a bloody sleeve.

"I'm not a coward, but I can't kill women and children."

"I'm as upset as you are, lad. It was horrible seeing them frying in the fire. I'll never forget the sights and smells of this day. Thank God it's over."

"I lost a boy from my unit, a child really, only thirteen. He volunteered with his older brother. I shouldn't have let him. I just buried him here, under this tree."

They walk together to the river where they help the wounded into boats which will bring them to Fort Saybrook. Ned confesses to Will that he can no longer fight in this war. Will says he understands. He silently gives thanks to God that his own militia didn't participate in the slaughter.

Seventy Pequot warriors have surrendered to the Narragansetts, and others have left their territory and joined the Montauks, but most have refused to surrender. The surviving warriors hold their *sachem* Sassacus responsible for this disaster.

Sassacus takes several hundred men and a lot of wampum with him and tries to convince the Mohawks to fight with him in the war. When the colonists learn of this, they're frightened. Mohawks are fearless warriors and may be cannibals. They're relieved when a Mohawk warrior comes to Hartford holding Sassacus' scalp. It's over.

* * * *

Reverend Wilson gives a sermon: "It was the Lord's doing, and it is marvelous in our eyes. There is sufficient writing in the Bible to justify killing women and children."

Roger Williams has a different opinion and quotes the Bible 2 Kings 2:6 that forbid punishing innocents for the sins of their fathers. He writes to Winthrop saying that *sachem* Miantonimo is disgusted and angry by the way the English fight. Why kill women and children?

Captain John Mason is considered a hero and is given a position a chief military officer of the new colony of Connecticut. He is given land for his own use. He has begun to develop a close relationship with *sachem* Uncas of the Mohegans and will get more land he hopes.

A treaty is signed at Hartford and signed by Uncas and Miantonimo which declares that the two tribes must let the English resolve any future conflicts between them. Many doubt if the treaty will guarantee peace between these enemies.

Winthrop wants the Pequot tribe to vanish. The name Pequot should never be used again; the survivors should be divided into the Narragansetts and Mohegans, with each getting eighty Pequot captives. They will have to pay the English an annual tribute in wampum for each person they have received.

Pequot land is now owned by the colonists by right of conquest.

34

BOSTON

Anne Bradstreet has severe headaches. Comfort gives her friend St. John's Wort, urges her to stay in bed. She closes the bedroom curtains, for Anne feels better in the dark, and takes Sammy to visit their neighbor who has a new baby.

The next week Anne begins writing a poem and says it is helping her feel better. Now it is Comfort's turn to feel overwhelmed with sadness. She can't stop sobbing at night, yet she is not exactly sure why she's crying.

"Is it about Ned leaving?" she asks Comfort.

"Yes. He's leaving soon. A ship will bring his family and friends to Aquidneck Island. Houses have been built in the north end of the island and they'll call the place Portsmouth. But there's something else bothering me. I don't understand exactly what's happening, but I feel I can't pray. Oh, Anne, it could have been my best friends Little Bird and Metacom who were burned alive in their sleep. I love and respect them. Not all Indians are evil, but I hear people now talking about wanting to kill all the natives."

"Of course some Indians are trustworthy. We have to continue to trade with them. We can trust some Indians to take our messages in their canoes and, using the rivers that connect our towns, they help us keep in touch with our friends. They were allies in this war. I hope this'll be the first and last war we ever have with them. You know the Wampanoags better than most people, so it is right that you feel concern for them after we have fought such a terrible war."

"Do you believe that it was our sins that caused God to bring about this war?"

"Some think the Lord is punishing us, but I don't. We can't understand His ways, but we must strengthen our faith by prayer every day."

"I'm angry at God for allowing so many innocent people to die. Will I go to Hell for thinking this way?"

"Take time for yourself, dear friend. Write in your diary. Writing my poem is helping me feel better. And pray. I believe the Lord will give you a sign, a new path for you to follow to give purpose to your life."

35

BOSTON

What is my destiny? How has living in Boston changed me? Two women named Anne have inspired me.

Ned's mother challenged the magistrates even though she knew it was dangerous. My birth mother, Dorothy, she didn't have the courage to live in this wilderness. Who am I like, Dorothy or Anne Hutchinson? Will I fight for what I believe? Do I even really know what I believe? I'm full of doubt about what I believe and what I am capable of doing.

Anne Bradstreet has a different kind of courage. She fights the pain and despair of a sickness called melancholy. She has great fear of dying in childbirth yet has said she intends to have many children. She has strong faith in herself and in God. She has confidence in herself, but she doesn't have the courage to disagree with her father.

Perhaps if I had grown up in London I would have more confidence in my abilities. Both these women knew many other educated, intelligent women. Both believe they are able to learn anything they want to learn. Anne Bradstreet studies her father's history books, and believes her poetry will be good enough to be in a book someday. Anne Hutchinson feels she is capable of teaching many people to recognize the power of God within their own hearts. What can I do? If I find a purpose for my life, will I have enough confidence in myself to achieve what I want to do?

Both women have husbands they respect and who respect them. Can I have this kind of marriage? I want to choose my own husband. Now that Ned is leaving, my parents may force me to marry someone they chose. They don't approve of Ned's mother. Sometimes I wish I'd been born a man. What will happen now? Will our love survive what might be years of separation?

I hate how people feel about Indians. I strongly believe they have souls, and they're in their own way as spiritual as we are. I love Little Bird and Metacom. Will they always be my friends?

I'm still young, and my future is uncertain. I should learn as much as I can from people I admire. Please help me Lord to be a good person and to find a way to contribute to this world which is so full of pain as well as promise.

36

Roxbury

Anne Bradstreet tells Comfort she should go to Roxbury to meet Reverend John Eliot who wants her help with his missionary work. "Go. If you become his assistant then your father will let you remain in Boston."

"But he betrayed Mistress Hutchinson's trust. He used what she told him in private against her during her trial."

"She spoke of her revelations as if they were more significant than the Bible. Reverend Welde wanted her banished, and John, being his assistant, had to agree. You must learn how complex a person's reasons are if you want to understand the world."

"Why does he want to talk to me?" She's annoyed that Anne is talking to her as if she were a child. Eliot could have followed his conscience, but he chose not to.

"I told him you speak Algonquian and have knowledge of their customs. He intends to preach to the Indians in their own tongue. He also plans to translate the psalms and, someday, translate then the entire Bible into Algonquian. What an amazing challenge he's given himself."

"Impossible. They don't have all those words. Well, I do agree he's an ambitious man and I will meet with him."

"Good. You'll like him. He's intelligent, and has a delightful sense of humor. And you can learn a lot from him. I've been talking with him about setting up a school so my boy can learn

Latin and Greek before he goes to Harvard. He's the perfect person to start such a school. I know Sammy's just a baby, but I must consider his future education. It may take years before a proper education can be offered here in Boston."

"Why do you think Eliot's the right one to start a school?"

"After he completed his studies at Cambridge University, he taught reading and writing in a school. He sees the importance of education for the future of New England. He has offered to raise money for Harvard from his contacts in London."

Comfort would like to learn how to teach, so she agrees to meet him and promises Anne that she won't discuss the Hutchinson trial.

"He lives in Roxbury, a village just on the outskirts of Boston. It gets its name from the many outcroppings of a special rock called puddingstone, a sandy colored rock with dark pebbles that looks like Christmas pudding I think."

Later that week she goes to Roxbury, a pleasant village with houses built around the church. She asks an old woman carrying a basket of vegetables if Reverend Eliot's home is nearby. The woman points to a modest home.

John's wife Hannah opens the door. "John will be delighted to see you." She has ruddy cheeks and a cheerful temperament, and is pregnant. "We want a large family," she says, rubbing the bump under her apron.

Reverend John Eliot is in his thirties and has dark eyes that sparkle with good humor. He invites her to take his cushioned chair while he sits on a stool. Hanna brings tea and apple cake. They talk about the Pequot War. He says he thinks it was wrong to kill women and children, and he hates slavery. The captured Pequot women should not have been sold into slavery. She likes him, and doesn't mention Anne Hutchinson.

"Anne and Simon Bradstreet speak most highly of you. They

say you're not only intelligent, but you speak the Algonquian tongue and have friends among the Wampanaogs. I want to learn to speak it and then develop a written language for it."

"Why do the Indians need to write their language?"

"To read God's words. After my new translation of the psalms which will be the first book printed by the new Harvard College press, I'll start my life's work. I intend to translate the entire Bible into Algonquian and use it to convert the natives. My London friends in the Society for the Propagation of the Gospel in New England will provide funds for this effort. Will you help me?"

Comfort is flattered. He's ten years older and well educated, yet treats her with respect. His idea of translating the Bible is interesting. "I'd be pleased to help you, sir. I can read parts of the Bible in Latin and Greek, but know only a little Hebrew."

"Do you still have friends among the Wampanoags?"

"Yes. They're not like the Pequots. My friend Little Bird is the daughter of their spiritual advisor Hobbamock. Her husband Metacom is Chief *sachem* Massasoit's second oldest son and may be the *sachem* himself someday if something happens to Wamsutta, the oldest son."

"Do you believe Indians can be good Christians?"

"Of course… if they want to. They despise adultery, lying and cheating. They love children and respect their elders. They respect all living things, even more that we do, I think. They provide for orphans, and no one starves. But I don't know if my friends would want to convert."

"I'll educate some Indians in an Indian College which will be part of Harvard. They'll be preachers. I'll set up villages where they can live together around a church. I've acquired land eighteen miles from here for the first village, Natick. If people get to know Christian Indians, they'll be more likely to accept them as good neighbors."

"Won't this take many years?"

He smiles. "Yes, of course, my dear. Everything worthwhile takes time. I must find Indians whose hearts are open to Christ's teachings. John Sassamon is such a person. You've met him, haven't you? He'll be my first Praying Indian preacher."

"He's a good man. I like him."

"We must civilize them if we are going to co-exist in peace in this New England."

"I'd like to help keep peace. I'm only a young woman, but I want to have a worthy purpose to guide my life. It would be an honor to work with you sir."

"Good. Then move to Roxbury, teach me Algonquian, and help me begin my translation work. You may live in a small cottage in back of my house if you wish. It's modest, but adequate. Hannah will see to it you have what you need. I'm going to go to London to raise money soon. I'd like you to come and help me convince rich merchants to provide money for my work."

"You'll take me to London?" Her heart is pounding. She can't believe she's going to see London at last.

37

Boston

The excitement of beginning work with John Eliot is the only thing that keeps her from weeping when Ned tells her he's leaving for Aquidneck in a few days.

They walk hand in hand around unfinished houses being built for refugees coming to Boston from Connecticut towns attacked by the Pequots. It is early morning and the carpenters have not yet begun their work.

Ned confesses that he's angry at his mother for getting them banished. "She should've lied." He says. "I'm going to miss you."

"I'll miss you too." She doesn't want him to blame his mother.

"Galileo is still conducting experiments because he disavowed his beliefs when forced to do so by the Inquisition. That's what her trial was really, an Inquisition."

"So don't blame her. She's a brave woman. I admire her."

Ned leads her into the wooden skeleton of a house. "Let's pretend this is our kitchen, darling. May I kiss you in our kitchen?" He kisses her, and she smiles. They walk into another unfinished room. "This is our bedroom. Take off your clothes, sweetheart and we'll make love." She looks at him shocked, and then pushes him away, laughing.

"But it'll be a long time before I'll see you again, kiss you, and hold you in my arms." He touches her face, then kisses her neck. They leave the unfinished house. The playful moment is gone.

They walk in silence, wondering if love will last.

"I was so worried you'd be killed by the Pequots."

"I saw things... terrible things... and those images are... well, they're burned into my head. They'll never go away."

"My father has nightmares."

"Enough. I've good news. Coddington has promised to take me to London with him to buy his new ship. We'll stay with Henry Vane and his new wife Francis. The King has appointed Henry as Treasurer of the Navy. Imagine that! My friend is important now. I can't wait to ask him questions about ships. I need to learn a lot if I'm going to have a successful shipping business."

He takes a folded paper out of his pocket. It is a drawing of a ship. "This is the one Coddington wants to buy. It's square-rigged, which means the main sails are at right angles to the ship's length. It will be fast, though not as fast as a Spanish galleon."

"I have good news also," she says. "I'm going help the Indians to read their own language. Algonquian tongue is only a spoken tongue now. Reverend John Eliot wants me to help him translate the Bible into Algonquian. And, guess what? I'm going to London too. He said he'll take me to help him raise money. Wouldn't it be wonderful if we could be there at the same time?"

"If we are, maybe you'll marry me there. Then I'll finally get to use a real bedroom and won't have to just imagine kissing you everywhere, your toes, your legs, your breasts. How about practicing?" He takes her hand, kisses each finger, and then he whispers in her ear "No one is here" and unbuttons her blouse. She pulls away. "I can't."

"What about Sarah Bowles? I saw you looking at her with lust in your eyes, so don't deny it. She's going with you to Aquidneck. Maybe you'll marry her."

"Well, I do like red hair... which reminds me... Susanna has begged me to bring her to say good-bye to you. I thought Beacon

Hill would be a good place to meet tomorrow for she loves it up there. I do want to marry you, darling. Promise you won't let your parents arrange your marriage to that...pig farmer."

"I promise."

38

BEACON HILL

"Look how clearly we can see the ships," Ned says, proudly holding out his new spyglass. Comfort takes it from him and looks down the hill towards the harbor. She sees several fishing boats, a larger boat that brings people and goods to towns along the coastline, and two ocean going ships. The coastal boat is being loaded with the household goods of Ned's family. They will be leaving today for Aquidneck Island. A group of people has gathered on Long Wharf to say good-bye to Mistress Hutchinson. She gives him back the spy glass.

"Isn't it truly an amazing invention?" he says.

"Yes. I wish you didn't have to leave today."

"I'll write. Roger knows a trustworthy Narragansett who paddles his canoe here with letters."

"Penelope waited for her husband Odysseus for ten years after the Trojan War. Don't make me wait too long, darling. I don't want to be a thornback like my Aunt Mary."

He leans over, kisses her, and smells her hair. "Rosewater, right?"

Five year old Susanna is sitting on the grass behind them and has been stuffing blueberries into her mouth by the fistful. She holds up her sticky fingers. "See?"

They sit next to her, and Ned wipes his little sister's fingers.

"I've a gift, sweetie," Comfort says. She takes out of her pocket a string of purple and white wampum beads and puts it around

Susanna's neck.

"It's pretty."

"Come," Susanna pleads.

"I can't, darling, but I'll write."

"I'm learning to read."

"Good." She takes a notebook from the picnic basket and hands it to Ned. In it, she's drawn pictures of plants and indicated the ways Indians use them.

He looks at a few pages. "This is great. I'll share it with mother." He opens the spyglass case, and removes a piece of blue velvet. He gets a small knife from the basket. "May I have a lock of your hair?"

"Only if you give me one."

Ned cuts off a curl, wraps it in the velvet, and puts it in his case. She cuts a lock of his black hair and wraps it in her handkerchief.

"Me too." Susanna grabs a fistful of her red curls and holds it out. Comfort cuts a curl and puts it in her handkerchief.

They're startled by the blast of a trumpet signaling the arrival of the Governor of Plimouth. Will's come to get a book from Coddington and then he'll take Comfort home for a visit with her family.

They walk down the hill to the wharf where she will greet her father, and he will help his father load the family's belongings onto the boat leaving for Aquidneck Island.

Her father is talking with Coddington and tells her to wait for him on the fishing boat.

"I've brought a surprise for you."

Little Bird is in the boat. "*Cowammaunsh, netop*, I love you, my friend. My mother and I made *honckock*, goose for you. Do you still eat *honckock*?"

"Yes." Comfort hands her friend a small mirror. "For you."

Little Bird looks into the mirror and smiles. She takes off her bracelet which is decorated with blue glass beads and gives it to

Comfort who puts it on.

"I know a new bear story. Want to hear it?" Little Bird asks.

"Of course."

"A woman is walking in the woods and sees a big, black bear and is afraid. The *pawwaw* has told her if you call a bear "*wasick*", husband, it won't attack you, so she calls him "*wasick*". The big bear stands up on his hind legs and growls. She stands still, looks down, and acts submissive. Then the bear goes away."

Comfort doesn't understand this story but the word "husband" makes her cry.

Little Bird caresses her hand, not understanding why she's crying. "Metacom waits at my father's house. He wants to see you Sky-Eyes and ask if many Pequot captives became slaves."

She's not surprised. Metacom has told her how much he hates slavery. Winthrop supported the sale of adult males to the Caribbean islands so they couldn't cause trouble after the Pequot War. Some women and children are slaves and continue to live in the colony. Winthrop has three, a boy and two women. What should she tell Metacom? Perhaps she should lie. She sighs. The war is over. Can't we just forget about it?

Part Two

1641-1642

LONDON

Comfort wakes, feels the rocking of the boat, and listens to waves hitting the hull. The Griffin isn't moving. They have arrived in London at last. It's quiet and dark in the sleeping quarters below deck, but she hears voices, footsteps on the narrow stairs, banging on deck. She dresses quickly and climbs the creaking stairs to get her first look at London.

On deck sailors are climbing on high masts checking ropes and sails. Near her, a muscular redheaded Irish boy is singing a bawdy song as he hoists a heavy barrel onto the deck.

How she has dreamed of this moment! She breathes the morning air, heavy with cold fog. What's that strange, unpleasant smell? Then she remembers that John Eliot told her the air smells foul because of the coal which is burned for heat. She leans over the railing and watches apples bobbing around small, wooden pieces of broken barrel.

There are many huge, square-rigged ships in the harbor. She strains to see the buildings on the shore but the morning fog is still too dense. All she can make out is a forest of ship masts. Between them, small boats with lanterns dart about ferrying people and goods. The watermen! It's all just as Ned described it in his letters. He's been here a year already working with Henry Vane.

She leans over and can see the crew of the ship next to them unload its cargo. They are lowering barrels and baskets onto a smaller boat which will bring this cargo to warehouses along the shore.

The fog is lifting, so she walks to the bow straining her eyes to see London Bridge. There it is! She can see all those big buildings on it. She's amazed even though she's seen engravings of the bridge in the book she's treasured since childhood.

Coming and going under London Bridge are the "shooters" which Ned told her are boatmen who successfully struggle with the fearsome rapids below the bridge. The drawbridges on both ends are raised to let two tall ships pass. Isn't that St. Thomas Becket's church on the bridge?

Fog no longer hides the shoreline. She sees hundreds of church spires. Along the riverbank she imagines there are horses-drawn carriages waiting to take passengers to the inner city. Is Ned waiting for her in one of them?

Reverend Eliot comes up behind her and gently places his overcoat around her shoulders. He's been so kind these past four years. He's only about twelve years older, he's thirty-three, but she feels like he's her father. He's learned enough of the Algonquian language to speak it with Indians like Waban, a Nipmuc, and his first convert. Now he has taken her to London to raise money for his new village for converts, Natick, and she's feeling grateful.

"I'm so excited to see the city I forgot about the morning chill."

Together they watch the busy harbor come to life. "Commerce. That's what London's about. Stock companies make rich people wealthy. They are investing around the world, bringing all the best commodities back. See that large vessel? She's likely returning with barrels of sugar from Barbados to put into thousands of cups of tea. That other ship's unloading tea and spices from China. Our people must drink sugar and tea every day, but don't think about where it comes from or who is getting rich bringing it here."

They watch the activity all around them. Eliot points out a ship coming from far off India, and then he wants to get busy. "Come. Let's bring up our small bags of clothing and my Bible. They'll deliver the rest to Henry's house. I can't wait to get on shore again and eat a proper meal. After two months of what that terrible cook gave me, I'm longing for fresh vegetables and rare roast beef."

They climb aboard the waterman's ferry which moves quickly through rough water to the steps which take them to the road above. They see Roger Williams and a portly gentleman standing beside a black coach and two chestnut-colored horses. Ned hasn't come to greet her.

John Eliot introduces her to Reverend Mashfield from The Society for the Propagation of the Gospel. "He'll be our main contact for our fund raising effort."

She's happy to see Roger who hugs her. He was the one who brought Ned to London last year to meet with members of Parliament and bring back an official charter for their new colony. Rhode Island needs a charter now; Indian deeds don't provide enough legitimacy to protect the boundaries of the colony and land speculators in Boston covet land that's less rocky and more fertile.

The carriage bounces over cobblestones. The noises and images fascinate Comfort and overwhelm her senses. There's a cart piled high with chairs. Another passes by stuffed with squealing pigs. Wagons piled high with barrels of rum are being unloaded in front of the door to a tavern. Handsome carriages trimmed in gold are bringing rich merchants to their warehouses. The streets are filled with broken boxes and foul smelling garbage. Beggars and pigs rummage in piles of rotten food at the intersections, even as gentlemen with high hats and silver-tipped canes stroll by them in fine clothes. What a strange mixture of sights and sounds.

Eliot has given up trying to speak to the pastor because of the noise. She hears him say softly to himself, shaking his head, "Dear God, please protect us from such chaos. May Boston never become like this!"

At last the coach leaves the inner city behind and they're in a residential area.

"Has Parliament granted you a charter for Rhode Island yet?" she asks Roger.

"Not yet. All the talk of war has kept the members on the New England Committee very busy, but several have assured me I'll get it. I forgot to tell you, Ned's grown a beard the color of his sister Susanna's hair. He'll be at dinner tonight."

It'll scratch my face when he kisses me, she thinks, but I won't complain.

2

Fairlawn Manor

Ned wrote to her about Henry's two residences, Fairlawn Manor on the outskirts of the city and an ancient castle called Raby Castle further away. His father, Henry Vane the Elder, acquired the large castle from the King and gave it to his only son Henry upon his recent marriage to Frances. Henry's father is a member of King Charles's Privy Council, the powerful group of men who advise the King. Since Ned's friend Henry was elected to Parliament, he has chosen to stay in Fairlawn most of the time. The King has knighted him, so he is now known in Parliament as Sir Henry Vane the Younger.

Comfort's room has a large window framed with dark blue velvet curtains. It looks out on a formal garden. The canopied bed has a velvet coverlet. There's a charming ebony writing desk inlaid with mother-of-pearl, and furnished with fine paper, quill pen and ink. The high ceiling has wooden beams. On the walls are paintings of rural landscapes with hills, meadows, cows and sheep and thatched cottages.

Molly, a lively Irish maid with sparkling green eyes, brings Comfort water in a large blue and white bowl and soap which smells of roses. She puts on a white nightdress, lies down in the soft bed, and falls asleep immediately. When she hears knocking on the door it startles her awake. She opens the door thinking it's Molly.

"Look at you!" Ned says. "You're so beautiful."

"My hair's all tangled! I'm in my nightdress!"

"My angel, you're adorable. I couldn't wait. What do you think of my red beard?"

She touches it. "It makes you look older."

"We are both older, love." He kisses her, then slides his hands down her back, and caresses her buttocks. "I remember how you loved me to kiss your neck." He kisses her neck and smells her hair, then gently takes her to the bed. He kisses her on her neck and ears. He whispers: "I've dreamed of this moment."

She can't breathe and doesn't stop his hands from reaching into her nightdress and exploring her breasts. Waves of sensual pleasure overwhelm her resistance, and she yields to touch.

Someone is at the door. "Who's there?" she says, annoyed.

"Molly, Madame. I've come to help you dress for dinner. Two gentlemen are waiting for you downstairs."

"Please Molly; I want to rest a little more." She hears Molly go downstairs.

Ned sighs and gets up. "My darling girl, these dinners are very formal. The gentry love to dress in finery. I must go and change. I'm ecstatic you're finally here."

Molly returns and helps Comfort put on a lavender silk gown with lace trimming on the large wide collar and sleeves. Anne gave it to her as a going away present, saying it's the right style for fashionable London.

Molly brushes her hair. She looks into the mirror. Her cheeks are still burning from Ned's prickly beard. She feels beautiful and confident.

As she descends the staircase leading into the Great Hall, she admires her reflection in a gold framed mirror. Above the stone fireplace is a large woven tapestry of a hunting scene. The high ceiling is painted with enchanting cherubs floating on clouds, splashing in a river, and playing flutes. Here and there in the room are chairs and small sofas covered in green silk fabric.

A man with long black hair wearing a dark blue velvet suit is writing, bent over a small desk. Roger is sitting in a chair reading. He sees her, comes to greet her and introduce her to one of his oldest friends, John Milton.

"Stop scribbling, John," Roger says. "The world can wait a bit longer for your new poem. This charming lady is my good friend. It's her first visit to London."

John Milton stops writing, folds the paper, puts the quill pen down. "Ah, so this vision of loveliness is Miss Bradford." He kisses her hand and his dark eyes examine her from the pointed toes of her new shoes to the butterfly hair ornament in her hair. "It's an enormous delight, my dear, to welcome so lovely a visitor. Perhaps you'll accept me as your companion tonight for dinner so we can get to know each other better."

Milton's being his usual flirtatious self, Roger thinks. He'd be a good guide to the culture of the city for Ned is busy with Henry, but I must warn him Ned adores her. "She loves poetry so I'm sure you'll enjoy her company."

"My friend Anne Bradstreet is a poet also. She gave me your long poem Lycidas."

Milton's dark eyes twinkle. "So at least one of my poems has reached the far shores of Boston, has it? What did you think of it?"

"I felt its melancholy deeply. Anne told me it was written about a young friend of yours who drowned. My birth mother Dorothy drowned when I was a young child, so I thought of her when I read it. Your poem made me cry, sir."

"The Bishops hated it. Milton didn't care and dared to call them corrupt and he predicted their ruin," Roger says.

Milton nods. "They want to censor everything that's published. I'll always insist on the liberty to write what I want without fear.

I prize free speech above all liberties. We must do away with all censorship if England is to become a democratic republic."

Roger knows Comfort loves learning languages and tells her about his relationship with Milton. "John and I've been friends since Cambridge student days. I've been teaching him Dutch, and he's been helping me expand my Hebrew vocabulary. John reads Hebrew, Latin, Greek, French, Spanish, and even Italian. He even conversed in Italian with Galileo a couple of years ago when he went to see the great scientist."

"I've looked through one of Galileo's telescopes. Is he still under house arrest?" she asks.

They're both impressed that she knows of Galileo. "Yes. When I visited, he'd just published his final book in Leiden, since people here were too fearful to publish it. It describes experiments on motion and the relationship between speed, time and distance. It'll be the foundation of the study of physics. I admire him very much."

Comfort says she was born in Leiden. "My father told me Leiden is special because of the excellent universities there. Do you know any scientists from Leiden?"

"I do indeed. My good friend, Samuel Hartlib studies agriculture, medicine, and education," Milton says. "He wants to spread new discoveries through education. It's unfortunate you've missed his recent speech to Parliament in which he told them of using scientific experiments to increase crop yields and cure diseases."

Ned comes to join this conversation about science. "I've met Hartlib's neighbor Robert Boyle who is also a scientist," he says proudly.

"Our charming guest should go to the science meetings Samuel has in his house. If you can't take her Ned, well, I'd be happy to do so. They might like to learn about the natives. I understand you know their language. Do they have stories similar to stories in our Bible?" John asks.

"I've heard one about a great flood." she says.

Before she can continue John Eliot, Oliver Cromwell, and Henry Vane and his wife Frances arrive along with several servants bringing wine. Everyone sits, is introduced, and they drink wine.

Comfort admires Frances Vane's green brocade gown. Ned has written to her about Frances, so she knows Frances comes from a noble, wealthy family, and her father, Sir Christopher Wray, is a member of Parliament. Like Henry, Frances calls herself "a Seeker" who is a person who has separated from The Church of England and is opposed to state interference in religious matters.

Oliver Cromwell is not an attractive man. She notices his poorly tailored jacket which is tight on his stomach. He has long, straight hair, a big nose and an ugly mole near his lower lip. While he isn't handsome, Comfort is impressed with his commanding voice and extreme self-confidence.

"I almost left for Boston myself, Miss Bradford," Cromwell says. "Had Parliament not published the Grand Remonstrance, I might have given up efforts to limit the King's power and joined your bold experiment in New England. After I got it passed, I had to stay here and lead the effort to prepare for war should the King not change his behavior."

"What's a Grand Remonstrance, sir?" Immediately she heard in her head Alice's voice reminding her not to ask many questions. But how can she learn, if she stays quiet?

"A list of grievances against King Charles," Henry says. "Oliver made sure it got enough votes in the House of Commons to pass."

Oliver smiles. "If it hadn't passed, I was ready to sell all I have and leave here the next morning for Boston. Roger tells me you are not afraid to ask intelligent questions, so please ask me anything."

"What city do you represent, sir?"

Again Henry replies for him. "Oliver not only represents Cambridge, but has so many cousins who are elected representatives people think his family controls Parliament. What's the count now, Oliver, eight or nine?"

"Nine, including the Speaker of the House of Commons, Mr. John Hampden. He's a hero for publically refusing to pay the ship tax. Crowds cheered him as he walked to Westminster that day to deliver a speech against the tax," Oliver says. "You know, it is a very old tax meant only for port cities during wars, but our King now wants all counties to pay it. He needs money for his wars."

Roger tells her that Hampden was part of the group with Lord Brooke and Lord Saye that hired John Winthrop Jr. to establish Connecticut. "So you see our destiny is closely tied to what happens here. We depend on Parliament for legitimacy and on the stock companies to finance our colonies."

Oliver's commanding voice and passion totally captivate her attention. "We'll turn this country upside down. We need a new constitution to insure Parliament's right to meet every three years. Do you know that His Majesty dismissed Parliament for eleven years? The people's voice must be heard. We must not allow him to do this again."

Henry continues. "We're destined to be the greatest commercial power in the world. Four of Oliver's cousins belong to The Providence Island Company which invests in the Caribbean. At first they planted tobacco and cotton, and now its sugar cane."

"Will there be war between Parliament's army and the King's forces?" she asks.

He looks solemn "We must be ready. I've thousands of volunteers. As Treasurer of the Navy, Henry's increasing our naval fleet. He knows thirty five war ships are not enough to protect London. King Henry IV of France may provide aide to Charles for his wife Henrietta Maria is a Princess of the House of Bourbon. She's disliked here, not only because she's a Catholic but also because she can't speak English well."

Henry tells her Ned is helping him keep good accounts of navel expenditures. She sees that Ned is pleased.

"Will the King agree to Parliament's demands?"

"He's not going to compromise." Henry says. "He believes God made Him King. However times have changed. In feudal times a King could be rich by taxing his nobles, but now merchants in London create our wealth. Parliament controls taxation now."

Cromwell turns to Ned. "Show her the ramparts, Ned. Thousands of men, women and children are creating an eleven mile earth-wall around the city with deep ditches in front of it. The People will stand with us."

"The East India Company is building forts with cannons in strategic places along these ramparts," Ned adds. "It will protect the city."

"But doesn't the King have a large army?"

John is so impressed with her questions he decides to tell her about the military situation. "Parliament's soldiers are called Roundheads because of their cropped hair while the King's men are called Cavaliers and have long hair." He runs his hand through his long, curly hair. "As you see, I wear my hair long, but I'm not a soldier, just a vain poet and everyone knows I support freedom."

"You'll help us tell the world our cause is just, John," Henry says, and then turns to Ned. "Take her to read pamphlets in the taverns. This year more than a thousand were printed."

Ned nods. "John and I often go to the taverns to listen to farmers, tailors, shopkeepers and to read the latest pamphlets. The English people want democracy. Before my father died, he was proud of me and of our cousins who've joined Cromwell's volunteers."

"Your father's dead? You never wrote me about that. I'm so sorry."

"His heart couldn't take the stress of starting over after we were banished."

Oliver puts his arm around Ned's shoulder. "You and I lad, we're stronger men for having lost a father at a young age. Mine died when I was eighteen, leaving me to care for seven sisters. Responsibility early on in life makes a man stronger."

"Your mother and the others, are they still living on Aquidneck Island?"

"No. Mother took the rest of the family to a small English settlement in a place called Pelham Harbor which is in Dutch territory. She says the Indians and Dutch are allowing this religious settlement, but I'm worried about their safety."

"The Dutch and Indians are fighting," Eliot says. "Governor Kieft has stolen Indian land and forced them to pay tribute to him."

"She won't change her mind," Ned says. "When I go home, I'll try to convince her to come back to Rhode Island."

"When will you return home?" The answer she fears most is the one he gives her.

"As long as Henry needs me, I'll remain; if war breaks out, it might be years," Ned says with resolve. He'd hoped to delay discussing this with her. She's waited four years already to marry him. Is it fair to make her wait longer?

Lady Frances takes Henry's arm. "Let's eat, dear friends. My niece will entertain us with harp music and the roast pheasant mustn't get cold."

John Milton takes Comfort's arm. "We'll drink more wine. Frances always serves the best Madeira from Spain with pheasant."

Comfort sees platters are piled high with roast pheasant, beef, potatoes, fruit and vegetables. In one corner of the dining hall, a girl with long black hair wearing a red velvet gown is playing a harp.

John says his father was a composer and inspired his love of music. "Please allow me to escort you to performances. I know musicians, actors and writers. Life must be a balance between work and the enjoyment of music and poetry." She agrees to let this charming man be her guide to London's scientific and cultural events.

3

LONDON

In the first month Comfort is in London, she rarely sees Ned. He's helping Henry plan the expansion of the navy fleet. Comfort attends meetings with Reverend Eliot in the homes of rich merchants willing to fund his missionary work. These are held in in a newly developed square called Covent Garden.

The next month Comfort has time to explore the city. John Milton arranges for his niece Sally Wroth and her friend John Lilburne to show her around. Lilburne is a handsome soldier with a thin mustache, small beard, and passionate disposition. He's a leader of a group called the Levellers who have a written manifesto called "Agreement of the People". Many soldiers in Cromwell's army belong to this group.

In its manifesto the Levellers demand suffrage for *all* men over twenty-one not just property owners. All men have "natural rights": freedom to worship, freedom from compulsory conscription, the right to be treated equally before the law, the right to be tried by a jury of twelve men of their neighbors, the right to remain silent and not to be forced to testify against themselves and the right to call witnesses for their defense. Levellers want parliamentary elections every year, a new constitution guaranteeing these rights, and a free press without censorship. They meet in taverns and inns, one of which is called The Rosemary Branch. He takes Comfort there one evening and points out the men are wearing a sprig of rosemary in their hats to identify like-minded people. If she could join such a group, she would, she tells John.

John and Sally take her on long walks around London pointing out interesting places and telling her about changes currently going on in England.

"The center of the city is only a mile square," Sally says, "and it's surrounded by an ancient wall. The city is growing rapidly outward because people from the countryside are flocking here for work. Cloth factories have closed, and harvests have been poor for years. Thousands are migrating to the West Indies and New England looking for land and new opportunities."

"He really cares about the poor" Sally says. "That's why I love him."

"Wealthy families own half the land and more than half our people are now wage earners. Monopolies control foreign trade, but only a few actually profit from this new wealth. Swampland is being drained, but this newly reclaimed land is sold to the rich, while poor farmers are put in prison. It's unjust."

"To change society to benefit the laborers everyone must vote," Sally says.

"Will women ever vote?" Comfort asks.

John shrugs his shoulders. "Not any time soon."

"Women can organize petitions for the poor, hold meetings in their homes on spiritual matters, and address Parliament on behalf of the poor." Sally adds.

They pass Fleet Prison where John was a political prisoner because he imported seditious books. "The Star Chamber, a corrupt court controlled by the King, put him there without officially charging him with a crime. Thank goodness it's been abolished."

Sally looks at John. "He was arrested, fined over 500 pounds, pulled behind a cart and flogged for two miles, then his head and hands were put in the holes of the pillory and he was beaten.

I saw his back dripping with blood."

"Stop talking about the past. I'm going to ride in a military parade on Thursday. Come and cheer."

They agree.

They join the crowds lining both sides of the main road leading to Westminster. Hundreds of foot soldiers parade by holding pikes. They wear silver helmets with large red plumes and silver breastplates, white stockings, black breeches to the knees, and red jackets. Others march by with guns and they wear black hats and red, green or blue jackets. Soldiers pass carrying flags of green, gold, or red and others bang small drums. They see John sitting proudly on his brown horse wearing a silver helmet and breastplate. They wave even though they know he can't wave back.

One day Sally wants her to go to the House of Commons to hear Mistress Attaway petition on behalf of the poor. Comfort thinks of Anne Hutchinson. If women can speak out here, why can't they speak out in Boston?

John wants to show her a pub, and they wander the narrow streets in search of the oldest one called "Ye Hoop and Grapes." They can't find it, so go instead to Bishop's Gate, one of the old Roman gates in original wall. Comfort wishes she knew more about the history of England.

"Of course you must see the Tower of London," Sally says. She takes Comfort to the courtyard where Anne Boleyn lost her head. She's surprised to learn that it's a torture chamber, a prison, an arsenal, and the place where the crown jewels are kept."

"I fear our Queen will steal the crown jewels and sell them to the French King, Henry IV of France, who's her father. There are rumors she's raising a lot of Catholic money for the Royalist cause."

John Milton, who loves gardens, invites her to see the garden of Old Saint Paul church. He tells her he's writing a long poem about the Garden of Eden.

"Eve will be a character in my poem. She'll be as curious and beautiful as you are." She's flattered. She is attracted to him. Perhaps if Ned would pay attention to her, she would resist John's charms. Ned is always too busy to take her anywhere.

Finally, Ned says she must come with him on a barge along the Thames River to see Whitehall Palace. He's a good guide, but not affectionate. What's wrong?

"This castle was built on the grounds of a medieval castle built by King Henry VIII. There are 2,000 rooms. Henry lived here when he was a boy and sometimes went riding with the King. He hopes to get the King to compromise and prevent the civil war."

"Boston must have seemed so small to him," she says.

"There's the Banqueting House," Ned says. "Those outside stairs lead to the musicians' gallery where I stood and I looked down to the hall below where people were dancing. Women whirled around the room in colorful silk gowns, with necklaces which sparkled in the candlelight!"

On their return on the barge, Ned stares into the waves and is silent. He sighs. "I'll never be rich." He's still not looking at her.

Her heart is breaking. He hasn't been affectionate all day.

"I don't care. I just want to know if you're coming home to marry me." As soon as she said this, she felt humiliated and wished she hadn't asked him.

"There'll be a war, Comfort, and it may last years. I've promised to help Henry. I do love you, there is no one else, but perhaps you should be free to love someone else. Let's go back now. I've a meeting."

4

MOUNT HOPE

The Pequot War is over, but there is continuing hostility between the Narragansetts and the Mohegans. The English fear they may have to get involved in this inter-tribal conflict. Uncas has the strong support of the Bay Colony leaders and of Captain John Mason in Connecticut. They're suspicious of Miantonomo. So is Metacom.

The Narragansett Chief *sachem* has been invited to come to Mount Hope tomorrow. Metacom and his father, wrapped in moose hide cloaks against the cold, sit in front of a fire and share a long-stemmed pipe of tobacco. The village is bathed in the light of a full moon. A brown horse nibbles frost covered blades of grass. Metacom looks over at his own *wetu* where Little Bird and his daughter Laughing Like Water are sleeping. How can he protect his family if he doesn't know what his father will do tomorrow?

He looks at the sky. The Great Bear constellation reminds him of his spirit guide the bear. It gives him courage to confront his father.

"Why are you allowing the *sachem* of the Narragansetts to come here? He's our enemy. His tribe has claimed our land."

Silence. Massasoit continues to smoke.

"When I was a boy, you told me that the Narragansett *sachem* Corbitant captured you and Squanto. He would have killed you if the Englishman Miles Standish hadn't arrived. Why invite this Narragansett *sachem* into our village?"

Chief Massasoit puffs on the pipe. "Miantonomo comes with only five advisors and his young son to talk about Uncas. If there is to be a war between them, we must know about it."

"What does their hatred have to do with us?"

"Uncas, son of Oweneco, is a dangerous man. I believe Miantonomo wants us to help him kill Uncas. Their hatred is very strong."

"But the English support Uncas? Why should we risk their anger for Miantonomo's revenge? Do you want to bring the thunder of English guns against us?"

Silence. Wolf-dogs howl at the moon.

Metacom doesn't want a war. If his father should die in battle, his older brother Wamsutta will be chosen *sachem*. But he's often sick. What if he dies? Then Metacom will have responsibility for his people. He feels he has a right to know what his father is planning to do.

"Be calm, my son. Neither Miantonomo nor Uncas threatens us or our English neighbors. The English in Plimouth have been trading partners for more than twenty winters and we have an alliance. I don't believe Governor Bradford wants war."

"What should I say to the Narragansetts when they come here tomorrow?"

"Just listen to Miantonomo with respect. He's an intelligent leader of a large tribe. Don't worry. I won't jump into the fire of war."

Metacom throws several twigs in the flames then speaks. "I believe they'll use Miantonomo's desire for revenge against Uncas for their own purpose, to get more land. They've already lied to him. They promised to allow Narragansetts to hunt in Pequot forests after the war, yet now don't let them. Many ships come bringing more strangers wanting land."

"It's wise to be cautious, my son. You'll be Chief *sachem* someday and must seek the truth. Go to sleep. The Narragansetts won't be here until the sun is high in the sky."

Metacom rests beside Little Bird on the sleeping bench. His fingers touch the sharp bear claws he wears around his neck, proof of his courage. He remembers that the old *pawwaw* saw a vision. He will be brave leader and fight for his people. He falls asleep and dreams he wears his father's long wampum belt signifying leadership of the tribe.

Miantonomo, his advisors, and young son arrive the next afternoon. Massasoit greets them with hospitality. Women bring corn cakes and venison, for travelers will have eaten only *nokake*, dried corn powder mixed with spring water. Today they are guests and must be treated with hospitality.

After the meal, Massasoit puts around his neck the long ceremonial wampum belt, nine inches wide, with geometric designs made of white and purple beads. He prepares the sacred tobacco, puts it into the stone bowl shaped like a man's head and passes it to his guest. The two *sachems* smoke in silence, sharing the long-stemmed pipe.

Miantonomo thanks Massasoit for allowing him to visit and calls him *ketasontimoog*, a Great Chief *sachem*. He speaks slowly, thoughtfully, and with eloquence.

"We are all one people, *nestadooltee-ek,* you are my brothers. We lead free nations. My language is like yours, and so is the food I eat. There have been disagreements in the past, but I come today to ask you to be my ally against an enemy."

Miantonomo's, son Canonchet, who will be sachem someday, is a restless boy and can't sit still. Miantonomo tells an advisor to take him and his pony to the nearby spring to get water. Then he continues.

"Life is a circle, a sacred hoop, which connects all. We all come from the same original seven sparks of the Creator. We are all People of the First Light."

Chief Massasoit nods. "I will now hear your complaint against Uncas."

"The strangers have chosen sides. They've chosen Uncas, but I can't trust Mohegans. They fit their name, for they act like wolves. Uncas wants power and has tricked the foolish English."

"Yet you fought alongside both of them and against the Pequots." Massasoit says.

"I didn't know then how cruel these English are. I saw elders, women and children cut down by swords as they fled from the burning flames. I knew then I could never trust them."

"Didn't you desire the Pequots' hunting grounds? Didn't you sign a treaty with the English to have the right to use these forests?"

"They were once our own. We are a large tribe and have many mouths to feed. Now Uncas has killed my young nephew. I must revenge his death. Uncas must die."

Silence.

"I believe the English want to take all our land."

"Some are good trading partners and don't wish us any harm," Massasoit says.

"Uncas wants to kill me and the English will let him. Join me in fighting Uncas and his lying English friends."

"You are a wise and brave man. I'll meet with my advisors and send a messenger. Respect my decision. I must do what is right for my nation. *"Ga'chun benadooee,* the door is always open. You may come to talk."

After the Narragansetts leave, Massasoit speaks with Hobbamock who goes into a trance and tells Massasoit that he is right to reject Miantonomo's request to fight against Uncas and the English.

Later that night Metacom tells Little Bird she need not fear. "Your father, in a vision, saw an eagle fall from the sky with broken wings. That eagle was *sachem* Miantonomo. We won't protect him."

Metacom knows it's hard to be the Chief *sachem*. He must understand these English, for their arrival has changed everything. They have many guns. He has a matchlock, but he should get a flintlock, many flintlocks.

5

BOSTON

Miantonomo, a deerskin over one shoulder and five eagle feathers in his black headband, stands tall and dignified facing the eight magistrates in Hartford, Connecticut. He is on trial for attempting to poison Uncas. He was captured by Uncas and brought to face English justice. The verdict of the magistrates is about to be announced.

On the left side of the room, seated on the wooden floor, are his young son Canonchet and five unarmed Narragansett warriors. Their faces and chests are covered with stripes of black war paint. Behind them stands Captain John Underhill and several of his militia, the barrels of their flintlocks glinting in the sun streaming through the window.

Across the room, also on the floor, sits *sachem* Uncas wearing a red English coat with silver buttons, a gift from Governor Winthrop for his loyalty during the Pequot War. He has been allowed to bring with him ten unarmed warriors. Other Mohegan warriors wait outside in a meadow away from the meetinghouse. They carry bows and arrows and hatchets. English militia watch from a distance.

The magistrates for this trial represent the United Colonies, a new alliance formed since the Pequot War. It combines men who serve in the militias of the Bay Colony, Plimouth Plantation, and both New Haven and Hartford which are currently two separate settlements in Connecticut. Rhode Island has not been invited to join this coalition. It is too full of heretics. Winthrop calls it a "sewer" because it dares to welcome all religious groups which is an abomination and will spread heresies. Winthrop would like to own the western part of Rhode Island. This trial is the first joint action of the United Colonies.

John Winthrop announces the verdict: "Guilty of planning harm against our loyal ally Uncas."

Chief **Sachem** Miantonomo isn't surprised. The magistrates rejected his request to be set free based on the fact that his tribe has paid a large amount of wampum to Uncas already. According to Indian custom, his ransom payment of wampum should have been sufficient to buy his freedom. Uncas accepted the wampum, but then denied it was paid. Miantonomo has no proof of payment.

"You have a right to make a statement before you are turned over for punishment to Chief **sachem** Uncas," Winthrop tells him.

Miantonomo turns and faces the people in the meetinghouse. His strong, thunderous voice startles those in the room. "I, Miantonomo, King of a free nation, don't recognize your laws or your verdict. What is English justice? Is it English justice to sign treaties then break them? Is it English justice to take our tribe's western hunting lands away by treachery? Is it English justice to give strong waters to local **sachems**, get them drunk, and demand they give you our land? Is it proper to make them sign papers they cannot read? They don't have the right to give land. Only I, the King, can sell it. You may find me guilty, but you'll never destroy the Narragansett Nation." Simon Bradstreet, as Secretary of the magistrates, writes down what Miantonomo has said.

Canonchet and the other warriors with him stand making loud noises of defiance "Aieeee!! Aieee!! Aieee!!"

The soldiers rush forward and poke the barrels of their

flintlocks into their backs.

One soldier lifts his gun to hit young Canonchet on the head with the barrel of his flintlock. Governor Winthrop shouts "Stop! No violence!" He asks Captain Underhill to tie Miantonomo's hands behind his back. He announces the sentence and asks Simon Bradstreet to record the sentence.

"We, the legally elected representatives of The United Colonies, do hereby give over the heathen named Miantonomo to our loyal friend Uncas to get justice for the terrible attempt on his own life. This meeting is now adjourned. Captain Underhill will make sure the militia escort all Indians out of English territory as soon as possible."

Winthrop asks Captain Underhill to come closer and whispers in his ear. "Take your men and go with Uncas. See to it that they kill him on their own land, not ours. Report to me when the deed is done. We have asked Uncas not to torture him."

"We should put all militias on alert," Underhill advises. "The Narragansetts may seek revenge on us."

"Do it."

Late that night Captain Underhill returns with the news that as soon as Uncas arrived on his own land, one of his warriors put a hatchet into Miantonomo's back six times.

Has English justice has been carried out? Simon Bradstreet isn't sure.

6

LONDON

Reverend Eliot is meeting with a friend and doesn't need Comfort to come with him. Ned, as usual, is busy with Henry Vane. Comfort spends the day with John Milton in the Red Lion Inn and Tavern reading political pamphlets. "There are so many pamphlets and newspapers here," Comfort says. "We don't have any in Boston."

"My printer friend says two thousand pamphlets were printed this year. I'm writing one myself; it's against censorship."

He leans over and takes her hand. "How would you like to see a masque in Whitehall Palace tomorrow evening? My friend Inigo Jones has produced it for the King."

"I'd love to go. What will it be like?"

"Inigo's musicals are dazzling spectacles with exquisitely painted sets, imaginative and colorful costumes, ballet dancing, thunderclaps and original music. The masque tomorrow night is based on a play by Ben Jonson. Inigo has produced twenty-five masques based on Jonson's plays for the King's father. He's the King's architect and developed the plans for the new Banqueting House where the masque will be performed. That's certainly a building you must see."

"Have you ever collaborated with your friend Inigo?"

"No, I don't want to. He changes the poet's words, re-writes the story. Also, he feels special effects are more important than words."

"Does King Charles I love masques as much as his father did?"

"Oh yes. Two are produced every winter. The King has acted in them since childhood because his mother, Queen Anne, adored them. The present Queen Henrietta Maria grew up in the French court and also loves theatricals. When she was pregnant with their son Charles she allowed Inigo to put wires on her to make her fly over the stage. It caused quite a commotion in the court when it was discovered that she had put the future heir to the throne in danger."

The waiter brings a wooden trencher of salt beef and pewter mugs of cider. They eat and drink in silence. John looks into Comfort's eyes, and takes her hand. "I'll be proud to have such an intelligent and beautiful woman as you are as my companion."

She doesn't pull her hand away, even when he kisses each finger and says he loves her smooth complexion and beautiful eyes. She's vulnerable to his flattery. Didn't Ned say she should be free? Didn't he clearly tell her he won't marry her for many years? Her heart and body are ready for love, and he's betrayed her. She understands there may be a civil war, but she has been waiting four years already and thought they would marry here.

Milton tells her the masque is to honor the engagement of the Princess Royal. She's only nine and is engaged to marry Prince Willem, heir to the House of Orange, who's only fifteen. His father is Commander of the army of the five provinces which make up the Dutch Republic. "They're always political, these royal marriages. Our King hopes by agreeing to this engagement he can prevent a war with the Dutch, our greatest competitor for trade."

"She's only nine?"

"Yes. You and I, we're the proper age." He smiles. "I'll tell you about the last masque I saw at the palace. It was political."

Why not flirt? Why not let this charming man entertain her?

Comfort moves her chair a bit closer to his because the room is noisy. He smiles, taking it as a sign of her interest in him.

"The main character was a misunderstood King who saved his people from a rebellion planned by evil members of Parliament. The set was a painted cityscape of London. The subjects were blamed for creating disorder. That's how he sees us, darling, as stubborn subjects. He doesn't understand that we hate him for being a tyrant who refuses to compromise with Parliament."

"What about the masque we're going to see? Do you know the story?"

"It's a satire on newspapers, a free press, as well as modern science. Are you aware of the new science of astronomy?"

"I've looked through a telescope made by Galileo."

"Ah, Galileo. I visited him in Florence last year. He showed me the tower from which he points his telescope at the moon. The moon is important in this play."

"What does he see on the moon?"

"Dark areas. He says they are mountains and valleys. This masque makes fun of such ideas and ridicules the newspapers reporting his findings. You know of course that our King until recently demanded strict censorship over all books and newspapers."

"Who prints all the newspapers?"

"Those who can get licenses approved by the King. There's a great thirst for knowledge about all things scientific. A few years ago John Winthrop Jr. from your town, Boston, brought us the strangest creature, a horseshoe crab. What an ugly thing it was and someone drew a picture of it for the newspaper. This masque we're going to see is called 'News from New World Discovered in the Moon' and Inigo will definitely use many mechanical tricks. I can't wait to see who'll be flying in the air this time!"

* * * *

On the evening of the masque, Frances Vane lends Comfort a blue silk gown with a tight bodice and a gold necklace sparkling with rubies. She looks in the mirror and sees Lady Bradford rather than a farm girl from Plimouth.

Milton has rented a carriage and two white horses for the journey to Whitehall. In the carriage he calls her "beautiful princess" and kisses her on the lips. She doesn't push him away.

They arrive in time to attend a betrothal ceremony in the Chapel. The walls and columns are made of grey marble and the light coming through stained glass windows inspires prayer. She loves the violins and the high voices of the choir boys.

The young girl standing at the front is the nine year old Princess Royal, Mary Stuart. She has long reddish brown hair and wears a crown of pearls and a pearl necklace around her neck. Her dress, a shimmering light blue with gold embroidery, shows off her tiny figure. She stands so confidently that she appears older. Besides her, a bit taller, stands fifteen year old Prince William II of Orange in a red satin cape, red satin pantaloons ending at his knees, and an embroidered vest with a wide white collar trimmed in lace. He holds Mary's hand.

When the ceremony is over, they walk to The Banqueting House. On the way, Milton tells her Sir Anthony van Dyke, a famous Flemish painter, painted over forty portraits of King Charles I and thirty of the Queen. "Our King considers himself a patron of the arts. He thinks by giving paintings of himself as gifts his monarchy will be celebrated around the world. His Majesty has erected a monument to Van Dyke at Old Saint Paul's. Next time we go there, I'll show it to you."

The Banqueting House is a white building with columns and a triangular pediment in the Greek style. It was designed by Inigo Jones to honor King James I, the King's father. Rubens painted the exquisite panels on the ceiling.

Comfort examines the nine paintings on the ceiling. The center one shows King James wearing a flowing red robe and holding a scepter. He has one foot on a globe, and the other on the wing of a flying eagle holding a thunderbolt in its talons.

"It represents Justice," Milton says, "and the King, by Divine Right of his birth, is in charge of Justice, so he claims." He points out the figures representing Zeal, Religion, Honor, and Victory. Above the King there are cherubs holding the crown and orb and several cherubs with glowing trumpets. The painting in the south panel shows Peace and Plenty. Minerva drives Rebellion down to Hell where Satan, attended by monsters, awaits.

"Does this painting intend to show those who oppose the King are Satan's devils?"

"Of course" he says. "I'm willing to claim that ugly monster as representing myself. Our King is shown as being capable to trample Rebellion. He'll be less arrogant when he loses the war." The musicians in the gallery are tuning their instruments and they take their seats.

The curtain opens on the first scene, a conversation between Herald, a printer, and a newspaper columnist. He only cares about the cost of printing not the content of his newspaper. Others on stage discuss how hard it is to believe what they read in this newspaper. The character Herald says: "I'll give anything for a good story now, be it true or false, as long as it is news!"

Milton whispers: "until recently we didn't have many newspapers and only one printing company controlled by the King."

The main story is about Galileo. He has looked through his telescope and seen mountains as well as aliens on the moon. They can't speak; they use signs to communicate. The lawyers on Earth are frustrated because they can't interpret what these aliens are saying.

These aliens have sex, and the females lay eggs out of which are born little creatures who are half bird and half men called "volatees". The actors' costumes are funny, and Comfort can't help laughing aloud as they jump about on the stage. This is the first play she's ever seen. Milton loves the fact that she's enjoying the play so much.

After the masque is over, they return to Fairlawn Manor. He says goodnight, holds her face gently in his hands and kisses her. "I'm so glad you came tonight."

"Ned and I... we were going to marry."

"Hasn't he told you? He definitely won't get married for years. Will you try to change his mind?"

"No."

"You're beautiful inside and out. If you were to stay, well, maybe..." He kisses her passionately. "I'll miss you."

"I'll miss you too," she says. "I'll never forget tonight."

7

Boston

Anne Bradstreet sits by a window holding Comfort's last letter. She is pregnant and fears she will die in childbirth. Her poor children can't understand why she's so irritable, but Comfort understands and knows how to calm her anxiety.

On the table are the toys Comfort has sent with the letter: a wooden whistle for Sarah, seven, a tipcat game with its two wooden sticks to bang together for Dorothy, a red wooden top and a knucklebone game made of sheep ankle bones and a leather ball to be shared by all of them. These toys will keep the children busy and give her peace so she can finish writing her new poems.

Simon is attending an emergency meeting at John Winthrop's house. "I must go. There are rumors the Narragansetts are attempting to get Mohawk help. They may be planning to attack us in order to take revenge for our compliance in Chief *sachem* Miantonomo's murder."

"Does one war always create another?" she asked him.

"Please don't worry, darling. We've shown the Pequots we're not cowards. We've God's protection against any new conspiracy the heathens may be planning."

She decides she'll write to Comfort about the trial and murder of *sachem* Miantonomo. Also she wants to tell her that hundreds are coming to Boston because of their fear of a possible civil war in England. She hopes Comfort will come home soon. She'll need her support when this baby is born.

How will a war in England affect us? There is already a shortage of good farmland. Will more of the newcomers go to Connecticut? Will that lead to a war with the Dutch who have many fur traders in that area? She has asked Simon about these things, but he says she must stop asking questions and just be a good mother.

That evening Simon comes home very anxious about the meeting. "Captain Mason insists we start another pre-emptive war, this time against the Narragansetts. There is no proof that the rumors about the Narragansetts are true, but he feels we need to act first. Perhaps Uncas is spreading these rumors, I told them, but Captain Underhill said the Pequots who were adopted into the Narragansett tribe are probably convincing them to attack us to get revenge for the massacre at their fortified village."

"We killed so many" Anne says. "Was it a mistake?"

"Maybe. We profit from the wampum we get from the remaining Pequots and the River Indian tribes. The Mohegans and Narragansetts pay us an annual tribute for each Pequot we allowed them to adopt. Uncas has given Captain Mason most of his tribal land in Eastern Connecticut. This is evidence they accept our dominance."

"My father says we can never trust them. He says Long Island tribes are refusing to pay tribute to the Dutch who've been fighting a war with them for several years now. These tribes can refuse to pay us tribute and could attack us."

She is so nervous. Simon holds her tightly in his arms. "Be calm my love. It's not good for the little one inside you."

"I don't want to live like this, constantly afraid of attack. Where can we go? London isn't safe anymore. I had a dream we were in Barbados and the children were splashing in the calm, blue waters of the Caribbean. Maybe we should move there."

"No. If we remain faithful to our covenant with God, we will survive. Our Lord wants us to bring civilization to these heathen and to practice our faith in the true way we have chosen." He rubs her stomach and feels the baby kicking. He caresses her stomach gently until the baby is calm.

"I love you Simon. You're wise, and shouldn't let professional soldiers force you to agree to something you have doubts about. Promise you'll try to get them to wait for proof that the Narragansetts plan to attack."

8

Pelham Neck

In a small English settlement on Long Island in Dutch dominated territory, Anne Hutchinson and her daughter Susanna, nine years old, are stuffing pieces of cloth into small spaces in the walls. A cold wind whistles through these chinks between the wood.

"Willie is cutting more logs for the fire" Anne says. She gets a sweater from a basket on the floor and gives it to her daughter.

She's worried about Susanna. Her youngest daughter no longer sleeps peacefully. The Dutch and Indian fighting in this area has increased and it gives her nightmares. She no longer combs her tangled red hair and lets it fall over her eyes.

"Come here," Anne says, taking a blue ribbon out of her pocket. "Tie your hair back. Help me set the table."

Together they set out thirteen places for their family. "We've a rabbit stew for supper. Be thankful your older brother's such a good hunter." Then they read psalms aloud while waiting for the oldest daughters, Katherine and Faith, to return from visiting a neighbor.

Was it was a mistake to bring her family here? So far the local tribes, the Wecqueasgeek and Siwanoy, have been friendly and have left them alone; it's the Dutch they hate. But now several of her followers have returned to Aquidneck Island with their families fearing attacks on Dutch traders will lead to attacks on them.

"Why did you have to bring us here, mama?"

"You know why, dearest. After your father died, the Lord told me to come. We heard the Bay Colony was trying to take control of all of Rhode Island. That's why Roger Williams had to go to London to get a proper charter. If those who banished me should take control, I'd be a prisoner again. A Dutch trader arranged a land sale for us here."

"My friend said he never gave our wampum to the Indians but rather kept it for himself. If that's true, the Indians have reason to hate us. I want to go home, mama."

"This is our home. Tell Willie to stop chopping and bring wood in. It's too cold."

Susanna goes out. Before she can talk to her brother, she glimpses an Indian face in the bushes. Terrified, she hides behind a large boulder.

Seven Indians quietly sneak towards the house. Three carry war clubs, two hold hatchets, and one has a flintlock. Susanna hears a gun go off, but doesn't dare get up to see what's happening. Her sisters have returned home and are screaming. She stays hidden.

In the house an Indian smashes her mother's skull with a war club. The plates, splashed with Anne's blood, fall to the floor.

A young Indian finds Susanna's hiding place, snatches fistfuls of her red hair and pulls her to him. She screams. He holds a hatchet over her head, ready to cut it open, but changes his mind and instead drags her by the hair into the bushes. She faints.

When Susanna opens her eyes, she's freezing and realizes she's on the snow. The young Indian talks to her, but she can't understand a word he has said. He kicks her, pulls her up, wraps a deerskin around her, and then pulls her along with him by her arm. She notices his leggings are covered with blood. The other Indians ignore them.

They stagger together through the snow for hours, stopping to rest only for brief periods. It's getting dark. Her Indian abductor puts corn paste in her mouth, but she spits it out. He touches her hair gently. He has never seen red hair. She's terrified, expecting him to cut off her scalp, but his touch is surprisingly gentle. She prays silently to God to let her die before these devils torture her; she has heard terrible stories. But her captor is gentle now and helps her up when she slips on the ice. Finally they reach his village.

Children come running to greet them. Wolf- dogs run towards her and she screams. Her young Indian master takes her home to his mother's wigwam. The woman's wrinkled face isn't friendly. She leads her to a bearskin covered sleeping bench and gives her a gourd of spring water to drink. Susanna drinks, then cries herself to sleep.

The next few weeks are spent doing chores for the old woman. They communicate with gestures. Every day she goes with her to get water from a nearby spring. Together they gather twigs for the fire and make a stew. Night after night the screams of her sisters invade her dreams and she wakes up sobbing. The woman sings to her when she has these nightmares until she falls asleep. She is calmed by this singing.

Months later Susanna realizes she understands what the old woman is saying, and she can say short sentences in Algonquian. She doesn't think of the past or future, and concentrates on the daily tasks she's ordered to do. The old woman no longer hits her ankles with a thin branch when she does something wrong or too slowly. She eats what is offered even though she dislikes it and sleeps through the night. This has become home. She's becoming a Siwanoy, a member of a small band that pays tribute to the Wappinger tribe. The old woman and her son are her family now.

9

Raby Castle

Ned leaves London for Raby Castle immediately after reading the letter from Captain Underhill telling him about the murder of his family. He rides fast, north and east towards Scotland, to Henry Vane's castle where he can mourn in private. "My sadness is like a boulder on my chest and I can't breathe. I'll come back as soon as I can lift it off. I'm no use to anyone now."

Raby Castle is a medieval castle. It has a twelfth century tower, a moat, and hundreds of acres of land. Some land is cultivated by tenant farmers and the rest is forest suitable for hunting. There is a small hunting cottage in the woods.

Inside the castle there is an Entrance Hall with gothic pillars, a Banquet Hall with walls covered with family portraits, a Baron's Hall which is an octagonal room which has a high beamed gilded ceiling and candelabra, and many beautifully furnished guest rooms. All the splendor of the castle is ignored by Ned as he falls deeper into despair.

He stays upstairs in a dark room in the tower thinking of his beloved older sister Faith who helped raise him, remembering her patience as she taught him to read the stories of dragons he enjoyed. He cries for Susanna. Did they cut off her beautiful red curls? Maybe, even though she was still a child, they raped her? He can't seem to drink enough wine to become unconscious although he tries, consuming more every day.

He forces himself to read Captain Underhill's letter again and again, forces himself to accept the fact that he no longer has a family. He wants to throw the letter into the fire, to throw himself into the fire. He doesn't feel he can survive the pain he feels, the guilt he feels. He's alive, so far away, and he wasn't there to try to defend them. Perhaps he could have done so. He's a good shot. At least some of the barbarians would have died.

"Dear friend, we can't know why such terrible things happen. God's ways are mysterious. Grieve for them, but remember that now their souls are happy in Heaven.

May your prayers give you the strength to survive this greatest of all misfortunes. All of us who loved your saintly mother will keep her memory alive for future generations of believers."

Did I believe in her conversations with God? No. I've never believed in them. Do I think what happened to my family was God's will? No I don't. Why would God kill her, a visible saint on earth, who inspired so many?

Is God punishing me for leaving home after my father died? Should I have written to them, tried to convinced them not to live so near Dutch territory where there has been conflict with local tribes? Would mother have listened to me? Probably not. Why did God allow this to happen?

Some people say that by bearing afflictions, God shows us the value of His presence. I don't feel His presence. I want to kill all savages, thousands of them. I want revenge. Will I ever be able to pray again? Right now I wish the sun, moon and stars would disappear and leave me in darkness forever.

He gets up to drink another glass of wine. The bottles in his room are all empty. He goes downstairs to get more.

* * * *

In London, Frances Vane is sitting at her vanity in her nightdress, while Henry's in the room getting ready for bed. She must think of a way to get Ned to return to London where she and Henry can help him. She fears he might kill himself if they leave him alone.

"Comfort must go to see Ned right away. I'll take her," she says to Henry. "I believe he still loves her and he needs her now." She starts brushing her long, wavy brown hair with a silver brush.

Henry comes over to her and kisses her neck. "Yes, my love. You're right. Take her to Raby Castle."

"I'll visit our tenant farmers. The harvest is poor and they're practically starving. I'll give them money to buy food."

Henry takes the brush from her hand and gently brushes her hair. "John Milton has been flirting with Comfort for months. Now he's told me he has decided to marry the sixteen year old daughter of his father's business partner, Mary Powell. I told him not to do so, for she is still a child. Besides her father is a strong supporter of the King. I believe he'll regret it. I don't know if Comfort has fallen in love with him. "

Frances takes the brush from Henry's hand and puts it on her table. "I don't think so, but I'll ask her. If she is willing to get Ned to return, his work may keep him from melancholy. Come, my love. I need the sweet comfort of your warm body so I can sleep. Otherwise, I'll worry about Ned all night."

"Glad to oblige, my darling wife."

10

RABY CASTLE

Vane's elegant blue and gold carriage passes through the narrow cobblestone streets of the city and heads northeast. It passes the Royal Exchange where merchants negotiate contracts and proceeds down the major road out of town called "City Road."

As Comfort looks out the window she remembers watching the Honorable Artillery Company's parade down this road with Sally. They came to watch John Lilburne ride by, one among hundreds of Cromwell's soldiers on horseback and foot, proudly displaying their readiness to fight against this tyrant King who refuses to share power with Parliament.

"It'll be dark when we arrive" Frances says. "I'll have the servants prepare a simple meal. Tomorrow Ned can show you the grounds. I'll leave you both alone while I visit my tenant farmers."

"Was your wedding held at Raby Castle?"

"No. Whitehall Palace. Henry's mother insisted, wanting to show off the Vane family's high position. His mother will surely support His Majesty in the civil war, even though her son is one of the leaders of Parliament. Henry's committed to the just cause of democracy, but he'll keep trying to get a compromise."

"Did your father arrange your marriage?"

"No. My father and Henry's know each other, but we decided to spend our lives together. We're both Seekers, and believe everyone should find their own way to God. We believe church and state must be completely separate. People in London and Scotland must make their own decisions in religious matters. My father almost made me call our wedding off when Henry put the Earl of Strafford on trial."

"Who's the Earl of Strafford?"

"Didn't anyone tell you?"

"No."

"He was a favorite of the King, but hated by many in Parliament because he urged the King to ignore their demands. One night Henry stole his father's keys and opened a secret red velvet box containing the King's personal letters. He copied a letter written by Strafford and made it public. They tried him for treason and he was executed. The King punished Henry's father for not protecting his private papers and removed him from the Privy Council. His father has never forgiven him for this humiliation."

"I've disobeyed my father too," she says.

"What did you do?"

"After Ned's mother's trial, my father forbade me to see Ned anymore because he thought she was a heretic, but I kept seeing him. Oh Frances, I still want to marry him, but I don't think he wants to marry me."

They reach Raby Castle just as the sun is setting. Comfort has seen etchings of castles, but the size of this medieval castle astounds her. Frances tells her about its history as they get closer. For over hundreds of years those who owned this castle have played important roles in the history of England.

Comfort is overwhelmed by the size and beauty of the rooms. Frances leads her to the Baron's Hall. "Here in 1569 seven hundred knights planned a rebellion which failed. I pray our rebellion now doesn't have a similar fate."

She rests for a while, then changes into a green silk dress. Will Ned even care what she looks like? When she comes to dinner, she's alarmed to see that the table is set for only two people.

"Has Ned left?"

"He takes meals in his room. I've invited him to meet me in the library for a glass of wine. I didn't tell him you're here."

"He might not be happy to see me."

"I'm sure he will. He told Henry he'll always love you."

They eat quickly and go into the library. Four bottles of wine and three gold goblets have been set out on a round mahogany table. In a corner is a small table with a telescope and a globe of the world.

Comfort examines the two portraits on the wall. The artist captured Henry's handsome oval face, clef chin, small mustache, wavy dark hair, and large brown eyes. In Frances' portrait, he's painted gold light in her flowing, blond hair. She's wearing a dark blue dress with a large lace collar.

"I love your portraits," Comfort says. "The artist has captured your elegance and intelligence."

"This library is Henry's favorite room." She picks up a book from the table near the large cushioned chair. "He sits here when he comes, reading this book. She shows it to Comfort. "Meteors and Shooting Stars" is the title. "I'll take it back to Fairlawn. He's just finished reading William Harvey's book on the movement of blood through our bodies. I prefer history. I'm reading John Speed's 'History of Britain.' Henry says he'd rather change history than read about it."

"He is changing history," Comfort says.

Ned walks into the library and is very surprised to see Comfort. He's thinner, pale, his hair and beard untidy, and his clothes disheveled. He doesn't talk to Comfort but pours a glass of red wine for himself and drinks it quickly.

"Are you well?" she asks.

"How can I be well?" He replies curtly.

Frances decides to get her business with Ned over quickly so she can leave them alone. "Henry hopes you can review the new navy budget before he authorizes payment to the sailors." Frances gives him papers and he puts them in his pocket without examining them.

"I'll be visiting our tenant farmers in the morning," Frances adds. "Take Comfort to see the grounds. The servants will bring lunch to the cottage. I'm tired, so goodnight dear friends." She leaves.

Ned refills his glass and fills one for Comfort. He drinks his quickly standing by the table, and then pours himself another before giving her the wine and sitting down in the large chair. He looks wretched. "So, I suppose you've come to say good-bye," he says, not looking at her. "You shouldn't have come. I'm poor company."

"Eliot has bought our return tickets on The Lyon. I couldn't leave without seeing you."

"Well here's to your safe voyage," he says, raising his glass. "Please join me in another glass. It's good Spanish wine. Most nights I finish two bottles." He gets up and refills her glass again.

"It makes me sleepy." She drinks.

"Be grateful. My nightmares are…well, you don't need to know the bloody pictures in my head. I don't know if I'll ever sleep a whole night without waking up terrified."

She tries to get him to think of happier times. "Doesn't this room remind you of John Winthrop Jr.'s library? We had such lovely evenings there looking through his telescope. That telescope over on the table, is it just like John's?"

"Yes" he says, twirling the wine in his glass, not looking at her or the telescope. "Say hello to those intolerant magistrates in Boston for me. Tell them they got their wish. God has punished my mother and her children."

She's angry. "Don't talk like that. She didn't do anything. It's a tragedy and those who loved her will never forget her." She gets up and goes to him. She takes the empty wine glasses and puts them on the table. She tells him to stand.

"Aren't you even a little bit glad to see me? Don't you care about me at all? Nothing will change what happened, but I want you to know I still love you."

He looks at her. "You deserve more than I can give you now." He touches his heart. "In here… there's burning anger. In here… there's regret for what I didn't do to protect my family." He looks down. "Perhaps someday I'll feel well enough to love again, but now what I need is wine. It's the only thing that dulls my pain."

She watches him fill his glass again. It can't end like this. This can't be her last memory of him. She gets up and kisses him. He doesn't push her away but doesn't return her passion. He goes to the window and looks into the dark night. "I feel dead."

"I don't want to remember you like this. Please talk to me."

Ned walks to a small sofa, sits and puts his head in his hands. Finally he speaks in a very low voice. "All those I love die."

She sits down next to him. "Look at me. Say you love me and I'll wait forever."

"You deserve better. Go home, marry, have children. You've waited long enough."

She kisses him again. This time he returns her passion. Tears fill his eyes. He touches her face gently with his fingers, then turns away and looks out the window again. He speaks without turning to look at her. "Who knows what'll happen when the fighting starts? I don't know how long it will last. Cromwell's army and the King's Cavaliers seem evenly matched, with thousands on both sides. I feel I can't leave until it's over. Henry wants me to stay."

"Do you still love me? Knowing you love me will sustain me until you come home." She's crying now. He turns back to her and sighs deeply.

"Come, my sweet girl. If you can love me now, when I'm full of rage, and despair, then I will accept your gift of love. God knows how much I need it." He takes her hand and leads her upstairs to his room.

It's cold and dark; there are only embers burning in the fireplace, so he puts a few logs on the fire. After watching the dancing flames in silence, he goes to the canopy bed, pulls open the curtains, takes off his shoes and rests on the bed. She lies down next to him. They don't undress and cuddle as they did long ago in Metacom's wigwam on the snowy night when they brought Roger and his family to Mount Hope.

After a while she stands up, turns away from him, and slowly begins to take her clothes off. He's never seen her naked. He watches her white petticoats fall to the floor exposing her beautiful back. When she's naked, she climbs into the bed. He gets up and undresses then pulls the curtains around the bed. They make love for the first time. They don't feel guilty, but rather relief for finally being able to do what they have longed for.

Ned shares his plans for life after the war. "I want to live in Newport Rhode Island because of its fine harbor. I'll buy a ship and bring fish and timber to the sugar plantations in the Caribbean. Could you share such a life with me?"

"I'll live with you anywhere in the world darling."

They stay in the hunting cottage for four days and nights, suspended in pleasure. Ned agrees to return to London.

FAIRLAWN MANOR

When she arrives in London, there is a message from John Milton for Comfort.

Dear Comfort: A poet's function is to search for truth, yet I've betrayed truth by not being clear about my intentions. I was blinded by your intelligent, curious mind, your knowledge of Greek literature, your desire to bite the apple of knowledge, your softness and your sweet attractive grace. I'll treasure my memory of our conversations in that small garden, that fragment of Eden, near Old Saint Paul's, as the noon sun warmed my skin and I stared in your amazing eyes and secretly called you my Eve.

Whenever I see a masque I'll think of you and that evening we spent together at the Palace. I adored seeing your excitement at discovering music and theatre. I'm a butterfly who knows it's landed on a rose not yet fully opened but sure to blossom into an exceptional flower. I couldn't bring myself to fly away once I found you, and couldn't stop myself from wanting to hold your slender waist and taste your sweet lips. God intended Adam to delight in Eve's beauty.

I won't blame Satan for seducing me to kiss you, for I believe in man's free will, and if we fall it's our own fault. God wants us to be challenged by temptation. I feel guilty for desiring to win your heart even though I thought you might still love Ned. I took a bite of forbidden fruit because it was so beautiful.

Can you forgive my bad behavior? Can we still be friends? I sincerely hope I won't lose you. May I write from time to time to let you know what's happening here? When I finish my long poem which I shall call "Paradise Lost" I'll send it to you. I'm flattered by your interest in my poetry.

Before you leave and there's an ocean between us, let's spend one more evening together enjoying intelligent conversation. This Thursday there is a meeting of that "invisible college" I told you about. Please come with me to meet my friends.

John Milton

Comfort goes with him on Thursday evening. Milton's friends meet regularly in the home of Samuel Hartlib who lives in a townhouse in Covent Garden Square. Among them are doctors, businessmen, researchers and educators.

Samuel Hartlib shares Milton's interest in educational reform. He tells her that both speakers are from the Bay Colony, John Winthrop Jr. and his friend Dr. John Child. She says she's borrowed many books from John's extensive library.

Samuel also has a large library. Every wall in this room is filled with books. He points out a section of science books which he hopes schools will acquire.

She's introduced to other guests: John Bainbridge, a physician and student of astronomy, William Harvey, a physician who studies blood circulation, and Margret Cavendish, the Duchess of Newcastle-on-Tyne, who's published poetry and plays. Margret tells Comfort she's studying the new scientific reasoning and gives speeches on the humane treatment of animals.

Robert Boyle is only seventeen, and tells Comfort he intends to live in London and become a scientist. He recently saw Galileo. "He uses mathematics to explain motion. I want to use it to explain air and gasses." What is so mysterious about air and gasses, she wonders. She thinks his passion for experiments could change how people think about the natural world.

She mentions that she's helping Eliot translate the Bible into Algonquian. He's interested. "I'd like to see the Bible translated into the Irish Gaelic language," Robert replies.

"What I like most about this 'invisible college'" John Winthrop Jr. tells her," is that these scientists consider the practical uses for new knowledge. Tonight I'll talk about my ironworks project. But first Dr. Child's will tell us about his visit to the King of Denmark's cabinet of curiosities. You'll be fascinated."

Dr. Child has visited the home of Ole Worm, doctor to King Christian IV of Denmark. He describes the collection of various preserved animals, fossils of plants that no longer exist, various samples of minerals, and a cloak covered with feathers from a tribe of Indians the Spanish explorers have exterminated. It makes Comfort very sad to see this beautiful cloak covered with colorful feathers. Is this all that is left of a proud nation? She thinks of Massasoit's wampum belt. Will that be kept in someone's cabinet of curiosities?

John Winthrop Jr. discusses his 'bloomer' which is used for smelting iron, and his forge that makes tools in New England. He plans to experiment with methods to desalinate sea water so it can be used for drinking and irrigation. John Milton tells friends that would be a blessing for all mankind.

In the carriage going home, John says he's feels optimistic about the future after attending these meetings. "This vast city will be a place of liberty. People will do experiments, and will feel free to publish their results without prior censorship by the Bishops or a King's advisor. No one will be jailed for heresy or for using their intellectual gifts no matter what they're interested in. Eventually democracy will spread throughout the world. We'll have a bloody war, but we will be victorious."

"I hope this war won't be too bloody. I know many will die. I don't like war. Are you sorry you're not in Parliament now?" she asks him.

"No. I'm a poet and essayist. I want to educate the masses. I've faith in ordinary folks. General Cromwell will lead us to victory, but I fear he won't be democratic. Power corrupts, and Oliver thinks he knows best about everything. I hope we don't rid ourselves of a King who is a tyrant only to replace him with a professional soldier who will become dictator."

When the carriage arrives at Fairlawn Manor, they are reluctant to say goodnight. He longs to kiss her one more time. He's surprised when she moves closer and kisses him passionately. "Thanks for everything. I'll never forget you." she says.

"Come back when these tumultuous times are over. Our world is filled with hatred and strife. Why must we endure cruel wars? Why do we want to destroy each other? I'm going to write poetry to get men to think about these things."

"I hate war. At least you have a vision for a better future. I hope the war will end quickly."

"My dear girl, it won't. The King says God made him King and wants him to keep his power and wealth. He's not going to compromise. He's not going to give up any of his power."

12

The House of Commons

Comfort wants to say goodbye to John Lilburne and Sally. They were so kind to show her the city. She's delighted when they invite her to sit with them one more time upstairs in the gallery of the House of Commons.

Parliament is discussing the expansion of the navy fleet. They want to make sure the King will not be able to bring his ships down the river to attack the city. The volunteers have finished building the long ramparts and four more cannons have been placed in strategic areas. They can fire on any ships that come to attack. Sir Henry Vane is telling the members that he has just returned from Scotland and the Scots have agreed to send their army to join Cromwell's soldiers and protect the city of London. This is a major accomplishment. Now the King will most likely move his army further north.

Everyone is shocked when King Charles marches in followed by more than a hundred armed soldiers. Comfort is dazzled by their uniforms. They wear green and gold velvet suits with large red feathers coming out of tall hats. She sees the King go to the podium where Henry Vane has been standing. His Majesty says something to Henry who immediately leaves the podium. The members of Parliament wait anxiously for King Charles to speak.

"Hundreds more Cavaliers are outside," says a man who has just come in. He sits next to Comfort and can't catch his breath.

"I saw them... Do you think the King...will he dare to disband Parliament again? "

"We can't let that happen" Lilburne says.

His Majesty speaks loudly to the astonished representatives. "I have come here to arrest five men for treason against the state. He calls out their names: Pym, Hampden, Haller, Hazelrigg, and Strode. Stand up immediately." There is whispering as everyone looks around the large hall. These five are the most prominent elected members of The House of Commons. Comfort leans over the railing to see where these men are. No one stands up. The members are talking among themselves. The King is banging his scepter on the podium. "Get up now. I order you."

Henry shouts for silence. "They're clearly not present here today Your Majesty." He speaks in a calm voice as if this is just a common circumstance. "I'm sorry. Perhaps they are sick."

"So the birds have flown," His Majesty replies. "Who warned them? Did you Sir Vane? Anyone who has warned them is a traitor. He will be executed no matter who he is. These men have spoken treason against me. I'll have their heads."

"Your Majesty," says Henry, "the members of this body have a right to speak their minds freely in this hall. You cannot arrest us for doing so."

His Majesty glares at Henry. "Why do you dare to betray me? I'm God's representative. You are my subjects and must obey me."

"I didn't warn those men, Your Highness, I can assure you, and I don't know who did. Since you're here now, please feel free to continue to address us. We want to hear what you have to say. We continue to be open to a compromise, a new approach for shared responsibility for the welfare of this great nation we all love."

The King speaks in a loud, angry voice. "It's for me, and only for me, to decide how our nation is governed, how my subjects are ruled, and how our church is organized. This is ordained by

Almighty God. It's not proper for subjects to question Royal prerogatives. I don't wish to discuss this. Accept it." Then His Majesty and the Cavaliers leave and join the other soldiers outside. They march away with trumpets blaring, red feathers on their large hats blowing in the wind.

"The war will begin; the only question is how soon. We don't know exactly where the King's forces will strike first," John Lilburne says to a soldier near him. "I doubt hostilities will start in London. Our army is too strong here. I think it will happen in the north, but war is always unpredictable."

Then John stands up, leans over the railing and shouts to the members who are still sitting in shock: "May our just cause triumph!" Some of the members join in and repeat his words.

Henry Vane orders two hundred barges into the Thames River with two thousand armed sailors onboard to protect the city from attack by the King's forces. Ned organizes messengers who will bring Vane's orders to all the ship captains.

His Majesty, fearing for his safety and that of his family, leaves the palace for the north. He has decided where he wants the battle to begin. Prince Rupert of the Rhine will lead the King's army towards London from Edgehill. He intends to win the war quickly.

13

EDGEHILL

The King's Cavaliers are on top of a steep hill. The King is on his white horse looking down at Parliament's army still getting organized below. Cannons have not yet been wheeled into position.

Both armies are large: over 12,000 soldiers, about 2,000 on horses, 700 dragoons which are soldiers who use horses to move into position then dismount to fight the enemy on foot. The rest of the men are foot soldiers. The King's army has an advantage since they're on the hill.

Captain John Lilburne is serving in Lord Brooks' regiment. He looks up the hill and sees King Charles himself on his white horse, wearing armor, riding from regiment to regiment, encouraging his soldiers. He tells Lord Brooks he thinks the King's forces are being told to rush down the hill and begin the attack. Lord Brooks passes this information to Lord Essex. The battle begins.

In an open field, between the towns of Radway and Kineton, foot soldiers fight man to man with guns, swords and pikes. Some wear helmets, breastplates, and back plates but armor is too heavy and too expensive, so many men wear thick leather coats to protect them from sharp swords and pikes sixteen feet long, tapered on the end.

The pike men stand shoulder to shoulder in a row. Some are holding the pike with their right foot, and bending so they can push the pike into a horse. The noise and smoke of cannons, the screaming of men attacking, and the neighing of wounded horses frighten the soldiers who are not experienced in warfare.

Both sides kill five hundred of their enemy and wound fifteen hundred others. Many boys in Parliament's army run away after they see the slaughter.

The King has brought his young son Charles with him but, seeing the carnage, orders an officer to take him off the battlefield. He is the heir to the throne and must be protected.

The sun is setting and Parliament's army retreats, leaving cannons and guns behind.

At dawn, Captain John Lilburne comes with others to search for wounded men among the scattered bodies and dying horses. A row of pike men lay dead on the ground, their long pikes tossed in every direction. He sees the mangled body of his young friend Mathew. He says a prayer then takes the boy's thick leather coat off to give to another soldier who needs protection. There are some men still alive. John asks a soldier to help him pull a heavy wheel off the body of a boy breathing, but with deep cuts on one arm.

Neither army is victorious after this first battle of the war. However, the King has gained command of the road leading into London. He moves his forces close to London to Oxford which he intends to use this as his headquarters for the rest of the war.

Captain John Lilburne is taken prisoner and sent to the King's prison in Oxford. When he is released in a prisoner exchange and returns to his unit he organizes a political group within the army among the artisans and workers. "We are fighting for universal suffrage. Lack of ownership of property must not prevent us to have our right to vote." He gives speeches about natural rights, rights not given by any government but rights that belong to men at birth.. "A poor man is as equal before the law as any high born man. We will be a democratic republic."

14

Fairlawn Manor

Roger, John Eliot, Comfort, Ned, Henry and Frances sit around the breakfast table. This is the last breakfast they will have here before the ship leaves for Boston later this afternoon.

"Are you satisfied with your charter for Rhode Island" Eliot asks Roger.

"Yes. It guarantees religious tolerance. Henry, since he's on the Parliamentary committee, was of great help. He's as committed as strongly as I am to the idea that government must stay out of religious affairs and everyone should be allowed to worship according to his own conscience."

"But I've noticed you are very anxious, my friend. What's been worrying you?"

"Well I don't know what's going to happen with the Narragansetts. *Sachem* Canonicus may take revenge on us for the murder of his nephew *sachem* Miantonomo. Although it was *sachem* Uncas who killed Miantonomo, the murder was done after the Bay Colony demanded Miantonomo come to Boston. The murder happened with Winthrop's compliance. My wife Mary wrote that Canonicus is furious with all the English."

"Do you still have influence with him?" Eliot knows another Indian war would certainly hinder missionary efforts.

"Maybe. He's used my home hundreds of times for tribal meetings. But I can't be sure. I'll find out as soon as I get back to

Rhode Island."

"Didn't Miantonomo have a young son called Canonchet?" Comfort asks. "Could he be the one advocating revenge?"

"Of course. I'll meet with him. Speaking of sons, I've a new one. Mary has named him Joseph. He's our sixth, born soon after I arrived here."

"Congratulations, Roger," Frances says. "Since we are on this subject, I will tell you our good news. I'm pregnant with our first child."

"The Lord has blessed us" Henry says, taking her hand and kissing it.

Comfort smiles at Frances, but then notices Henry's face. It's as if it has been suddenly drained of all his boyish happiness over being a father and is now the face of a man who has swallowed bitter medicine.

"My dear friends, we're fighting for a just cause, but this war will last for many years. As you know, the first battle at Edgehill was inconclusive. Our forces are inexperienced. We have only a few trained officers. The King's trying to arrange a truce with the Irish rebels so their army will join his Cavaliers. We will have the Scottish Parliament's army since they also oppose the King's and his bishops' imposition of church rituals. Thousands of young men will die this year so our sons can enjoy religious freedom and be free of a tyrant's absolute rule."

"Although we leave here today, and there will be an ocean between our colonies and England, our prayers will be with you," Roger says. "Our destiny is entwined with yours."

Henry continues to discuss the war with Eliot and Roger. Ned asks to be excused. Shortly after he leaves, Comfort says she must finish packing her things and follows him.

When she opens the door to her room, Ned is waiting. "I want to kiss you everywhere," he says, unbuttoning her blouse. Her heart is beating wildly.

They fall on bed, satisfying their aching desire. They are about to be separated again for years.

"I'll worry," she says, as she gets dressed. "Please write often."

"I'm not going to be in danger" he says. "I'll help Henry in London. We will prevent the Royalists from taking over London. Of course I'll write, but by the time you get my letter many things will have already changed."

"I'll pray for you and for victory every night" she says, tearing. He goes to her and kisses her tears away.

"You know, darling, I don't believe in God anymore. Your love, that's all I need."

"I'll try to rescue Susanna," she says.

"Even if she's alive, she'll never be the same. She was only eight when those devils took her."

"I've heard captured girls are treated with kindness. My friend Metacom says young girls are adopted into a tribe."

"They're all barbarians. You're never going to convince me otherwise. They murdered my family. I'll never be able to trust any of them." His voice is harsh.

He takes her into his arms. "Please, don't go into hostile Indian villages looking for Susanna. I couldn't bear to lose you too."

"I wish we had married here," she says.

He takes a small book of Shakespeare's sonnets from his pocket. Inside the cover he has written "Remember the hunting cottage." He gives it to her as they walk out to the rose garden. They sit on a stone bench. He starts to read a sonnet he knows she likes:

Shall I compare thee to a summer's day?
Thou art more loveley and more temperate.

He drops the book and kisses her passionately.

"We'll have a good life in Newport. I can't come to see you off this afternoon. I've arranged a meeting with Oliver Cromwell and Lord Essex about treatment of the wounded soldiers."

15

ATLANTIC CROSSING

Comfort, leaning over the railing, watches the shore recede as the large square-rigger moves slowly out to sea. She is thinking about John Milton. He came to see her off. He brought her a book of Ben Jonson's plays and a book of his own poems. He said that music and poetry are food for the spirit especially in hard times. She said she would share these books with her poet friend Anne Bradstreet.

"When we defeat King Charles, kings throughout the world will know that just power must come from the consent of the people," he said. "We must educate the masses, allow a free exchange of ideas in debates and in print, and have leaders who are tolerant and don't oppress those with different ideas about religion, politics or scientific matters."

"Be well, John," Roger said. "Practice speaking Dutch, for you can help Parliament because you know so many tongues. Don't read all night long by candlelight. You've lost sight in one eye, my friend, and England needs to benefit from your passionate ideas and your poetry. I'll miss you."

Frances came to the wharf bringing Comfort a package of silver buttons, needles, pins, blue satin ribbons and white lace. "I was told such things are not easy to find in Boston." They hug. Comfort said she'll pray that her child is born healthy.

I've been so lucky, Comfort thinks, as she bends over the railing of the ship feeling nausea. I made new friends. In addition to Milton and Henry and Frances Vane, I'll miss Sally Wroth and John Lilburne. I wonder if I'll ever get a chance to return.

The ship has reached rougher waters. It's headed towards the endless dark waters of the ocean where it will travel for at least two months. The sky is gray, the wind howls, and her stomach feels bad. She goes below. She can't eat for days, though the others do not seem ill. She vomits into a bucket every morning, and must carry it upstairs and empty it into the ocean. She stays below the first two weeks.

Finally, she's well enough to go up to the deck to join John Eliot and Roger Williams. They have been arguing about how to open the hearts of the Indians to Christ. She doesn't interrupt, but sits and listens. They have different ideas.

"Don't try to change everything they believe. They must feel you respect them," Roger says. "It was a good idea to learn their language and try to invent a way to write it. I approve of your Indian College plan to educate preachers, but I've concerns about your plan to set up separate villages for your converts."

"I must provide safe and productive places for them and their families. They must give up their false gods, cut their hair short, change their lazy ways. They need to learn to farm, to be black-smiths, carpenters. I will teach them to read their language" Eliot says.

"Do you really think cutting their hair short matters? Why try to change everything about them. Is that necessary in order to bring their hearts to Jesus?"

"The outer man must change in order to change the inner man. Those who have accepted Christ must live apart so they can practice their faith. The new villages will be built around a church, just like in my hometown, Roxbury," Eliot says.

"Their *sachems* won't want their people to leave. Preach to those really willing to change. Don't try to force conversion. We don't need more hypocrites," Roger says.

"The heathen must give up their wild and scattered manner of life as well as their *manitoo*. Only by converting them to Christianity can we keep peaceful relations in New England," Eliot says.

Comfort listens for a while longer, and then walks around the deck. She remembers that Metacom was angry when he learned that Reverend Thomas Mayhew and his son had successfully converted many of his people living on Cape Cod. Will he be angry when he learns I'm working with Reverend Eliot? What will I tell him and Little Bird? I don't want to lose their friendship. She goes below again, thinking that she's still very far from Boston and may be vomiting during the entire journey home.

Part Three

1643 - 1656

CAMBRIDGE

Four months have passed. It's the morning of Dorothy Dudley's funeral. Comfort is in bed at Anne Bradstreet's house listening to the church bells announce her mother's funeral. Anne asked her to come here from Roxbury to help her keep the children quiet during the funeral and reception.

Morning sunlight creates shifting shadows on the wall, the long sleeved black dress, the table near the bed where the gold mourning ring and a pair of black gloves have been placed. The ring's decorated with a skull, and next to it is the elegy book of psalms, and includes a poem Anne wrote about her mother The pages have pictures of skeletons and hour-glasses in the margins.

Will the dress hide her pregnancy? Will she be cast out of Boston as a sinner?

No one must realize she's pregnant. Comfort stands and examines her body in the mirror. She slides the black dress over her head. It'll hide what must be hidden.

She walks to the meetinghouse with Anne, holding the youngest child. Many people stop them to tell her that they admired her mother; saw her as a visible saint.

Two tall candles are on the bier platform next to the coffin. A pile of elegy books are on a table ready to be distributed to the mourners.

In the front pew the bearers, dressed in black suits and wearing funeral gloves, are sitting. The under-bearers will carry the coffin, and the pall-bearers will hold the corners of the bier-cloth, a black velvet cloth spread over the coffin that will be lifted and held over the heads of the under-bearers as they carry the coffin through town to the gravesite.

As is custom, there isn't a sermon. Silence is the preferred way of mourning. There'll be no prayers at the gravesite either. The elegies will be read aloud at home after the burial.

The funeral procession begins. The bearers lift the coffin, the pall-bearers hold the cloth, and the mourners walk through town. On the way, more people join the procession, while others stand in the street or watch from windows. The procession passes silently through muddy Cambridge streets to the gravesite.

Afterward, when the magistrates are in the Dudley household drinking beer and eating, Reverend Wilson says to Thomas "your wife was a paragon of womanhood."

"There was not a bit of heresy in her beliefs, nor did she tolerate it in others," adds John Winthrop.

"She was an obedient wife who knew her duty," Thomas Dudley says. "Please, Reverend Wilson, read aloud from Proverbs 31 in the elegy book."

"Who can find a virtuous woman? For her price is far above rubies. The heart of her husband does safely trust in her… She stretches out her hand to the poor…Strength and honor is her clothing… She looks well to the ways of her household, and eats not the bread of idleness. Her children call her blessed; her husband also, and he praises her…Favor is deceitful, and beauty is vain, but a woman that fears the Lord, she shall be praised."

When all guests leave, Anne asks Comfort to talk with her while she nurses her baby daughter. The child falls asleep and Comfort puts her into the cradle.

Exhausted, she lies next to Anne on the bed. Where will her baby sleep?

If only Ned had married her. He doesn't know about the baby. No one must know the truth.

"Why won't you let me find you a husband?" Anne asks. "There are four men to every woman here. I saw Thomas Hawkins today. His wife died giving birth to a son. Shall I invite him to dinner?"

"Please no. I told you I'll marry Ned when he comes back from London."

"Do you really want to live in Rhode Island? I'd have to ask my father to give you a permit and I'm not allowed to go there. Father says the place stinks of heresy."

"Why would I need a permit?"

"We require permits from anyone from Rhode Island. Father doesn't want our people to be infected by heretical ideas. I don't agree, but can't say so."

"Oh Anne, have the courage to tell him you disagree. In London I met women who dared speak out and even to present petitions to Parliament saying they're opposed to debtors' prison. I remember once ----"

"Go home to Roxbury. I've no strength left for a debate." Anne turns away.

"I'm sorry. It's been a difficult day. Forgive me." She gets ready to leave.

2

ROXBURY

COMFORT'S DIARY

Last night I had a nightmare. I'm standing in front of the magistrates. Light coming from a high window illuminates John Winthrop's angry red face. He's pointing at me.

"Your child is a monster! Because of your lustful behavior you'll burn in Hell."

He describes what my baby looks like to everyone in the meeting-house. "Your child's ears stand upon its shoulders and over his eyes are four horns, hard and sharp, and its nose is hooked upward. All over its breast and back are sharp scales. The navel and belly are where the back should be, and the back and hips are where the belly should have been. It has arms and legs, but instead of toes it has claws with sharp talons. Your sin has created this monster. It's the Devil's own creature."

Then he reads the verdict: "Comfort Bradford is guilty of the sin of lust. The father is a son of the banished heretic who was excommunicated. This deformed child is proof Comfort Bradford is a witch. We hereby sentence her to hang until dead."

The crowd screams: "Hang the witch! Hang the witch!"

I woke up; my nightdress was soaked with sweat. Could there be a monster inside me? I got on my knees and prayed.

In the morning the Lord answered my prayers. Reverend Eliot asked me to go to Mount Hope. He realizes that he needs more words for his Algonquian dictionary if he is ever going to be capable of preaching in their tongue and creating a written language for his Algonquian Bible.

Eliot told her he's converted Little Bird's cousin who plans to leave Cape Cod and go to Mount Hope to help Little Bird deliver and care for her second child. This girl, now called Rebecca, will live with Little Bird in a separate wetu until the baby is born. The Wampanoag custom requires this because the spirit of a pregnant woman is thought to be dangerous to a man; it takes away his power to be a successful hunter.

Eliot wants to convert Little Bird because she'll be Queen when Philip becomes King someday. Rebecca will try to convert her. She can help me discover which Algonquian words are most appropriate for prayer. Eliot told me to become friends with Rebecca and to stay in Mount Hope all through the spring and summer months."

I'll tell Little Bird and Rebecca I'm pregnant and ask them to keep my secret. Little Bird's mother is an experienced midwife and I trust her to help me when my time comes. I'll say a prayer of thanks to God every night and teach Little Bird to say this prayer as well. I can't wait to go.

3

MOUNT HOPE

Comfort is dressed as a Wampanoag woman in a mantle *(squaus auhaquet)* stockings (*nquittetiangattash*) and shoes *(mockussin-chass)*. Her hair is braided. When it's hot, she and Little Bird take off their clothes and Rebecca brings them cool water from the spring to bathe. She looks at her friend and is sure she'll give birth first. They splash each other with the cool water and laugh.

Rebecca brings vegetables and fruit. "You must eat good food every day," she says. She gathers nuts and berries, and cooks savory vegetable stews. During pregnancy a Wampanoag woman doesn't eat meat.

In the evenings, around a fire, Rebecca and Comfort tell Bible stories. Rebecca is a good storyteller. Comfort writes down the Algonquian words she uses.

"*Wuckaudnummenes manit peetaugon wuche Adam*," Rebecca says. This means God took a rib from Adam and out of that rib he made a woman.

The three women take walks in the woods to a special pond where they swim naked. Comfort remembers how much she wanted to do this as a girl, but had to sit on a log watching while Philip, Wamsutta and Little Bird had fun splashing each other.

Little Bird's mother comes to talk and brings her work. She softens doeskins by pounding and pulling them over a post. She shows Comfort how to use a needle of bone and threads of sinew to make tiny deerskin tunics for the babies to wear in winter. Little Bird shows her how to paint small birds on the tunics.

Philip is making two cradleboards. A child must stay with its mother so it's strapped in a cradleboard which is either in front, when it's nursing, or attached to her back, facing forward with its head above her shoulder, watching her as she works in the fields. The child won't grow up to be lazy if he watches her work. If it's a boy, a tiny bow is attached to the cradleboard. Philip has made two bows hoping for two boys. The board uses moss as padding to make it softer. Each baby will be swaddled, wrapped in soft doeskin, and then strapped into the cradleboard. He is proud of his good work.

One day he shows Comfort how to tie the cradleboard around her. He touches her arms gently and looks into her eyes with affection. Does he think she has decided to be his second wife? A man can take a second wife when he's the Chief *sachem* of the tribe.

Little Bird has given birth to a son. Comfort can't believe how brave her friend was during the birth. She gave birth sitting up and the child fell on a blanket which was put over a pile of leaves beneath her. There was no crying, no begging for the pain to stop. Rebecca washed him in cold spring water to make him resilient. Little Bird has plenty of milk.

"This is our way," Rebecca says. "We must show courage, just as our men show courage in hunting bears and in battle. This is the cycle of life."

Little Bird teaches her new words. A sucking child is a *noonsu nonannis*, breasts are *wunnunoganash,* and breast milk is called *munnunnug.* Her milk flows when the baby cries, and continues even after he has fallen asleep on her breast. Philip and Little Bird call their son Little Thunder.

At last it's Comfort's time. At first she finds it hard keeping quiet when sharp pains cut her like a knife. But as soon as Little Bird's mother sings to her and holds her hand, she is able to be calm. Finally the baby is born. Her sweet son isn't deformed like in her nightmare. He has lots of black hair and brown eyes so Little Bird says he looks like a Wampanoag baby and Philip gives him the Algonquian name which means Little Raven. She'll call him Tommy, and hopes Ned will like that name. If only Ned was here.

When Tommy tries to nurse, he cries and Comfort's nipples hurt. Little Bird's mother gives her a soothing plaster, but nothing helps so Little Bird nurses Little Raven also. He sleeps peacefully on her breast.

It's a painful decision, but Comfort will leave Tommy here with her friend. She'll visit often until she can figure out a way to bring him to Roxbury. Little Bird says she'll love this English boy as much as she loves her own child. "They'll be friends forever," she says, "just like us."

When Comfort returns to Reverend Eliot's cottage, his wife Hannah thinks she has a worm in her stomach because she cries so often. John Eliot is pleased that she brought back so many Algonquian words, he says. "Soon I will give a sermon in Algonquian."

She helps him pronounce the words: *Netompauog* means "Friends", *Manit anawat, cuppittakunnamun wepe wame* means "God commands all men repent now", *Paucuck naunt manit* means "There is only one God", and the longest string of words, *Quttatashuchuckqunnacawskeesitinnes* means "Out of nothing in six days He made all things."

Over the next two years, whenever she can, Comfort visits Tommy. She stays for a week with Rebecca, who has remained in Mount Hope in a *wetu* of her own.

Tommy is always happy to see her. He puts his little hands in hers and looks longingly at her, asking for a gift. She brings him little wooden toys Anne's children no longer play with, boats and animals Simon carves out of wood.

She's sad that Tommy doesn't call her *nitchwhaw*, mother. He calls her "English lady". While he speaks Algonquian fluently he only says a few sentences in English. He loves Little Thunder and Laughing Like Water, calls them *weticks*, sister and *weemat*, brother. Comfort's glad Tommy is loved by this family, but she longs for the day Ned will see his charming son. She doesn't want to tell him about the child in a letter for she knows he wouldn't want his son living with Indians.

* * * *

NED'S LETTER

The war continues with no end in sight. Oliver Cromwell is now called Lieutenant General of the Horse. He wants to continue the war until the King is captured or killed. Unlike Henry Vane, he doesn't want the King to compromise. The army has been re-organized. It's now called "The New Model Army." It is a standing army rather than what it was before, a confederation of part-time militias. The King's nephew, Prince Rupert, leads the Cavaliers. Did I tell you that he rides on his horse with his pet poodle by his side?

Oliver appoints officers according to their ability, not according to their social status as gentry or their religious views. The army shouldn't be caught up in the ongoing religious and political dis-agreements in Parliament, yet, in these times of great uncertainty about the future, soldiers argue amongst themselves. To win this war will be difficult, but to design a fair and acceptable government without a King will be another tremendous task.

I strongly hope this year, 1645, will be the year the King'll be defeated. Henry Vane still holds out hope His Majesty will compromise and we will have a constitutional monarchy, but this is very unlikely.

I send you warm regards from Frances who has just given Henry another son. John Milton's eyesight is worse so he no longer writes letters. He dictates letters, essays and poems to a daughter. He's angry that all the theatres in London are still closed by our Puritan Parliament for religious reasons. His writer and actor friends are starving and fleeing the country. He asked if you ever think of him.

Love,
Ned.

COMFORT'S LETTER

My life here continues just as I wrote in my last letter. Reverend Eliot gave a sermon in Algonquian. The Indian converts laughed at his mistakes, but they respect him for trying so hard. I help by teaching the Indians to read the Bible in their own language. Our work on translating the Bible into Algonquian continues. I visit my friends at Mount Hope often to collect more vocabulary.

Good News: Roger Williams says the Narragansetts are not going to go to war any time soon. His biggest concern is that folks from Connecticut are taking land that belongs to the western part of Rhode Island.

She doesn't tell Ned that his sister Susanna may have been found by Captain Underhill.

4

BOSTON

The black robed magistrates sit at a long table in the meeting-house facing the large crowd. Comfort and John Eliot watch from the back of the room.

Captain John Underhill has come to ask for money to pay for his men and for ransom money. He wants to rescue English children captured by Indians in the Dutch area they call Lange Eylant which is not far from New Amsterdam. The Indians call the place Paumanok which means Island Pays because it's where they gather shells to make wampum.

Standing next to John is a blond ten year old boy dressed in a breechcloth and shirt. He doesn't look at the crowd or the magistrates, and sits on the floor twisting his braided hair nervously.

"Look, the devils have made him one of them," a man shouts, pointing at the boy.

"Quiet! I want quiet!" Winthrop says. "Many of you know Captain Underhill as the former leader of our trainband. He has been hired by the Dutch to subdue the savages. He's a mercenary, like his father. While he no longer lives here, we've agreed to listen to his request out of respect for his past service to our colony."

Thomas Dudley addresses the crowd. "The Captain is offering to bring back captured English children like this poor boy. This lad's family was brutally murdered and only he and his father survived the attack. By God's mercy, and with Captain

Underhill's help, the lad has been brought back to civilization. You may address us, John."

John takes his hat off and puts it on a chair next to his flint-lock. The boy keeps his head down while John addresses the crowded room.

"I know how to fight in the wilderness, learned their tricks. I've turned over many Indian heads and hands to Dutch Governor Kieft and been paid well for them. My men—I've thirty now—are experienced and brave. I come here today to ask you to hire me and my men to go back to Dutch territory to rescue captured Christian children."

He reaches down to touch the boy's head, but the lad moves further away from him. Now he sits on his haunches, Indian style, staring at the young girls in the room. A woman whispers "I think he's forgotten how to speak English."

"To rescue this lad cost ten English pounds in wampum. The Dutch provided it for him but they told me they won't pay for the rescue of any more English captives. The savages didn't want him, so it was easy to take him."

Reverend Cotton speaks next. "Let us all take a moment to pray for this poor lad's soul. "Lord may he receive your sanctifying Grace. We are grateful that he's been mercifully returned to us."

After the prayer, Underhill continues. "I hope you fine folks will agree to save others."

"How many are there? What'll it cost?" Winthrop asks. His face is somber.

"Don't know exactly, sir. Dutch traders have seen several. They saw a young girl with red hair, most likely the daughter of Anne Hutchinson. I believe she's being held in the same village where I found this boy," he says, pointing to the boy who's still looking down "but they were hiding her. The savages like to keep our girls and give them to their boys. Give me fifty pounds and I'll save her from lustful bondage."

"Not the heretic's daughter. Not her! I won't pay to ransom her!" shouts an old man sitting in the first row. "You supported that woman, didn't you? Did you sleep with her? Is the girl your daughter?"

"Don't accuse me of that. I respected her. Maybe you, old man, lusted after her." He's angry. He stamps his foot, lifts his hand and leans towards the man as if to strike him.

"Quiet! Quiet!" Winthrop bangs on the table. "Let's have order. We magistrates will decide this matter."

Thomas Dudley has made up his mind. "I will vote against your request Captain, for economic reasons. The civil war in England continues to hurt our trade. While the King's men were defeated at Marston Moor in Yorkshire, and again at Naseby in Northhamptonshire, this civil war is far from over. I oppose any new expenses at this time."

"Mr. Dudley speaks the truth," a woman says, standing to face the crowd. "My dear sons have joined Cromwell's New Model Army. It's short on gunpowder and there's conflict between a radical group of soldiers called Levellers and their officers who they call Grandees. Fighting within Cromwell's army will help the King win; who knows what the King will do if he wins! There's a rumor he'll appoint a royal governor and force us to pay a lot more taxes. I wouldn't spend a shilling on that heretic's child at this time."

Comfort touches Eliot's arm. "Please," she whispers, "speak in favor of Underhill's proposal. I must save Susanna. It's not right to blame a child for her mother's beliefs. The Bible says that, doesn't it?"

Eliot tells her to be quiet. "Everyone should have a chance to give their opinion," he says.

An old man stands. "Damned if I'll let my younger brother die for want of gun powder. He's in Cromwell's "Ironsides" brigade, that's the regiment of his bravest fighters who dare to dash before swords and cannon. I say let's give our money to this brigade so we can win this war." Others shout agreement.

A merchant speaks. "Our vessels no longer trade with England so we have no profit. Shipping's our lifeblood in this colony. We've begun building some of our ships here, and need more. If I hadn't provisioned a ship going to the Caribbean with cod and timber I'd be bankrupt. I say we shouldn't give money to Underhill, but rather spend money on building more ships for the Caribbean trade."

Finally Eliot stands and addresses that merchant. "Profit is important, dear neighbor, but when young Christian souls are suffering at the hands of heathen, surely the Lord wants us to save them. Let's hear this boy's story before we abandon poor Christian children."

Simon Bradstreet gets down from the platform and bends to talk privately to the boy. Having young sons, he's able to talk to the boy and convince him to tell his story.

"They killed my ma and sis, and took with them me, my da, and that red-haired girl. They dragged us through the forest. My feet were frozen and bloody. One savage gave her moccasins, but no one gave me anything for my poor feet. We ate acorns, green hurtle berries, and roasted snake. I vomited everything. We slept on the cold, hard ground. That girl, she cried a lot, but I told her to be brave." He pauses.

Simon urges him to continue. "We need to know the truth, lad."

"When we got to their village, a woman pushed us into an icy river and rubbed us hard with her hands as if to wash away not only dirt but who we are. The girl was dressed in a doeskin tunic and they braided her hair. They cut mine - one side long, one short - so I could shoot arrows quickly by holding the bow against my head. I liked to shoot arrows, was good at it, but I wanted to get away. I ran but they caught me and tied me to a tree for two days and starved me, so I gave up trying. I had to wear this here stupid thing." He turns his back to the crowd, lifts the breechcloth exposing his naked backside. The young girls and boys laugh and point. Simon warns the lad to behave properly.

"They made me watch when they painted my da red all over with smelly stuff, and then made him run between two rows of men who beat him with branches."

"They're devils for sure" shouts a woman holding a baby.

"They hit me with a stick if I spoke English to my da. The girl learned their strange tongue quickly, but da and I had a hard time with it."

"What did they force you to do?" Simon asks.

"I had to clear brush so deer could be hunted easily. The girl fetched water and gathered firewood. The Indian boys taunted us and their wolf-dogs chased us. Mosquitoes bit us all over. I was flogged often with a branch but she wasn't." He lifts his shirt and shows scars on his back. "One day, by the river, my father said he'd swim away and bring back help."

"At first light he swam off, but one of them shot him. I heard the shots and knew. You shouldn't be selling them guns!" he says to Simon, shaking his fist at the magistrates. He wipes away tears with his arm.

"Enough." Simon says, but the boy shakes his head. He wants to continue.

"After da died they were kinder to me. They taught me to make arrows and set traps for beavers. I got good. They let me join their games with hoops, and wrestling. I'm strong, see" he says, showing off the muscles in his arm.

"The red-haired girl, Red Bird they called her, was treated special. She was adopted by her master. The woman was head of the turtle clan. She was crazy, that one, and wore lots of necklaces and stank from bear grease, but she liked the girl."

He sits down again on the floor and looks down. "Now that this man has saved me where will I live? I've no family."

There is silence. The boy's story has gained him some sympathy, but his manner is crude and no one wants him.

Reverend Eliot stands. "I'll take you boy; with the Lord's help, you'll heal. I've set up a Praying Indian village called Natick. You can help me. If the magistrates will give Captain Underhill ransom money to bring the red haired girl back, I'll be her legal guardian and yours."

"Maybe she won't want to come back" says the boy. "Maybe the crazy woman won't give her up."

Winthrop talks to the other magistrates. They have decided. The colony won't give Underhill any money to ransom Susanna. He can be the guardian for the boy if he wants to keep him.

Eliot knows he can't convince the magistrates to change their minds. He returns to Roxbury with Comfort and the boy.

Comfort can't bear the thought that if the girl really is Susanna she will remain a captive for the rest of her life. She begs Eliot to help ransom the child.

Eliot knows it would break his heart if his daughter were captured. The Bible says one shouldn't punish a child for a parent's sins.

"I'll give you some of the money you helped me raise in London. Dudley took a lot of it to establish Harvard College, so I can spend some to rescue this child. It probably is Susanna. I'll give you ten pounds worth of wampum. Give it to your Wampanoag friend Philip and ask him if he'll help you."

5

Siwanoy Indian Village

It's been four years since her capture. Susanna is thirteen, has a new name and a new family. She braids her hair, then ties it with a strip of doeskin. She puts on two white shell bead necklaces, adjusting them around her neck. Her fingers dip into a broken shell with bear grease, and she applies it to her arms and legs to protect them against mosquitoes. Because her skin is white, boys say she's ugly, yet she saw them peeking from behind the bushes to stare at her white nakedness as she swam in the river.

She has a secret place under the sleeping bench where she keeps a scrap of blue linen spotted with blood and a cloth doll with red wool hair. When she has a nightmare, she sees blood falling like rain around her and clutches these possessions to her chest.

Her mother, also the mother of the **sachem,** often sings about the seven sparks from The Creator from which seven kinds of people came to this land at Dawn Time. In that song these sparks created fifty fires, each a different band, some called Tappans, others Lenape or Wiechquaesqecks or Siwanoy and others whose names she forgets.

Susanna gossips in Algonquian with her girlfriends at the spring as they wash themselves and clothes. Once she met strangers whose language is a little different, but her mother says they're all are part of the same hoop, the same circle. She's proud to have been adopted into the turtle clan. They call her Red Bird and she remembers no other name.

Today visitors from another village are coming to buy beaver pelts to trade with the Dutch since a peace treaty has been signed. There will be a feast and dancing. Her mother places on the sleeping bench her best tunic, the one with the pretty red birds on it made out of quill.

"You're lovely, my child," her mother says. "I shouldn't call you child, for you are a woman now."

Last month, mother took her to the *wetu* where women live apart on days when the sacred blood comes. The women fussed over her, fed her sweet strawberries, and told her funny stories about their husbands. She looks forward to staying there again next month.

Everyone welcomes their kin and friends who are visiting today from another village. The men go fishing; soon there's plenty of fish for a feast. The fish are strung up on horizontal poles off the ground and a fire is lit under them to smoke them. Red Bird loves smoked fish and waits patiently to get her share. While she waits, a young man from another village named Runs So Fast tells her about his home.

"Our village is on the shore of a river where I can catch many fish with my hands, and we always can dig for clams. Sometimes the sky darkens with thousands of birds arriving to eat the green eggs of horseshoe crabs. You'll love swimming in my river's cool water."

"I'd like to see birds darkening the sky," Red Bird tells him. She knows he likes her. She thinks he's handsome.

After the feast, there's dancing. She loves to move her legs to the rhythm of drums. Sweating, Runs So Fast leaps near her, touches her hair, and then then pulls his hand back quickly. "Oh, you put me on fire." He laughs, jumps away again, then comes back. He caresses her arm. "I like you Red Bird." They feast and dance until dawn.

When he leaves for his village, he gives her a copper bracelet. "Don't forget me."

"I won't. Next time you come, I'll have a gift for you." She wonders what she can give him. Perhaps she'll kiss him.

* * * *

It's a warm night. Bark mats from the top of their *wetu* have been removed to let in breezes and the moonlight. She lies next to her mother thinking what it would be like to kiss that boy.

"Do you like Runs So Fast?" her mother asks.

"Yes."

"He went on a vision quest and fasted alone in the woods. His guardian spirit, a large grey wolf, watched over him. He's the son of the *sachem* of the wolf clan. They live on the Delaware River. He'll be your *sannup*, daughter."

"I don't want to leave you, mother. I don't know people in that village."

"I'll plan a wedding feast as soon as the pumpkins ripen. Someday Runs so Fast will be *sachem*. Be glad he wants you for his wife."

Her mother sings and Red Bird falls asleep. In a dream she's riding on a brown horse with Runs So Fast. Her arms are holding him, and she smells sweat mingled with bear grease. She sees mother standing outside the *wetu* getting smaller and smaller as she rides to her new home on the river where thousands of birds arrive each year making the sky dark.

6

Mount Hope

Why is Philip taking so long to decide? Does he think she'll give him her son in exchange for his help to save Ned's sister? That's not going to happen. She's grateful he and Little Bird have been substitute parents, but she wants to take Tommy home to Roxbury soon. It's too painful leaving him here. She should be the one singing him to sleep, bathing him in the river, teaching him new words, words in English.

Tommy is almost three years old now and Little Bird still gives him her breast whenever he demands it. She indulges him and he's become a willful child. If he's to grow up to be a God fearing, obedient, English boy, she must teach him how to behave properly.

Little Bird notices Comfort's frowning face. "As long as I have milk, he can have it. Little Thunder has no more interest in *wunnunnoganash*, breasts, but this one is **noonsu nonannis**, a sucking child. Laughing Like Water nursed for five years, and Little Raven can also nurse for five years if he doesn't bite my breast."

Later Comfort watches Tommy and Little Thunder play with a red spinning wooden top she has brought for them. They're truly behaving like brothers, one minute laughing, the next pushing, taking away the red top.

Philip arrives with two horses, one black and one the color of golden honey. He asks her to ride with him and she mounts the golden horse. They gallop across a meadow and walk the horses slowly through the woods until they reach another meadow, this one filled with blue wildflowers. They get off and let the horses nibble at the grass while they stretch out and enjoy the sun. She listens to bees buzzing the purple clover. She's waiting for him to talk.

"So, Sky-Eyes, you want me to ransom a girl from the Siwanoy nation. My father says I should help you because of his respect for your father. I don't think it's a good idea."

"Why?" She is very disappointed.

"We might not find her. The Siwanoy move to the ocean in summer to fish, swim and collect shells for wampum. I've been there. I spent a summer with them a long time ago."

She tries to make him consider their long friendship. "Remember when we were children and one summer you tried to teach me how to drill holes in shells without breaking them?"

Philip laughs at the memory. "You broke them all. Sky-Eyes, I want you to realize that the Siwanoy could be anywhere along the beach. It's a very long shore."

"I was told Susanna lives with the mother of the *sachem* of the turtle clan. Have you met that *sachem*?"

"*Sachem* Wampage. Yes. He once told me all the beaver will be gone soon because of English greed. We're greedy too. We desire English and Dutch things so we compete to kill our cousins the beaver. If we can't pay our debts for beer and blankets, English and Dutch traders demand land as payment, land that only the Chief *sachem* has the right to give to these greedy strangers. It makes me angry."

"I'm not a fur trader, Philip. I'm your dear friend, and I'm begging you to ask the *sachem* to let my Susanna come home."

"What if the *sachem* doesn't want to let her leave? I don't want the Siwanoy to be my enemy, Sky-Eyes."

"You can offer him all the wampum I've brought."

Philip laughs. "I told you already, they collect the shells used for wampum. They don't need any of yours." He's silent for a long time. She's sure he isn't going to help. Her eyes fill with tears.

He surprises her with his answer. "I'll go but only if you come with me. You must say she's your lost younger sister. We respect requests to bring kin home. Are you brave enough to come?"

"Of course I'll come. But why would he care about an English woman's kin?"

"I'll tell him you're my wife, captured as a child. You grew up with me at Mount Hope; that's true, right? So this Red Bird, well, she's my kin too. He'll accept that, I think."

"But does *sachem* Wampage know Little Bird is your wife?"

"It doesn't matter. As a son of the Chief *sachem*, I can have two wives. I've chosen only to have one, but he won't know that. You know our language and ways."

"What will I have to do?" Comfort nervously twists the blue ribbon in her hair.

"You'll cry, say you miss your sister. You speak in our tongue, call me Metacom, never Philip, and he'll believe us. Do you think I want to sleep with you? Ha! I wouldn't mind at all, my dear, beautiful Sky-Eyes, but I wouldn't hurt you and I'll never want to bring pain to Little Bird."

"I can pretend to be your wife, Philip...I mean Metacom."

"I'll bring gifts - an excellent bow and strong arrows I've made myself, and copper bracelets for his mother."

"I'm so grateful you'll do this for me." She wants to hug him, but instead gently brushes his hand.

"Never call me Philip again, Sky-Eyes. In fact I'm tired of that English childish name. Treat me with great respect; I'm a future Chief *sachem*, not your childhood friend. Speak to me only in Algonquian. Feed me first. Follow our customs. It will be dangerous if the *sachem* thinks we are playing a trick on him."

"When can we go?"

"Tomorrow at dawn. Little Bird will give you her clothes and prepare food for our journey. Two friends of mine will come along. You know them. They're good hunters so we'll have meat on the journey. You're not frightened of bears, are you?"

"Why should I be afraid, dear *sannup* when I'm with such a brave man? You've killed the largest bear in the world, haven't you?"

"You used to call me Trickster Wolf? Are you no longer afraid of my tricks?"

"We'll need all your tricks, Metacom."

The next morning Little Bird rubs Comfort's body with bear grease to keep away mosquitoes. She has mixed red pigment into it to give her skin a copper color. She darkens her hair with a black soot mixture, and braids it into one long braid. She gives her a doeskin tunic to wear and leggings to protect her legs from scratches.

She gives the men dried cornmeal for their pouches to mix with spring water for a quick meal as well as dried meat and corn cakes. Comfort carries a small pouch around her neck filled with nuts.

When she is dressed and ready to go, Comfort bends down to talk to Tommy. He hugs her. "English lady smells like mommy," he says in Algonquian.

They ride all day, then rest. Metacom kills a rabbit and shows her how to skin and cook it. The men eat first, and then she eats alone next to a birch tree. Metacom asks her to gather leaves for their beds. He speaks to her in Algonquian and she replies with respect. He and his friends share a pipe of tobacco by the fire while she watches them from a distance and fetches twigs for the fire.

She tries to sleep under the birch tree on a pile of leaves covered by a blanket, but is too anxious. What if it's not

Susanna? What if it is her, but she doesn't want to come with me? What if the *sachem* discovers the truth and becomes angry and kills us?

7

SIWANOY INDIAN VILLAGE

Late the next afternoon they reach a long, sandy beach. They camp in a grove of trees nearby and the men leave to search for the tribe's camp. While they're gone, Comfort tucks her skirt up into the waistband and walks in the water along the shore collecting shells. What a fine necklace Little Bird can make out of this *quahog*, she thinks, as she gathers more clam shells that have purple parts to bring back to her friend.

Metacom returns with good news. The Siwanoy camp is close by. The *sachem* is happy to see him again.

Comfort washes her face in the cool water, and re-applies the red pigmented bear grease. She puts on two copper bracelets which she will take off and give to the *sachem*'s mother.

Metacom wraps some tobacco in piece of deerskin, takes the bow and sheaf of arrows he has made as a gift, and the small wampum belt his father gave him to give the *sachem* as a promise of friendship between their two nations.

They ride into the village. Many men, *aumauog*, have gone fishing. Women and children stare when they see them enter the village.

"We come in friendship. We are also of the First People" Metacom says to the *sachem* who they find sitting in a clearing where fish are drying in the sun. They both clap their right hand on their hearts. The *sachem* orders a boy to bring mats for the visitors to sit on.

"*Neestadooltee-ek,* we understand each other, *sachem* Wampage replies.

"*Nowecontam,* I'm glad your war with the **Swannekins** is over," Metacom says.

"We can never trust them. They pay well so we trade. We no longer live *loo-weh-woo-dee,* in anger and fear. These **Swannekins** call us *wilden,* but it's they who don't respect **manitoo**."

Metacom introduces Comfort. "This is Sky-Eyes, my *weewo,* wife. *Neesekea,* I have two. **Swannekins** have killed many of her kin. She has lived with my people since she was a child. **Eenan-towash,** she speaks our tongue. She asks for your help. Please listen with an open heart."

She speaks in Algonquian, repeating the words Metacom has told her to say. "I know the turtle clan has suffered many losses just as I have by the **Swannekins**. The one you call Red Bird is my dearest younger *weticks,* sister. I'm happy she's alive. Thank you for your kindness to her."

Wampage looks confused, then alarmed.

"**Sachem,** please let me see my only surviving kin, this girl with hair, *wolquasamough,* like the setting sun. Is she here now?"

This causes sounds of dismay among several older women present. One of them goes to whisper something to the *sachem.* Comfort is afraid that he'll deny Susanna is living there because his mother is so fond of the girl. The *sachem* stares at her and takes his time responding.

"Red Bird has lived with us for four *quaqusquan,* summers. My mother has adopted her as a daughter. She's happy here," the *sachem* says. Then he asks a boy to tell his mother to come here to meet Red Bird's sister. Metacom smiles because the *sachem* seems to have accepted Comfort as the girl's sister and as his wife. He believes this may end well.

The sachem tries to convince Comfort to leave Red Bird here. "You who have eyes, *moos-seh-geeq-chamough*, as blue as the summer sky, you know your people can be happy among us. Your sister has learned our language, and will marry one of our people, as you have done. Red Bird has been chosen by Runs So Fast, son of the *sachem* of the wolf clan. Their children will give grandchildren to my mother. It's a good marriage."

"Please may I see her? May I visit with her alone for only one night? I want her to know I miss her and I'm happy she's alive." She feels her heart beating faster, excited to see Susanna. Has she come too late?

A few minutes later, a plump, older woman comes and sits beside the *sachem*. This must be his mother. She wears a white doeskin tunic and many long strings of shell beads around her neck. Her long hair is piled on the top of her head in a strange manner of many braids. It shines with bear grease. She whispers to her son and frowns. It is clear she isn't happy they've come here asking to talk to Red Bird.

Comfort takes off both copper bracelets and holds them out to the old woman. "Please, take my gift. I most humbly ask to see Red Bird. She's my only living kin."

The woman examines the bracelets then puts them on her arm. "The girl you speak of is my kin now. I'd sooner part with my heart than lose this girl."

The *sachem* says something to his mother. They argue, and she leaves.

"The girl has taken a canoe and gone with Runs So Fast to his village, home of the *Muncee,* the wolf clan. She should return soon. I'll look into her eyes and learn if she wishes to see you. Then I'll decide. If she'll speak with you, I'll send a messenger to your camp on the shore."

There is nothing more they can do at this moment except go

back to the beach and wait for Red Bird to return. Two days pass. Comfort is losing hope. She fills the time remembering how she took care of Ned's sister. Susanna was only five when her family was banished and eight when they were killed. Would Susanna recognize her dressed as an Indian woman? Would she say they aren't really sisters? Will she want to leave rather than stay and get married? Comfort knows Metacom will not take her away by force. He will not make an enemy of this nation.

On the third morning, she sees two young people approach the shore in a canoe. She stays in the trees and watches them.

Susanna looks healthy and strong. Her red hair is long and braided. She wears a sleeveless tunic and short doeskin skirt. She has tan, muscular legs, and climbs out of the canoe to help Runs So Fast pull it onto the sand. Runs So Fast is a tall young man with long black hair. He wears only a breechcloth, so she sees his smooth chest, his muscular arms and legs. Will want to leave this handsome, well-built young man?

That evening a messenger tells them Red Bird does want to see her sister. Does she think one of her real sisters has survived the massacre and come here? Unsure of anything, they return to the village.

When Susanna sees Comfort, she touches her face and her hair. Then tears begin to run down her cheeks. She doesn't talk, but seems to know her. She doesn't say her name.

Comfort dares to speak to the *sachem*. "Please, be kind; let me see her alone for one night. It is right to let sisters mourn together for their dead kin now in the southwest where the dead live. Let us remember those kin who no longer walk on earth, but who loved us."

Sachem Wampage speaks. "There's a small *wetu* near the shore which my boys use when fishing. My men will take you there. Wait there. Red Bird will come when the sun falls into the water.

My men will stand outside while you talk and sleep. At first light, they'll bring Red Bird back home to my mother's *wetu*."

Metacom assures the *sachem* that he is grateful for this kindness. He and friends will sleep in his village as hostages until Red Bird's safe return.

Comfort is escorted to the fishing *wetu* and waits anxiously. She has a Bible, and prays. She hopes she can find the right words to convince Susanna to come with her.

The hide flaps open and Susanna arrives carrying a small basket which she places on the sleeping bench. She takes out corn cakes; they eat in silence. When Comfort tries to touch her, she pulls away, frightened.

"I'm not a ghost Susanna. I'm really Comfort. I took care of you when you were little and lived in Boston." She says this both in Algonquian and in English, for she doesn't know if Susanna still understands English."

For a long time they stare at each other. Finally, very slowly, Comfort reaches for Susanna's hand and puts it on her own face. "See, I'm flesh and blood. I love you Susanna. My heart is filled with joy at knowing you're alive. Are you happy to see me?"

Now Susanna moves her hand across this familiar face then touches her hair. Comfort has washed the soot out so it's blond again. "You do remember me, don't you?"

Susanna nods yes, tears in her eyes. "I know you."

"Remember how we used to play, you, me and your brother Ned. We picked blueberries on Beacon Hill. Ned is alive. He's in London and wants me to bring you back to Boston. Ned and I are going to marry when he comes home. Oh, darling girl, you belong with us. We're your real family. You'll be happier with us."

Now Susanna sobs. Comfort gently rubs her back. She gives Susanna the Bible. "This is Ned's Bible. See, his name is written in it, his and the names of everyone in your family. Come back to

Jesus who loves you." She shows her the names written in the first page of the Bible. "It's Ned's handwriting. Do you recognize it?"

Susanna nods. "Jesus abandoned us," Susanna says softly in English. "I heard their screams, Faith, Katherine, William, mother, all the others. He did nothing to help us." Susanna lies down on the sleeping bench, curled up, facing away. Comfort tries to touch her, but Susanna moves away, so she lies beside her.

After a while, Comfort opens the flap of the *wetu* and looks outside. It's still dark. She fears when the dawn comes Susanna will be lost to her and Ned forever. This is her only chance to reach Susanna's heart and make her want to come home.

Susanna has fallen asleep clutching a small cloth doll. Comfort recognizes it as the one she made for her before the family left for Rhode Island. She reaches over and takes the doll.

Susanna wakes up and grabs it out of her hands.

"I gave it to you. You've kept it all these years because you want to come home with me. Dear Susanna, I love you so much. It's time to come home."

"Why did God let my family die?"

"We cannot know His mysterious ways. But the Lord brought me here to bring you home, to live again with Christians." She opens her arms.

Now Susanna falls into her arms then lays her head in Comfort's lap. Comfort strokes her hair and kisses her forehead. Then Susanna speaks to her in a high, childish voice. "I hid behind a boulder, heard screams. I held my ears, closed my eyes tight. I should have tried to help mother who was inside alone, but I couldn't move. Then someone grabbed me by the hair and held a hatchet to my head. Another Indian boy pushed him away and carried me into the house. It was raining blood. Then all went dark." Susanna sobs, has trouble catching her breath.

"I don't remember much more of that horrible day. There was

a big forest, I was very cold, and I was given moccasins for my frozen feet. I clutched this doll I had been holding when he dragged me for hours."

Comfort asks about her life with the Siwanoy. She wants Susanna to speak English and tell her what happened.

"I had to work hard and was hungry. The old woman held up a stick and threatened me. I never knew when she would get angry, so I tried hard to please her. I learned their words. I needed to feel safe. The nightmares were terrible. I'd hear screaming. I shouldn't have survived. I tried to drown myself in the river, but someone pulled me out."

Comfort now hugs her. "The Lord was with you. Jesus wanted you to live."

"The more I spoke their language, the better they treated me." Then she started hitting Comfort. "Why did it take you so long to come for me? Why? I was so alone, afraid. Why did you wait until now to find me?"

Comfort looks into her sweet face and sees the child she once held. "I'm so sorry, brave girl, and so very sad for your loss, your pain. I didn't know you were alive or where to find you until now. I love you. I need you to come and live with me."

Susanna pulls away from her and stands up, and opens the flap. She looks at the moon and doesn't speak for a long time. Then, not looking at Comfort, she says "I belong here now. I will be married soon. I love Runs So Fast."

"No, No. Please don't marry him. They're kind people, but Ned and I need you. You need to be with your own people. Come, rest." She stands and brings her to the sleeping bench. She rubs her back, and sings an English folk song Susanna used to love. They both fall asleep.

At dawn, the Siwanoy men bring them back to the village. Comfort and Metacom are anxious. Will all go well? Does

Susanna want to leave? Will the *sachem* let her leave if his mother refuses to give her up?

A council meeting is called. The *sachem's* mother sits on one side of her son, Runs So Fast on the other. Wampage says "Red Bird, we have adopted you. Runs So Fast wishes to be your *sannup*. Let me look into your eyes. Tell me truly what's in your heart."

Susanna speaks in Algonquian. "You and your mother have cared for me. I will always be grateful. Runs So Fast is kind and has a strong spirit. I'll miss him." Then she hesitates, her eyes close, she bends her head down and sobs.

Comfort fears she won't leave the handsome young man.

She wipes away the tears and looks at the *sachem*. "I'll always be a stranger here. Please, let me return to my own people. I have a sister and a brother still alive. I'll always be grateful to you and your mother, but I can no longer be happy here knowing they want me to return."

The *sachem's* mother gets up, and says something to her son. She's bent over and trembling and looks like she's about to fall down. Runs So Fast puts his arms around her and starts to leave. Then he stops and goes to Susanna.

"You are not a good woman. I no longer I wish to marry you. You have caused great pain to this woman who was a mother to you. I never want to see you again."

"Don't hate me. I'm sorry. I won't forget." She's sobbing and Comfort puts her arm around her.

Sachem Wampage speaks. "Know our door is open, Red Bird, and you'll not be forgotten. I won't force you to stay. Go quickly."

They leave right away before he changes his mind. Susanna gets on Comfort's horse and holds on tightly leaning her head on her back. She doesn't speak at all when they stop to eat and spend the night.

When they arrive at Mount Hope, Comfort introduces her to Little Bird and Tommy. They spend a week. Tommy likes Susanna right away, and she takes him to the pond where she teaches him to swim.

Comfort tells Little Bird she is ready now to take her son back. She has decided she'll tell Reverend Eliot that she's rescued this little boy also from the same tribe who captured Susanna. They'll live in the cottage and help him with his missionary work.

When they leave for Roxbury, Comfort's heart aches. Tommy screams, holds his little arms out to Little Bird "*okasu*, mother, I don't want to go with the English lady." He runs back to her, hugs Little Bird's knees. He's desperate. Then Little Thunder and Laughing Like Water both pull him, and try to drag him back into the *wetu*. Tommy cries *weemat*, brother, *weticks*, sister. Little Bird is sobbing. Even Metacom wipes a tear from his eyes.

"*Nickattash*, leave quickly, Sky-Eyes" he tells her. "Promise to bring him to visit us. We'll all miss our boy Little Raven."

"I'll bring him back often, I promise. *Cowammaunsh*, I love you."

* * * *

That evening, Reverend Eliot and his wife welcome them home. Eliot prays, gives thanks to God for saving these two poor children from the heathen. Hannah prepares a special meal.

Susanna and Tommy are exhausted, anxious and feel confused. Comfort sleeps with Tommy curled beside her. Eliot's servant brings a mattress and quilt for Susanna. Comfort is unsure how she will heal their pain. She prays that Ned returns soon to help.

Over the next few weeks, Susanna and Tommy have nightmares. Tommy cries for Little Bird. Comfort rubs his back and sings songs, but he pushes her away saying she isn't his mother and he wants to go home. Susanna wakes up screaming, reliving the massacre, seeing gruesome details she had forgotten.

John Eliot says she must be firm and reinforce good behavior. The natives indulge children too much, so the boy is too willful now. He will act as a father and help with discipline. They will pray to God, and He will have mercy and help them heal.

Her friend Anne also gives her advice. "Religious poetry should be read aloud every evening, just as I do with my children. I am writing a book of proverbs for my children and I'll give you a copy."

One day she discovers that Susanna has packed a bundle with her Indian clothes and keeps it under her bed. Is she planning to run back to that Indian boy?

"Runs So Fast is handsome, but not the right husband for you. You will find another man to love."

"Why would he have been wrong for me?"

"My darling, remember those Indians took you by force; perhaps you were a replacement for a daughter lost to smallpox. They killed your family. You're a Christian. Pray and God's Grace will bring you peace."

"But I don't know who Susanna is anymore. I often feel like Red Bird."

"In time you'll know who you are and what you need, my darling. Ned will return and we'll be a family."

8

Natick

One hundred forty-five souls, about thirty families with children, live in a Praying Indian village called Natick. They are converts from the Massachuset tribe. Chief *sachem* Cutshamoquin is a convert and has come here with his people. Reverend Eliot is happy he's here because it proves tribes will respect their *sachems* even if they convert to Christianity.

Eliot, Sassamon, Susanna, Comfort and Tommy will spend all day at Natick, and return at sunset. Eliot will preach in Algonquian and English, John Sassamon will answer questions about the sermon in Algonquian, and Susanna and Comfort will teach English to the children and help the adults learn to read their own language. Tommy's job is to distribute apples to the children.

Natick is the first of fourteen towns Eliot wants to establish, all within twenty-five miles of Boston. Like Natick, they'll be agricultural towns. Every family will be given their own small plot of land which he hopes will sustain them for generations. They'll have water rights. He'll insist they stay here throughout the year, rather than move in summer to fishing places then move again in winter. Limited hunting will be allowed. Eliot will teach them how to plant orchards and raise cattle. They'll learn to be diligent, work hard for six days and keep the holy Sabbath on the seventh.

Each town will have a meetinghouse and a school. Eventually

native preachers will live in these towns. Someday, when he completes his Algonquian language Bible, these preachers will use it to teach the words of God. He also intends to teach carpentry and other skills so they can build English style homes and streets. He's forty-one and hopes he'll live long enough to see his dream realized.

Comfort doesn't talk to Metacom about her work with Eliot. He fears the missionaries will lead his people to lose respect for their leaders and customs. She often brings Tommy to visit Little Bird and her children who love her son. Sometimes Sassamon and Susanna come with them. Metacom has decided to let Sassamon help him write deeds for people who want to buy Wampanoag land.

This morning they're all traveling in Eliot's small sailboat, heading north on the Charles River towards Natick. It's a warm day with a moderate breeze.

"May I have a biscuit, sir? Please," Tommy begs politely. Eliot always packs biscuits because he can't digest native foods.

"Take a biscuit. Remember to be polite when you give apples to the children and speak English so they can practice."

"I will sir." He puts both hands into the basket and pulls out two biscuits, one in each hand and holds them up. "Can I have two?"

"Sure," Eliot says. He laughs. He's fond of Tommy.

Eliot turns to Sassamon. "They've cut their hair, they're covering their nakedness with proper English clothes, and they're getting good at blacksmithing and carpentry. I want you to record the names of those who are the best artisans."

Sassamon takes out a small notebook he is keeping for Eliot.

"They've given up hunting, gambling, and dancing to drums. It's harder to get them to forget about **manitoo,** and to stop asking for their *pawwaw* when someone is sick, but that'll change in time. They confess their sins to me and feel shame. I know most of them love our Lord. They feel safe and happy living at Natick."

Susanna says something to Sassamon in Algonquian. She'd be a good wife for him, Eliot thinks. Sassamon is also an orphan. He sees they're holding hands.

He convinced the magistrates to sell him land. "My converts will be loyal citizens. Not only are we saving souls, but these people will be allies."

Sometimes Eliot stays overnight in a large room above the meetinghouse in Natick. Sassamon will live here when he finishes studying at the Harvard Indian College.

When their boat arrives at Natick, they're greeted by young Indian boys shouting in English: "Hello, preacher. Do you have stories for us? Boy, do you have apples?"

"Hello, *netops*" Tommy answers. "I'll give you apples, and **wuttahimneash**, strawberries also." These boys remind him of his brother Little Thunder.

The meetinghouse is crowded. Eliot gives his sermon. People laugh at his mistakes in Algonquian. Sassamon says a prayer in English and Algonquian. Eliot hopes these Indians and English Christians will attend services together in the future.

Let us lift up our eyes to God in heaven, and say
Heavenly Father, we are poor worms under thy feet.
Bless our souls and help us all to rejoice in the Lord.
Our pleasures and delights are all sins which provoke His wrath.
Bring us into the Light. Christ will give us life. Amen.

Tommy gives out apples. Comfort and Susanna begin English lessons.

Late in the afternoon they leave for home. Sassamon and Susanna sing psalms to Tommy who's falling asleep on Comfort's lap. It's been a good day, Eliot thinks.

9

FAIRLAWN MANOR

The King has been captured and is under house arrest in Hampton Court Palace. Ned and Henry are in Henry's study talking late into the night. They're tired, but can't sleep; so much is as stake. Who will shape the future, Oliver Cromwell and his generals or Henry Vane and his followers in the House of Commons? They have different ideas about how to proceed. With victory on the battlefield comes the responsibility to define the future.

Henry still holds out a slim hope that King Charles will accept a constitutional monarchy with Parliament keeping control of all taxes and determining guidelines for freedom of the press, tolerance for religious practice, judicial reform, and the expansion of suffrage. Oliver wants the New Modern Army to play a dominant role in the control of governance as well as in religious matters. Of course, as the General who brought about victory, he feels he is the one who should shape the future.

"Our future will depend on the resolution of disagreements within The House of Commons as well as within Cromwell's army," Henry tells Ned.

"Even though the King won't negotiate, will the monarchists in the House of Commons still support him?" Ned asks.

"Yes. Many do. At the same time thousands of soldiers are demanding democratic reforms. Oliver must find a way to prevent mutiny in the army."

"Many representatives think the answer is to disband the New Model Army and establish a new militia. Will Oliver allow that?" Ned asks.

"Never. I fear he might do something drastic to stop it," Henry says.

Ned sighs. "It would be a pity if one tyrant was replaced by another."

"His soldiers have legitimate cause for anger. They haven't been paid in a long time. Their families are starving, but we just didn't have the money. We'll have to raise taxes even though that won't be easy. Trade has been disrupted for years."

Henry gets up and opens a bottle of wine. He fills two glasses. "Let's toast to our victory. More than one hundred thousand men have died and the economy is in shambles, but we've won."

They drink a toast, and then finish the bottle of wine in silence, thinking of the problems that now must be addressed.

Henry is trying to decide if he believes the House of Lords can be abolished.

Ned believes Cromwell wants to control not only Parliament but local governments. Do people really want their villages run by generals? All those farmers, carpenters, small shop owners died for what they called "the just cause". They died for freedom and new rights not for military control.

"These have been hard years," Henry says, breaking the silence. "Everyone has been hurt by poor harvests, the plague, overcrowding and crime in our cities."

"What are you most afraid of now," Ned asks.

"Anarchy. Or the return of Charles' son. Go to the taverns, Ned, and listen to the soldiers and our citizens. Let me know what they are thinking. Now let's go to sleep."

* * * *

Cromwell proposes a debate between the Levellers and his officers. He calls the radicals "The Agitators" and the officer group
"The Grandees". Cromwell and his son-in-law will control the
debate. It's to take place in a small yellow church in Putney which
is in the southwest of London and is the current army headquarters. Henry has asked Ned to attend and report back to him.

John Lilburne, the leader of the Levellers, is now called "Freeborn John". His group demands "native rights" which they say
belong to all men as a birthright, not as something a government
confers on them. These rights include having a voice in government and equality before the law regardless of income. Ned tells
John Lilburne that Henry Vane supports most of what he and
the Levellers want.

"I don't trust Sir Henry Vane or Oliver Cromwell," John says.
"They'll both keep us everlastingly in bondage and slavery as
laborers on farms, in coal mines and textile factories. Without a
vote we'll never improve our lives. They are rich powerful men
and want to keep their privileges."

The Levellers have thousands of followers in the army and
among the citizens. He and his friends have written a document
called "The Agreement of the People" which they hope will be
the basis of a new government. He stands up in the church and
reads aloud the demands in this manifesto.

"All native freeborn men should have an equal voice in elections
for Parliament. These should be held every two years. In addition there must be an end to imprisonment and torture based
on poverty or religious views. We also have specific suggestions
about legal reform and a new constitution."

At the end of the day Cromwell says there will be sometime in
the future a mass meeting of the army in which "The Agreement
of the People" manifesto will be discussed. However, he has no
intention of having such a meeting.

Ned talks to the wounded soldiers in the church, many missing a leg or arm, and feels sympathetic to their demands. He returns and tells Henry.

"Oliver Cromwell doesn't trust the masses," Henry tells him.

"Won't the merchants, landowners, and the monopolistic joint-stock companies really be the ones who profit from this war?"

"Yes. Cromwell wants commercial interests to grow stronger. He thinks the English and the Dutch should divide the world between them. Let the Dutch take Asia and Africa, and England will take both Americas and the Caribbean. He will propose it to the Dutch, but I know they won't agree," Henry says.

Cromwell wants the royalists who support the King to stay out of office for five years. He's demanding all soldiers sign a loyalty oath before they can get the back pay owed to them. This oath promises loyalty to the army and not to the Parliament.

* * * *

King Charles escapes from Hampton Court Palace. All negotiations within the military and Parliament cease until he can be captured again. He is captured and this time he's put into a medieval castle on the Isle of Wright. His Majesty tells Henry he will now negotiate in good faith, but actually he secretly attempts to raise an army in Scotland to continue the war.

After this escape attempt, Cromwell wants the King brought to trial. His generals march into Parliament and arrest forty-five members of the House of Commons who disagree with conducting a trial. Now Cromwell's supporters have a majority and they agree to a trial.

Henry Vane is not arrested, but he's furious at Cromwell for using force to get his way. He decides not to attend Parliament in protest of this illegal military purge. The House of Lords objects to the trial, but is ignored.

A High Court of Justice is established which will try the King for treason. Members of Parliament are appointed by the army to be on the jury. Many refuse to serve and go back to their country estates. Sixty eight men agree to sit in judgement.

* * * *

Spectators crowd into the upstairs gallery of the Great Hall at Westminster to watch this unprecedented event. Never before has a King been put on trial.

A large crimson velvet chair is in the middle of the room facing the podium and the Judges are seated on benches on both sides of the podium.

King Charles is escorted into the hall. Twenty officers before and behind him march him in. He's dressed all in black, wearing his large, shiny silver star, the Order of the Garter, around his neck, sits rigidly on the crimson chair. He stares with anger at the members of this court on both sides of the room and at the spectators in the gallery who are leaning over the railing to watch his humiliation. He taps his jeweled heels on the floor. He doesn't remove his high black hat for that would show respect for those who are judging him. He tries to stop the clerk from reading the charges by hitting him with his silver headed cane. The top of the cane falls off.

A clerk reads the act which Parliament passed to set up this court: "Charles Stuart, King of England: The Commons of England Assembled in Parliament, being deeply sensible of the calamities that have been brought upon this Nation (which is fixed upon you as the principal author of it) have resolved to make inquisition for Blood, and according to that debt and duty they owe to Justice, to God, the Kingdom, and themselves...have resolved to bring you to Trial and Judgment."

"By what power I'm called here? I'm your lawful King. What sins you bring upon your heads, and the Judgment of God upon this land, think well upon it before you go further...I have a Trust, committed to me by God. I will not betray it. Let me see a legal authority warranted by the word of God, or warranted by the constitution of the Kingdom and I will answer a plea."

The attorney says the Law is his superior, and all the people in England accept this fact. "It is Parliament, the sole makers of law, the representatives of the people, which judges you. The ultimate purpose of law is Justice, and a King is but an officer in trust of Justice. If there are wrongs, the only remedy the people have resides in Parliament. You are charged with being a tyrant, a traitor, a murderer, and a public enemy to the Commonwealth of England."

"Ha!" he says. He refuses to answer the charges against him.

The decision is read to him: "For all the treasons and crimes this court does judge against you, Charles Stuart, we find you a tyrant, traitor, murderer, and a public enemy. You shall be put to death by the severing of your head."

All the members of the court stand up to show their assent to this sentence.

Fifty-nine members sign the death warrant including Oliver Cromwell. Henry Vane can't bring himself to sign it. He didn't want to kill this King. He had hoped to limit his powers.

The execution will take place in one week.

Parliament quickly passes a law preventing the King's son Charles from being declared King after the execution.

10

Fairlawn Manor

Henry Vane sits at his desk in a dark corner of his study. The only light comes from a small candle. The heavy red velvet drapes are closed. He is signing papers to release government money to pay soldiers and sailors back pay.

He knows that a large wooden scaffold has been set up in front of the central window of the Banqueting Hall. The King will have to climb out of the room through this window. He has refused to witness the execution which is taking place now.

If only the King had accepted the last compromise he offered him. There would have been only a House of Commons and the appointed House of Lords would be abolished. It would have prevented the interference of bishops and the people would select their own ministers and rituals. The poor would not be thrown into prison because they owed money. Free expression of ideas without censorship would be guaranteed. He had worked long into the night to get Oliver Cromwell to agree, but Oliver then changed his mind and demanded the King be executed. Soon it will be over. He's so weary of war. There's so much more he must do. He puts his head down on his desk and falls asleep.

Henry's elderly mother, her thin gray hair flying wildly about her small sad face, is ushered in by his guard. He awakes to see her collapsed in a chair near the fireplace. She's breathing heavily.

"So, are you happy now, son?"

"I didn't want him executed mother. I asked the others to let him finish out his days as a prisoner at Carisbrooke Castle on the Isle of Wight. I didn't sign the warrant for his execution. I didn't want this to happen, believe me, but he wouldn't compromise, so we didn't have a choice."

"How could you let them kill him? He adored you when you were a child. He taught you to ride that black pony on your eighth birthday. Did you forget he permitted your father to buy Raby Castle so you could have it as wedding present?" She's taking deep breaths, and seems fragile.

"I remember, mother, of course I do. All of it - the early morning rides in cool, fragrant air, and how he taught me to be a good hunter. But those days are gone. Absolute monarchy must give way to democracy. We will be a great commonwealth, you'll see. It will take time, but England will be better for what we have done today."

"Your father's a broken, lonely, old man, a ghost of himself, and it's entirely your fault. You betrayed him by stealing those documents about Lord Strafford. Your actions helped kill Lord Strafford and humiliated your father. You may as just as well have killed me and your father today, for we no longer wish to live. We've lost our position, our income, and our friends." Her body is shaking.

Henry goes to her and hands her a handkerchief, but she shoves his hand away. "I won't ever forgive you, Henry, nor will your father. You'll pay dearly for what you've done. May God have mercy on your soul." He tries to help her stand and to hug her, but she pushes him off and leaves.

Henry pulls open the heavy drapes and stares into the darkness. He's surprised to feel tears on his cheeks, but doesn't wipe them away. They're not for the King, but for his parents and all the other gentry who don't understand or accept why their comfortable world has been destroyed.

* * * *

"It's over" Ned says. He has come to report about the execution.

"Tell me." He falls into the chair, his head in his hands.

"There was a battery of guns mounted on a platform near the scaffold just in case the crowd turned out to be difficult to control. There were many spectators but they remained quiet because they wanted to hear his final words."

"What did he say?"

"First he asked for bread and wine, and then he walked to the middle of the scaffold. He was wearing a white cap, black breeches, a white shirt and doublet, and a black cape. 'I'm being punished by God because I allowed Parliament to kill my dear friend Lord Strafford' he said. Of course that didn't win him any sympathy, but I guess he wanted to say it before he died."

"What else did he say?"

"He spoke about wanting peace and liberty for his subjects. He called himself a martyr."

"God help us if many see him as a martyr," Henry says.

"He said the people of England are 'subjects' and they have no right to rule. They must obey their King who was sent by God to protect them. The crowd booed and many people raised their fists in anger."

"Did he die with dignity?"

"He took off his doublet, but wrapped the black cloak around his shoulders again. The bishop came over and tucked his long, gray hair under his white cap. His neck was now exposed and he placed it on the block, and stretched out his arms. I could hear him saying to the Lord that he was ready to die just before the axe fell and severed his head."

"And when it was over? What did the crowd do then?"

"The executioner ripped off the King's cap and seized his flowing hair and held his head up for all to see shouting 'Behold the head of a traitor!' He shouldn't have done that, for that angered His Majesty's supporters. They started to attack the soldiers with sticks so they were removed with force. They won't accept this, the monarchists, and they'll try to bring back his son Charles from France. I don't want to be here when that happens."

"What will you do when you return?" Henry asks. He gets up and goes to his desk and gives Ned the papers he signed regarding the soldiers' back pay.

"I'll establish a shipping company in Newport; I'll bring codfish and timber to the Caribbean. Oliver wants a law to require merchants to use English ships only; he says we mustn't let the Dutch control the seas. That will help me succeed. I hope Comfort still wants me. I'm ready to have sons."

"I'll miss you, Ned, you know that. We've turned the world upside down, haven't we?"

PLIMOUTH

The colonists are busy with spring planting. Husbands, sleeves rolled up, work preparing the hard earth, while wives and daughters, long skirts tucked up, walk behind sowing five corn seeds in each little mound of earth. Their young children are picking up rocks and putting them in baskets to clear the fields.

In addition to corn, they are planting barley, oats, wheat and peas. The multicolored Indian corn will provide a hearty porridge.

On the other side of the palisade fence, Hobbamock's wife is working in her garden. She planted her corn earlier and it's already as high as her hand, so she's planting pole beans that will twine their vines around the corn plants climbing up each ear as it grows. She will plant melons with broad leaves to keep weeds down and the earth moist. She and Hobbamock still like to spend summers here.

Comfort and Tommy have come to see her parents. Will was sick most of the winter. This is the first time she's bringing Tommy. Will knows she has adopted a boy, but doesn't know the boy is his grandson, nor does Tommy know Comfort is his birth mother. The secret must be kept until Ned returns and she's properly wed. She's received a letter saying he'll be home in a month.

"We're here, my sweet" she says. She ties up the horse. "See that small boat in the harbor. Would you like to go on it?"

"Can I go now?"

"I'll ask my father if we can go tomorrow."

Tommy picks up a small pail of water. "Drink up, horsey" he says.

Comfort takes his hand and walks towards her house. "We're staying at the house I lived in as a child."

"I like houses made of bricks better."

She's changed so much, but this house is the same. She walks around noticing all the familiar things. She lifts her father's pewter tankard and smells beer, puts her hand into dried marigold petals heaped in the spice basket ready to be used in a stew. She picks up books in Latin, Greek and Hebrew piled on the table next to her father's chair. She sees the clay jug she made as a child filled with blue wildflowers. Elder Brewster's Norway pine chest has his name carved on it. It was bequeathed to her father in Brewster's will.

Tommy sees a wooden trencher with several corncakes and she gives him one. He wants two, so she gives him another. He grins and nibbles on both of them.

The Bible is open on its stand near the window and her father's spectacles are on it. On the wall is the sampler she made to practice her sewing. The tiny crooked stitches say: "Comfort Bradford is my name. Lord guide my hand so I will feel no shame."

She takes his hand and leads him to her father's study. "This is where I studied Greek and Latin." She lets him sit on the worn red velvet cushion in her father's chair.

"Don't touch his journal." It's open and she reads his last entry: "The beavers are nearly extinct. We had few pelts. This has changed things with the Wampanoags. We must have a town meeting soon."

She reaches into a drawer in a chest and pulls out the Mayflower Compact. "See this paper, Tommy. It was signed by all the men who agreed to work together when they first arrived here. My father wants me to make a copy and keep it safe in our house."

"Are they dead?"

"Many are."

They sit at the table in front of the hearth and she tells him how father taught her to write well. She takes a quill, paper and ink and lets him write a few sentences about their journey as they wait for her parents to return.

Will arrives carrying a pail of freshly caught fish. Tommy rushes over to see the fish flapping against the sides of the pail. Cautiously, he pokes one with his finger. Then he smells his finger and scrunches up his nose. "They stink."

Will laughs. "Do you like to eat fish, little fellow?"

"Only dead ones, when they're cooked."

Will places the pail of fish near the hearth, and asks Tommy to give him small branches for kindling. As she watches them make a fire, she feels sad she can't tell her father the boy is his grandson.

Alice comes from the community oven with freshly baked bread. She puts Tommy to work setting wooden trenchers and spoons on the table.

"I can count to ten." He proves it.

"We're only four today."

After they've eaten, Alice pulls out a large metal basin and boils some water. "It's been a long time since I've had a little boy to bathe," she says, smiling. After scrubbing Tommy's thin body with a cloth, she hands him a shirt too large for him. They both laugh. She takes him upstairs to the loft to tell him the story of Noah and the flood, and to put him to sleep. When Comfort goes upstairs to see if he's asleep, she finds her mother asleep next to her son.

Will asks Comfort to go into his study so they can talk. She examines books on a shelf and doesn't face him. "Please forgive me, father. I've disobeyed you."

"Is it so bad a thing you've done you can't bear looking into my eyes? Don't be afraid, my angel."

"I've disappointed you."

"I'm listening."

"I couldn't stop loving Ned Hutchinson, though you didn't want me to be with him. I'm going to marry him. He'll return soon from London and will start a shipping business in Newport, Rhode Island. We intend to live there."

"I knew you were waiting for him. Is he a heretic like his mother? Is he a fanatic?" he asks. "What a sad ending there was to his family."

"He's not at all like her," she says. She decides not to tell him that Ned has lost his faith in God. "I've loved him since I was seventeen. We saw each other when I went to London with Reverend Eliot."

"Well I'm glad you won't be an old maid like your aunt Mary. I wouldn't have chosen him for you, but I'll accept your decision. God wants us to have a mate to help us survive the losses we all must face in our lives."

He motions for her to sit beside him on a chair. "I've never told you that I held your Ned in my arms once."

"When?"

"During that Pequot massacre. He'd put his flintlock on the ground and was leaning against a large elm crying. He was just as sick as I was at the brutality of our soldiers, at seeing the children burning …." He can't go on.

"You never told me."

"I held him tightly in my arms for several minutes. There was no need for words. We both felt that the killing of innocent women and children was unjust. So you see, dear daughter, I've seen your young man's good soul." He smiles and she feels relieved.

"Tell me the truth, dear. Did he ask you to risk your life to rescue his sister Susanna?"

"No. It was my idea. I couldn't have rescued her without Metacom's help. He said he helped me because you treated his father with respect for many years. You've kept the peace, papa, and it matters."

"Now I need to tell you about my will. This house and our farm will go to Willie as the oldest son, and the younger boys will get small parcels of land. You'll only get the furniture after Alice dies if you want it and a small amount of money, but I've left my journal and books in your hands. I know you'll keep them safe."

"Oh please papa, don't talk of dying."

"I don't fear death. God decides the timing, and I must accept His plan. I've done my best for this colony. It'll survive without me. Come, it's time for bed, and I get little sleep these days. I get up during the night and spend hours working on my Hebrew dictionary. I want to read the psalms in Hebrew."

The next day Alice tells Comfort that she will accept Ned as a son-in-law, but doesn't want to go to Rhode Island because it's full of heretics.

They spend the next afternoon sailing in the harbor. The water is still very cold so they can't swim. Tommy is delighted that Will lets him catch a fish. When they return to the house, he takes a nap.

Suddenly she decides she'll tell her parents that Tommy is their grandson. She says Ned was lost when he learned his family was murdered. He was drinking and wouldn't go back to London to work with Henry Vane. She slept with him for a few nights in a cottage and conceived Tommy.

"Does Ned know?"

"No. What good would it have done? He wouldn't leave in

the middle of the war. You're the only ones who know."

"He's a sweet boy. I'll be a good grandma." Alice hugs her. "I'll love you and those you love as long as I live."

12

Boston

Ned arrived last night from Rhode Island on a ketch he bought. It was made in Boston's busy shipyards for the coastal and Caribbean trade.

He slept at the Red Lion Inn last night and he plans to leave early this afternoon. He has arranged to meet Comfort and Susanna here. He has asked the ship's captain to perform a marriage ceremony. Susanna is coming for a short visit.

He walks downstairs and sees the tavern owner putting logs on the fire in the hearth. The room has a beamed ceiling, an orange colored wide-board floor, and a long table set with trenchers of bread, cheese and butter. He hopes he can order hot porridge with milk and sugar. There are pewter tankards for beer or cider.

"I know you. You're Ned Hutchinson, right?" says the older man sitting at the table.

His face is familiar, but who is he? His beard and hair are gray and he has a scar on his left cheek. Ned doesn't feel like talking to him. The man may ask about his mother's trial and murder. If he says she deserved to die because she was a heretic, he'd have to punch him. He doesn't want to feel all the pain and grief of the past. He knows he doesn't control his anger. The long, bloody civil war has changed him; it's made him a more suspicious man.

"Don't you know me, lad? I'm John Underhill. I heard your saintly mother preach. I've been excommunicated myself, twice in fact, once for adultery. Can I help it if ladies jump into my bed? Even married ones desire the excitement I offer." He winks and asks the tavern owner for more beer. Is he drunk so early in the morning?

"After they kicked me out, I was a mercenary for the Dutch in Long Island, fighting the savages. I ransomed several English children held captive by them. Now I'm a privateer in the Caribbean; this means I'm a pirate with a license to steal, that is, so long as the bounty I steal is from the Spanish or Dutch ships and not ours. It's too cold here for my old bones anyway. So what're you doing here?"

"Just passing through. I'm off to Newport this afternoon."

"Why?"

"I'm starting a shipping business."

"Caribbean trade?"

"Yes. I'll bring cod and timber to Barbados. I hear there are thousands of English living there and more come every year. Portuguese Jews from Brazil learned how to grow sugar cane and now live in Bridgetown. Wealthy royalists from London have bought land for large sugar plantations. They're all going to be very rich; I'd like some of that profit."

"They've brought indentured Irish servants and Pequots, but I hear they're starting to bring over black slaves from West Africa," Underhill says.

"I'll need to make a good profit since I'll be risking storms and pirates."

"The tavern owner told me you were in London. Cromwell's army? "

"No. Remember Henry Vane? He was Governor here for a short while."

He nods. "He admired your mother."

"He's still fighting for religious tolerance. Henry's a leader of the Independent Party in the House of Commons. I assisted him during the war."

"I once dreamed of being a post-captain on one of those man-o'-war ships, the kind with fifty guns; sixth rate I think they call them. I went aboard one when I was in England writing my memoir about the Pequot War. Did you go on any big ones?"

"A fifty gun ship with three hundred men is a called a fourth rate, John. I went on a first rate one with one hundred guns and eight hundred men, three decks of cannon, and more on the quarter-deck and forecastle."

"It wasn't the famous Sovereign of the Seas, was it? The ship King Charles spent so much money on? I wish I'd had a chance to see her," John says. "Tell me everything you know about her. She's the grandest man - o'- war ever built."

"Well, she's a three decker, has a triple planked hull, and carries one hundred guns. On the main she has twenty-eight big cannon, on the middle twenty-four broadside cannon. On the upper deck there are twenty-four more broadside cannon and four lighter chasers. She's over one thousand tons and needs a crew of six hundred. You know she was partly to blame for the civil war. It was because she cost so much the King had to impose that hated ship tax on merchants. Parliament took her away from him when war broke out."

"A Dutch sailor told me they call her the Golden Devil. You know we might soon be fighting mighty battles on the seas with the Dutch for control of trade, don't you?"

"Yes. Well, that ship was an extravagance Parliament didn't approve of. There's an equestrian statue of King Edgar at her beak head, beneath the bowsprit, and under the horse's hooves are carved the bodies of seven kings covered with gold. The stern head is crowned with a gilded figure of Cupid riding upon a pouncing lion. On the upper gun deck are carved golden goddesses, mermaids, dolphins, lions, unicorns and dragons. I saw the bill the King gave to Parliament. She cost the treasury over sixty-five thousand pounds!"

"Well I'll be damned! The Golden Devil caused King Charles to lose his head!"

"It was the spark that set the fire." Then Ned calls over to the tavern owner and asks if anyone has come asking for him this morning.

"A couple of ladies have just arrived, sir" he says. "I led them outside to the garden; that's where lady visitors wait."

"I need to go, Captain," Ned says, putting a few shillings on the table. "Come see me if you ever get to Newport."

"That I will, lad. We'll share stories about light brown girls, pretty offspring of plantation owners and their African mistresses. Anyway, Rhode Island's the only colony tolerant enough to accept the likes of me."

In the garden he sees Susanna holding the hand of a boy. Comfort runs into his arms. Susanna and Tommy wait. Then Ned motions Susanna to come into his arms.

She comes closer with Tommy. She hugs her brother and they both cry with joy to touch each other again. She introduces him to Tommy.

"He was rescued from the Indians. We live together."

"They're both coming," Comfort says, smiling at Tommy.

Ned ignores the boy, and focuses his attention on his sister. She looks so like his mother that his eyes are tearing. If only his mother could have seen how beautiful she is grown-up.

"I'm a teacher to Christian Indians, so I can only stay with you one month. John Sassamon, an Indian preacher, needs my help. I intend to live at Natick with John after he finishes his studies and we get married."

"What? My God, haven't you had enough of savages? After what they did to us, how could you want to have one as your husband?"

"John's studying at the Indian school at Harvard College. He's a good man. I'd be proud to have his children."

"Your children won't be accepted. I hate Indians. It's going to be hard for me to accept one of them as my kin."

He turns again to Comfort, takes her hand, and they sit on the bench. "I've asked the captain to marry us as soon as we get settled onboard. I can't wait to make you my wife. But I must warn you, love, the civil war has changed me. I've dark moods and I'm quick to anger."

"Love is strong medicine," she says.

He looks around. "Where're your things? We sail in an hour."

"Reverend Eliot is bringing them to the wharf. He and Anne Bradstreet are coming to say goodbye."

"Come here," Comfort says to Tommy, opening her arms.

The boy shakes his head no, and refuses to move. He looks down, angry at being ignored by this stranger who doesn't like him.

"Can't he stay with Eliot?" Ned asks.

"Of course not. He's ours now. I adopted him," Comfort says, going over to Tommy and putting her arm around his shoulders. "Tommy loves boats. You'll show him around the ketch, won't you? I've told him you've been working with the navy."

Ned doesn't want to take care of someone else's child. "I've too much work to do, starting the business. Maybe if I pay Eliot, he'll keep him." He looks at Comfort, his eyes pleading for understanding.

Tommy is trying hard to hold back tears, but failing. "He's going to live with us."

Ned thinks perhaps he'll find a good family in Newport who will adopt the child.

They all walk towards the wharf, and see Anne Bradstreet waiting.

Anne hugs Comfort. "Here's a copy of my book of poems, recently published in London by my brother-in-law. People are surprised it was written by a woman and blame the printing errors on me, even though I wasn't even there to fix them."

"I'll write my friend John Milton and tell him to buy it." Ned says. "I'd be flattered to have such a famous poet read it."

"Here's my translation of Genesis into Algonquian," Reverend Eliot says, handing Comfort papers. "Please correct my mistakes. I'm depending on you to continue to help me. I'll send sections to you as I finish them."

"Of course I will," Comfort says, and hugs him. "I'll always be grateful for all you've done for me."

"Don't thank me. The Lord, dear friend, has brought us together for this important purpose."

After they board the ketch and store their belongings, the Captain, a man with a broad smile on his weathered face, brings out a bottle of wine. He performs a brief ceremony on the sunny deck. They drink a toast to their future happiness. Susanna sings a psalm. Tommy asks for bread to feed the seagulls.

Ned and Comfort go to their cabin. At last, after so many years of waiting, they're together again. His touch is gentle. He appreciates the softness of her curves, the smell of her hair, the wonder of having her, finally, as his wife. She's shy, nervous, hoping she can please him. As she rests her head on his shoulder, she decides to use this sweet moment to tell him Tommy is his own son.

"What? Why didn't you tell me? Does Susanna know? I can't believe this. You never wrote me about him."

"I had to hide my pregnancy. I couldn't face Eliot and my parents as a sinner. My Wampanoag friends helped me. Tommy lived for a while with them and their two children, and I visited as often as I could. It was so painful to leave him and I cried a lot, but I would've been humiliated, an outcast in Boston if people knew I wasn't married. What good would it have done to worry you about me?"

"He looks a bit Indian… all that black hair, those dark, sad eyes."

"Are you accusing me of lying? He has your brother's face. I named him for your brother Tom. He's a gift from God, a blessing for us." She starts to cry. "You wouldn't have left London, I knew that."

He's ashamed of himself for doubting her. She gave birth without a husband at her side. She suffered pain and the fear of humiliation because of his lust and his reluctance to marry in London. What if she'd died giving birth? What would have happened to this boy, his son?

"I'm so sorry. I'll be a good father, I promise, my love. When he learns to love me, we'll tell him the truth."

That afternoon, Ned takes Tommy for a walk around the ketch. He tells him that a ketch is bigger than a sloop, though both vessels are used in Newport for trade with the Caribbean islands. He tells him that someday he will learn to sail a ship like this one.

Tommy touches everything, the ropes, and the sails. "What kind of wood is used for the keel? What does this ship weigh? How many cannons does it have?"

Ned tells him that most ships of this type are between twenty and eighty tons and have three or six cannons.

"Can I touch the cannons?"

Ned lets him touch one. "It's loaded with cartridges by a powder boy."

"What does he do to get it to fire?"

"A powder boy puts a bag with six pounds of powder in the muzzle of the gun and rams it down until it can be felt with a priming iron thrust through this hole. Imagine I've a bag" he says, pretending. "Then the powder boy puts it in and rams it and cries Home!"

"Home!" says Tommy pretending to put an imaginary powder

bag in the muzzle. "Home!" he shouts again. "But we need the round shot first, don't we?"

"That goes in next," Ned says, and he puts in an imaginary round shot. "It's made of iron. Now I must follow it by a wad that also is rammed down hard." He lets Tommy pretend to ram it all in.

"I'm the captain of our team, Tommy, and I must fill it with more powder from this horn I carry. Now we're ready to fire the cannon. But we also need a spark from a flintlock, a kind of glowing wick from a gun. I'll give you the order, and when I do, you'll light the spark and put it into the powder. Are you ready?"

"I'm ready." Tommy's face is flushed with excitement as he pretends to create the spark to shoot the cannon.

"Stand back men. Fire!" Ned says. They both say "Boom!" at the same time then laugh afterwards, for they are startled by a loud noise as a sailor drops a barrel on deck.

"Can I do it for real? Can I be a powder boy?" he asks. That afternoon Tommy begins a life-long fascination with guns and receives his first warm hug from his father.

13

MOUNT HOPE

It's the largest council meeting Metacom has ever attended. The many tribes and small bands that make up the Wampanoag Nation have come from every part of their nation. Their lands are smaller now than in Dawn Time. The Narragansetts have taken much of what the English call Rhode Island, and many new English settlements are being established close to their villages. Chief sachem Massasoit wants to discuss the future.

People have come across the big bay by small birch bark canoes down narrow inlets as well as by large dugout canoes holding twenty people. Many arrive on horseback. Chief *sachem* Massasoit tells Metacom to greet their guests at the shore and help them with their canoes. Little Bird escorts them to temporary *wetu*s in the meadow.

The *sachems* haven't come alone; they bring advisors, wives and children. They bring gifts of tribute for Massasoit. He's been their Chief *sachem* for over thirty years. As tribute they bring hides, corn, squash, pumpkins, beans, clams, scallops and alewives. When Massasoit sent a messenger telling them this would be an important council meeting, they didn't hesitate to get ready to come. Everyone is anticipating long speeches around the fire, a delicious feast, and dancing to drums. They look forward to connecting with siblings who now live with families in other villages.

Old *sachem* Annawon has come from the north, near

Squannaconk swamp. He and Massasoit are childhood friends. Wamsutta, Massasoit's oldest son, whom the English call Alexander, and his wife Weetamoo, whose hair is shiny from bear grease, cross the river at Pocasset. She brings a servant girl to fix her hair and help her dress in a new tunic with red quillwork. She looks forward to gossiping with *squaw sachem* Askamaboo. These two women like to share stories about women elders.

English settlers have settled very near Cordibant's village. He tells people that they call their settlement Swansea after a place in a country called Wales. Tispaquin brings his daughters from Assawampset Pond, Place of White Stones, a lake four square miles, in the hopes that they will find husbands. Many bands visit there in the spring when thousands of alewives come into the nearby Namasket River, the Place of Fish.

Sachem Tyasks comes from Acushaet, west of Cape Cod, which is also called Cushnea, Peaceful Place Near Water. He helps his old mother out of the canoe. She's here to take care of her mischievous grandchild. Totoson's band comes from Mattapoisett, a place of swamps and sandy shores. They bring clams.

Coneconam comes with the Manomet, a band that lives on a big hill near Plimouth Plantation. He tells Metacom many Wampanoag people have been converted by a missionary named Thomas Mayhew and his son.

Metacom doesn't like this. "A squaw named Rebecca came from that place and tried to convert my wife. Little Bird liked her, and so did my children, but I made her go away. We don't need to be saved."

Piawant crosses the Taunton River from Assonet Bay with his oldest boy. From the far off island the English call Martha's Vineyard, Nohtooksaet's band arrives with Pahkepunnasso whose band is called Chappaquiddick and their village is called Noepetchepi-Aquidenet. They bring Metacom oysters, and tell him that some English have established among the salt marshes, red cedar woods, blue heron and other birds, a town they call Edgartown.

Sachem Massasoit's messenger told them it is time to talk about these strangers from across the Great Waters who buy or take land, cut down trees, bring cows, hogs, chickens, chase deer away from our meadows. It's time to decide what to do when hogs and cattle trample our corn fields and eat our sacred crops: corn, squash, and beans. It is time to consider those people who worship Lord Jesus and reject our **manitoo,** and refuse to pay appropriate tribute to our Chief **sachem** Massasoit.

Soon the great meadow is filled with people. The smoke from cooking fires fills the air with the smell of roasting fowl and deer. Little Bird listens to the women gossiping as they pound corn in hollowed out logs and then put it in large kettles to be boiled. She walks from one group to another, welcoming them, showing appropriate hospitality especially to the young and the old.

A small circle of young boys surrounds an old man who is drawing a picture of a wolf on the cheek of one of their friends using a sliver of bone and black dye. Little girls gather leaves to make beds for dolls made of rushes or hide.

Old women are comparing the quality of their quill work. They show the young girls how to soften the quills in their mouths and then sew them carefully into the hide. They point out patterns most admired by their husbands.

Young adults looking for mates gather near the men beating drums. A boy speaks softly to a shy young girl with red pigment on her forehead and chin. The girls wear short tunics and are admired by the boys for their muscular legs. They begin to lift their legs to the rhythm of the drums. Little Bird remembers the time when she was young and first danced with Metacom, choosing him secretly in her heart to be her husband. Someday her daughter Laughing Like Water and her son Little Thunder will join theses dancers to find the ones they want to marry. She hopes they will give her many grandchildren.

When the dancing and the feasting are over, and the games boys who have been playing with painted rocks or with throwing hoops have already been won or lost, the meadow is quiet. In the darkness, small fires dot the meadow and mothers sing babies to sleep.

Metacom makes sure the fire on the sacred council ground in front of the longhouse is burning well and there's plenty of firewood nearby. Now he sits near his father and his brother Wamsutta and watches the *sachems* and their advisors and oldest sons gather here for the council meeting. They sit cross-legged on mats placed around the fire in a semicircle facing Massasoit and his sons.

Chief *Sachem* Massasoit has past his sixtieth year. His skin is wrinkled from the sun. He wears around his neck the ceremonial wampum belt which is over nine inches wide.. He also wears a thin one with a star made of purple beads. A red headband with three eagle feathers is on his head and around one shoulder is a mantle of soft doeskin. Little Bird has decorated it with a painting of an eagle.

Massasoit puts tobacco into his long- stemmed stone bowl shaped like a man's head. He hands sacred tobacco to Metacom and asks him to throw some into the fire for the *manitoo*. He puffs on the ceremonial pipe, and then passes it to the *sachems* from the largest bands.

There is silence. Everyone waits patiently. Finally old Hobbamock, Little Bird's father, stands and says a prayer:

"We, the Original People, People of the Rising Sun, thank you Maushop for the warm sun and flowing rivers with bountiful fish, for letting loose the wind eagle's wings so cool breezes blow, for this sacred tobacco, for deer, bear, fox and beaver, for teaching us how to make the canoes that brought us to this sacred council under a star filled sky."

Metacom points out to his brother Wamsutta his constellation, the Great Bear.

Hobbamock continues. "We are a part of all things on earth and in the sky. We are a part of all that was, all that is, and all that will be. We are together, each part of a whole, for we are one people, one nation. Tonight let each say what is in his heart, and let everyone listen with respect. Let us understand the truth."

Chief *sachem* Massasoit speaks. "I thank you for your gifts, and for your blessings. I will give more land to those whose families have had children."

He puffs on his pipe and pauses. "There is sad news. We have killed our cousins the beaver for guns, iron tools, blankets. There are fewer than ever this year, and soon they will no longer be our neighbors. Some of us owe wampum to the strangers for trading goods, so they have given away land. They forgot that all our land belongs to the nation and only I can give or sell it. It's time to think about our future." He passes the pipe to the other *sachems*.

"We have lived in peace with the English for over thirty years. We have taught them how to survive in our nation. They have signed a treaty with us to protect us from our enemies. But will peace with these strangers continue for our sons and grandsons? Too many are coming and they all want our land. What will be left for The First People? We have a guest tonight who wishes to discuss these things."

Massasoit introduces Cushamakin, the Chief *Sachem* of the Massachuset people, who stands, takes off his wampum belt, and holds it up to the sky with both hands. "In the markings woven here I see the history of my nation. This line is broken so I can remember a time of great sickness. Here is a design which reminds me a white man called Hunt kidnapped my grandfather and made him a slave in a distant land. I don't want any more sad stories woven here. My people say the English will protect them, but do we need protection from the English? We are an ancient people who have always lived here. I ask you, my friends, to think about these things."

Nahtooksaet, from the island the English call Martha's Vineyard speaks next. He says many in his village admire a white preacher and don't call a *pawwaw* when their child is sick. And if two men fight they want the preacher to solve it, not the elders."

Hobbamock speaks. "We don't need a Great Book to know about the **manitoo**. We don't need a Book to teach us to be hospitable to guests or how to treat our families and friends. We can heal sickness. Our elders should decide if there is conflict. We are not inferior to these strangers; we should not pay tribute to them."

A younger man shouts: "We are not inferior" and other young men join in chanting these words until Massasoit silences them. "Nothing need be done now, but it is good to share our thoughts." He ends the meeting with these words:

"We are the Original People. We must remain a free and independent nation. We must pray to Maushop and respect all living things who share this earth with us. Our hearts will tell us which promises to trust. Rest well and we'll feast again tomorrow."

That night Metacom holds his flintlock in his hands and examines it in the light of the full moon. He feels the smooth wood of the stock. It is much lighter than the musket Governor Bradford gave him years ago. He will learn all the secrets of this gun. He will protect his people.

Part Four

1657 - 1677

NEWPORT

"Tommy, stop cleaning that flintlock. You've been at it all morning. Your father's ship will be here this afternoon. I want you to come with me to welcome him home from the Caribbean." Comfort has finished cleaning the large kettle and places it back near the heath.

Her son is fifteen. His interest in guns and cannons has never pleased her. Now he wants to join his uncle's militia in Plimouth. She's refused to let him go.

"Uncle Willie and Ben Church have invited me to train with them next month," he said this morning as she served him a third helping of porridge with milk and lots of sugar. She's amazed at how much a fifteen year old boy eats.

"Wait until you're eighteen. That's when your father began."

She and Ned argue about Tommy's future. She hates war and doesn't want him to be a soldier, but Ned feels he'd be a good soldier. He was always interested in the stories about the civil war Ned told him.

If only she'd had a daughter. Her father, just before he died last year, told her how much he enjoyed having a daughter who loved languages, history and literature. During his last illness, right before he died, he told her he was proud of her. Tears filled her eyes. He said she must always use her language ability to keep the peace with the Wampanoags.

Her brother Willie says the new Governor, Thomas Prence, has been bullying Wamsutta, Massasoit's oldest son. Since Chief *sachem* Massasoit has died, Wamsutta has been ordered not to sell land without Prence's approval, but he's not obeyed. Willie's worried and wants her come to translate next time Wamsutta visits. She'll wait until Ned leaves again in two weeks, for he hates all Indians now and doesn't want her to be involved.

Tommy puts his flintlock away, and goes to visit Mary Dyer's son Peter.

Comfort takes in the clothes put outside to dry in the sun, folds them and puts them away. If only she had a daughter to help with the chores. God didn't bless them with any other children, only Tommy. Anne Bradstreet just sent her a book of proverbs she wrote for her eight, four girls and four boys. Maybe if she had been able to give Ned several children, her marriage would be stronger now. She certainly wouldn't be so lonely.

He goes away for long periods of time. His shipping business has been successful. He takes timber, cod, and horses to Barbados and brings back sugar and molasses. William Coddington supplies the horses used in the sugar mills to crush the cane. Ned says it must be processed quickly before the juice ferments and spoils. African slaves on Barbados have discovered a way to make rum from the cane and Ned brings some back. She thinks he stays away longer than necessary because he's dazzled by the wealth of the Plantation owners. He probably enjoys drinking the rum and flirting with their daughters. He says he likes to stay there because she argues with him too much when he returns home.

Of course she argues. He's supporting slavery. Rhode Island has passed the first law against slavery in New England; in Boston slavery is legal. She and Mary Dyer organized meetings with the

Quaker women and asked them to encourage their husbands to vote for it. West Africans are replacing Irish indentured workers and Indian slaves. This must stop. By working with the slave owners, and bringing them food for the slaves, Ned is supporting this immoral practice.

Why can't he bring fish, apples, and vegetables from Rhode Island's fertile farms to the coastal towns here? There are many new towns; more people arrive every year. But Ned refuses to change, no matter how many times she begs him to do so.

A ship captain has delivered a letter yesterday from Henry Vane. The letter explains why so many people are leaving England. Cromwell has started a war with the Dutch. Also people dislike the fact that Oliver Cromwell is behaving like a king who has absolute power. She reads it again before it putting in Ned's correspondence box.

HENRY VANE'S LETTER

Cannon smoke fills the air over the Atlantic Ocean. Many English and Dutch war ships have been destroyed. Oliver wants to expand our Empire's control of trade. I am trying to convince Parliament to pass another unpopular tax, for I need money to repair our ships.

I confess, dear friends, I can no longer hide my dislike of Oliver Cromwell. He wants to be a dictator for life and intends to pass on absolute power to his son. Some generals are even urging him to accept a crown. This is totally unacceptable. We fought so long and hard to rid England of a King who wanted absolute authority. Oliver no longer cares what I think. The Irish Catholics are still being persecuted and he's imposing his religious ideas on everyone. He's closed the theatres, making our friend John Milton angry. Many people are leaving London. Don't be surprised if many of them arrive in Rhode Island.

Not only have more English come, especially Quakers, but

Protestants called Huguenots have left Catholic France and come to Newport. Also Jews, forced to leave Portugal and Spain because of the Inquisition, are seeking refuge here. Comfort and Mary Dyer help newcomers adjust to life in Newport. Sometimes her Irish servant Maggie comes with her to meet those coming from Ireland.

This year Ned built another room on their home for a pretty Irish girl, a former indentured servant, named Maggie whom he brought from Barbados. She has long red hair and sparkling green eyes and a mature woman's curves. She works with Ned to help him keep his accounts and warehouse organized.

When Ned is gone, Comfort attends Quaker meetings held in John Easton's home. John and his father Nicholas were followers of Ned's mother and came to Rhode Island with her. Now they are prominent officers here and have become Quakers who believe the Spirit of God is within, decisions should be made by consensus, and fighting in a war and supporting slavery are not acceptable. Mary Dyer, also a Hutchinson follower, became a Quaker missionary in England and is Comfort's friend.

She sends Maggie to bring Tommy home from the Dyer's house, for it's time to leave for the harbor.

When they arrive at the wharf, they see Ned's ship has arrived, but he isn't finished supervising the unloading of the large barrels of sugar and molasses. His workers are bringing them to his warehouse.

"I want to go with my father to Barbados when he returns," Tommy says.

"No. I won't allow you to go."

What would he see if he went to Barbados? He'd see Africans, bent over, covered in sweat, cutting cane. Nearby, the burly overseer is ready to use his whip. Inside the mill young boys are sweating, standing over huge vats of boiling cane mash, stirring the boiling mixture. Outside men are trudging up the hill hauling huge bundles of cane. These slaves work sixteen hours a day. No, Comfort doesn't want her son to go to Barbados with his father.

Tommy sees a wagon close to his father's warehouse. A man is talking with his father. Is this stranger coming for molasses? The man, a huge fellow, is dressed like a farmer. Ned goes inside and comes out with two black children about twelve years old, a girl and boy. Are they slaves he's brought back from Barbados? They're barefoot and the lad is wearing torn black trousers and doesn't have a shirt. Tommy notices scars on his back. The girl wears a dirty, ripped, grey dress and keeps her head down. She has scars on her legs.

The boy turns, sees Tommy staring at him and spits in his direction. Then Tommy sees the man give Ned a bag of coins. Ned counts them. They're probably those newly minted pine tree coins made in Boston. He guesses this farmer has come from the Bay Colony where slavery is legal. The man forces the two frightened children towards his wagon by beating their legs with a whip. They climb in the back of his wagon. The wagon leaves and his father goes back inside.

"They're slaves, aren't they?" Tommy says, wiping away tears with the sleeve of his sweater. "Let's leave, mom."

* * * *

Later that evening she confronts Ned about the African children. "How could you do this? I worked so hard with John Easton to get the new anti-slavery law passed, and now you openly disobey it."

Tommy can't stand their arguments and he goes to the Dyer house again. He takes his gun to practice shooting.

"Stop trying to change the world! All nations accept slavery—England, Spain, Portugal, and the Dutch. Slaves provide needed labor. I'm sorry Mary Dyer's converted you into her Quaker faith. I can't stand hearing your shrill voice and seeing your disapproving face! You've become ugly to me."

"But why do you support this evil practice? Your mother spoke out against it. She didn't approve of selling Pequots into slavery. What you are doing now, selling children into slavery, makes me furious."

"I'm warning you for the last time, stay out of this or I swear I'll divorce you."

"I won't stay out of it, even if you do divorce me."

"You're too much like my mother," Ned says, his face red, his voice loud. "I resented her; she was obstinate, caused our exile, and that killed my dad. She took my sisters and brothers into hostile Indian country. I hate you for being like her."

She watches as he goes out the door. She's sad and exhausted. She knew this would happen, but now it's real.

"I'm going to the tavern. Living with you is like being put on trial."

2

PLIMOUTH

Governor Prence orders Willie to take an armed militia and force Wamsutta, also called Alexander, to sign the same treaty his father Massasoit signed years ago. He wants him to stop selling land to Quakers from Rhode Island.

"I like my new home in Eastham," the Governor says. "I'm thankful my Wampanoag neighbors on Cape Cod are Praying Indians. I'd rather have them as neighbors than Quakers. Many more settlers are coming from England and we need more land."

"Perhaps we shouldn't confront the young Chief *sachem* so quickly after his father's death," Willie says. "I'm going to ask my sister to come. She's known him since childhood."

As she rides quickly towards Plimouth on her brown mare, Comfort is thinking about her father and his relationship with Massasoit. He respected Massasoit for keeping his nation united even though there are many Wampanoag bands, and each has their own *sachem*, and they live in villages scattered about their territory. He tried to do the same as Plimouth became a plantation of scattered villages. They understood each other and trusted each other. What will happen now that both have died?

She remembers how much the Massasoit and the people of Plimouth respected Will Bradford. Respect. That's the key. Without it you can't lead your people or negotiate with others. Without it, everything falls apart, even a marriage.

When she arrives at the harbor she sees two large Indian canoes moving towards shore. English soldiers with flintlocks are sitting among the Indians in these canoes. Other armed soldiers are standing on shore waiting to escort them to the meeting which will take place in the house she grew up in that now belongs to her brother Willie.

* * * *

Chief *sachem* Wamsutta is seated on the floor Indian style. The five warriors who have come with him are standing against a wall. The Indians carry bows and arrows, but do not have guns.

Comfort greets Wamsutta in Algonquian. "*Aspaumpmauntam sachem,* how is the King?"

"*Asnpaumpmauntam,* I am well, Sky-Eyes," he says and smiles.

She watches as he stares at the armed militia. He's scowling, clearly angry to be forced to come to this meeting. Sending soldiers to bring him here and having so many armed men watching him shows great disrespect. He's the newly appointed king of an independent nation. He's wearing around his neck the blue and white beaded wampum belt, the symbol of the Chief *sachem's* authority.

Governor Prence speaks in a loud voice and stands over him. "You know why I've brought you here. Do as I have asked, Alexander. Promise to sell land only when I allow it. I will give you a treaty that promises your people our protection from your enemies, the Narragansetts. We will ensure that the land surrounding Mount Hope will be Wampanoag land forever." He holds a paper and a quill pen dipped in ink in his hand and, bending down, he pushes it in Alexander's face. "Enough delay. Sign now."

The *sachem* pushes his hand away forcefully. The quill pen and the treaty fall on the floor. The Governor picks them up, glares at Alexander, then turns his back and puts them on the table. He keeps his back turned for several minutes, trying to control himself.

Alexander talks politely to Comfort in Algonquian. "Tell him, Sky-Eyes, you are *netop*, my friend, so make him understand that I no longer use that English name Alexander which your father gave me when I was a boy. *Ntussawese*, I am called Wamsutta. I'm Chief *sachem*, King of an independent nation, and not his subject. I'll continue to sell my land to Quakers. I like them; they show respect."

Governor Prence grabs a flintlock from a soldier standing next to him and points it at Wamsutta's head. "I demand you sign the treaty."

The Wampanoag warriors prepare to shoot arrows. Willie looks at Captain Josiah Winslow. "Stop him," he says pointing at Prence.

Josiah Winslow puts out his hands and the Governor gives him the flintlock. Governor Prence leaves the room. He knows he won't be able to persuade this stubborn Indian to sign the treaty today. He speaks to Wamsutta in a respectful voice and asks Comfort to translate.

"Chief *Sachem* Wamsutta, your father went hunting with my father. Your father signed this treaty. It's in the interest of both our nations. Don't you want to keep harmony between us?"

"No, I won't sign it," Wamsutta says in English. "I must be the only one to decide about selling our land. Already we have sold *wautacone-nuaog*, coatmen, too much land. It is much more valuable than the things you give to us for it. We must keep it for ourselves."

Winslow sighs. "This is not a good time to sign a treaty. I invite you and your friends to a feast. I hope you'll return soon and you will be ready to sign. We are neighbors. We have traded for many winters. Your father helped us when we came here and we are grateful. Accept our hospitality now."

Four girls bring in trenchers of roast pig and tankards of beer. Wamsutta knows his men are hungry and decides to enjoy the feast. He eats a lot and drinks several tankards of beer. Comfort sees that he is touching his stomach and seems ill. She knows he's always been sickly but thinks this is probably only indigestion.

When the Indians leave, Winslow tells her and Willie he's hopeful the treaty will be signed. Comfort's not so sure. Wamsutta knows their land is worth more than they get for it, and fears too much is being transferred into English hands. The Wampanoags want to continue to be an independent nation.

"He felt insulted," she tells her brother after hugging him goodbye. "The Governor shouldn't have used force. Wamsutta must prove his independence." She leaves for Newport, wishing her father was still alive.

Shortly after he arrives at Mount Hope, Wamsutta dies. Metacom sends a messenger to Governor Prence accusing him of poisoning his brother.

3

NEWPORT

Roger William's canoe moves slowly between two large sailing ships anchored in Newport harbor. Even though he's in his sixties, he has great strength in his arms and usually paddles his canoe from Providence. The sun is beginning to set, and the pink and orange clouds bring thoughts of calm weather; but Roger's mind is not calm.

Most of the cargo has been unloaded from the large vessels and is piled on the dock. A sailor lights a lantern on a ketch, and nearby an old man is washing the deck of his fishing boat with buckets of water.

As he gets closer to the wharf, Roger hears bawdy songs coming from the tavern. Rowdy sailors will be handled by the night watchman. He ties up his canoe and walks to Ned's house, his lame leg hurting with every step. He's using the walking stick his son Joseph has made for him. Roger isn't working the land anymore. He has given most of his land to newcomers. With Joseph's help, his trading post in the north now provides enough income to feed his family. He has come tonight because he knows Ned will be leaving for Barbados again in a few days, and wants to tell him that he should go to London instead.

Comfort tells him to sit in the cushioned chair by the fire and she asks Tommy to help him take off his wet shoes and put them near the fire to dry. She brings his favorite drink, a brandy made from pear juice. She's always glad to see him, but sees his somber face, so she expects he's bringing bad news.

"Ned's upstairs going over last month's accounts with Maggie. I'll tell him to come down." Roger fills his pipe with tobacco.

When Ned comes down, he shares some bad news. "I've received a letter from John Milton. He says he has lost hope for reform. Our revolution of the people has been lost."

"It was lost when Cromwell made himself Protector," Ned says. "What's happened now?"

"King Charles' son has returned from exile in France and has declared himself King Charles II."

"Were there riots?" she asks Roger. "Milton wrote to us that many were tired of Cromwell and his corrupt generals controlling the towns. I didn't think they'd welcome the monarchy back."

"Well they did. They lined the main roads, cheering, and shouting 'Long Live Charles II.' They want stability. They like having a King. It's part of our history, our identity as a nation. Of course, the king's son came back from France with twenty thousand armed men on horseback. It would have been a bloody massacre had there been any resistance."

"Why do you think this happened?" Ned asks.

"The economy has been bad for a long time. Cromwell was a cruel dictator, especially towards Irish Catholics; thousands have been killed. You know he sent Irish children to be indentured servants on the sugar islands. You've seen them in Barbados and you've brought Maggie home with you." He takes out a letter and puts on his spectacles. "John Milton always says things better than I can. I'll read parts of his letter."

JOHN MILTON'S LETTER

We couldn't save the freedoms we won...too many disagreements, too much taxation of merchants who didn't want to pay for an army which was meddling in their affairs. So much was won, only to be lost again. We won the right to worship according to our conscience, to petition Parliament, to write and publish without censorship. Oh how I had hoped our example would inspire the world! Keep the lamp of freedom burning in the New World, my friend, for it's gone out here.

Comfort closes her eyes and remembers John's intense eyes, long wavy hair, and the blue velvet suit he wore. She blushes, thinking of his passionate kisses in the carriage when they were returning from the masque. He took her to see the medieval garden at Old St. Paul's, to attend the performance of Inigo Jones' masque at the palace, and to meet his 'invisible college' friends. His spirit must be crushed by the return of the monarchy. Perhaps his actor friends will return again to stages in London. He'd be happy about that.

"How's John's health?" she asks, fearing the worst.

"Not good. He was arrested briefly by King Charles II. Thankfully they let him go because he's famous; he's also blind. He spends his days dictating a long poem called "Paradise Lost" to his daughter. John's worried sick about Henry Vane."

"Has Charles II decided to get revenge on those who killed his father? Has he called Henry a regicide even though Henry didn't sign the King's death warrant?" Ned asks.

"Listen to the rest of John's letter." He reads it aloud.

There is such madness going on. They've dug up Cromwell's corpse, cut off his head and hung his body at Tyburn, then put his head on a pike. Sir Henry is charged with treason and locked in a dark, cold cell in the Tower of London. He won't beg for mercy. He doesn't have a lawyer. I believe they'll hang him. Come here as quickly as you can and help me convince him to beg for mercy. Others who have done so have been freed. Our dear friend is too proud to do so.

"I've booked passage on The Abigail leaving for London next week. The King promised clemency to many, but wants to make an example of Henry. While in London, I'll ask our new King to renew our charter. We need protection from land speculators in the Bay Colony who continue to desire our land. I'll pay for your passage Ned if you come with me. Perhaps we can get Henry a lawyer who can free him."

"I owe Henry so much. Of course I'll come," Ned says. "I can pay for my passage."

"Good." Roger smiles for the first time since he arrived. He drinks a little pear brandy.

Ned looks at Comfort. Their impending divorce must be postponed. "Will you keep the business going while I'm gone?" he asks Comfort.

"I'll do what's needed." She won't allow the sea captain to bring more slaves here, but she doesn't say so.

That night she tells Ned to be careful. "Don't say anything in public against the King; he might arrest you. Poor Frances. Go to see her, Ned. Henry once wrote us he was in charge of selling the King's art and possessions to have money to pay the army. His Majesty's son might take all of Henry's wealth and Raby Castle to punish him."

"I'll be careful and you need to be also. I fear Metacom will take revenge for his brother's death. Don't go to Mount Hope. That's an order." He doubts she'll obey.

"John Sassamon spends time these days helping Metacom write land deeds in English. He says he thinks Metacom no longer believes Wamsutta was poisoned. His brother has often been sick. I'm invited to Metacom's coronation; I intend to go. It's necessary to have his friendship if we are to have peace."

"When will you stop getting involved with these savages?"

"When you stop supporting slavery."

"I only brought two children and the farmer promised to treat them well. They'll be better cared for here."

"Ha! From small beginnings, good things blossom, my father used to say. Well I say evil acts can seem small, but can have huge consequences. People must never accept slavery. I'm helping John Easton enforce our colony's anti-slavery law. If you bring more children to sell into slavery here, I'll have to report it to John."

Ned slaps her face. They stare at each other. He says he's sorry, but she ignores him and tucks her pillow under her arm, and goes downstairs. She will sleep with Maggie until he leaves. Her marriage is broken, and with another long separation and an ocean between them, it'll stay that way.

He knows he shouldn't have hit her. Most wives obey their husbands, so why can't she? She's too much like his mother and will bring disaster again into his life.

Comfort can't sleep. She endured loneliness before, but she's concerned that there will be gossip about her. Some will blame her for not being a good helpmate. Tommy will blame her for the divorce. She'll confide in her close friends, Mary Dyer and John Easton. John wants to go with her to Mount Hope for Metacom's coronation. His wife died last year, so there'll be gossip.

4

MOUNT HOPE

They've come from more than thirty villages, and represent the nine bands of the Wampanoag tribe. Today Metacom is being celebrated as their Chief *sachem* and will be honored with feasting and dancing. Temporary *wetus* have been set up everywhere in the village.

Comfort and John Easton walk through the village with several small children following them. A girl asks to touch Comfort's hair and clothing. The youngest giggles when she says "*askutta-aquompsin*, how are you?" John imitates her words, for he desires to learn the Wampanoag language. He bends down and gives the children sweet cakes he has brought.

She recognizes Weetamoo, *squaw sachem* of the Pocasset band, Wamsutta's widow and Metacom's sister-in-law. She says she's so sorry he is *mauchish*, gone.

"He has gone to *Kautantowwit*, the great south-west God." Weetamo is wearing a tunic with red quillwork flowers. Comfort admires it.

"*Taubotneanawayean*, thank you" she says.

Comfort recognizes Awashonks, *squaw sachem* of the Sakonnets and greets her in Algonquian. "*Aspaumpmauntam committamus*, how are your children?"

"*Konkeeteaug*, they are well."

Comfort points out Cordibant to John. "His village is nearest to the English village Swansea where Susanna and Sassamon live with their sons. And over there is Coneconam from Manomet, a village near Cape Cod, talking to Nohtooksaet who is the *sachem* from Martha's Vineyard. Next to them is Pahkepunnasso *sachem* from Chappaquiddick Island. They all recognize Comfort and welcome her.

They see Little Thunder, Metacom's son, sitting in a circle playing a game with painted stones. Tommy is with him, also throwing these stones. She hasn't seen him for a few weeks because she finally agreed to let him stay with his uncle and become part of the Plimouth militia. This is gambling game, and Tommy knows Comfort disapproves of it. He continues playing, and doesn't speak to her. He's blames her for making his father want a divorce.

Comfort remembers Tommy's screams as a child when she took him away from Mount Hope. *Neemat*, my brother," he yelled, holding his little arms out to Little Thunder, demanding to be rescued from this woman he called "the English lady".

Willie has brought Tommy here as well as Ben Church. They're both Captains in the new United Militia. Rhode Island was not invited to join. John Easton is introduced to Willie and Ben.

Ben, a plump, cheerful young man, is full of curiosity about Indian language and customs and asks Comfort questions.

"Did you tell Ben how you used to wrestle with Metacom when you two were boys?" Comfort asks her brother.

"He usually won," Willie says.

When the men talk about training soldiers, Comfort leaves to seek out Little Bird.

She's supervising two women stirring large clay pots of stew.

"Sky-Eyes, *netop*, friend, *notammaun*, I'm busy. Where is Little Raven?"

"Over there, with Little Thunder, *asauanash*, playing a game," she says, pointing.

"Ask him to say hello to me. Come, see what we're going to be eating today."

Comfort peers into the pots. Little Bird says this one has sweet fish, *osacontuck*, with wild leeks, and that one has venison stew, and the other has *aupuminea-naw-saump*, boiled corn porridge.

"Help me fill these baskets with nuts and berries." They work together, until all are full and Little Bird goes to give them to the *sachems* of each band.

"Don't forget. Tell Little Raven to come see me."

In another part of the village, boys are getting tattoos. She and Tommy watch as an old man finishes painting a picture of a wolf on the chest of a boy. He uses two mixtures of animal fat, one with black and another with red pigments. He paints with a sliver of bone."

"I'm next" Tommy says, unbuttoning his shirt.

"Don't you dare."

He laughs. "Just teasing, mom."

"Find Little Bird. She wants to see you."

Metacom comes over to the old man. He is wearing a breech-cloth; his chest is bare. His arms and legs have tattoos on them. He greets her warmly. "Sky-Eyes, I'm happy you've come."

"You'll be a good *sachem*, as wise as your father, *netop*."

"If your people stop trying to convert my people there will be peace." He says something to the old man, and sits down to get a tattoo. "Stay. See how well he draws my spirit guide."

Does he blame her for the missionary work? She's only a translator and teacher. Doesn't he want his people to read their own tongue? Today is not a good day to argue with him.

The old man has been told to draw a standing bear on his chest. He mixes more black pigment with fat, and takes a new sliver of bone and draws the bear. She admires it. "You look very handsome, *netop*."

Metacom smiles. "***Taubotne aunanamean***, I thank you for your love."

Comfort feels better and goes to find John Easton, Ben Church and her brother Willie.

"A part of me will always belong to this world," she tells Ben Church.

"I've bought land for me and my new wife Alice from the *squaw sachem* Awashonks. I'm determined to be her friend. I want to learn their language also."

They watch as the ceremonial platform is being covered with a large blanket made of raccoon skins. The tails have been left on and hang down the front of the platform. In the inner circle around it, the *sachems* of the nine bands sit with their oldest sons, and around them, making a much larger outer ring, are the grandparents, wives and children who have come for the feasting and dancing after the ceremony.

Metacom climbs on the platform wearing Massasoit's ceremonial wampum belt around his neck. It's nine inches wide and reaches almost to his ankles. Another one, shorter and thinner, with a star made of the purple shell beads, rests on his chest. He also wears several strings of wampum beads and his bear claw necklace. On his head he wears a red headband with three eagle feathers. Around one shoulder is a mantle of hide painted with red geometric designs. He wears a breechcloth and moccasins decorated with quillwork. His skin shines from bear grease. He sits cross-legged on the platform. Next to him is his father's war club, a large wooden club with a handle of inlaid white shells. He lifts it up and shows it to the crowd, and then places it back on the platform by his side. Comfort thinks he looks very much like a king.

Little Bird joins him. Her shiny black hair is braided and she's wearing a light colored doeskin tunic with red flowers and a small bluebird painted on it. There is a turtle tattoo on her cheek indicating her clan. She looks happy and proud.

The *pawwaw*, a spiritual leader, lifts Massasoit's long-stemmed ceremonial pipe with its bowl carved like a man's head. Comfort recognizes it and remembers how her father used to smoke it with Massasoit.

The *pawwaw* points the pipe to the East, West, North and South, and then offers it to Metacom who puffs the sacred tobacco. Then the *pawwaw* passes it to each of the *sachems* of the nine Wampanaog bands.

It's time for Metacom to speak.

"I'll translate," Comfort tells John.

Metacom acknowledges the presence of each *sachem* and their band.

"Ah-iee! Ah-iee!" the people say after each leader is named.

He speaks about his dead father and brother. He says that their names should never be given to anyone else, out of respect for them. "This is their custom," Comfort whispers to John.

"We are the People of the First Light, the Dawn People. We've lived on this land a long, long time. We are a free nation and will remain so forever. I'm proud to be the Chief *Sachem* of the Wampanoag Nation."

"Ah-iee! Ah-iee!

"We live with all our cousins, owl and bear, deer and beaver. All creatures have *manitoo*. We are grateful for the sacred sisters, corn, squash, and beans."

He pauses, puffs the long-stemmed pipe and passes it around again to the *sachems*.

"Long ago Maushop, he who watches over us, turned into a whale. When strangers came to hunt him, he swam away. He comes back at the right season to make sure we have not become slaves of the strangers."

"Ah-iee! Ah-iee!"

"I invite you to feast, drink, and dance to the drums until you fall down happy and exhausted." He gets off the platform and walks about greeting everyone. Little Bird joins him and they admire the babies, and speak kindly to the elders.

Soon the teenaged boys and girls begin to dance in a circle to the drums, stomping and howling, and flirting. Many will find their mate tonight, Comfort thinks.

It's time for the English guests to leave for Plimouth. This feasting and dancing will continue until dawn. She wishes she could stay, but knows she'll always be a stranger.

5

LONDON

JOHN MILTON'S HOME

John Milton is fifty-two years old. The last few years of his life have been full of fear and despair. It's early morning and he's the only one awake. He's sitting in his book lined study thinking about the past. His guests, Roger and Ned, are still sleeping. He remembers those student days in Cambridge when he used to wake up early and tickle Roger's feet and offer to teach him Hebrew vocabulary in return for his assistance with Dutch grammar. Those carefree college days are like a hazy dream of pranks, debates, and competition for beautiful girls.

Reading by candlelight 'til one in the morning then getting up early for his class, that was his habit despite his poor eyesight. For years, the beautiful colors were fading, and now there's been only total darkness for eight years.

Roger's so tired of waiting for permission to see Henry Vane. He thinks someone may have murdered him. So many murders have taken place in that dreadful dungeon. Last night they stayed up talking and drinking past midnight, trying to understand what the consequences will be now that they have a monarchy again. Parliament passed a law against Charles II claiming the throne, but twenty thousand soldiers and the people's disgust with Cromwell's corrupt generals forced us to repeal that law.

Milton wrote a pamphlet:

"If we let a king dominate us we're not free but servants. We should depend on God, reason, virtue and industry. In a Commonwealth a leader can be removed and punished but it's difficult to remove a tyrant who claims he's chosen by God. The happiness of a nation shouldn't depend on a single person."

Charles II sent soldiers to arrest him. This was after they made him watch them burn his books in the square. Thanks to his friends and blindness he was released. The regicides, those who signed his father's death warrant, they have already lost their heads. Henry didn't sign the warrant, but he's going to be put on trial if he's still alive.

* * * *

It's late afternoon that day, and the three friends are sitting in the rose garden drinking Madeira wine. Ned has decided to share his pain about his failed marriage.

"We aren't compatible anymore. We've both changed. I can't live with who she's become. If I don't leave her ...well... it will be horrible for both of us. I must confess that I slapped her face hard right before I left. I felt so guilty about it, but she wouldn't let me apologize. She took her pillow and left the bed."

"How could you hit her?" Roger is angry. "What made you so angry?"

John says. "We won't judge you. We want to understand."

"She's become a Quaker, a fanatic, and is acting like a crazy person. She's says she must stop slavery. I don't approve of slavery, but the sugar industry in Barbados requires large plantations and African slaves to work on them if it's going to be profitable. I have to protect my business and accept this situation."

Roger turns to John. "Have you heard that thousands of West

Africans are being brought in slave ships to our plantations in the Caribbean?"

"They outnumber our people on Barbados. It started small but now there may be as many as fifty thousand already," Ned adds. "I must continue my shipping business there. What can I do about slavery? Comfort's being unreasonable."

"Our new King's planning to give a royal charter to a company that wants to promote the African slave trade. We can't stop this immoral practice. It's part of the effort to build a world-wide trading empire" John says.

"Slavery is legal in Boston, but we've passed an anti-slavery law in Rhode Island," Roger says. "Ned, you need to consider our new law and the strong anti-slavery feelings of the many Quakers living in Newport."

Ned is furious. "It's easy for you to say Roger. You've a trading post that provides income for your family. I'm still in debt to London merchants who have invested in my company. I've put all my money into buying the ship and warehouse."

John gets up and Ned takes his hand. "Let's take time out; I want to smell the roses in my garden. At least I can still get pleasure using my nose." Roger watches them. How fragile John seems to him at this moment. He's thinner than he's ever seen him. He needs that cane, and he needs Ned's arm to hold him.

When they sit down again, John changes the topic. "I've had enough of legal and controversial issues. It's time now for me to begin to write my epic poem. I can't see light, color, or the beautiful eyes of a woman, but I can smell these fragrant roses in my garden. Writing poetry, listening to music and smelling roses provide pleasure, but I want to find another wife. Two have died already, but I must have companionship. I long for the smells and soft skin of a young woman's breast; I long for all the pleasures of wild sexual passion." John looks at Ned. "May I ask you a personal question. "What is happening, or not happening, in your bed? Is there any passion between you and Comfort?"

"No. Well I travel to Barbados. I'm gone a lot. I had a young Irish mistress in Barbados. I've brought her home."

"Ah. I see. Sex is important, but when it's not an expression of love, it won't bring happiness. You loved Comfort so much once. I was jealous when I realized she was still in love with you. I rushed into a marriage with Mary who was half my age, immature and a royalist. A big mistake. She left me right after the wedding. I took her back years later. Love is essential for happiness, so if you don't love Comfort, I believe divorce is justified. You've read my scandalous essay about divorce, right? Does Comfort want a divorce?"

"I think so. She's probably worried about money. I assure you, I won't let her starve. Tommy is grown and wants to live with her brother Willie in Plimouth and join his militia."

Roger has remained silent. Ned sees the sadness in his eyes. He thinks of all those times she helped him: when he first arrived and was interested in learning Algonquian, and when he escaped banishment by going to Mount Hope for that winter. "I've known her since she was thirteen. I admire her for following her con-science and for wanting to keep peace with the Indians. I'll still need her help. I want to remain her friend and yours."

"What do you think is the basis of happiness?" John asks him.

"I've a wonderful family; that's a blessing. But for me following one's conscience is essential for true happiness. We all have lost loved ones, known pain and disappointment, but if we give up our values, we'll be denying our faith in God. Christ has given us free will to make choices, hopefully good ones. I must get the new charter, and it must guarantee freedom of religion and democracy, or I won't be happy. I don't love all the Quakers in my colony, they're sometimes difficult, but I always try to find compromise. Comfort is a valuable citizen and I hope, whatever you decide to do, Ned, you'll support her and help her make a new life for herself."

John agrees. "The Quakers believe in tolerance, oppose war and support equality between rich and poor, men and women. I've heard they've been persecuted in Boston. Is that so?"

"Yes. The magistrates have banished them, cut off their ears and used a hot iron on their tongues. It will get worse, I fear." Roger sighs. "Do you still have hope things will get better here?"

"I do. Let me tell you what gives me hope. The King has invited the Jews to return after hundreds of years of banishment. He'll certainly be more tolerant of Catholics since he has a Catholic mother. Oliver was far too brutal against them and their churches and the Irish will always hate him. Our invisible college will soon become a Royal Society to support science. Our trade is expanding to the East, bringing new textiles, spices and more jobs. The merchants supported the return of the monarchy and they will profit from that but I also hope they'll be willing to help educate the masses, for without that we can't have a republic. We fought for a democratic Commonwealth; we'll get it I'm sure, but might not for a long time. When we do, I want educated people to vote. Meanwhile I am proud of Rhode Island; it's a fine experiment in democracy and tolerance thanks to your hard work, Roger."

"Hopefully the King won't try to control the colonies or tax us unfairly." Roger replies. He gets up. "I'm off to bed earlier tonight. Perhaps we'll be lucky tomorrow and get permission to see Henry."

Ned spends a difficult night, tossing about, feeling guilty. Roger and John made him feel sad about his divorce. Perhaps, he'll wait a while longer. Maybe, when he returns home, she'll have changed.

6

RHODE ISLAND

As she walks to John Easton's house for the Quaker meeting, Comfort is remembering the many pleasant days she has spent with John this month. On chilly days, she and John have sat near the fire practicing Algonquian pronunciation. On sunny days, with fluffy white clouds over Goat Island, they have spent afternoons reading Anne Bradstreet's poetry outdoors. He's a widower and she knows he finds her attractive. Mary Dyer says John's the most intelligent and kindest widower in Newport, and Comfort should accept if he asks her to marry him after her divorce is final.

She smiles, remembering that evening prayer meeting in the woods for those Narragansetts interested in Quaker beliefs. Comfort and John attended. The Indians liked the idea of a spirit within each person, for they also believe people have a *manitoo,* spirit. After the meeting John walked her home. He kissed her goodnight, not as a friend, but passionately, holding her tightly in his arms. She didn't push him away. That was their first kiss.

The Quaker meeting today is very important because they must decide what to do about the persecutions in Boston. Two women Quakers from Barbados are in jail and their books were burned in the marketplace. They're old friends of Mary Dyer. They will be sent back to Barbados and Mary is very angry.

Ann Coddington tells those at the meeting about what she

saw in Boston on her last visit. "They whipped a woman with a knotted rope. I saw her back, all bloody and bruised. Then they dragged her behind a moving cart and kept on whipping her." She has to stop speaking because she's sobbing. John says there's a new law which requires giving the death penalty to anyone making a third attempt to establish a Quaker meeting there. Mary Dyer says she'll go again to challenge that law.

"You'll be in grave danger. Don't go," John says.

"My friends William Robinson and Marmaduke Stephenson are in jail. I must support them. God has spoken to me."

* * * *

The next week John learns from a visitor who has just come from Boston that William Robinson and Marmaduke Stephenson have been hung. Will Mary be next? He goes to Comfort's house to talk about this.

"My friend, Anne Bradstreet, wrote to me and said that her husband Simon was the only magistrate who voted against the death penalty law. Simon feels this persecution has gone too far and he's been trying to stop the madness."

"He obviously has failed. Do you think you could convince him not to hang Mary?"

"Maybe. I want to try. I'll go to Boston right away. I'll ask him to save her and I'll ask Anne to arrange meetings with women willing to try to convince their husbands to demand repeal of this terrible law. Mary was brave during Anne Hutchinson trial; I was too young and too scared and stayed silent then. I won't stay silent now."

"Don't tell them you're a Quaker. I couldn't bear it if anything happened to you."

7

Boston

Comfort searches in the crowd at Boston Harbor for Anne Bradstreet's lovely face. Time has not changed the affection they feel for each other. Anne sent her a poem last month about age.

My memory is short, and brain is dry
My almond-tree hair does flourish now,
And back, once straight, begins apace to bow.
My grinders now are few, my sight doth fail
My skin is wrinkled, and my cheeks are pale.

"You don't look old at all." Comfort says. She hugs her tightly. She notices that Anne is thin and has a cough.

"This body which has produced eight children isn't healthy anymore. Seeing you is good medicine."

Anne sets up meetings with women who might be sympathetic to saving Mary Dyer. Many remember Mary was their midwife years ago. They believe there's only a small chance Mary can be saved.

Over dinner at Anne's home Comfort listens as Governor John Endecott argues with Simon.

"We whip them 'till their backs are bloody, yet they return," he says. "Even after we cut off Christopher Holder's right ear, he returned. I tell you, John, it's not working. They're getting more converts because we're being too cruel. I don't see any end to the flow of Quakers. Perhaps it's time to change our policy."

"Never. It'd be a dark stain on my conscience to let them spread their poison in this colony," the Governor replies. "Tolerance is a weakness."

"But are we succeeding?"

"We will. After we exiled Hutchinson, we had peace. I won't change my mind."

"Please, John don't hang Mary Dyer," Anne says. "She has six children. I feel very strongly about this and so do many women."

"A woman with six children should stay home, not come here to confront us. Simon, make arrangements for a trial. We'll use that same tree on the common land to hang her. The soldiers must be armed in case we have trouble controlling the crowd."

Simon is upset. "Many will be angry to see a woman hang."

"You're wrong. They'll bring children to watch and use this to teach children not to disobey our laws!"

That night Comfort cried herself to sleep.

* * * *

Mary Dyer's trial is over quickly. She confronts the magistrates. "I came in obedience to the will of God who desires you to repeal your unrighteous laws. The Lord sent me to stand up for the right of individual conscience to worship as Our Lord reveals to us."

Endecott points a finger at Mary. "Your words speak of love, but you are such as Christ spoke of: outwardly you wear sheep's clothing, but inwardly you're a dangerous wolf come to destroy the public order."

Mary replies calmly. "My blood is on your hands. You'll suffer in this life as well as in the next."

"A prophesy" a woman shouts.

"She's a witch! Burn her!" screams a man from the back of

the room.

Comfort remembers that twenty-two women have been accused of witchcraft recently and eleven were Quakers. Mary isn't afraid to be called a witch or to be called a dangerous wolf. She is prepared to die, to be a martyr. Comfort sees defiance in her face.

Governor Endecott quiets the crowd. "I'm not afraid to judge you, Mary Dyer. Tomorrow you shall be hung by the neck until dead. This sentence will be carried out at three o'clock and all who wish to witness your punishment can gather at the large elm tree where we hung your two friends. This trial is over."

* * * *

The next afternoon a crowd gathers around a large elm. A ladder is placed and ropes are put on the platform. People have bought children and sit on the grass eating and drinking beer. How can they bring young children to witness this dreadful event? Comfort thinks. She stays close to the tree so she can speak words of love to her friend.

Just before three o'clock Captain James Oliver and a hundred armed militia lead Mary from prison to the platform under the elm. Many move closer to get a better view.

Comfort recognizes Reverend Wilson. His back is bent and his long, stringy white hair is blowing wildly in the breeze. He's taunting Mary: "Repent! Repent!" He shakes his walking stick at her when she tries to speak.

"I will not repent." Comfort hears her strong defiant voice despite the drumming by soldiers told to drown out her voice.

"Let her speak," several women are yelling. Others cry: "Free her! Free her now!" and "You'll not be forgotten Mary. The Lord loves you."

Mary prays silently as the executioner puts a rope around her neck. He ties another around her legs so her long skirts won't fly up when she swings in the air.

It's over quickly. The crowd rushes to leave, pushing one another across a small wooden bridge. Below it the Charles River is flowing rapidly below due to the rain this month. Too many people get on the bridge. It begins to creak and sway. It breaks apart, throwing screaming men, women and children into the water.

Many can't swim. Although some try to help others, they're pulled under by the rapid current as well as by people pulling on their clothes in panic. Comfort wasn't on the bridge, but she goes into the water to help a little girl clinging to her mother as they're swept away. She saves the child but the mother drowns.

When Comfort returns to the Bradstreet home, Anne says she'll see to it that the child is returned to a family member. Exhausted, Comfort sleeps, but cries out in the middle of the night.

"The Lord punished us for hanging Mary" Anne tells Simon. "I'll never get over this day. The wilderness has changed us, Simon; it's changed us into savages. We came to be free from an oppressive king and his bishops, but we have forgotten how to be compassionate. How should I explain this to our children?"

"I couldn't change Endecott's mind. And that bridge… I told him two years ago to get it rebuilt. My fear is that the new King, when he learns what we've done, will take away our charter, our independence. We're foolish if we think that just because we're on the other side of the ocean we can do anything we want. I may have to go to London to defend our laws, but in my heart I believe we're wrong. While I don't like these new religious sects, they're part of our times, our struggle for freedom."

Comfort leaves the next day. "At least we tried, Anne."

On the boat going to back to Newport she cries for Mary and her children. Why is it that men who were persecuted for their religious beliefs, are cruel to others seeking the freedom to worship? Without separation of church and state, such conflicts can't be resolved. God has compassion for us, so why can't we have more compassion for each other?

John Easton is relieved when he learns she's home and safe and goes to see her. "I'm so thankful you weren't on that bridge. Let me hold you." They spend an hour in silence, just kissing, caressing, holding each other, happy to be together.

Later that afternoon they help Mary's family plan her funeral. "Her funeral will be a testament to our determination to live free of religious persecution. Let's invite all our neighbors Jews, Huguenots and Baptists," John suggests.

"Does the new King know about this cruelty?" Comfort asks.

"He will. My friend Edward Burrough will go to London and tell him these laws against Quakers will continue to create dissent. This King's more tolerant than his father."

"Will the magistrates in Boston obey if he demands they allow Quakers to practice their faith?"

"Maybe. They know the King might send a Royal Governor to rule us; he's done that in the Caribbean colonies. We'll lose our independence."

8

MOUNT HOPE

Metacom has refused to sign the treaty with Plimouth. The Governor has asked John Easton and Comfort to go to Mount Hope to convince him to sign. Metacom's friend Tobias escorts them to his *wetu* without smiling or greeting them properly, so they think they won't be successful.

Metacom is angry. He doesn't want to talk about the treaty. "*Netop*, why do English torture and kill Quakers? They're honest, and respect us."

"We're Quakers, Chief *sachem*," John says. "We believe everyone has a seed of God's spirit within and Rhode Island doesn't interfere with our religious meetings. We have come to see you because we want peace with all our Indian neighbors."

"Ah, *aquene*, peace. Good neighbors. Not always." He gets up and walks back and forth for a few minutes, then looks into Comfort's eyes. "Sky-Eyes, I don't like those who convert my people. *Nummusquantash*, I'm angry. We have our ways and don't want to be like you. Praying Indians don't show proper respect to me, their King. Understand?"

"*Cummusquawname*, are you angry with me? I'm not converting anyone. I'm teaching people to read their own language. John Eliot is not forcing anyone to become Christian and people chose to live in his villages." She doesn't continue, for his furious expression scares her.

"*Nowetompatimmin*, we are friends, Sky-Eyes. *Tuppauntash*, consider what I say. We don't need *manitoo wussuckwheke*, God's book, to tell us to be good. Make your own people good first. Tell them to leave us alone. We like our ways."

John whispers "keep quiet."

Metacom gets up and tells Little Bird to show proper hospitality. She heats the porridge. He leaves the *wetu.* Little Bird gives them bowls of hot corn porridge and berries. She asks if Tommy is well, and Comfort asks about Little Thunder and Laughing Like Water.

When Metacom returns a little while later, he's calm and smiles.

"I know you want me to sign the treaty with Plimouth. I haven't decided. I don't like Prence. You're my friend, Sky-Eyes, just as our fathers were friends. John, you're honest. *Coaumwem*, you speak the truth. People in your colony are good neighbors to the Narragansetts. I'm glad to see you both. "

When they're ready to leave, Little Bird gives Comfort a small basket as a gift. Comfort takes off her bracelet made of blue glass beads and gives it to Little Bird. "I love you, my sister," she says."

On the journey home, John is worried. "Will he sign the treaty? I don't think so."

"Let's ask Reverend Sassamon to talk to him about it. He helps Metacom write land deeds and lives nearby in Swansea."

"What does Eliot think about Metacom's rejection of his missionary efforts?"

"He will work until his last breath to bring God's Grace to those open to learning about our faith. He keeps asking Sassamon to try harder to convert Metacom, but I told him that it will never happen and he shouldn't try to force him."

"Have you told Eliot you intend to divorce Ned as soon as he returns?" John asks.

"Yes. I told him Ned's bringing young African slaves back from

Barbados and selling them to farmers in Boston. Eliot is angry. He doesn't believe Indians or Africans should be slaves. All men have souls, and must not be used by other men like horses and oxen he said."

9

SWANSEA

Swansea, a town made up of three small villages, is about forty miles from Plimouth, near the Kickamuit River. It's very close to Mount Hope. The land is fertile and the settlers are tolerant. Many Baptists and Quakers from Rhode Island live here.

Reverend Sassamon used to live in Natick, but moved here with Susanna and their two sons. He's a preacher in Swansea and in the nearby Wampanoag village of Namasket. When he goes to preach in that village, he often stays in his cabin on the shore of Assawompsett Pond.

There have been conflicts lately between the settlers and the Wampanoags. The communities are too close; they're only separated by two marshy, tidal rivers. Pigs and cattle owned by the English are trampling Wampanoag cornfields and frighten deer away.

Metacom has demanded that Sassamon tell these settlers to build fences. He did but they haven't done so yet. They continue to bring cattle to graze on Wampanoag land which is used for hunting. They still haven't built fences. The sows have twenty piglets in a litter and two litters a year so many pigs are eating the Indians' corn.

Chief *sachem* Metacom and his son Little Thunder are hunting near the meadow the settlers use to graze their cows. It's Wampanoag land. Little Thunder is ready to shoot a doe entering the meadow from the bushes just as Sassamon's son Peter and five cows enter the meadow from the Swansea side. The doe is startled and runs into the woods.

Little Thunder aims an arrow at the boy.

"Stop" Metacom says. "That's Peter Sassamon. He has the red fire hair of his mother. Aim for the calf not the boy." The calf falls to the ground, and the other cows scatter. Peter runs home to tell his father.

"I told you to keep our cows away from that meadow," John says. "It's not our land; they hunt there. It's close to the woods."

"What should we do?" Peter says. "I saw Metacom and his son."

John gets two flintlocks and hands one to his son. "Let's get our cows home first. I'll call a town meeting when we're sure our cows are safe."

That night the Swansea meetinghouse is crowded with angry settlers. "My wife is shaking with fear. Let's take care of them before they kill all our animals," says a young fellow who has recently built a house near the river. "I can't afford to lose my cows."

"Does anybody know how many guns they have?" another newcomer asks.

"Too many" John says. He urges calm. "It's a misunderstanding. I know Metacom. He trusts me. I'll speak with him."

"My wife wants to move back to Rhode Island. We never had trouble like this from the Narragansetts. We've just had another baby, and I must keep my kids safe."

"I ain't leaving. I'm too old to start again." An older man picks up his gun. "I say strike fiercely, and strike first. Burn their wigwams and their cornfields. Let them go hunt somewhere else."

"Not a good idea," says another, shaking his head. He lifts his shirt and points to a long scar on his chest. "This here's from the Pequot War in '36. I was ready to take them on then. Don't do it, lads. They fight like wolves; attack where and when you least expect it."

"But if we show weakness won't they kill all our cattle and maybe us?" asks a newcomer.

"It's the fault of the Quakers; let's send them back to Rhode Island," says a man. "I never wanted to live among them."

"We're living too close to Mount Hope." John Sassamon says. "We must start building fences quickly. It'll show Metacom we mean to stay but also respect their hunting rights."

"I say force him to obey us. That's what we did in Boston in '45. We put that Narragansett Chief Miantonomo on trial and made him pay us thousands of wampum. Then we told that Uncas fellow to kill him. It worked, didn't it?"

"No. I say let's build those fences," Sassamon says. Finally they agree to do so.

Later that night Susanna asks John if he's sure that Metacom still trusts him.

"I think so. Eliot keeps urging me to convert him, but I've stopped trying."

"Perhaps we should return to Natick. It'll be safer for our boys."

"No. I like it here. I'm converting the Indians at Namasket. I love my little cabin on Assawompsett Pond." He likes the solitude, and enjoys fishing in summer. In winter he fishes through a hole in the ice. He hunts for wild turkey.

"But you saw your son's face. Peter's scared. I'm scared."

John doesn't want to discuss leaving Swansea. "We'll build a garrison house." He goes to sleep.

* * * *

One cold, snowy Sabbath afternoon shortly after this incident, Metacom and Little Thunder enter the meetinghouse in Swansea in the middle of John's sermon. They've come in to get warm. Little Thunder is carrying a large dead rabbit. He puts it on the bench. Every one stares at them.

"I'm glad to see you Chief *sachem*. You're always welcome. However, you must leave the dead animal outside. Our Lord forbids hunting on the Sabbath."

Little Thunder stands and holds up the dead rabbit. "You can't tell me what to do. I am not your subject. I only obey my father, the Chief *sachem*."

"Then I'll have to ask you to leave. It's our holy day. I respect your ways; I'm asking you to do the same for us."

Suddenly a nine year old boy stands up and grabs the dead rabbit. Little Thunder grabs it back and hits the boy on the head with it. The boy falls off the bench, and his father gets up and is ready to hit Little Thunder with a wooden walking stick he holds in his hand. John quickly tells the man to sit down.

"Treat my son with respect" Metacom says to the man. "We come as your guests today, but you are guests in my country."

Metacom walks up to Sassamon and grabs a silver button from his coat. He rips it off, and throws it on the ground. "I care as much for your God as I care for this button." He and his son walk out, leaving the door open, letting in howling wind and snow.

10

PLIMOUTH

Josiah Winslow is elected Governor of Plimouth. He decides to try again to force Metacom to sign the treaty.

He writes to Governor John Endecott of the Bay Colony to ask for support. "Send a representative here to the meeting I will hold with Metacom. We have a united militia; let's show him we'll act together."

Endecott refuses. "Chief *sachem* Metacom is your problem."

Winslow asks John Easton and Comfort Bradford to attend the meeting. If they're present, perhaps he'll agree to sign. He orders Willie and Ben Church, who are known to Metacom, to escort Metacom here. Tommy goes with them.

On the day of the meeting, Comfort and John Easton arrive early. Comfort wants him to understand what her childhood in Plimouth was like. She takes him through the fence to what once was Hobbamock's house. He and his wife have died and the compound is abandoned. All that is left is an overgrown garden and the bent poles of the *wetu.*

Comfort's mind is filled with fond memories. "This is good for your toothaches," she says, pulling up a plant and wrapping it in her handkerchief. She picks blue wildflowers to take to her parents' graves when they go up the hill.

"You were happy here. Why?"

"I loved the freedom to enjoy nature and see how they live life in a different way. I picked wild berries with Little Bird and her mother. When Metacom came, he'd tell us stories about bears and whales. He was funny, mischievous, and handsome. Little Bird and I called him 'Trickster Wolf'. When he chose Little Bird for his wife, I was jealous. Does that shock you?" She looks at him.

"No." He takes her chin in his hands and tilts her face up, looks into her eyes smiling, and kisses her. "I'm not very handsome, and far too serious, but I'll try to be more mischievous if it would please you."

She laughs. "I love you for who you are. Remember, I'm not divorced yet; please don't kiss me in front of my brother and son."

They go up the hill to her parents' gravesite to put the wild-flowers on their graves. She prays: "Please Lord, give me the strength and wisdom to help keep the peace."

"If your father were alive, would Metacom sign this treaty?"

"I think so, but times have changed. More new towns have been set up close to Wampanoag villages. John Sassamon told me about the problems in Swansea. New settlers don't respect the fact they're living on Wampanoag land."

* * * *

"Do you think Metacom will sign today?" John asks Governor Winslow.

The Governor points to the document on the table. "It's the same as the one his father signed. He must sign it."

Metacom arrives with twenty warriors. Their faces and bodies are decorated with black war paint. He has brought his father's war club and a flintlock. Most of the warriors are told to stay outside with the English soldiers. Some carry flintlocks, while others carry bows and arrows. Some warriors have shaved one side of their head so they can aim their bows and arrows quickly, while others have shaved both sides, leaving only a shiny band in the middle of their heads. Willie, Church and Tommy escort Metacom and his two closest advisors, Tobias and Mattashunannamo, inside.

Metacom stands before the Governor and speaks: "***Wautaconuags, Ketasontimoog, ahtakosog, Pokanoket.***"

Comfort sits at the table next to the Governor and translates. "Coatmen, I, the Great Chief, am here with my advisors, from Mount Hope."

Governor Winslow begins. "I thank you for coming and welcome you as my neighbor. Kindly speak English; I know you speak it."

Metacom replies in English. "I want to speak with your king, not you, for I represent a free nation."

"For over forty years we've been good neighbors," Winslow says. "Some of your people are killing our cattle and swine. We want you to sign this treaty and we insist that your people don't kill our animals. We want to approve all future land sales."

"Tell your people to keep their ugly pigs and cows off our land and not to steal our land. I know the boundaries of my land. I'm not stupid."

"Our people don't steal your land. We buy it."

"***Cuttiantacompawwem***" Metacom shouts.

"What did he say?" Winslow asks Comfort. He doesn't like this anger.

"He says you're lying."

"We have given you many things for land: kettles, hoes, many fathoms of wampum, blankets, warm coats, knives."

"Newcomers get men drunk then take land. These men can't sell tribal land, only I can. You want too much land. Go home."

"We have deeds with your mark. Put your mark on this treaty. Enough delay." He holds out a quill pen.

Mattashunamamo points his gun at the Governor. "Show respect."

Immediately, Willie demands the gun. Metacom says something in Algonquian to Mattashunamamo, and he gives Willie his gun. Comfort sees that Tommy's face is pale; he's very frightened.

Comfort speaks in Algonquian to Metacom. "*Tawhitch yo enean*, why are you doing this? *Netop*, friend, *aquie iackquessaaume*, don't be so hard," she says. *Wunishaunto*, let's agree. *Cowetompatimmin*, we're friends. *Awepu*, be calm."

Metacom tells his advisors to stay calm. Then he addresses the Governor with controlled anger. "You're greedy. Everything is about wampum. You want more beaver to sell, so our cousin the beaver will soon be gone. You convert my people and tell them not to pay tribute. I'll decide who to sell land to."

Winslow is more respectful. "Chief *sachem* Metacom I'm asking to please make your mark here. Give up all your guns; we'll protect you."

"You English think your ways are the only good ways. Here is my gun." He points to Comfort. "It was a wedding present from her father when I married *Wootonekanuske*. If you take back gifts, how can I trust your promises?"

"It's the truth; the gun was a gift," Comfort says to Winslow. Then she addresses Metacom. "Chief *sachem* Metacom please honor our fathers' friendship by putting your mark on this treaty."

He ignores her. He addresses Winslow. "You have more men and guns, so I will sign." He picks up the quill pen, dips it in the ink pot, and makes his mark: ".P."

"Bring me all your guns," Winslow says, knowing he won't comply.

Metacom doesn't answer. He and his warriors turn around, walk out, say something to the others outside and they all go down the hill to their canoes. Mattashunamamo knows Metacom is very angry.

Milton's Garden

"Tell us about your epic poem," Roger asks Milton.

"It will be an allegory about moral choices, and the fall of man. I've decided to have a sympathetic Satan in the story to be Christ's strong adversary. Eve convinces Adam to eat the forbidden apple because he doesn't want to lose her."

Ned wants to talk about the new telescope Charles II has brought back from France. "Do you suppose we can see what the moon looks like through the new telescope?"

"Maybe," Milton says. He's remembering that the masque he took Comfort to see was a satire about aliens on the moon and it made fun of Galileo. Milton can't bear staying in his garden another day. They still don't have permission to visit Henry.

"I want to hear music. Let's see the new masque. While I won't be able to see the costumes and scenery, you'll describe everything to me Ned. I'm sure they'll be plenty of big yellow turbans, long white cloaks, and gold. The water will be blue and there'll be white sails for the Sultan's fleet."

"I'd like to go," Ned says.

"William Davenant has written a new masque in honor of Charles II's coronation. He's calling it an opera. Inigo Jones is producing, of course. My friend William is now Poet Laureate."

"What's the story?" Roger asks.

"It's about a battle between Muslims and Christians for

control of an island in the South Aegean during the 16th
century. Sultan Suleiman ruled during the Golden Age of the
Ottoman Empire. It's called 'The Siege of Rhodes' and is being
performed in the new Lincoln's Inn Field's Theater, built on
the old indoor tennis court near the Inns of Court. For the
first time a woman will be acting in a woman's role. I'm told
she's a dark-haired beauty. You must describe her to me, Ned."

"I will. What have you heard about the new theatre?"

"It has the latest inventions: the stage is sloped upward towards
the back to show perspective, and the scenery slides into place
and can be changed often. I've been invited to sit in a box seat
among the aristocrats, so we won't have to be in the pit on the
benches with the noisy crowd."

"So many religious and political wars have been fought," Roger
says, "it's no surprise poets write plays about them. But how did
you and Davenant become friends if he sided with a monarchy
and is a Catholic?"

"We admire each other's work, and I helped him get out of
prison, and when I was arrested he helped me get out. Do you
know he was Lieutenant Governor of a new colony called Mary-
land for a short time?"

"I know. It's a refuge for Catholics."

"His Majesty will be there and openly flirting with his mistress
Nelly. So you'll both come? "

"Sure. Perhaps we'll meet someone in that box who can us get
us permission to see Henry," Roger says.

* * * *

They arrive just as the musicians are tuning their instruments.
The orchestra pit is covered by the apron of the stage which, for
the first time, has a proscenium. Suddenly they hear a trumpet

fanfare. King Charles II enters wearing a gold colored brocade suit and his mistress Nelly is with him wearing a gown of crimson velvet. The Queen enters later with the visiting ambassador from Portugal.

"Queen Catherine is Catholic, from the royal family of Portugal, and this marriage has brought us territory: Tangiers and the islands of Bombay. The music was written by five composers."

Milton enjoys the singing, and Ned describes to him the trapdoor tricks, the actors who fly across the stage on wires, the costumes, painted scenery, and the fireworks at the end. "Tell your friends back home you saw the first English opera," Milton says.

12

The Tower of London

At the masque, they met one of the King's advisors who helped
them get permission to visit Henry Vane in the Tower of London.
They decided to meet first with a lawyer who was present at
Henry's trial.

"Was it a fair trial?" Roger asks the lawyer, a grey-haired man
with a paunch.

"No. The show was over in less than half an hour. They didn't
even allow him to have a lawyer. Such is the poor quality of our
justice system today. It's sad that so brave and honest a servant
of the people couldn't get a fair trial."

"He must beg for mercy," Ned says.

"It's helped some of the others, but our Henry has too much
pride," John replies.

Next they visit Frances Vane and their eight children who
are living in a small house on the outskirts of the city. They are
shocked to see such a reversal of fortune. "Our castle, farms,
paintings, and all our money have been taken. My children have
no future," Frances laments. John gives her a hug. He's surprised
to feel how thin she is, and promises to visit again next month
if his oldest daughter will bring him here.

The Tower of London is a dreary, dark maze of buildings.
"This place is filled with ghosts; so many men and women were
murdered here" John says. He's holding tightly onto Ned's left

arm. They walk slowly, carefully, on the slippery cobblestones of the road. John hears the clicking of Roger's walking stick and the lapping of water against the wharf where prisoners and their guards get off. "Here comes an armed guard. Show him our papers, Roger," Ned says.

John hears the rustling of papers and the coughing of the guard. A door is opened then closed. They climb a circular staircase. John is out of breath when they reach the third landing. He hears the deep voice of another guard demanding to examine their papers again. This one tells them the rules: "You must be brief and you can't excite the prisoner. If I suspect something, anything, you're out of here at once. I'm in charge." Another heavy door creaks and it opens into the cell.

There's a sliver of light from a high, bared window, and Ned can make out the hunched back of Henry who's writing at a small table. Next to him is an iron bed with a stained and lumpy straw mattress. He turns to look at them. When he recognizes them, he smiles and hugs them. "Welcome, old friends. I'm so pleased to see you. I can only offer you a seat on this mattress. John, you may have my chair."

Roger notices his grey hair hangs limply around his gaunt face. His dark eyes, once sparkling with wit, are half closed slits. He's an old man at forty-nine. Roger remembers Henry at twenty-five, the Governor of The Bay Colony. It's so sad to see him like this, he who was knighted, an Admiral, in charge of expanding the navy, a respected leader of Parliament during the civil war.

Henry asks them about their families. In other circumstances Ned would have told him about his desire to divorce but he can't now. Instead he tells him of their visit to his family. "Your children are well. We admire Frances' courage, will visit her again."

"My oldest boy, only eighteen, feared for his life and fled to Denmark. He died there, all alone. I can no longer protect my family." He wipes away a tear with his finger. He gets up, paces the small room, and continues speaking. "Someday there'll be democracy here; I regret I won't be alive to see that. Perhaps the youngest of my children will experience the reforms we tried so hard to bring about."

"I'll ask my friends to establish a fund for your children's education," Ned says.

"Thank you. You've been my dearest friend."

"Of twenty-nine arrested, only ten have been executed" John says, refusing to give up hope. "Don't be too proud to beg for mercy."

"I won't get a pardon. King Charles has promised me a knight's death: beheading. I'm ready to die knowing the seeds of liberty have been sown. You must make them blossom in Rhode Island, Roger."

Henry lifts a corner of mattress and takes out a package of papers and hands it to Roger. "Keep this, copy it, and share it with those you trust. It's John Lilburne's 'The Agreement of the People.' I have included my thoughts about legal reform." Roger opens his shirt and hides the package inside.

"My faith is strong. I'm at peace."

They hear banging on the door. "Your time is up. You must leave."

* * * *

On the day of his execution, Sir Henry Vane shows great dignity. He wears a black suit and cloak, and underneath, a scarlet silk waistcoat to show defiance; scarlet is the color of victory. He takes off his hat, and salutes the thousands of spectators who have come to honor him. He takes out of his pocket a prepared text and begins to read: "The work which I am called to do in this place is to die. However, I was not brought here under any proper law of this land."

Trumpets blare and drums roll in an attempt to prevent the crowd from hearing his final words. The crowd demands to hear him. He has given his friends a copy of his speech. He knew they would try to prevent his words from being heard.

"I've always defended the rights of the people. I never signed the warrant for the king's death. Those men who say I profited from the war are not telling the truth. I did my best in dark times."

Then he prays, removes his black cloak, and opens his scarlet vest. He bares his neck, and turns to the black hooded executioner holding the sharp axe. "Please do not hurt these blisters on my neck." He spreads out his arms and lowers his head to the wooden block. The sword is sharp; blood flies in the air. Many in the crowd scream and cry out. "You'll never be forgotten."

The next week the King's advisors give Roger a new charter which guarantees religious freedom and democratic governance. Ned and Roger make plans to leave for home. John Milton dictates a poem to his daughter that begins with these words: "Vane, young in years, but in sage counsel old, than whom a better senator ne'er held."

13

Newport

When Ned arrives home, things are calm for the first week. Comfort tries to please him by preparing food he likes best. She sleeps in Maggie's room, for Maggie's visiting a family from Ireland who has just had a baby. Tommy has come home from Plimouth to see his father.

"Will you divorce her dad?" he asks. They are fixing the broken barn door.

"That's my business, not yours." Ned says curtly. Does she know Maggie was his mistress in Barbados? Gossip will hurt his business. He'll tell Comfort how much money he can give her after he checks his profits from the business.

"Will the new King build more ships?" Tommy asks.

"Yes. We compete with the Dutch. I'll make profit from white pine. It grows over one hundred feet tall here and is perfect for a ship of four hundred tons."

Comfort comes over to them bringing cider. "Do you want another war with the Dutch, Ned?"

"Don't be so quick to accuse me of greed. I think His Majesty is going to impose new taxes. He's appointed men to Parliament and they'll do whatever he wants. Politics are too complex for a woman to understand."

"What? Have you forgotten I was friends with John Lilburne? That I went with him to hear Parliament debate? I was there when the King marched into Parliament with his Cavaliers to arrest those five members before the war started. I may be only a woman, but I've opinions and I deserve to be heard."

"I've heard your opinions too often. Do you ever listen to me? I ordered you to stay away from Boston. You could've drowned when that bridge collapsed! A wife should obey her husband."

"Have you no feelings? They hung Mary. She was your mother's best friend. I did the right thing to try to save her life."

Ned sighs. "You interfered with Governor Winslow's efforts to subdue that arrogant savage Metacom."

She takes a deep breath. "Negotiation requires respect for their leaders. What's the alternative? Another war? Do you want Tommy to fight them? I work for peace; you profit from slavery and war."

"I see you haven't changed; I hear the same shrill voice accusing me. This marriage is over. We'll discuss the details tomorrow." He throws down his tools. "Son, I'm going to the tavern; join me."

"He's just come home. Don't you think it was hard for him to witness Henry Vane's execution? You shouldn't act this way, mom." He follows his father.

Comfort sits alone drinking chamomile tea to calm her. What'll she do for money? A woman isn't allowed to own property.

14

MOUNT HOPE

Metacom gave his old gun to Winslow, but has many new ones. Instead of giving the English all his guns, he's gathering more and hiding them in all the Wampanoag villages. He has asked those who trade with the French to buy guns and hide them.

Little Bird doesn't ask him about the guns. In the evenings, she makes mats for the *wetu* while he makes arrows. Sometimes, in the middle of the night, she hears him outside speaking to Great Bear in the sky, asking his spirit guide for advice.

One night, after Little Thunder brings guns into the *wetu* for Metacom to hide, she asks about his plans. "Don't the English have more guns?"

"I know what I'm doing," he replies. "I must defend our freedom and ancient ways. My father taught me to welcome advice. When it's time, I'll ask for yours."

That evening Metacom and his friend Mattashunnamo hold a meeting of advisors. Tobias and his son are invited. Little Bird listens as she sews quills on a new pair of moccasins. "It is time to ask the *pawwaw* to tell us the future," he tells them. "I'll meet with him alone. I don't want angry young warriors there."

The old man comes late at night He throws the sacred tobacco into the fire. He is in a trance. He speaks in the strange voice of one who sees visions. "I hear horses, see warriors, blood dripping from their eyes, fire-arrows flying. I see the strangers' houses burning and their dead cattle ripped open and covered with flies. Our people scatter like seeds in the wind. Find the true ones."

Metacom asks Mattashunnamo to find warriors with kin in other villages and tell them to visit and hear complaints about the coat men. He will visit the elders and *sachems* of the bands to thank them for their loyalty to his father Massasoit and to remind them they owe loyalty to him. He'll ask advice.

He visits Agawam and Assonet, then Cohannet, and Cooxissett, Kitteaumut, Mattaposet, Nasnocomacack, Patuxet, Shawonet and Wawayontat. There are more than thirty Wampanoag villages; most are on the mainland, but several are on Cape Cod, Martha's Vineyard and Nantucket. He does not to speak with the Praying Indians for he doesn't trust them to be loyal. " Don't talk to John Sassamon about what we're doing, for he may be a spy," he tells Tobias.

Metacom, with Mattashunnamo by his side, visits the *sachems* of other nations seeking allies. They visit the Nauset, Niantics, and even their old enemies the Narragansetts. They go during planting time and again during fishing time, and yet again as red leaves fall before the snow covers them. He brings gifts and offers protection. He listens to stories of land stolen by traders who made their brothers drunk with rum and took their land. He promises to protect all who join him. "Your women and children will never become slaves here in our country or far away."

Metacom reminds the Narragansetts of the treachery of the English who told Uncas to murder Miantonomo. They're not interested in fighting a war with such cruel strangers. Their elders remember the Pequot War and the screams of Pequot women and children who were put on fire. This is not an enemy they want to fight.

Little Bird brings together groups of women to sew doeskin cases for the hundreds of arrows Little Thunder and his friends make. At night she can't sleep. Will Little Thunder and Laughing like Water live long enough to give her grandchildren? Will she be alive to teach them stories about the wisdom of the elders?

15

ASSAWAMPSETT POND

Branches snap under the weight of ice. Deep snow covers the path. The wind howls. As he rides through the snow covered woods near Assawampsett Pond, John Sassamon feels a sense of dread. He's worried that Metacom doesn't trust him anymore. He's been fishing through a hole in the ice near his cabin at Assawampsett Pond. Now he's riding home to Swansea. A bitterly cold wind is whipping his face. It's getting dark.

He has been reporting to the Plimouth Governor about Metacom's hidden guns and the growing support among his people for a war against the English. Does Metacom know he's a spy? He must move Susanna and their sons back to Natick; Swansea is too close to Mount Hope.

Suddenly, three men on horseback appear through the woods and ride towards him. They're wearing red English coats, but as they get closer he realizes they're Indians. They begin screaming and encircle his horse. His horse rears up in fright. Sassamon falls into the deep snow, hitting his head on a snow covered rock.

The three Wampanoags get off their horses. Blood stains the white snow around Sassamon's head. Tobias examines his body and tells the other two that John Sassamon is dead. Mattachunnamo says "Good. Hide his body."

Tobias drags John's limp body towards the frozen pond. His son gets off his horse and makes a hole in the ice with his

tomahawk. They push the body under the ice. They'll tell Metacom. It is good luck that the *manitoo* of the rock killed this spy.
Another Indian whose name is Patuckson has been watching
from a hill nearby. He's too far away to see clearly. When the
others leave, he rides down from the hill. He sees a body under
the ice and works hard to pull it out. He recognizes the corpse
as Sassamon. He'll take it to Swansea and ask for a reward. He
needs wampum. He has gambling debts to Mattachunnamo. But
wasn't that him on the black horse? He'll report to the English
that Mattachunnamo killed this Praying Indian. Then the English
will kill him and he won't have to pay his gambling debts.

* * * *

The next afternoon, Comfort is surprised to see Susanna at her
door, her blue coat dusted with fresh snow, her face red from the
cold wind. Her hands are so stiff Comfort has to help her out of
the wet coat, boots and gloves. She wraps her sister-in-law in a
blanket and makes her comfortable by the hearth. She makes
tea, then goes out to get Ned who is in the barn checking on a
sick cow. They plan to divorce in the spring.

"Why did you come in such a snow storm?" Ned asks when
he sees Susanna.

"John's dead. An Indian found his body under the ice at
Assawampsett Pond not far from his cabin. I don't know what
to do." She's sobbing. "My boys are bringing his body here . I
want to bury him here with our family. I'm taking my boys back
to Natick."

"Did he fall into the ice while fishing?" Comfort asks.

"I don't know. The Indian who brought his body says he was
murdered."

"Does he know who did it?" Ned asks. He's ready to get his gun.

"He says he saw Metacom's friend kill John. He was on a hill above and says he could see everything clearly." Susanna is sobbing and Comfort gives her a handkerchief.

"Do you know him?" Comfort asks.

"Yes. His name's Patuckson. He's from Namasket. John tried to convert him, but stopped when he found out he's a drunk and gambler. Patuckson says he saw three men. He recognized Mattachunnamo, Metacom's close friend. He said the other two were Tobias and his son."

"Maybe we can't trust Patuckson, Susanna. Maybe it was an accident." Comfort is worried about this unreliable witness.

"How dare you!" Ned's face is red. "How dare you defend the savages who killed your brother-in-law! Is it because they're Metacom's friends? My God, woman, get away from me. Go upstairs."

Comfort hugs Susanna then goes upstairs. She is tired of fighting with Ned. She's worried because John Easton told her Sassamon has been spying for Governor Winslow. Did Metacom send his friends to murder Sassamon? It's possible.

The next morning John Sassamon's sons bring his body. They help Ned use axes to dig a grave in the frozen earth. Susanna and her sons leave to spend the rest of the winter at Natick.

* * * *

Comfort visits John Easton to ask him what he wants to do to prevent war. He has already received a letter from Governor Winslow telling him Plimouth has captured the three men Patuckson identified as the killers of Sassamon. He will keep them under guard and put them on trial when the General Court meets in the early spring. The Bay Colony again told him the Wampanoags are Plimouth's problem.

"We must try to prevent Metacom from interfering with the trial. This could be the spark that ignites the flames of war."

Comfort tells Ned she and John Easton are going to talk to Metacom about the trial before it begins in the spring.

"You're crazy. Rhode Island is neutral; we're not a part of the militia of the United Colonies. The Narragansetts are old enemies of the Wampanaoags so they won't join Metcom."

"We have to try to keep Metacom from starting a war."

"I'd like to kill all those savages. I'll join the war and shoot your friend Metacom myself. Perhaps I'll make your friend Little Bird my slave."

16

MOUNT HOPE

Comfort and John are riding to Mount Hope now that spring has arrived. The General Court in Plimouth will begin the trial of Metacom's friends soon. They stop in a meadow, spread a blanket on the grass and eat brown bread and cheese. The birds have returned: golden plovers, terns, oystercatchers, and ducks. Spring has always been her favorite season. After so many dark winter days, the return of these birds cheers her heart.

"How should I speak to Metacom? You know him better than I do."

"Don't shout. He's proud and will react badly if he feels he's being humiliated. Be respectful. Let him take time answering your questions, for this is valued. Never raise your hand quickly for he might think you're going to strike him. Don't call him Philip, the English name my father gave him, for he hates it. Don't mention his brother for he still thinks Winslow might have poisoned Wamsutta."

John listens carefully. "I'll be respectful, but I must show strength. He must realize there'll be grave consequences if he dares to interfere with this trial. He must believe all the colonies are united even if we aren't. Do you think you can appeal to childhood memories of peaceful times when your father was Governor?"

"Perhaps. But now we have so many more settlers, and I've

been told that the Wampanoags don't have much land left for themselves. I wish my father were alive to advise us." Her eyes fill with tears.

"Will Little Bird be pleased to see you?"

"I hope so. If she isn't, it could mean Metacom has already made up his mind not to cooperate. John Sassasmon is a spy. He told Winslow Metacom is hiding guns in all the Wampanoag villages. I fear Tommy will have to fight his son. Those boys were like brothers."

"Don't think of that now. Our goal today is just to keep him from going to Plimouth and interfering with the trial."

"He's smart, you know. He sees through a bluff. He respects Quakers, so let's remind him that we're Quakers."

"Yes. We'll speak honestly, try to understand what he's thinking, and do our best to prevent conflict."

* * * *

When they arrive at Mount Hope, they're escorted to Metacom's *wetu* by two young warriors in black paint carrying flintlocks, which isn't a good sign. John says *aspaumpmauntam sachem*, how are you king? Metacom doesn't reply but continues making an arrow.

"*Keen netop*? Is that you, my friend?" Little Bird asks. She puts corn cakes on a hot stone to show proper hospitality. She asks about Tommy, calling him by his Indian name Little Raven. When she learns he's a Captain in the militia and lives with her brother Willie in Plimouth, Little Bird is angry. "Your brother came with soldiers and arrested our friends. He's no longer welcome."

Metacom, a large pile of arrows beside him, continues sitting on the floor whittling away at a piece of wood. They watch as he attaches a stone arrowhead to the end. Then he speaks: "This stone stays in a wound, causing much pain just as your people who stay in my land are causing us harm. *Tawhitch peyahettit*, why do they come? It's not their country."

John doesn't want to talk about this, but rather to focus his attention on the trial. "We've come to talk about the *miawene*, the court gathering, which is about to start, Chief *sachem*," he says. "We invite you to observe, but you must promise to stay silent and may bring only ten men and no guns, war clubs, knives, or bows and arrows. Do you wish to observe?"

"*Machaug*, no. You've no right to judge *meshnowahea*, innocent men. This matter must be settled in the Wampanoag way. The accused are said to have killed an Indian, so it must be settled by Indians. These men not *kemineiachick*, murderers."

"John Sassamon is *kitonckquei*, dead. He was the brother-in-law of your friend Comfort." He looks into Metacom's eyes. "She wants justice. You know we're Quakers; we speak honestly and care about justice."

"I never told anyone to kill him. Bring the three accused men to me. I and my *taupowauog*, wise elders, we will decide their fate. If they're guilty, I'll provide furs and food to his family, to the red-haired woman who is his wife and was a girl I once rescued. This is the proper way to get justice. Your trial challenges my leadership and the sovereignty of my nation. *Aquie kekaumowash*, do not scorn me."

Metacom looks at Comfort with sad eyes. "I'm sorry for the loss of your kin, Sky Eyes. *Nnowantam, nloasin*, I grieve for you."

John raises his voice and demands obedience. "You agreed to follow our laws when you signed that treaty. These men will be tried by a jury of twelve men. We have a witness. Our people govern by law. It will be a fair trial."

"Fair? When are your people fair? Your greedy people use more land than we've sold them, all the nearby woods and meadows. Your *cowsnuck*, cows and *pigsuck*, pigs trample our cornfields. No one is ever punished and no wampum is given to us. Is that fair? You promise to let us continue to fish and hunt, but then take back this promise whenever you want. Some of my people can't feed their families so we all have to help them. I don't believe this trial will be fair. *Aumaunemoke*, take away the accusation against them."

Metacom gets up and walks back and forth in the room shouting. "You've only one witness, and he's a drunk and a gambler who owes much wampum to one of the accused." He turns and stares at John. "Doesn't your law require two witnesses? It says so in your Book of Laws. Sassamon explained it all to me."

John is surprised. He didn't expect Metacom to be so well informed. He answers in a calm, quiet voice. "There may be other witnesses; we won't know until the trial is held."

Metacom pauses, and then goes outside the *wetu*. They don't know if he's coming back, but he does return to continue arguing with them.

"If twenty honest Indians testify against one Englishman, you'll ignore them, but when you have one lying Indian, you chose to believe him." He sits down again and works on another arrow.

"Six Indians will be amongst the judges" Comfort tells him in a quiet voice.

"Ha. Why do you mock me, old friend? You know I'm not stupid. Only Praying Indians will be chosen and they always lie to please the English. Besides, according to Sassamon, these Indians can only give advice, they can't vote and so they don't matter. *Sunnaumwash*, speak the truth." He picks up the arrow and makes them wait and watch him attach a stone at the end.

Metacom now speaks softly to Comfort. "Sky-Eyes, when you convert my people, they turn away from me and our ways. I told you a long time ago to stop working with John Eliot. You told me you're just a teacher, but you're translating the Bible so Eliot can convert us. We have **michachunck**, souls, and we have our own Heaven. We don't need to change."

John wants to talk some more about the trial. "The accused men will have a lawyer" he says.

"**Nummautanume**, I've spoken enough. You have a **sachimauog**, a King. Why not take me to him? Or you can bring him here and I'll show hospitality. I'll negotiate only with the King of your **sachimauonck**, monarchy. Isn't he the owner of everything you've taken from us?"

Comfort wants him to remember an event in the past. "When we were children, three Englishmen were put on trial in Plimouth for the murder of a Narragansett man. You were there, don't you remember? You were visiting with your father. Those Englishmen were hung. Justice was done by an English jury. Please don't interfere."

"**Netop**, your father was honest. I don't trust this Governor. Give him my message. Tell him **manoweass**, I fear no one. I've many allies. Tell him **Konkeeteahetti**, let my friends live. If they're hung, **ntannoam**, I'll take revenge."

Metacom takes two arrows with stone ends from the pile, wraps them together with a snake skin, and gives them to John. "This is my answer. Give this to the Governor." He gets up and walks out of the **wetu** without looking at them again.

"My heart is full of sorrow." Little Bird says as she gives them two corn cakes for their journey home. "I have no words for the pain in my heart. Metacom's friends are innocent; it was an accident. I want **aquene**, peace, but fear it isn't possible."

Comfort hugs her. "I'll always love you, sister."

When they get back to Rhode Island, John says he'll insist Rhode Island stay neutral if there is a war. "Why should we fight?

The other colonies didn't invite us to join the United Militia. We must make sure the Narragansetts stay neutral also."

17

PLIMOUTH

The magistrates sit at a table in the front of a crowded meetinghouse. John and Comfort are seated near the people from Swansea who have come to see justice done.

The Praying Indian Patuckson, the only witness, stands before the magistrates and testifies. "I saw three men on horses surround Sassamon and force him off his horse. They killed him, then dragged his body to the pond, cut a hole in the ice and pushed him under the ice. I was on a hill above and saw it all clearly."

The defense lawyer begins. "There's no way to know how the victim's head and neck were bruised. These bruises could have been caused by a fall from a horse. There were many rocks nearby covered with snow. They say he fell and hit his head on a rock and died. It is certainly possible John Sassamon died as these three men claim he did, by accident."

The prosecutor now introduces facts about the victim and asks questions. "This poor man was a Praying Indian, a learned preacher who went to the Indian College at Harvard. He served Reverend Eliot well by preaching to the converts living in Natick for many years and then took his family to Swansea to preach to the English and the Indians who lived nearby. Do these savages admit to pushing his body under the ice?"

"Yes, they admit they did that, but said he was already dead" says the defense lawyer.

"If they were not guilty, why did they work so hard breaking frozen ice to hide his body?"

"They feared being falsely accused of murdering him," says their attorney.

"Do they recognize the witness Patuckson present here today?" the prosecutor asks.

"Yes, they do. All of them say he never speaks the truth. He would've been too far away to see anything because he was drunk."

"Didn't they say they couldn't see him?"

"Yes."

"So how could they know he was drunk?"

"They said he's always drunk and he owes them a lot of wampum for his gambling debts. They think he doesn't want to pay his debts so that's why he has accused them of this murder."

The defense lawyer adds that according to the Bible and English law there must be at least two witnesses. However, the magistrates remind him that it was winter and the snow was heavy. "This murder happened in the woods during a blizzard, so one witness is sufficient under those circumstances."

The prosecutor sums up his case: "These men knew Sassamon had a cabin nearby the pond. They admit they pushed his body under the ice. They murdered him because he was a spy and was revealing the fact that Metacom is planning a war against us. I hope the jury will find them guilty as charged. They can't murder a good man, a Praying Indian, and get away with it. The verdict of guilty will be a warning to Metacom to stop collecting and hiding guns for the purpose of planning a war against us."

The jury considers the testimony for only thirty minutes. All three Wampanoag men are found guilty of murder and are sentenced to be hung by their necks until dead. The six Praying Indians say they agree with the verdict and the punishment.

"I am not surprised," John says. "Now we must wait and see if

Metacom uses this trial as a reason to begin a war."

Two of the prisoners die quickly, but the rope around the neck of Wampapaquan, Tobias' son, is frayed and breaks. The man, trembling, is forced admit that Metacom ordered him to kill Sassamon. He claims he was only watching when they murdered him. They shoot him.

18

Swansea

It's a warm day in Swansea. Susanna's on her knees in the garden pulling up the last of the carrots. She's startled by gunfire coming from a house close by. She and her two boys rush into the garrison house for safety. A woman already there tells her they should abandon their home. "It was our refuge, but it's no longer safe here," she says.

Susanna knows that many of her neighbors came to escape the problems back in London: poverty, a great fire, religious persecution of Quakers, an outbreak of the plague. It was a safe haven, a place to start again. She sees fear in their eyes, and in the way their young children are holding onto their mothers. Indians must have come to kill them today. They don't know who was shooting, but they stare anxiously at her sons, Sassamon's children, and are afraid. Her boys are Christians, but also half Indian.

"I saw Metacom" a teenage boy shouts, running into the garrison house. "He saw me kill that boy and asked why I did it. I wasn't scared. Cause he's a thief I said. "

"But he was hungry and looking for food in an abandoned house Metacom said to me."

Susanna asks if that was true.

"Don't know, don't care. I told Metacom killing an Indian is of no importance at all." He's puffed up with pride at what he dared to do and dared to say.

Susanna is distraught. "Foolish boy! He may have been kin. Even if he wasn't, to insult Metacom was stupid." She decides to go back to Natick immediately. The Praying Indians loved John Sassamon; her boys will be safe among them and they'll also be protected by the militia in Boston.

The next day five Wampanoag warriors return to Swansea, find the teenager who shot the boy and kill him, his father and five neighbors.

* * * *

When Susanna's wagon reaches Boston, she sees young soldiers building a ten foot wall around the center of the city. She asks if war with the Wampanoags has started.

"Not yet, but we'll win it. We've a new Governor; name's Leverett. He's ordered this wall. He was a fighter with Cromwell's army, and is a Major-General."

"It's going to happen, lady. I've seen a lunar eclipse and a cloud shaped like an Indian bow. Bad omens. I'm glad we've got Leverett on our side," says an older boy.

"Don't worry, God's on our side," says the older man supervising the youngsters.

"Do you think Leverett plans to negotiate with Metacom?" Susanna asks.

"Doubt it. This Metacom is the worst devil of them all. He wants to force us to leave. Well, we're not going. This is going to be a war for survival. It's our country now." He goes back to building the wall.

Susanna is relieved to receive a warm welcome by old friends in Natick. A boy says he'll show the English that Praying Indians are loyal. "If they'll let me, I'll join the militia."

19

PLIMOUTH

Metacom's warriors have attacked the scattered villages of Taunton, Dartmouth and Middleboro. People from these towns go to other villages without knowing if those will be attacked next.

"Just as we feared, it's going to be hard to protect all our villages." Captain Willie Bradford tells Captains Ben Church and Tommy Hutchinson. They are sitting on a bench inside the empty meetinghouse smoking pipes. It's a warm night, the sky is full of stars, and there's a full moon.

"They know we're weak because we're so spread out," Tommy says.

"This'll be a different kind of war," Ben replies. "In the civil war in England there were huge battles between Parliament's forces and the King's army, but here many innocent people will be killed by surprise attacks on villages on both sides. Fear will make our people demand we kill as many of the Indians as we can. We must try to negotiate with Metacom. If that's not possible, we must capture and kill him."

Tommy is thinking about the Pequot War. "My grandad told me about the Mystic massacre. Hundreds of women and children were burned to death while they were still alive. What did he tell you about it Uncle Willie?'

"He was sickened by the smell of burning flesh and had

nightmares for a long time" Willie replies. "His screams woke me up and I had bad dreams also."

Tommy knows what happened in Long Island, Dutch territory. "Indians murdered my grandma, aunts and uncles, except for my dad and Aunt Susanna. Dad hates all Indians. I don't. Of course I'll obey orders, but I sure hope I won't have to burn entire villages."

"They hide in swamps," Ben says. "They build fencing with trees all around their hiding places. We must find friendly Indians to be our scouts. They can help us find these fortified villages in the swamps."

"I hate swamps." Tommy says. "I get lost in those labyrinths of water. I hate snakes and bugs. It's a Hell on earth. You can't even see the sun in those wet jungles of vines."

"Who should I recruit to be scouts Willie?"

Willie thinks for several minutes. "Mohegans. Chief *sachem* Uncas was loyal when we fought the Pequots. Narragansetts were allies also, but I don't trust them."

* * * *

The Plimouth militia goes to Mount Hope only to find that it's been abandoned. Willie decides to build a fort there to prevent Metacom's men from returning to get corn at harvest time. Ben organizes a small force of farm boys, all good hunters, and finds Mohegan scouts willing to hunt Metacom. Tommy will go with Ben Church.

"He's been spotted on the other side of the Sakonnet River," a Mohegan says.

"I must build the fort and also send our boys to protect our fields at harvest time. I won't go with you," Willie says. "Find him quickly so we can end the war."

* * * *

On a hot, cloudy night Ben, Tommy and his small group of soldiers and scouts are waiting for two boats to take them from the Mount Hope side of Narragansett Bay across to the other side. The farm boys are cleaning their guns.

How well do these boys shoot? Ben is thinking. He's worried. A flintlock is good at fifty to one hundred yards. With a bayonet, it's six feet long and weighs ten pounds. How quickly can these boys bite off the end of the envelope with the ball and powder, ram the charge and place priming powder in the pan before they fire? If all goes well, flint strikes steel, producing sparks that ignite the powder. They must do seventeen separate motions well and quickly. He gets off three rounds a minute, but these boys will surely be much slower as they are inexperienced and haven't been well trained. They'll be exposed to the enemy's guns and arrows as they shoot.

He looks at the pike men sitting and sharpening their sticks, turning them into bayonets. He feels they'll be of little use, but his boys are less afraid because of them. They believe the pike men will protect them while they are getting ready to fire.

After midnight, a small group of soldiers arrive with two pinnaces to take them from the Rhode Island side to the swamp where they believe Metacom is hiding. The boats glide across Narragansett Bay as the sky is getting darker. He has warned the boys to be absolutely quiet. Any noise will frighten birds and warn the Indians of their arrival.

When they finally arrive at the swamp, it's already almost dawn. He orders the boys to split into two groups and encircle this place. Tommy and his group put tobacco in their pipes and smoke while they await a signal to attack. They light a small fire.

One of Metacom's lookouts smells smoke. All the Indians

escape. To make matters worse, Tommy and his group have left all their provisions behind. Hungry, tired, and ashamed Tommy slogs along in the swamp to the place where boats are supposed to come to take them back to Rhode Island. He catches a shoe on a vine and falls in the water. Another humiliation.

In late morning the small group finally emerges from the swamp and walks towards the bay. Then they come upon a few abandoned English houses. Three have been burned to the ground, and two others are partly burned. They see a garden planted with peas. Tommy bends down to gather a handful of peas. He eats them raw. He's starving.

Suddenly he's being shot at from above. He looks up. He can see guns glittering in the sun. Confused and frightened, he and the other boys waste gunpowder shooting in the air even though it's clear the enemy is too far away. Then the Indians rush down the hill.

"Take cover. Find a wall, a tall hedge, anything" Ben orders. A shower of bullets continues for hours. At dusk, with gunpowder almost gone, Tommy starts praying. A young boy, thirteen years old, sitting next to him wipes away tears with his dirty sleeve.

At last Ben sees the sloop he's expected. They get onboard, grateful to get away.

As they go across the bay, Ben talks to them. "I guess we had three hundred savages shooting at us. You held them off for more than six hours. You've made me proud, lads."

But Tommy knows he's let Ben down because of smoking around that fire. Metacom may have been in that swamp and his actions warned him. He must show Ben he has courage, even if it means taking risks.

20

NEWPORT

Ned Hutchinson has decided to contribute to the war effort in two ways. He has helped set up a headquarters fort at Wickford, Rhode Island and he brings the soldiers who are there more guns and food. Also he's allowing Comfort and the other Quaker women to use his barn as a hospital for wounded men. Now that their divorce is final and Comfort is living by herself in a cottage at Easton Point, she and Ned can cooperate in the war effort. She glad he's made their barn available for the wounded and has paid a lot of money to a carpenter to totally remodel it and paid for the beds, mattresses and other things needed.

The Governor of Connecticut, John Winthrop Jr., lives in New London which is not too far from Newport. He comes by boat from time to time to supervise Comfort and the other women working in the new hospital. In addition to his interests in the iron mine and astronomy, John has been involved with alchemically-based medicine for most of his adult life. He knows a great deal about healing and treats hundreds of people in Connecticut. New London, his home town, is called by many "the hospital town" because of John's work as a doctor with so many people in Connecticut. His recent membership in the new Royal Society of London has added to his prestige as a scientist.

John is used to training women as healers. Many of the wives of the leading men in his colony come to him to increase their skills as midwives and healers for sick children. Now these women must volunteer to care for the many English boys wounded by guns, knives and arrows.

Comfort and the other Quaker women who are helping the wounded in Rhode Island have met with John and appreciate his advice. "Arrows mustn't be pulled out, for the arrowhead will remain inside and cause infection and could lead to decay of the flesh. The whole arrow must be removed. You could make a poultice to prevent infection; people have used honey or sugar, crushed cranberries and such, but I'm sure you women know of herbal medicines used by midwives. The barber has tools for surgery. Knife cuts are easier to clean, don't bleed too much and can be stitched closed. If a gunshot shatters bone, there is no way to fix the bone. The entire leg must be removed. With bullets, the problem is that bits of cloth which are dirty get into the wound. Depending on where the bullet has entered, it might be necessary to leave it stay in the body."

Comfort asked him what to do for pain. "Those poor boys, I can't bear to hear their screams."

"Give them rum, or a stick to bite on. Some people use rose water, egg white, and licorice but that doesn't work. You can try comfrey root and wine; it'll help them sleep."

Today Comfort is busy washing a boy's wounds with soap and water when she's shocked to see her son Tommy among the wounded. He tells her he is now a Captain. "When an Indian was about to shoot Ben Church, I spun around quickly and shot that Indian, but his bullet grazed this leg of mine. Ben says I was quick and brave."

The wound's superficial. She washes it well then bandages it with a strip torn off a boiled sheet. "Please stay here with me in Newport, I'm begging you. Rhode Island is still neutral. You'll be safe here" she says.

"I've a duty to stay with my unit. Ben calls us his "Rangers" and there are only twenty of us and several Mohegan scouts. We're like brothers; we look out for each other. I won't leave them."

"At least stay in my cottage so I can help you get your strength back." She wipes his face with a wet cloth. "I've missed you, Tommy" she whispers, tearing. She knows he still blames her for the divorce. "Your father and I are working together to help the men fighting. Boys from Plimouth, Massachusetts and Connecticut are now in Rhode Island. Stay here."

"Only for a week. I've never seen your new cottage."

That week Tommy shares his feelings about having to fight the Wampanaogs. "Sometimes, at night, I dream I'm a child again, living at Mount Hope. Little Thunder is my older brother and Metacom is my father. I scream because you're taking me away from my family. I call you 'the English lady.' I wake up crying and wishing this war had never happened. I know Metacom feels his people have been treated poorly. I understand we must kill him if we're going to stop this horrible war. Someone will kill Metacom, but I hope it won't be me."

"The Narragansetts have signed a new treaty which says they'll stay neutral. If only we can get them to fight on our side, Metacom might give up." Comfort doesn't think he will. Tommy says he doesn't think the Narragansetts will stay neutral.

"They're openly giving refuge to Wampanoags, mom" he tells her. "Queen Weetamoo, Wamsutta's widow and Metacom's former sister-in-law, has married the Narragansett *sachem* Quinnapin . That man is a cousin of Chief *sachem* Canonchet who still wants revenge for his father Miantonomo's murder. He says Winthrop was responsible because he gave his father to Uncas knowing Uncas intended to kill him. Even though we forced them to sign this new treaty, Willie and Ben think that the Narragansetts will join Metacom and so do I. Our actions in the Pequot Wars have consequences for this one. Rhode Island will not be able to stay neutral, mom, even though you want to."

* * * *

Winter weather arrives. Snow blankets the earth and the ponds and swamps are frozen. There is no pause in the war. Metacom's warriors continue to burn villages, slaughter cattle, and kill families throughout Massachusetts, Plimouth and Connecticut. Nipmuc bands join him, as well as many but not all of the tribes along the Connecticut River. He asks the Mohawks to be his allies but they still refuse to get involved. Wabanaki bands, armed by the French, are fighting the United Colonies militia in the north.

To prevent the Narragansetts from joining Metacom, John Easton and Roger agree to meet with the most powerful Narragansett *sachems*: Pessacus (brother of Miantonomo), Canonchet (son of Miantonomo), Ninigret and Quinnapin. Their faces are painted with black dots and lines, so Roger thinks they have already decided to join Metacom's war. John Easton thinks Rhode Island needs The United Colonies soldiers to help Rhode Island survive.

They meet at Worden Pond, a large freshwater lake deep in Narragansett tribal territory in Rhode Island. It's shallow and therefore completely frozen. The *sachems* ask why all the colonies are involved in a war which should be between only Plimouth and the Wampanoags.

"We're under the same King and so we must help each other" John says.

"We're also under your King's protection" Pessacus says. "Roger arranged it."

"Not if you join Metacom against us" Roger replies. "You

mustn't join him."

"You were our ally before, and we expect you to remain friendly to us." John adds. "Stay neutral."

Chief *sachem* Pessacus is angry. "The English told me my brother Miantonomo caused the Pequot war and demanded I pay them six hundred fathoms of wampum as a penalty. I didn't have it so they took my land. I don't trust what you coatmen say anymore " Pessacus replies.

"Our old enemy *sachem* Uncas and your Captain Mason in Connecticut are thieves and want to profit from this war" Canonchet says. Uncas wants control of all Pequots still alive, to increase his own power. "Uncas murdered, *nosh*, my father; *Ntannotam*, I seek revenge. Know this: *Manoweass*, I fear no one."

21

Natick

Susanna and her sons come into the church along with a few of their Praying Indian friends. Everyone wears English clothing. They find seats in front and are waiting anxiously for their young Indian preacher and Reverend John Eliot to arrive. How will a terrible new law they've heard about change their lives once again?

It's not been as pleasant here as Susanna hoped it would be. Natick was the first of fourteen Praying Indian villages and has many English style homes, productive farms and farm animals, but now it's too crowded. Thousands have been forced to live in only five villages and these five are surrounded by armed English soldiers. Her sons say it's like living in a prison and want to leave, but Susanna doesn't know where to go.

Since the villages were established within a twenty-five mile radius of Boston, folks in the city fear they'll be attacked. Some of Susanna's Indian friends have fled north into French held territory. Others have joined the English militia to be scouts and fight Metacom. A few have joined Metacom. Susanna chose to stay. Today that may change.

Without enough food and warm clothing, life has been miserable for Susanna and her sons, but for those still living in temporary *wetus* it's a dangerous situation. Many are sick, some die and starving mothers have no breast milk for their newborns.

Their young Indian minister comes in with Reverend John Eliot. He is one of twenty-four Indian preachers trained by Eliot. He holds the Algonquian language Bible in his hands and tells everyone to be quiet for Eliot wishes to speak to them.

John is seventy years old, but strong enough to paddle his canoe here. He tells them that Praying Indians from a Nipmuc band have joined Metacom's warriors and are attacking English villages. The English soldiers have attacked one of his villages in revenge and many people have died. "I know you are all loyal, but I can't make English people believe they have nothing to fear. They don't want you living so close to them any longer."

"Where can we go? This is our home. We need our church. We don't want to go back to the old ways."

"There is a new law that demands all Praying Indians and their families must go to Deer Island in Boston Harbor and stay there until the war is over. I've arranged for boats to take you and your things . Take all your warm clothing. Bring wood to build temporary shelters and for fires. Pack as much food as you can. I promise I'll bring more food and warm clothing as soon as I can collect more."

"I know that island. It is a cold, windy, barren place. There are no deer, only wolves. It's not a good place to grow corn. We'll either freeze or starve to death."

Some young men say they'd rather volunteer to be scouts for Ben Church's militia. A Wampanoag man from Mashpee says he'll do the same, but a Wampanoag boy from the Gay Head - Aquinnah band has a cousin fighting with Metacom and whispers to his brother that he will join Metacom. "Better to die fighting to save our people than to starve on that barren island. The English intend to kill us all."

"We won't abandon you." Susanna stands up and goes to John Eliot. "I'll help collect food and warm clothing from the Quakers and other kind people in Rhode Island."

"I'll help also" says their young Indian preacher. "We'll pray together. God will be with you. Have faith dear friends, and you'll survive." He must ask Eliot for axes to cut through the ice to dig graves. He opens Eliot's Algonquian Bible. "Let us pray."

22

NEWPORT

Comfort is sorting clothing by size and by how much warmth each piece can provide. Next to her is the large basket of clothing Ned's servant Maggie has brought over to her cottage from the attic of her former home. It's filled with Tommy's old clothes. She also has clothes donated by Quaker, Huguenot and Jewish families. Eliot has asked her to collect warm clothing.

She holds up a small blue woolen jacket that was Tommy's. She pulls out a red wool hat and a pair of matching red mittens that fit Tommy's twelve year old hands. Suddenly, she is overwhelmed with sadness. Children are dying on Deer Island. John Eliot says there are many graves.

She hopes Tommy's hands are warm. He and Ben Church continue to search the frozen swamps for Metacom. She knows the danger of frostbite. She must try to get extra pairs of woolen gloves and socks to her son.

Susanna has written that there are four hundred Christian Indians still alive on that barren island and more are being exiled there. This afternoon, she'll come with John Eliot to get these warm clothes.

She reaches into the basket and pulls out an Indian moccasin. Excited, she searches under the discarded clothing for the other one and finds it. She smells the doeskin, clutches the pair to her heart. These were Little Bird's gift to her after her wedding feast, a gift from her *weticks*, her sister. Will she ever see her alive again?

Susanna and John Eliot arrive to ask for her help to save the Praying Indians. As she serves them tea, Eliot tells her that a mob of forty men from a village called Lynn in Massachusetts planned to go to Deer Island and slaughter all the converts. "People are going mad with fear. Thank Goodness, Simon Bradstreet stopped them." he says. "He's Deputy Governor now."

Comfort thinks of her friend Anne who has died of consumption. Simon has a new wife. Anne's spirit remains with Comfort always and she often reads her poems before going to sleep. Anne might have lost her strong faith if she had lived to see what has happened to these Christian Indians.

"Come with us to Deer Island, Comfort. Help us give out food and clothing. We must save as many as we can. They'll be loyal. They've faith in God," John says. "I've devoted my life to saving them, and I can't abandon them now." She agrees to go.

* * * *

The next morning John Eliot takes them to the Boston harbor where a friend rents him an old fishing boat. He helps John fill the boat with food and clothing. The boat is old and Comfort hopes it doesn't leak. The sky is dark, it's windy and cold, and waves are as high as hills. The cold water splashes her face and some gets into the boat. She and Susanna wrap a blanket around themselves.

Suddenly she sees a boat coming towards them. It's large, a fifty foot sloop rigged with a single mast, main sail and jib. It's following them, coming closer and closer. Comfort notices it has three cannons. It may have been a merchant ship used in the Caribbean against pirates, she thinks. What is it doing here? More icy water splashes over the sides of the fishing boat.

Susanna is shaking, terrified.

Eliot recognizes the Captain. He screams: "Stop what you're doing, Samuel Moseley. You'll have to kill me to stop me from feeding those poor wretches."

"Go back old man," the Captain screams. "Let the devils die!"

Their small boat is rocking in the waves. Two barrels roll overboard and break open. Cod fish and biscuits float in the dark waves.

"Who is this evil man? Why is he doing this to us?" Comfort shouts to Eliot.

"Captain Moseley is a soldier, and once was a pirate in Jamaica. He'd like to kill as many Indians as he can and sell the rest as slaves in Jamaica or Barbados. He hates me for protecting these converts, and tells people that they'll all join Metacom."

When Captain Moseley sees that Eliot's boat isn't turning back, he finally turns his sloop around and lets them go on to the island.

They arrive shaken. The Indians help unload the supplies. Comfort is distressed to see how emaciated they look. The children hold out their small hands, begging for food. Their mothers plead in weak voices: *teaqua natuphettit?* What can they eat? Susanna and Comfort pass out biscuits and dried turkey meat. John leads them in a short prayer:

Manitou wussuckwhere, God's book tells us, *wame, ewupaw-suck, manit, wawontakick,* all who know the One God, *ewo manit waumau sachick ka uckqushanchick,* all who love and fear Him, *keesaqut auog,* they go up to Heaven, *micheme weeteantamwock,* they live forever in joy.

Then they climb back in the leaky fishing boat, bail out water with wooden bowls, and leave for Boston in silence, too disheartened to talk.

In Eliot's cottage, Susanna and Comfort have wrapped a quilt around both of them, and in this warm cocoon they finally feel safe. They remember sleeping together like this when Susanna was rescued as a child and had nightmares.

"He tried to kill us," Susanna says. "He swamped our boat because he wanted us to capsize. We could've drowned. I feared we would float slowly down through the dark, deep water and rest forever at the bottom. I saw my husband's kind face, and I was ready to join him in Heaven."

Comfort smooths her hair. "You're safe. Shh. Try to sleep."

"I love you so much. " Susanna says.

"We'll survive." Then she thinks of Tommy somewhere in a frozen swamp looking for the Narragansett hidden fort. She prays he'll be safe.

23

THE GREAT SWAMP FIGHT

In a large swamp, north of Worden Pond, hundreds of Narragansett Indians are busy building a huge fortified village which will house over a thousand people. Small trees and branches are used as stakes for the high palisade being built in a tight lattice pattern. This tall fence is being backed by a mud wall many feet thick.

There is a single entrance. Several men are lifting and positioning a huge tree trunk at the entrance. On each corner of the wall there are blockhouses made with thick trees from which warriors can rapidly fire arrows and guns at soldiers trying to breach the fence. The entire hidden village of hundreds of *wetus* fills four acres inside a huge swamp. If this fortified village is attacked it will be a fight to the death. The younger warriors want to fight, the elders do not. They all hope to save the women, children, and old people.

Women with cradleboards on their backs help drag branches to the space in front of the palisade in order to impede soldiers from climbing over. Nearby, young boys are building a shelter for the horses, while young girls are lining deep pits with woven mats to store corn.

"The English are stupid," says Queen Wetamoo to her new Narragansett husband *sachem* Quinnapin. "They'll get lost. They'll never find us here."

* * * *

The English decide they must attack the Narragansetts first. A pre-emptive strike is planned. Willie and Ben are ordered to lead the effort. Ben has put together what he calls his "Rangers": a small force of thirty boys chosen for their ability to shoot well and twenty Mohegans he calls "Friend-Indians".

Tommy, second in command, hands each man a small sack with food, gunpowder and bullets. He hopes to get intelligence to help them find the Narragansett fortified village in the swamp. These Rangers will then join up with a larger force of Connecticut militia. Tommy's glad the ground is frozen, so it'll be easier to navigate through the quagmire of shrubs, trees and vines.

First they attack a small Narragansett village near Wickford. They burn the houses and corn pit. Among the captives is a man called Peter who says he knows where the fortified village is hidden. "I helped cut down trees for the fence. I'll lead you to it," he tells them. Ben promises him he can be a scout and will be given his freedom after the war if he takes them to the area north of Worden Pond where he says the Narragansetts are hiding.

They leave in a blizzard, their faces burning from the bitter cold. They meet up with the three hundred soldiers from Connecticut. Among them are one hundred and fifty Mohegan Indians. From among these, Ben selects a dozen more Mohegans to join his scouts and leads them ahead of the others.

They slog through the woods in deep snow, and in places they must dare to walk on ice. One boy stumbles and falls through a thin covering of ice into a hole with freezing water. Many boys are suffering from frostbite on their hands and feet. Tommy's glad his mother gave him an extra pair of wool mittens, three pairs of wool socks and leather boots.

An Indian informant called Peter by the English says they're getting closer to the fortified village. He tells them he knows where they can breach the wall. The weakest area is a six foot wide place over a stream with a thick tree trunk that they can climb on and get inside.

Ben and his boys lead the assault. They rush through the vulnerable spot and set fire to as many shelters as they can. They meet at great amount of resistance at first. Then many youg warriors know a way to escape and they flee.

Men, women, children and old people scream as their hair and clothing goes up in flames. The English set fire to the whole village. It is a hellish scene of blood, cries, and smoke. Fighting continues in all the spaces between the many houses and people have no way to escape the fire.

Tommy can't see. The smoke burns his eyes. He stumbles over the body of a little girl, still alive, screaming.. Without thinking, he bends down to pick her up, but before he can get up an Indian puts a hatchet in his back. Willie sees this and pulls his nephew's body away from the fire.

Ben is wounded by three bullets, one deep wound in his thigh, a superficial wound through his breeches, and a third bullet that goes through his pocket and is stopped by a heavy pair of mitten wrapped together. Willie has a bullet in his thigh that will stay there for the rest of his life. Even though they're in great pain, they urge their soldiers to continue. "Burn it all down. Destroy all the food pits" Ben yells. He wishes they could take the food, for his men are always hungry.

When the slaughter is finally over, the Narragansetts have lost a hundred and fifty women and children. Two hundred Narragansett warriors have escaped and gone to join Metacom. Canonchet will now lead warriors into battle against towns in Massachusetts, Plimouth, and Rhode Island.

They can't find Metacom right away because he has gone to

Albany to meet with the Mohawks to try once again to convince them to join him. They refuse and attack his warriors.

* * * *

Willie returns to Plimouth to bury Tommy. Then he goes to Newport to tell Comfort that her son has died and has had a soldier's funeral.

"I wrapped his body in my blanket and took it home. I gave my nephew a proper funeral. A carpenter made a simple box and the markers at the head and foot of the grave. I told him to write: 'Here rests Thomas Hutchinson, a brave soldier, grandson of William Bradford.' It's next to our father's grave on Burial Hill. Ben couldn't come, but Major General Josiah Winslow attended as well as some of the boys from Tommy's unit."

She's devastated. She goes to bed, pulls a blanket over her head, and cries for two days. She thinks of those precious hours in Raby Castle when he was conceived to parents who then loved each other. She remembers Tommy as a baby in Little Bird's lap, holding his tiny fingers on her breast, so content. How she hated to leave him there. Her friends named him 'Little Raven'. When she took him back to Boston, he screamed and didn't want to leave them. Would they care he's dead? Now he'll never give her grandchildren. Exhausted, she falls asleep. When she wakes, she asks Willie about the battle in the swamp.

"It was just as horrible as the massacre of the Pequots. Our father said he suffered nightmares for a long time, and now I will. I wish we didn't have to kill women and children. Many warriors escaped, and they'll hunger for revenge. What have we accomplished?" He puts his head in his hands and she stays silent for a while.

"Does Ned know?" she asks.

"Yes. A Baptist boy with Ben's Rangers went to tell him. Quakers here must agree to fight. The Wickford command center that Ned is helping supply is sure to be attacked at some point. Rhode Island is in fact no longer neutral."

Comfort makes Willie a plaster to ease the throbbing pain in his thigh where a bullet is lodged. It will stay in his body for the rest of his life, reminding him of the war and of the day his nephew died. "Use it before you go to sleep. I've no medicine for the pain in our hearts."

* * * *

John Easton comes to see her and she tells him Tommy is dead. She can't stop crying as he holds her tightly in his arms. "I don't want to believe it. A child should never die before his mother."

"I'm staying," he says, holding her in his arms.

He takes care of her as if she were a child. They drink wine, which calms her. She's so happy he's here, and doesn't want to talk, only listen to his soft, deep voice tell her about the life they'll have together when this war is over.

"We'll live in my house. You'll have that rose garden you've always wanted. I'll make a small table and chairs for our garden and in summer we'll eat our meals there. On the hot days in August I'll paddle our canoe to Goat Island where we'll swim. I know a secret spot where we can swim naked like the Indians. You'll read me love sonnets. I'll catch a few fish and cook them over a fire. Go there now in your mind, my darling. Watch the orange and pink colors of the sunset light up the clouds."

He puts water in the kettle to warm it for a bath, undresses her, and when the wooden tub is ready, she climbs in and he bends on his knees and washes her with loving hands. It's as if time has stopped and all her pain is melting away into the warm water. She looks into his eyes and smiles. "I've never felt so loved," she says.

"I'm so grateful I have you in my life, sweetheart." He dries her with a cloth and she gets into bed. He undresses and covers her body with sweet, gentle kisses. She falls asleep in his arms.

24

WICKFORD, RHODE ISLAND

The English soldiers at the command post in Wickford are busy with preparations for the hundreds of soldiers soon to be stationed here. Some men are reinforcing the stockade, while others are busy painting the barrels of their flintlocks brown so they won't glisten in the sun and be easily seen. Men are storing food and gun powder in two newly fortified buildings. Major General Winslow is in charge of the United Colonies militia. His assistant keeps an account of the guns, gun powder, food and clothing that Ned Hutchinson supplies this fort.

Every week Ned arrives with a wagon full of supplies: warm clothing, woolen stockings, overcoats, mittens and shoes, as well as food.

Ned leaves Wickford just before sunset. He's ambushed by three Indians who come galloping out of the woods. They shoot him in the chest and he falls into the back of the wagon onto his Praying Indian servant James. The poor boy is sprayed with blood and frightened. He wraps Ned's corpse in the blanket, says a prayer for him and drives the wagon home.

Maggie has been waiting anxiously for his return. She screams when she sees James alone in the wagon. They bury Ned next to the empty grave of his murdered mother. Maggie tells James to bring Comfort the sad news.

* * * *

Comfort decides to sell the house and asks Maggie to come live with her. After the war, she'll move into John's house and Maggie can stay in the cottage.

"Will the Narrangsetts attack us?" Maggie asks, as she puts two bowls of porridge on the table. She is happy to be with Comfort once again.

"They might. We aren't really neutral now because of the fort at Wickford."

Comfort sees tears in Maggie's green eyes. "My friend Anne wrote this fine poem about death. What I find it hard to accept is that so many boys will never have a chance to grow old."

When I behold the heavens as in their prime
And the earth (though old) still clad in green,
The stones and trees insensible of time,
Nor age nor wrinkle on their font is seen.
If winter comes and greenness then do fade,
A spring returns, and they more youthful made.
But Man grows old, lies down, remains where once he's laid.

"Irish songs are sad," Maggie says, and sings a song her mother loved to sing.

That night Maggie lies awake talking to herself. What a mess you left me with, Master Ned. What'll Comfort do when she finds out I'm pregnant with your child?

The next morning, Comfort shows Maggie a book of Shakespeare's sonnets. "Ned read these to me."

"Shall I compare thee to a summer's day?
Thou art more lovely and more temperate.

Rough winds shake the darling buds of May,
And summer's lease hath all too short a date."

"Oh I loved this one too," Maggie says. "I don't know how I'll live without Ned now that I'm pregnant with his child."

"I thought you were lovers."

"Oh mistress, he rescued me. My master beat me with a knotted whip, and Ned bought my freedom. Now I'm pregnant with his child and I don't have any money."

"I'll support you and his baby, Maggie. If it's a boy, will you name him Tommy? He can call me grandmother." She feels that this is a blessing.

"My ma's buried in Dublin, and Ned's mom is dead, so he'll need a grandma. I'll name him Tommy Hutchinson. He'll be proud to be your kin."

25

Newport

The war continues in Massachusetts, Plimouth and Connecticut. The Narragansetts and Wampanoags are starving and attack Lancaster, Massachusetts. Several women and children are taken captive. The Indians want to ransom these captives for money to buy food.

Reverend Eliot arrives one afternoon with Reverend Joseph Rowlandson from Lancaster. He meets with Comfort and John Easton.

"We've come to beg for your help in a matter of great urgency," says Eliot. "Listen to Joseph's story. Please consider undertaking a dangerous mission of mercy."

"What do you want us to do?" Comfort asks.

Reverend Rowlandson tells them about Lancaster. "It happened on February 10th. I was in Boston trying to get soldiers to come to protect us so I wasn't there when they attacked." He can't continue for a moment. He takes a few moments to calm himself and takes off his glasses to wipe his eyes.

"There no shame in grieving," John Easton says.

"My poor Mary and three of our children were among twenty taken captive. I thought they were dead. By God's grace, I've just received this letter." He takes out the letter. "It was brought by a Wampanoag messenger who told me Mary's Narragansett master was Queen Weetamoo, and now she has given Mary to

Metacom."

"Is Metacom willing to let her go?" Comfort asks.

"We hope so. He's sent a messenger demanding twenty English pounds or the equivalent in our new pine tree coins, two warm coats, half a bushel of corn, and a leather pouch of tobacco. Will you bring these things to him? I beg you; help me get my Mary back."

"My brother Willie and Ben Church have been chasing him since the beginning of the war. He may not be pleased to see me."

"You're my only hope. Let me read you Mary's letter."

Dearest Joseph: Yes, I'm alive. I am a servant to Metacom. We move often to hide in the swamps. Hunger is my constant companion. I never would have believed I could eat such awful things with great relish – a soup of boiled horse's bones and hooves. Yesterday I drank the liquid from the boiled bones filled with dead maggots.

That terrible day of the attack bullets rattled against the house then it was set on fire. I grabbed the children and ran, but we were captured. We trudged through deep snow all night and I heard the heathen singing, happy for their victory. For nine days they marched us through the woods.

Metacom has treated me with kindness. He asked me to knit a hat for his son who is ill. By chance I had yarn and knitting needles with me. I refused to work on the Sabbath, and he didn't force me.

Now Metacom is willing to release me. He needs money for food. This letter proves I'm alive. It will be delivered to Reverend Eliot by a man we English once called "John the Printer" because he helped John Eliot print his Algonquian Bible. He speaks English. Please dearest raise the ransom quickly. Pray for me.

Love,
Mary

"I know it's a dangerous mission," John Eliot says. "I'm too old and Metacom hates me for trying to convert him or I'd go myself."

"Do you think we can succeed?" Comfort asks, looking at John Easton.

"Let's try. They're starving; perhaps he's ready to surrender."

"We'll go."

"Tell him Governor Winslow has promised he can return home to Mount Hope and live in peace forever if he surrenders."

John Eliot gives Comfort a signed paper. Why would he suddenly trust Winslow?

They send a message telling Metacom that Comfort and John Easton will come. There's no answer. Finally a messenger arrives. Metacom is ready to release Mary.

John the Printer meets them in Providence , blindfolds them and takes them to Metacom's hidden refuge in a swamp. Comfort guesses they're someplace west of Mount Hope. They arrive wet, hungry and disoriented.

She removes the blindfold. What a sad place this is. She sees old men lying on mats, all skin and bones, holding their stomachs, writhing in pain. Dirty children with bloody scabs on their skinny arms and legs are digging for worms to eat. It is just as John thought, they have no food.

They are brought to a *wetu* to rest and wait for Metacom. Comfort falls asleep but John can't sleep. He might kill us. He'll take our bundle and knock us on the head with his club. Why did he put Comfort in danger?

Later they are brought to Metacom. He's sitting with Mary. Her gray hair is tangled, and she's emaciated. Metacom is also thin. John sees a war club beside him. Comfort sees long scars on his lean chest where there is a tattoo of a standing bear. She remembers when he got that tattoo. It was part of his initiation as Chief *sachem*. She remembers how Metacom looked with love at Little Bird. She wonders if her dear friend is still alive.

"Sky Eyes," he says, looking at her. "*Peeyaush netop*, come here friend."

Comfort moves a little closer and John sighs with relief. He still likes her.

Metacom motions to John to place the bundle on the ground in front of him.

"**Aspaumpmauntum sachem?** How are you king?"

"So, you must be hungry. *Pautinnea mechimucks*, bring something to eat," he tells a boy. "Your people destroyed our crops and storage pits. I've little to offer."

"We have brought everything you've requested, Chief *sachem*" John says. "We're grateful that Mary can return to her husband and children."

"*Nummokokunitch*, I'm robbed. You took my land and freedom. But Mary is a good woman and can go home." The boy comes with three corn cakes.

"My father and yours were *wauontakick*, wise men. We had happy days once." Comfort says. "I'm sad, *netop*, friend.

"*Kakitonckqueban*, they're dead," Metacom says. "So many are dead."

Little Thunder comes and sits next to his father. His face and body show the marks of small-pox. He keeps his angry eyes on John who removes a leather pouch from around his neck with the ransom coins and gives it to Metacom. Then Metacom tells his son to open the large bundle. Little Thunder examines two coats. He chooses a red one and puts it on. His thin arms stick out of the sleeves.

"Little Raven wore this coat," Comfort says to him. "He's dead now. He would have liked you to wear it. He never forgot you were once *weemat*, his brother."

Little Thunder is angry. He doesn't talk to her. He goes away.

"My son rarely talks anymore. Perhaps he's going to tell his mother you're here."

"Your messenger told us she's alive but *mauchinaui,* sick."

"Yes."

"May I see her?"

"I'll take you, but I don't know if she'll speak with you."

John speaks softly. "I'm a Quaker. You know I want peace. Return to Mount Hope with your people. You'll own the land there forever. Here is a new treaty signed by Governor Winslow. Sign it. All our people are weary of war."

"Surrender? Never! Your soldiers will cut off my head. My warriors would rather die than become slaves. Do you think you can own us as you own cattle and pigs? We know how to make gunpowder and have many guns. Other tribes have joined me. Leave our nations alone. You're no longer welcome in our country."

Metacom looks at Mary. "Have I treated you well?"

"Yes." She's trembling with fear.

A boy tells Comfort she may visit Little Bird. Metacom says she's to follow him.

"My daughter Laughing Like Water is dead from the smallpox. My son no longer speaks. If my son and wife are captured, will they be sold as slaves?"

"I hate slavery. Little Bird is my sister. I'll save her and Little Thunder."

"I choose to believe you Sky Eyes."

He pulls back the hide door of a small *wetu* and lets her in. He whispers a few words to Little Bird, and then leaves them alone.

Comfort hears coughing. When her eyes adjust to the darkness inside, she sees an old woman on the sleeping bench with gray hair and dead eyes; they look like stones on the bottom of a river.

"Hello, Sky Eyes. You still walk upon this earth I see."

"Dear *netop,* I'm sorry you're sick."

Little Bird coughs. "The *pawwaw* says it's not my time to die yet, but I long to go to *maugom manit wekick*, God's House."

"I gave your son Little Raven's red coat."

"Is he alive?"

"No. He and his father are dead."

"Do you believe you'll see them in your Heaven?"

"Yes."

"What about your brother Willie? Does he still search for Metacom?"

"He's wounded, but alive. He wants the war to be over."

"Does he still want to kill my husband?"

"If only Metacom had not started this horrible war."

"How dare you! How could we survive as a free nation?" She coughs for a long time and spits blood into a small piece of doeskin.

Comfort is crying. "Please ask Metacom to accept the new peace treaty we've brought. You could go home to Mount Hope. Wouldn't you like to go home and live in peace?"

Little Bird stops coughing, and her eyes fill with tears. "He'll never surrender. Leave me. Soon I'll be happy to be reunited with my dead father, mother and my dear daughter."

Comfort, John and Mary leave with John the Printer. Comfort is sure she'll never see Metacom or Little Bird again.

26

PROVIDENCE

Roger Williams, in his seventies, has twenty-five grandchildren and two more on the way. He lies in bed this morning thinking of his blessings. All six of his children have prospered thanks to the fertile land he received as a gift from Chief *sachems* Canonicus and Miantonomo. He's proud of protecting Rhode Island's fertile land from land speculators in Massachusetts and Connecticut.

This small house where he has lived for forty years was used by the Narragansett *sachems* for their meetings. Sometimes more than fifty men came to sleep on his floor and he provided food for them. The sloped hill a hundred feet above the house protects it from the wind. He loves his house and hopes to live here until he dies and is buried here.

He dresses, wraps a russet woolen scarf around his neck and sets out on his usual walk. One of his granddaughters' made this scarf for him and he's glad he has it because of the cool wind. He takes his walking stick, as his lame leg aches on cool mornings.

He passes through the meadow where cows graze, and pauses to look at the small fishing boat on the river. Both the Moshassuck and Woonasquatucket Rivers empty into Narragansett Bay. He stops again when he reaches the fresh spring, bends down and drinks from his hands.

He continues walking past the pond where he swims with his grandchildren in summer. The spring and pond were gifts from *sachem* Miantonomo, though he gave him some hoes and knives in exchange for it. The Narragansett leader also gave him the land at Nahiganset to set up a trading post which provides sufficient income.

Over the years Roger has given gifts to his Indian friends. Miantonomo admired his blue wool coat, so Roger gave it to him. To Canonicus, who loved sugar, he gave a ten pound bag. He let Canonchet, when he was young, use his boat and canoe whenever he asked for it. Later he bought a large dugout canoe that held twenty men and let him use it to ferry Naragansetts to Roger's house for meetings. He was proud of the reciprocity of his relationship with the Narragansetts over so many years.

Roger wishes the war with Metacom would end soon, for he fears the Narragansetts might attack and burn the towns of Rhode Island. He has prayed this morning to God asking Him to protect his beloved Providence. The massacre in the great swamp was wrong not only because so many innocent people were killed but also because such a massacre certainly will require the Narragansetts to take revenge.

As he walks home along the river, he sees a canoe with three Indians coming towards the shore. He recognizes Canonchet, Miantonomo's youngest son, paddling the canoe. He's wearing *mowi-sucki*, black war paint. He's alarmed but since there are only three, he thinks they're coming with a message and not to kill him.

Canonchet helps a very old man out of the canoe. Roger recognizes him as Yotoash, Miantonomo's brother, who served as the chief negotiator for the tribe after the Pequot War. He's surprised to see with them a young English boy dressed as an Indian. The boy introduces himself. "I'm Joshua Tift. *Ntouwiu*, I'm an orphan, and Canonchet *wauchaunat*, was my guardian and now is *nosh*, my father," he says. Roger invites them to his home and offers them refreshments, "*Nekick, Kekick,*" my house is your house. He offers *puttuckqunnege,* cakes, bread, cheese and beer.

"*Cowaump?*" Had enough, Roger says.

"*Nowaump.*" I've had enough, Canonchet replies.

Roger asks him why he has come. "*Tawhitch kuppee yaumen netop?*"

Canonchet replies "*kuttannummi,*" will you help me? But he's not ready yet to explain. First they must smoke together. He takes his *wuttammagon,* a long pipe, from around his neck, and asks for *wuttammaug,* tobacco. Roger gives him tobacco from his pouch and puts some in his own pipe. They smoke in silence. Finally Canonchet is ready to reveal the purpose of this visit.

"*Nissese,* my uncle, Yotoash is *nuppamen,* he's dying. He has begged me to bring him to you. He came here when Canonicus was dying and he saw your kindness to him. He remembers you wrapped his uncle in your own red blanket and said words from *Manittoo wussuckwheke,* God's book. This gave his uncle peace. Now he wants you to do the same for him."

"I respected Canonicus" Roger says. "I'll do what you ask" he says to Yotash. "I know you're a man who loves *aquene,* peace."

Old Yotoash starts coughing. "*Nchesammattam,* I'm in pain. *Masit,* medicine."

Roger takes a small bottle of a brown liquid from a shelf. "*Cotatamhea,* drink. It's for *Nchesammattam.*" Roger points to Canonchet. "*Witchwhaw,* his mother, she taught me to make it."

As Old Yotoash drinks the brown liquid Canonchet walks about the room and touches the books on a shelf. "I came here with my father many times. You let me use your canoe." He is anxious and tells the English boy to go to the canoe and wait there.

When the boy leaves, Cannonchet warns Roger. "Take my uncle and leave this house. Providence will burn tomorrow. *Kunnishickquock,* they will kill you. Don't delay. I've come to warn you because of your past kindness."

"We're neutral. Why are you going to destroy my town?"

"Attacks on my people are planned by the soldiers at Wickford. I'm warning you, **netop.** That's all I can do." He turns to go, looks back at his uncle and Roger once more with sadness, and leaves.

Roger takes down a metal box in which he keeps the charter for Rhode Island and the deed to his land. He shows the deed to Yotoash.

"See," he points to the paper, "this is Canonicus' mark, a bow. Here's your brother Miantonomo's, an arrow. Here are the marks of two witnesses, Sobash and Alsonmunsit. They sold this land to me and gave me more land as a gift. It was not **commotion,** it wasn't stealing."

The old man has another fit of coughing. He's trembling. Roger gently places a red blanket around the old man's thin shoulders. Then he takes two more blankets and the iron box. He will go to his oldest son Daniel's house and Daniel will come back here to gather warm clothes and food. They will gather all the family and flee to Newport. He wonders if Daniel's son would have time to take the goats by pinnace to a little island where they can be safe. Old Yotoash walks slowly, leaning on Roger.

Old Yotoash dies that night in Daniel's son's bed. Roger says prayers for his soul and he and Daniel dig a grave and bury him wrapped in the blanket. Roger places a rock on the gravesite and says another prayer in English and Algonquian: "*Ewo manit waumausachick ka uckqushanchick, keesaqut auog,* they who love and fear Him go to Heaven."

He sends his youngest son Joseph to warn the militia at Wickford that Providence will be attacked tomorrow. He sends a messenger to John Easton to tell him to prepare for a possible attack. Garrison houses will keep some families safe, but most must flee to Boston. He wonders if the people in Boston will be kind to Quaker refugees.

Three days later the town of Providence and the surrounding villages are attacked. The Narragansetts come at dawn and leave by late morning. Roger's house is one of twenty-seven burned to the ground.

He finds himself homeless for the second time in his life. Simon Bradstreet rescinds Roger's long standing banishment, but refuses to return to Boston. Rhode Island will be rebuilt someday, and he intends to help.

Sachem Canonchet is captured thanks to information given by a friendly Mohegan spy. It happens near a river. Canonchet takes off his English coat, tosses aside his wampum belt, the symbol of his power, and jumps into to the river hoping to swim to safety. Another Mohegan scout is waiting on the other side, captures him and brings him to Ben Church.

When Ben asks him to sign a peace treaty, Canonchet remains defiant. "How can I make peace? You burned hundreds of my people alive in the swamp."

He tries to escape that night and is shot by *sachem* Oweneco, whose father, *sachem* Uncas, thirty years earlier killed Canonchet's father Chief *sachem* Miantonomo.

27

Plimouth

Ben Church and Willie Bradford follow every lead the Indian scouts provide them but can't find Metacom's hiding place. All they have found are abandoned fire pits. They do not give up despite the disintegration of the United Colony militias. Many soldiers are deserting and fleeing with their families to refugee camps outside larger towns.

"Stay with me." Ben's wife Alice begs. She's given birth in Newport which hasn't been attacked. He holds his infant son in his arms; the newborn opens his blue eyes. "If I don't kill Metacom, I can't promise you peace, dear boy."

Ben knows there are growing problems in the conduct of the war. Major Willie Bradford told him there's no money to pay his men. There are problems of a lack of clear authority within the United Colonies militias. Some people are blaming Plimouth for starting the war several years ago when they used force to bully Wamsutta to sign the treaty. Some even wonder if someone in Plimouth poisoned Metacom's brother. A preacher in Salem is saying the cause of the war was the fact that so many newcomers don't join a church. "This war's God's punishment because too few are praying to Him."

"Metacom's alliance is also collapsing," Ben tells Willie when they meet in the woods near Plimouth to plan what to do next. "I heard his young warriors argue with him over strategy. Disease and starvation has reduced their numbers. The Mohawks refused to support Metacom and are now helping us. They've brought me information."

He continues after lighting his pipe. "Metacom's alliances are falling apart. My spies tell me they've met warriors who have fled. My scouts must be rewarded with Narragansett land after the war, Willie."

"The Bay Colony is sending too many soldiers to Maine to protect their trading post," Willie says. "This means we have fewer men to protect the remaining villages here. They're fighting Wabanakis who have been given many guns as well as gunpowder by the French. I think this fighting will continue even after Metacom is killed."

"I'll talk with *squaw sachem* Awashonks of the Sakonnet band and ask her to help us. Ever since I bought my land from her, we've been very friendly. I like her."

"Didn't she drown," asks a soldier sitting with them.

"No. That was Weetamoo, the other Queen. I saw her jump in the river trying to escape and go under the water," Ben says. "Metacom's wife and son were captured that same day. They were better swimmers, but couldn't escape the soldiers who jumped in the water and swam after them. They're captives now."

"Good. Did Metacom's wife tell you where he's hiding?" Willie asks.

"No. She went crazy, tearing her clothes, spreading dirt on her face and arms, howling in pain. Her son couldn't calm her. She mourned the loss of Weetamoo who was her half-sister. They're in a prison camp near Boston and will be sold. Selling slaves to the sugar islands will bring us needed money to pay our soldiers."

"Perhaps Queen Awashonks, the *sachem* of the Sakonnets, will help me find Metacom," Ben says. "She's Metacom's cousin, but she told me long ago she didn't want this war and she hoped she could remain neutral."

* * * *

Ben arrives at **sachem** Awashonks' camp bringing gifts of rum and tobacco. Because she fears being poisoned, Awashonks makes him drink the rum from his calabash first, but she is interested in his plan.

"Surrender and I promise your people can go to a safe place," Ben says.

She asks why he has waited so long to offer peace. "I want all of us, men, women and children to be safe. I don't want anyone to be enslaved," she says. "If you promise this, **netop**, I'll accept the protection of the English and my warriors will fight with you."

She talks privately with her son Peter. Ben stays overnight in her camp waiting for her answer. He trusts her and isn't afraid. At dawn she says that Peter has agreed to go with him and meet Major Willie at Punkateese. If they come back and Peter tells her it's safe to surrender, then she and ninety of her people will surrender.

Willie agrees with this plan. "Tell her to take all her people to a place called Sandwich on Cape Cod."

When Ben and Peter convey the good news, there is a loud shout of happiness by everyone present. A feast is prepared of bass, eels, flat fish and shell fish. Afterwards, people dance around the fire in a circle. Ben watches a warrior in black war paint call out the names of all the nations that are enemies of the English. He shakes his axe showing they'll defeat them all. Several volunteers ask to join Ben and he chooses those who look strongest to take with him as he continues his search for Metacom.

Ben tells his friend **sachem** Awashonks that Metacom has been sighted near Mount Hope.

"My cousin wants to die at home," she tells him.

28

A Swamp Near Mount Hope

It is just before dawn. Metacom is hiding in swamp at the foot
of the hill. He walks up the hill to see old Annawon with a heart
full of sorrow. This respected warrior has been his close friend
during the worst times of the war. He had been his father's advisor when Metacom was a boy. He takes with him the symbols
of his kingship: the nine inch wide wampum belt, his war club
inlaid with shells, and the smaller wampum belt with the star
which rests on his chest.

He finds the old warrior and his men resting. He takes him
inside a shelter and sits and opens his deerskin bundle.

"I've lost all hope of victory, old friend, I want to die in
Pokanoket. I'm ready for the joy of the Southwest." He sighs
and tells him he is sure his family is dead and waiting for him
to come.

Old Annawon, with tears in his eyes, accepts these symbols of
kingship. "Little by little they took all our land and our nation's
pride. Your father would have been proud of your courage."

"Stay here, old friend, and live."

* * * *

Ben and his men find Metacom's camp thanks to a deserter from
Metacom's warriors. They wait until dawn so can distinguish their

friendly Indian fighters from the enemy. They want the attack to be a surprise and it is.

Metacom's men are still sleeping in shelters with one open side for escape, when Ben's Indians attack screaming and shooting. Metacom, wearing only a breechcloth and stockings, throws his gun powder pouch over his head, grabs his flintlock but isn't ready. A Praying Indian scout named Alderman sees him standing and shoots him. Two bullets hit Metacom near his heart and he falls on his face onto the muddy ground. The Indian scout drags Metacom's body by his long hair screaming "I've killed the monster!"

Later he is given thirty shillings for Metacom's head and it's paraded around Plimouth to a cheering crowd. Winslow orders it to be placed on a tall wooden pike where it remains for twenty-five years as a warning to all Indians.

* * * *

One of the last warriors to be captured is old Annawon. Late one night he is ambushed near Squannaconk Swamp. by Ben Church and only six Wampanoag Indians who have surrendered and one English soldier. Ben knows Annawon.

He and his men are on a hill looking down at Annawon and his men who are preparing a feast. Big pots are boiling and many are seated eating. Their guns are some distance away in a pile unguarded. First Ben's men capture the guns and leave a guard. Then the others, with guns raised, tell the men to surrender and they do. They offer Ben's Indian scouts food. They know Metacom is dead. The war is over. Ben sees Annawon and goes with his gun to where the old warrior is sitting before a campfire eating.

"I've come to sup with you." Ben tells Annawon, and puts his gun down and sits.

"*Namitch, commetesimmin*, stay and eat. Do you want cow-beef or horse-beef?" Annawon asks, smiling.

"Cow-beef. I'm very hungry," Ben says, "thank you." He's not afraid. They eat.

"I see a new moon, *yo ockqquitteunk*. The Moon God is called *Nanepaushat. Awaun keesiteouwin keesuck?* Who made the Heavens?"

"*Pausuck naunt manit, keesiteouwin keesuck*, there is only one God and he made the Heavens and everything else in six days" Ben replies.

"*Awaun kukkakotemogwunnes?* Who told you so?" Annawon asks.

"*Manittoo wussuckwheke*, God's Book" Ben tells him.

"*Kautantowwit*, our God, made a man and a woman of a stone, but broke it because he was not happy with them. He made another man and woman of a tree. We have different stories, you and I, but we both have souls. *Mattux swowanna kit auog, michichonckquock*, yours don't go to the Southwest as ours do. Maybe you and I will be better neighbors in our separate Heavens than we were here on earth."

After they've eaten, they share a pipe of sacred tobacco. Ben says all of Annawon's men may go free, but he must take the old warrior to Plimouth. He'll try to save his life, but can't promise it. He says he objects to making men slaves.

Then Annawon gets up and Ben watches him, a gun in his lap, as Annawon goes into his shelter. He comes out with a bundle.

"You've killed Metacom and have conquered his country, so these things belong to you," he says, opening the bundle. He pulls out Metacom's long wide wampum belt made with black and white wampum beads. He hands this symbol of high office to Ben who puts it in his knapsack. Then he takes out the much smaller one which Metacom wore on his head. He gives this to Ben also. Finally, with tears in his eyes, he gives Ben the narrow belt with a star which Metacom wore on his chest. "We have no *sachim-mauog,* King, and no *sachimauonck,* Kingdom, so these sacred things are yours."

Ben tries but is unable to save Annowan's life.

29

BOSTON

Little Bird pulls a torn red blanket tighter around her shoulders against the morning chill. Little Thunder is still asleep. He was up all night talking with the other young men planning to escape. They decided it's impossible; too many guards.

"*Kunnishickquuock*, they will kill you, if you try to escape" she told her son when he came back in the dark.

"Weetamoo was lucky to drown," he replied.

She puts a basket on her back and walks to an area near the perimeter of the prison camp to find twigs for a fire. She passes Wampanoag and Narragansett families crowded together around small fires heating porridge. A young woman is holding a dead baby. That dead old man on the ground next to her is her father. Will the English allow us to bury our dead so *michachunk*, the soul, *sowanakit-auwaw*, can go to the Southwest and enjoy pleasures forever?

She passes the guardhouse. The guard, looks at her anxiously, raises his flintlock, but then turns away. She's an old woman and not a threat. If he knew who she was, he would have shot her. *Nuppamen*, I'm dying, she is thinking. I'll say *Annehick nowesuonck*, I've forgotten my name.

She searches the ground near the palisade for twigs left over from the building of the palisade. Without a fire she can't cook for her hungry son. She gathers twigs and puts them in her basket.

When she returns to the shelter, her son is gone. She decides to go to the small stream to wash the mud off her feet. She sees two young boys pushing a small piece of bark around in the water with a branch.

"Be careful," she says. The boys ignore her for she's just another crazy one.

"*Kosh*, your father, is he alive?"

"*Pauquanan*, killed."

"Do you want to hear a story? Do you know how *Maushop* captured the Wind Eagle?"

"No. Teach us to swim."

"*Nummauchemin*, I must go now. *Sauop*, tomorrow."

"*Sauop*, tomorrow, *npummuck*, I am shot." The boy turns from her and splashes the other boy with water, laughing. This is how they survive, one moment at a time.

Little Thunder is waiting when she returns. He's on the dirt floor, "*Nitchwhaw*, I can't escape. *Noonshem metesimmin*, I can't eat. *Mat wonck kunnawmone*, you'll never see me again. *Nummusquantum*, I'm angry. I'd rather die than become a slave."

"**Geezeegodwit**, I'm old bent pine tree, but you are young still, dear son. Try to stay alive."

"This morning a Pequot captive told me he'd been a slave. They gave him spoiled, smelly cod to eat and whipped him until he couldn't stand. *Loowehwoodee*, I won't live in fear and anger."

* * * *

Little Bird and Little Thunder join fifty Wampanoags and sixty Narragansetts who are forced to walk to the slave market on the Commons. When they arrive, she sees a platform and people are sitting on the ground all around it. The prisoners remain tied together. Who will want to buy her, such an old, thin woman?

Will they know she's Metacom's wife? Will she have to watch them sell her only son?

* * * *

Comfort is standing near the table set up for the magistrates waiting for Simon Bradstreet to arrive. On the table is a big wooden sign displaying the new official seal of The Bay Colony. It shows an Indian in a grass skirt and the words "Come Over and Help Us". How strange. Indians don't dress like that. The Indians certainly don't want more English to come here offering to help them. But now that the war is over, many more English people will come seeking land cleared of its inhabitants.

The meadow is crowded with wounded soldiers looking to buy and sell children since they haven't been paid for months, sea captains with business in Jamaica and Barbados interested in buying and selling slaves, and families wanting young slaves for labor on their farms. There's always a shortage of labor.

The males are dragged to the platform first. Comfort recognizes Little Thunder. Simon Bradstreet has just arrived, so she tells him she wants to buy this boy.

"No. Metacom's son is too dangerous to be kept here. A sea captain has already offered us a good price and says he will take him to Barbados. Others are also interested in buying him, but it would be better if we can send him far away. Metacom's wife is old and sick and will not bring us much money to use for reconstruction of our towns. You may buy her. Don't let anyone know who she really is or someone will surely try to kill her."

Comfort watches as a man and his son examine Little Thunder. The man pulls open his mouth to check his teeth. The son touches his chest where there is a tattoo of a standing bear just like the one his father had tattooed on his chest. Little Thunder spits in the boy's face. The boy kicks Little Thunder in the groin.

"I don't want him," the father says. " I don't need more troublemakers among my slaves in Virginia. I'll buy Africans for my tobacco fields." He and his son get in their wagon and leave.

Finally Little Thunder is sold to the sea captain who is waiting for him. He is holding an iron neck ring and chain. Little Thunder struggles; the sea captain kicks him in the groin.

She sees coming towards the platform the two little boys who were playing with the bark boat. They're holding hands. A woman buys them both and gives each one a piece of bread.

Comfort sits with a group of Quaker women from Rhode Island. She is waiting for Little Bird to come up to the platform.

"I want a young girl to help with chores. I'll let her free when she's old enough to marry. That's what our new law says. What do you think I'll have to pay for her?" she asks Comfort.

Comfort doesn't answer. How can Quakers, who have known such suffering themselves, buy children to be servants? It isn't right, but Rhode Island will be much better for these boys than Barbados, and they won't be slaves forever.

Finally Little Bird is brought to the platform. Comfort has already given Simon thirty shillings for her. She goes to the platform and tells the man holding her friend's rope she has already paid for this woman.

Little Bird remains silent during the entire voyage back to Newport. Her heart was like a stone. "I will always love you, **netop**," Comfort tells her.

30

Newport

"Maggie, heat water to fill the tub," Comfort says as soon as she takes Little Bird into her house. Maggie and Comfort carefully wash Little Bird's dirty limbs which are covered with mosquito bites. After the bath, they try to untangle her gray hair with a wooden comb without hurting her. She twists her mouth in pain, but doesn't make a sound. They put one of Ned's old nightshirts on her and tell her to sleep on a mattress placed on the floor of Maggie's room. She sleeps for two days.

When Little Bird finally wakes up, she sees Comfort sitting in a chair near her mattress.

"Sky-Eyes?"

"Yes, *netop*."

"Why did you save me? I don't want to live."

"You are *wattap*, a root of a great tree. You must tell the stories of the Wampanoag nation. Your husband wanted you to live. I promised him I'd save you."

Little Bird smiles. Sky Eyes understands that she mustn't say Metacom's name since he's dead and it is their custom not to say the name again.

"*Cuppompaish*," I'll stay for you. *Cowammaunsh*, I love you."

31

Newport

Comfort watches as Little Bird gently bathes Ned and Maggie's infant Tommy with a cloth soaked in warm water in a washbasin as she holds him on her lap. Morning light falls on Little Bird's face and she smiles. She's wiping him with a cloth, and his dark eyes are looking up at her. "Look, *wompissacuk* is smiling at me," she says to Comfort.

"Yes, I see *netop*." She doesn't mind Little Bird calling him "*wompissacuk*" which means eagle.

When she asked about that choice, Little Bird says she wants this baby to be *minikesu*, strong, courageous like eagles that live on treetops, free. "It's sacred. Eagles have a long life. I know many stories about eagles. When he's older I'll tell him stories about eagles and bears." She starts singing an Algonquian song to him as she carefully dresses him in a tiny linen short sleeved shirt. She puts tiny mittens on his hands so he won't scratch his own face.

"When he's older tell him the story of Ahsoo with the sweet voice that lured the monster fish from the sea. I like that story," Comfort says.

"I'm happy to have a baby to care for again. If only my children had lived. *Wenisuck*, I'm an old woman; I need grandchildren."

Comfort shares her pain. If only Tommy were alive and he could have given her grandchildren. If only he were here to celebrate the end of the war today. She doesn't tell Little Bird that

Reverend Eliot plans to go to Barbados to try to bring home some loyal Praying Indians who were sold as slaves. Even if he found Little Thunder alive on a sugar plantation, he couldn't bring Metacom's son home.

"It's time to put the baby in his cradle," she says. "I need you and Maggie to help me get everything ready for our guests."

Maggie is told to pick roses from the garden and put some on the trestle table in the garden. Little Bird is asked to sprinkle mint leaves and rose petals dusted with sugar in the hearth. "It'll make the house smell good," she says when her friend seems puzzled.

Many guests will soon arrive. John Easton has invited them to his home to plan the reconstruction of the towns destroyed in the war. After the meeting there will be a feast of thanksgiving to celebrate the end of the war.

Little Bird helps Comfort put on her new dress. She hasn't had one for years. Its sleeves have been copied from a picture of the latest London style with sleeves pulled in just above the elbow with blue satin ribbons. Little Bird is wearing an Indian tunic and her grey hair hangs down her back in a braid. She has refused to wear English clothes. She will stay upstairs with the baby today.

John will serve the beer, rum, apple cider and Madeira wine with a dash of brandy. He also made a special wedding drink in honor of their marriage since this is the first time they're having guests in a long time. It's called sack-posset and is made of ale and sack liquor, eggs, cream, nutmeg, mace, and sugar. When he tasted it this morning, he got some on his nose and she laughed. How good it felt to laugh again.

But it isn't just a celebration. They must try to understand what caused this war, and how to prevent a war like this in the future. Last night in bed John said he was going to write a pamphlet about the war. He said he wanted people to know Metacom had many reasons to be angry. He reminded her about his meeting at Trip's Ferry with Metacom before the war.

"He told me forty-seven reasons why he was angry. He said he'd consider arbitration by a neutral party."

"If only you could have negotiated a little longer, you might've prevented the war," Comfort said. "The trial of Metacom's friends wasn't fair, and John Eliot tried too hard to convert him. Those fences at Swansea should have been built right away."

"Prence and Winslow both knew he wouldn't give them all his guns. I know the Boston preachers will dismiss what I write as the false views of a passionate Quaker, but I don't care. The truth must be told."

Comfort thinks of all the boys like her son Tommy who fought and died here and in England during the civil war. "How can we reconcile the values of the civil war where we fought for freedom from the King's tyranny, with our demand that all the free Indian nations submit to us in everything? How can we justify selling them into slavery for profit?"

John sighed. "My love, as usual, you see the truth. We say we're "civilizing" them, and their land is "vacant". That kind of thinking has led to this war. We are no different than the Spanish Conquistadors though we think we are. We want to be a powerful Empire and our generals and merchants will do whatever they want to make that happen."

* * * *

This discussion with John last night kept Comfort from sleeping peacefully. She looks in the mirror. She sees an old woman of sixty years, with grey hair and puffy eyes. But she remembers that most of her guests are older than she is.

Roger William, John Eliot and Simon Bradstreet arrive. They

are ready to discuss how to care for thousands of refugees, both English and Indian. So many towns have been destroyed. People are living in shelters where their houses once stood. Towns must be rebuilt in every colony. They'll need to borrow money from London and will have more debt. They'll need to cooperate.

Roger Williams is eighty years old. When John asks him to run for Governor again, he laughs. "I'm much too old. I'll help rebuild Providence."

John tells him now that he hopes to write about the war and Roger urges him to do so. "Ben Church will write about the fighting, but that won't explain why the Indians chose to die trying to keep their people free. Metacom's views should be considered. History always seems to reflect the views of the conquerors."

John Eliot is seventy-four years old. He tells Comfort he is translating the Bible into Algonquian once again; all his Bibles were destroyed. Only a few of the Praying Indian villages will be rebuilt since they have become like prison camps. All males over fourteen must now live with the Praying Indians and they are watched by armed guards. Many have fled North.

Simon Bradstreet says he will organize another slave market. Mercenaries from the West Indies who fought for us now want to sell the sixty Indians they captured. He tells John he thinks we shouldn't ask the King for money to rebuild our towns. "The King could send a Governor to control us."

No one is here from Connecticut. Governor John Winthrop, Jr. died two months ago, and the new Governor is too busy rebuilding Middleboro and Taunton, Scituate, and Rehoboth.

Willie has come representing Josiah Winslow. He tells Comfort that Pilimouth recently sold one hundred and twelve Wampanoags into slavery. He says the pain in his hip from the bullet reminds him of the war every day.

After the meeting is over, Maggie helps Comfort put food on

the table. and then goes to sleep. John goes to his study to write a report of the meeting.

Little Bird and Comfort sit outside under the starry sky and a full moon.

"Remember those *wuttahimneash,* strawberries we used to pick?" Comfort says.

"We made good bread with them," Little Bird replies. "Remember when I taught you to make holes in the wampum beads and you broke them all?" Then she is silent and looks at the sky.

"Look, there are so many stars in the sky tonight." Little Bird says. "See, there's my husband's spirit guide, *Mosk,* bear."

"We call those stars Ursula Major," Comfort says. "It also means bear."

"*Mosk* watches over us Sky-Eyes. A mother bear fiercely protects her cubs. I couldn't protect mine." Her eyes fill with tears.

They are both thinking about Metacom. Little Bird closes her eyes and sees him as a young, muscular man running a race with his brother. Their chests and faces glisten with sweat and after the race is over, they rest in a meadow among blue wildflowers. She smiles, for she believes they are both together and happy in the Southwest.

Comfort closes her eyes and sees herself as young and dressed in Little Bird's clothing pretending to be Metacom's second wife in order to save Susanna. He tells her he respects her courage. She can't tell anyone that she was proud to win his respect and friendship.

She opens her eyes and puts her woolen shawl around her friend's thin shoulders to protect her from the chilly night air. "*Cowammaunsh,* I love you" she says.

"*Coanaumatous,* I believe you. *Nowetompatimmin,* we are friends, forever."

Epilogue

The Aftermath of the War

Many historians have called this war the most devastating in our history in terms of its proportionate impact on a region. From a population of about eighty thousand, ten percent of the people were killed, one third of them English and two thirds Native American. About three thousand Native Americans died from starvation, disease, or were killed, and more than a thousand were sold into slavery in the Carribean. Many fled to Canada.

Of the ninety English towns in New England, fifty-two were attacked and twenty-five pillaged, and seventeen were abandoned. Boundary disputes continued.

Reverend Eliot's Praying Indian Villages and Algonquian Language Bible

It took until the 1690's for the reconstruction of four of the Praying Indian villagees. Natick was the largest village rebuilt. There were relocation camps, foreshadowing the reservation system. There were armed English guards. Reverend Eliot spent years trying to bring back converts who were sold into slavery. He re-created his Algonquian Bible and there are copies in existence.

Roger Williams

He published "A Key into the Language of America" in London in 1643. It includes customs and vocabulary of Narragansett Indians. I used it for the Algonquian language.

African Slavery

African slavery continued to increase rapidly after this war and Newport and Boston became major seaports in New England for the African slave trade.

New England Tribes

Most of the surviving members of the Wampanoag Tribe who remained in the region settled in Mashpee on Cape Cod and Gay Head on Martha's Vineyard. The Mohegans remained on their land in Connecticut until Uncas's death in 1683 when their land was given to English towns and land speculators. Two Pequot groups were given reservations in Connecticut before the war and remained loyal to the English. They became known as the Stonington and Mashantucket Pequots. Ninigret's band of Narragansett tribe kept its autonomy, but his successors eventually sold nearly all their land to the English in Rhode Island. This war fundamentally changed the relationship between colonists and Native American populations. The settlers continued to challenge the sovereignty of tribes and refuse to accommodate native cultures and land use.

Memoirs and Plays

Several memoirs were published about the war praising the first generation's piety and the heroism of the soldiers in what was known as King Philip's War. Thomas Church, son of Benjamin Church, published his father's journal (1716). The Indians did not leave written documents except for deeds of land sales and treaties with their signature. In 1829 the famous actor Edwin Forrest performed in a popular play sympathetic to Metacom called "Metamora; or The Last of the Wampanoags" which toured all over the country. However, this didn't lead to restoration of Indian land.

QUAKERS

Quakers continued to come to New England. After the war they were allowed to worship in Boston. In 1677-1678 five large vessels with eight hundred emigrants, mostly Quakers, settled in a new area called West Jersey where religious freedom was guaranteed. William Penn, a Quaker, signed a treaty with the Delaware (Leni Lenape) Indians, and wrote a charter for West Jersey guaranteeing freedom of religion. In 1681 he founded the colony of Pennsylvania.

LOSS OF INDEPENDENCE

King Charles II was ready to impose greater control over the colonies although he did not challenge the Massachusetts charter until 1682. In 1685 His Majesty appointed Sir Edmund Andros as Governor over what was then called the Dominion of New England. Andros challenged all colonial property rights. He was finally forced out by protests led by Simon Bradstreet. In 1689 the Dominion ended and colonies in the region got new charters but they never regained their previous sovereignty.

THE ROYAL SOCIETY

The Royal Society of London became an important scientific organization in London. Scientists like Isaac Newton published books on methods of scientific analysis. In 1675 King Charles II established The Greenwich Observatory and appointed John Flamsteed as Royal Astronomer. This Society has played a major role in the history of astronomy and navigation.

NEW ENGLAND TRIBES TODAY

According to the 2010 census, people of Native American descent in the U.S. today make up .8% of our current population. There are 562 recognized federal tribes and others are recognized by state governments only. It is estimated that 6,058 Native Americans live in Rhode Island, 18,850 live in Massachusetts, and 11,850 live in Connecticut. Since the mid-1970's nearly all of the New England tribes in the region have sought recognition by the federal government. Federal recognition allows special financial assistance and the right to operate a casino.

The Mashantucket Pequots received recognition through an Act of Congress. The Wampanoags received recognition through the Bureau of Indian Affairs. The Narragansetts finally received recognition in 1983. The Hassanamisco Nipmucs are still seeking recognition.

The Pequots have a museum and research center in Mashantucket, Connecticut. The Narragansetts have a museum in Exeter, Rhode Island. The National Museum of the American Indian, part of the Smithsonian Institute, is based in Washington D.C. and New York.

The Wampanoags, like other tribes in the U.S. and Canada are teaching their young children the Algonquian language in a language immersion school under a 1990 federal law, The Native American Language Act, which helps support the preservation of native languages.